JAN WATSON

Torrent
FALLS

Tyndale House Publishers, Inc., Carol Stream, Illinois

Visit Tyndale's exciting Web site at www.tyndale.com

Visit Jan Watson's Web site at www.janwatson.net

TYNDALE and Tyndale's quill logo are registered trademarks of Tyndale House Publishers, Inc.

Torrent Falls

Designed by Jessie McGrath

Edited by Lorie Popp

Scripture quotations are taken from the *Holy Bible*, King James Version.

This novel is a work of fiction. Names, characters, places, and incidents either are the product of the author's imagination or are used fictitiously. Any resemblance to actual events, locales, organizations, or persons living or dead is entirely coincidental and beyond the intent of either the author or publisher.

Library of Congress Cataloging-in-Publication Data

Watson, Jan.
    Torrent Falls / Jan Watson.
        p. cm.
    ISBN-13: 978-1-4143-1473-0 (pbk.)
    ISBN-10: 1-4143-1473-6 (pbk.)
    1. Rural women–Fiction.   2. Widows–Fiction.   3. Kentucky–Fiction.   4. United States–History–1865-1898–Fiction.   I. Title.
    PS3623.A8724T67 2008
813'.6–dc22   2007035709

Printed in the United States of America

14   13   12   11   10   09   08
 7   6   5   4   3   2   1

For Terry L. Taylor

Proverbs 17:17

❧ ACKNOWLEDGMENTS ❧

Had I ten thousand, thousand tongues,
Not one should silent be;
Had I ten thousand, thousand hearts,
Lord, I'd give them all to thee.

–PRAISE SELECTION FROM THE BAPTIST HYMNAL, 1875

To Him be the glory.

Special thanks always to Jerry Jenkins and the Christian Writers Guild; Tyndale House Publishers, especially Jan Stob and Lorie Popp; Mark Sweeney, my agent; family: Charles, Catherine, Andrew, and Stephen Watson–plus Julie Ashcraft and Bob Taylor (I keep you close to my heart.); friends–you know why you are special to me; the Grassroots Writers Group; and *continual* gratitude to the outstanding staff of Bluegrass-Oakwood residential facility in Somerset, Kentucky.

To my dear and valued readers: thank you for taking Copper Brown into your hearts and loving her as much as I do.

To my eternal sweetheart, Chuck, who is just away for a brief moment in time: you are always on my mind.

PROLOGUE

1886

You'd have to be lost to find the place, set as it was up a holler overgrown with thorny locust, tangled devil's shoestring, and poison ivy as dense as mosquitoes on a riverbank. The sturdily built cabin was just one room with one door and two fair-sized windows looking out over a rough-sawed porch floor. In the mornings fog rose like smoke from the surrounding mountains, and at night panthers prowled the ridges screaming their lament.

Dance Shelton's thin hand parted tattered curtains as her husband, Ace, trekked across the yard. He paused in front of a rickety lean-to by the barn, rummaging around for the varmint Dance knew he would withdraw. Arms bowing from the weight of it, he strutted back to the house. As always on the mornings he left her alone, he raised the trapdoor in the porch and leaned it against the wall. He caught her watching and so lifted the turtle high. Its head weaved about like a blind man's.

Jumping back, Dance let the curtain fall. She didn't have to look to know he'd lower it into the gap, then grunt as if he was working hard while he tacked a piece of window screen over the turtle's hole to keep other varmints away from his prize. One morning after Ace left, she'd watched with apprehension as a raccoon clawed at the screen, hoping for a tasty meal.

Absently, she rubbed the stump of her right index finger against her chin. The motion was enough to take her right back to her childhood and the day a snapper much like this one grabbed hold of her. She remembered screaming in fright and pain that day at the creek. Everybody knew a turtle wouldn't let go until it thundered, but there was not a cloud in sight. Her little brother Dimmert pulled the turtle one way while she pulled the other until the end of her finger snapped right off. It never did grow back.

Cold sweat broke out across her forehead and under her arms. Her old man knew she'd never cross that porch. Just the thought of the thing being so close gave her the shivers. Dance was purely terrified of snappers . . . and hoot owls. Hoot owls would steal your soul if you stared into their knowing yellow eyes.

Ace left by way of the flooded creek bed, and Dance sat as she did every day in a straight-backed chair by the window, wishing her life away. The raw place on her arm was scabbed over, but still she kept watch on the poker. She wouldn't try sneaking out into the night again. Ace slept like a snake, with one eye open.

Maybe he'd be home before dark. If so, he'd take the turtle back to the lean-to and plug up the hole so she could cross the porch to chop weeds from the garden or kill a chicken for supper. Her stomach knotted at the thought of saving the entrails for the snapper. Seemed stupid to feed your tormentor. If she could have, she'd have turned that thought over. Once she was her mother's quickest young'un, always first to figure a riddle. But now it was easier if her mind drifted like a dandelion seed in the wind, never lighting for long.

Dance absently traced the mound of her belly and hoped seeing the turtle hadn't marked the baby. She remembered her mammaw Whitt and the Bible she kept close at hand. Mammaw always said, "Take your troubles to the Lord, Dance, and He will see you through."

She guessed it wouldn't hurt to try. Bowing her head like Mammaw did, Dance prayed, *Lord, if Ye see fit, I need for Ye to send me someone to help when it comes my time to birth this baby. It ain't a time I want to be alone, and Ace won't hear of me going to my family. I thank Ye. . . . And, Lord, since I'm asking, make sure whoever Ye send ain't afraid of turtles.*

CHAPTER 1

Copper Brown Corbett held her skirts ever higher. Rushing water lapped first at her ankles and then her knees as she ventured farther into the creek. The flood was receding, but it was too late to save her garden. Might as well pull her feet out of the mud and go back to the house.

A baby's cry drew her attention. Lilly Gray was awake. Hands on hips, Copper took one last look at the muddy water. That was the price you paid, she reckoned, for living on Troublesome Creek.

She'd asked for her father's ramshackle farm, and he'd turned over the deed. Now all the work and worry belonged to her. She knew Daddy would be back one day. By time that she was sure to have the farm up and running again so that all he had to do was sit on the porch and listen to the katydids and the whip-poor-wills. Longing for her family nearly dropped her to her knees right there in the spillover that drowned the green onions, what was left of the lettuce, and the cucumber vines no bigger than her little finger. A few more weeks and they'd have pickles. Copper had already scrubbed the crock.

Lilly Gray's cry escalated, gone from asking to demanding.

"Mama's coming, baby," Copper called as she mounted the stone steps. A dash of water over her feet sent a thin stream of mud off the side of the porch.

She entered her bedroom and smiled at her baby. Her pure pleasure. "Did you miss me?"

"Nursey!" Lilly Gray said, her cheeks still flushed from slumber, her eyes the dark gray color of a storm cloud. The contents of the crib were strewn about the room, flung as far as her chubby arms could make them go.

"You're still dry, Mama's good girl!"

After Lilly's quick trip to the wooden potty in the corner, Copper wrapped her daughter in a crib quilt and carried her and a cup of tea to the porch.

"Nursey?" Lilly asked plaintively as she snuggled against her mother's chest.

Copper settled into the wooden rocker that had been her father's favorite. Stroking her daughter's silky hair, she let the garden go. There was food to be found in abundance up the mountain—ramp and cress and mushrooms—and surely she hadn't forgotten how to hunt. Daddy's gun hung idly over the fireplace. Mam said he wouldn't need it where they were going:

Philadelphia. And there was an abundance of canned goods in the cellar. Her sister-in-law, Alice, had sent enough to feed an army, sure Copper would let Lilly starve without her help. A furrow formed between her eyebrows. Oh, that Alice.

The tea was just right, hot and sweetened with a teaspoon tip of honey. Tension melted from Copper's shoulders as she rocked. There was nothing more relaxing than nursing a baby. *I'll miss this. Lilly Gray's a big girl now. She'll turn two in November. I'll have to think about weaning her before fall.*

Could it have been just a month since she'd left Lexington and her life in that fair city to return to her mountain home? As the baby lay in the crook of her arm, Copper examined her palms. Calluses were forming where blisters had popped across her soft, tender skin. A little more time with the rake and the hoe, a few more wash days, a few more floor scrubbings and she'd have working hands again. Hands she could be proud of.

Shifting Lilly Gray to the other side, Copper let her mind wander—a dangerous distraction. Sometimes she wished she could go back in time to when she was a girl, innocent of pain and sorrow, happy to run wild up the mountain in search of whatever suited her fancy on any given day. She leaned her head back and laughed to herself remembering how her stepmam's desires, yanking her hair ribbons out and losing her store-bought shoes. Poor Mam, she tried so hard.

It turned out that Copper had needed every one of the lessons her stepmother so diligently taught, for she married a doctor and left her mountain home, ever grateful for Mam's foresight.

"Still, I had much to learn," she said as if Lilly could understand.

"A hillbilly girl set down in the city, I was a sight. I don't know how your father stood me."

Lilly Gray glanced up. She looked so much like Simon. Copper didn't know if she'd ever get used to seeing him there, locked in his daughter's eyes. A little heartache started up, but she pushed it back down. She was tired of grieving. "Let's climb the mountain, baby. Let Mama get her shoes, and we'll go find some wild onions for dinner."

Testing the path with a walking stick, Copper steadied herself as she climbed. It was difficult going with the weight of the child nestled in a sling pulling her backward. She'd lost her sturdiness since Simon died. Between that and nursing Lilly, she was as stringy as an old squirrel, no meat on her bones.

She pushed aside a leafy branch and peered into a quiet meadow lined on three sides by towering oak, beech, and ash. It had probably been a hundred years since they were acorn and seed. The early morning sun streamed through their leafy limbs, piercing the shadows. She could barely see a smallish tumble of water on the far rocky hillside. Even from a distance, the splash of falling water played a pretty song.

"Cow?" Lilly Gray asked.

Copper reached behind, her arms cupping Lilly's bottom, taking the strain from her shoulders. "Shh. Mama deer and baby fawns, Lilly. They're having breakfast."

"Shh," Lilly whispered in Copper's ear. "Nursey?"

"Yes, nursey."

They watched as the doe nibbled delicately on a patch of

clover while the twins took turns with her milk, knocking heads in their impatience. Suddenly, the doe's ears perked. She froze for an instant before turning to leap into the darkness of the forest, her twins close behind, white tails bobbing. Their crashing run reverberated across the meadow.

Copper was sorry for disturbing the mother deer. But the beauty of the place could not be ignored; the forest creatures would have to share with her and Lilly Gray.

The sun hitched higher in the morning sky and graced a line of pear trees with its light. A breeze kicked up, and a drift of fragrant white blossoms showered Copper and her baby.

Untying the sling, Copper slid Lilly from her back and let her dance in the midst of their sudden good fortune. Lilly grabbed handfuls of the silky petals and flung them in the air.

"Looks like snow, doesn't it, Lilly? You were just a baby last winter when we made snowmen with Auntie Alice and cousin Dodie." *Another thing I've probably done wrong, taking Lilly Gray from her family.*

Help me know I made the right decision in coming back, Lord, she prayed. *Please help me.*

Copper picked up Lilly, then settled her on her skinny hip. "Let's go find the waterfall." As they traversed the field, she took note of the small orchard, just a line of a couple dozen or so trees actually, as if someone had intended to farm this patch of land and then left for one reason or another. She and Lilly would come back to check on the fruit. Pear butter was good on biscuits.

They entered the forest gloom and popped out again before

a sparkling waterfall revealed itself. It tumbled from a high rock outcropping and was as pretty as a gemstone.

Oh, Copper wished she'd brought a bar of soap and a towel, but no matter, she and Lilly Gray would bathe anyway; her linen petticoat would serve to dry them. Lilly shivered in the needlelike spray. Copper could have stood there all day. The sluicing water, the moss-covered rock, the sycamore tree bent forward over the brook . . . peace, that's what it was. Peace as strong as communion and also sacred. It seemed God had designed this place and this moment just for her. An answer to spoken prayer.

Back in the meadow, Copper picked a bright patch of sunlight and sat with Lilly to dry her hair. She'd rest just a moment before starting home, although there was so much to do she couldn't afford the time. Eggs needed gathering, the milk from the morning needed straining, and she needed to see what she could salvage from the garden. How could she get everything done alone? Of course there was her neighbor John Pelfrey. John had been so good already, planting the garden and bringing her a cow and some chickens, but Copper didn't want to rely on that goodness. John had his own work to do, and the last thing she wanted was to be beholden.

Things sure had changed since she'd been gone. There used to be a houseful of Pelfreys right across the creek, but they'd moved away, leaving only John. Copper wondered why he hadn't gone with them. She felt a smile tugging the corner of her mouth as she remembered how she and John had once been sweethearts—at least they'd played at being sweethearts, children that they were. Well, that was in the past. She was through with all that. She'd never risk that kind of pain again.

Lilly was down for a nap, and Copper took the churn out to the porch. Up and down, up and down, the smooth wooden dasher slid through her fingers. Come supper, there would be butter on their corn bread to go with the soup beans that simmered on the cookstove. She'd make a wilted salad with the ramps and cress she'd gathered this morning. Her hands sensed the change in the milk as it formed soft lumps. Lifting the lid, she saw that it was nearly finished. Soon she could pour off the whey and put the solid in the molds. Lilly loved the butterfly that formed atop the butter from the mold.

A horse and two riders appeared from around the corner of the barn.

The dasher fell back into the churn as Copper stood. "Who in the world could that be?"

The old tomcat who lay beside the chair didn't answer, busy as he was licking a splash of whey from his foot.

The horse ambled across the yard, taking his own sweet time. The riders, a girl of about fifteen and an older boy, stared at Copper. The girl smiled.

"May I help you?" Copper asked.

The boy reached out an arm. His muscles stood up like knots on an apple tree limb.

The girl grasped it and swung herself down. "Mammaw says you need some help."

"Do I know your mammaw?"

"Everybody knows Fairy Mae Whitt. She's lived up Crook-Neck Holler for seventy-five years, give or take." The girl marched up on the porch and settled her ample hips in the chair at the churn, taking over the dasher.

Copper knew of Fairy Mae Whitt. She'd visited up Crook-Neck with her daddy on occasion when she was a girl. Daddy would go checking on neighbors after a storm or some such thing. Fairy Mae was a good woman, widowed as long as Copper could remember. Copper reckoned Fairy Mae wouldn't send trouble to her door. Besides, her daddy taught her to never turn away a stranger. "We might be entertaining angels unaware," she'd heard him say at least a dozen times.

"Come on up," Copper said to the boy. "Rest a spell and have a glass of water."

The young man stayed on his horse; his Adam's apple bobbed in time to the churn.

The girl beckoned, so the boy slid off the horse, looping its reins around the porch rail. The horse was a fine-looking animal. Its coat, brushed to a shine, glinted red in the sunlight. Oddly its hooves shone too.

"Stove blacking and sheep tallow," the girl said as if Copper had asked. "Dimmert polishes them every night."

The quiet fellow eased over to stand behind the girl. His own bare feet could have used some attention. Taking the water Copper offered, he drank it down in one gulp.

"Thank ye," the girl answered for both of them. "Darcy Whitt," she said, releasing the dasher and sticking out her hand.

Copper's face colored. Why, this girl had better manners

than she did. "Pleased to meet you, Darcy." She shook the proffered hand. "And you too, Dimmert, is it? I'm Mrs. Corbett, but please call me Copper."

"My brother don't waste words," Darcy said as Dimmert stood with downcast eyes.

"Well, now," Copper said, trying to take charge of her own porch. She wished she had some spectacles to adjust. That's what Mam would have done, pushed her glasses up on her nose and made everything fall into place with that one motion. "I've got leftover cold breakfast pie. Who'd like some?"

Dimmert raised his hand as if he were in school.

"Is it blackberry?" Darcy asked. "I like blackberry, but I'd say no to rhubarb."

"You're in luck then. I'll just dish up a couple of bowls." The screen door squeaked as Copper opened it. A little grease would fix that, but she loved the sound of a screen door. She slid the pan of cold biscuit from the pie safe, nearly dropping it when she turned back around. Darcy stood at the table pouring whey from the churn into a stoneware bowl. These two were quiet; she'd give them that.

"Where do you want this butter, Miz Copper?" Darcy asked.

Copper put two molds on the table. "These should do it. We'll make two so you can take one home to your mammaw."

"We weren't figuring to go home for a right long spell." Darcy patted the butter neatly into the copper molds, pressing out air bubbles. "These here sure are pretty."

"I thank your grandmother for thinking of me," Copper replied, "but I'm not sure—"

"We won't be no trouble. Dimm will sleep in the barn, and I'll be fine right there in front of the fireplace if you can spare a quilt."

"I'll have to think about this. I can't promise you anything right now."

"Can you think right fast?" Darcy screwed up her freckled face. She was a spunky, brown-haired girl and charming with a ready smile. The opposite of her lanky brother, she was short and stout. "Mammaw cain't afford to feed us all."

"How many are there?" Copper asked.

"Well, let's see. There's me and Dimmert; that's two. Then there's Dance, but she don't live at home, so that's minus one. How many's that?" She counted off her fingers, holding up three and dropping one. "Huh, still two. Dilly's the baby and next is Dory, Dawn, Delia, and Dean." Her tongue poked out the corner of her mouth, and she knit her brow as she counted. "I'm leaving someone out." She tapped her toe as she stared at the floor. "Ezra," she crowed triumphantly. "I almost left out Ezra. How many's that? A bunch, I reckon."

Copper's head swam. Ezra? Wonder why they hadn't named him Dezra. "That's a bunch, all right. I don't remember Fairy Mae having but one girl living with her."

"Oh, we ain't been here long. We're from Virginia."

Adding a little water to the beans, Copper gave them a quick stir, then hung her apron on a peg behind the door. "Darcy, will you listen for my baby? She's sleeping in the next room. I won't be long."

Copper needed to think. Truth was she did need help, and

there was something about Darcy she liked. She paused to mull it over. Dimmert could be a help for sure. Every farm needed a man's strength. She wished she could talk to John. She wandered down to the creek. There was Dimmert, a ring of blackberry stain around his mouth, shovel in hand. The trench he was digging had already begun to divert the muddy water from the garden. He held up the shovel, a guilty look across his face.

Copper couldn't have been more surprised if the tomcat had hitched a team of mice to the plow. "You've saved the cucumbers. Thank you." She could have hugged him. Not only was he smart, but he had the decency to know he should have asked to use the shovel.

It looked as if she had a couple of hired hands. Darcy could have her old room, and with just a little fixing, the tack room in the barn would work for Dimmert. "Thank You, Lord," she whispered, tears in her eyes. God was good.

CHAPTER 2

The long summer days on Troublesome Creek took on a familiar rhythm. Mornings and evenings Copper milked her cow. Mazy was not charming like her favorite, Molly, had been. She was flighty. Copper had to watch closely to keep her from kicking over the bucket, and sometimes Mazy would smack Copper right in the face with the end of her long tail. But she produced beautiful, creamy milk, and Copper never had to go hunting for her. The bell that hung from her neck tolled like clockwork every evening as she made her way down the mountain right to the stable door. Copper liked that in a cow.

Dimmert had fashioned a tall-sided wagon, somewhat like a crib on wheels, to keep Lilly out of trouble while Copper milked or mucked out the stable. As soon as the milking was finished, the milk strained, and the buckets washed, she and Lilly Gray would go in for breakfast.

What a treat. Darcy was as good a cook as any grown woman, and Copper was more than happy to turn over that chore. On this particular morning thick-sliced bacon and eggs over easy, as well as biscuits, gravy, and fried apples, waited on the table.

Copper, Lilly, and Darcy had just sat down and finished grace when John poked his head in the door. "Smells mighty good," he said.

"Don't stand on ceremony. Come on in." Copper tucked her bare feet under her long skirt. "Your place is set as usual."

"Morning, girls," John said, sliding his tall frame into a chair and hefting a white ironstone mug. "Darcy Whitt, you make the best coffee on Troublesome Creek. Sure keeps me coming back."

Deep dimples played hide-and-seek in Darcy's cheeks. "Thank you, Mr. John."

Copper wondered if it was indeed the coffee he kept coming around for. Truly, she hoped so, but her heart told her differently. She never should have opened her home to him so readily. She should have kept her distance, protected herself, but he was a man alone and who could help but feed him? They had once been as close as kin, after all.

"Cat got your tongue, Copper?" John interrupted her reverie.

"Goodness, how my mind wanders." Copper pushed back her chair. "Do you want some more eggs, John?"

"Couldn't eat another bite, but I'll take a biscuit and bacon with me if you girls don't mind. It will make a fine noon meal."

"Please help yourself." Copper opened the screen door. "Dimmert, do you want some more breakfast?" she asked, but the porch was empty, Dimmert's plate and mug stacked neatly on the wash bench right beside the full water bucket. He never let the bucket get empty. The door slapped closed behind her. "Where are you working today, John?"

"I heard tell of a job felling timber over on Lost Creek. I thought I'd mosey on over that way."

Copper couldn't help but laugh. "That's a sight I'd like to see, you going slow enough to mosey. Sounds like some kind of dance."

His green eyes met hers across the table. "You think I can't dance? Try me. There'll be fiddle playing and dancing at the schoolhouse come Saturday night. Think you might go along?"

She could feel the hateful blush creep up her chest and spread across her face: the curse of a red-haired woman. "Oh no, I don't think so." Quickly she busied herself scraping the plates, dumping the scraps in the slop bucket for the shoats Dimmert had bartered for last week. Lilly loved the piglets, and they were cute. Round pink snouts and tails curved like springs. She'd have to watch, though, when they got bigger. A hog could kill a baby as quick as anything.

"Copper?" she heard as if from a great distance. "You all right?" John stood close, too close. He touched her shoulder.

She jerked away. "Of course I'm all right. I'm just cleaning up."

"I'm sorry," John said, stepping back. "But you seemed so far away."

"There's nothing wrong with me!" Sorry for the hurt in his

eyes at her outburst, she reached for the biscuit and the bacon, wrapping two helpings in waxed paper, an unspoken apology. "I'm fine. Don't fuss over me."

"Sorry, Pest. . . . Oops, sorry again. Didn't mean to call you that." He put on his wide-brimmed felt hat and made for the door. "I'd better get out of here while we're still speaking."

Standing at the screen door, Copper watched him stride across the yard. Tears shimmered in her eyes. *Pest.* He called her the nickname he'd given her years ago and rightly so. She'd been his shadow on treks up hollers and through the creek, even to the top of the highest mountain and as far away as Quicksand. She leaned her forehead against the door. He'd never once complained. Just teased her sometimes. Those were good times.

Careful, her mind screamed, but her heart yearned for the easy relationship she'd once shared with John. *Best get busy. "Idle hands are the devil's workshop," Mam always says.*

"Can I take Lilly Gray to the garden, Miz Copper?" Darcy asked. "We want to check on the tomatoes and hoe a few weeds from the corn."

"Of course. Just put her bonnet on and take the wagon. I don't want her down on the ground. Remember that copperhead we saw last week?"

Darcy's eyes grew as round as the biscuits she'd made for breakfast. "Yes, ma'am. He was a big one. Too bad you missed him with the hoe!"

"Just be careful. You really should wear your shoes."

"I'll be watchful, but I never could stand to work a garden in shoes. Takes the fun out of it."

The kitchen was lonesome without Lilly and Darcy. Copper poured boiling water in the dishpan and then cooled it with a bit of cold. She'd rather be in the garden herself, but she couldn't always leave Darcy with the tedious inside duties. With a memory of their own, her hands worked at their task. Soon plates, cups, knives, and forks stood drying in the wooden rack.

Holding the door open with her hip, she sluiced the dishwater over the porch floor. *Ping!* What was that? A glint of gold met her eye. Her wedding ring rolled right off the porch and disappeared in the grass. On hands and knees she found it and slid it back where it belonged, where Simon had placed it three years before, where it was never to be removed. "Until death do us part," she heard him say.

"'Til death and beyond," she said as she grabbed the broom and scrubbed the floor. *Ping!* She heard it again. This time the ring fell through a knothole. "For pity's sake!" She'd have to crawl under the porch. Hopefully the copperhead hadn't made himself at home there.

Most cabins up and down Troublesome Creek sat on short stilts or rocks, making a crawl space underneath them, and Copper's was no exception. It was a fine space for hound dogs to lay on hot days, and it helped keep the dank out during rainy seasons. Lying on her belly, Copper peered into the gloom. There it was, shining brightly in the light from the knothole. She dragged it out using the broom handle.

Back in the house, she sat on the side of her bed. The bed she had brought all the way from Lexington, the bed she'd shared with Simon. She cried and cried until she hiccupped, then cried some more. The ring wouldn't stay on. Her once plump finger wouldn't hold it. Finally spent, she lay back on the bolster pillow and remembered the day he died. Remembered and wished she had died too.

One moment's carelessness took her husband's life. It had been a beautiful fall day when Simon set off to visit a patient way out in the country. Copper remembered as if it were yesterday how she said good-bye to him. Sunlight played across his shoulders as bright as butter on a biscuit. He cupped her chin, and his parting kiss was gentle and sweet. Then he set off for the livery station to get a horse, for his was being shod. She remembered how glad she was that day, how full of joy.

Simon was found by the side of the road, battered and alone save for the old blacksnake that lay dead beside him. The snake they surmised that had spooked the unfamiliar horse. It took Simon more than a week to die. Days of hope and nights of fear.

Why couldn't all that stay behind where she'd hoped to leave it? Why did it have to follow her across the rolling hills, over the mountains, and clear up the holler to Troublesome? Before she'd left Lexington, she'd gone to their special place and retrieved two willow saplings. One she'd carried all the way to Troublesome Creek, and the other she'd asked Reuben to plant at Simon's grave. Maybe she could bury some of her sorrow when she planted the willow by the creek.

Copper heard the creak of Lilly's wagon from the yard. How long had she lain here? Standing, she unbuttoned her shirtwaist, then looped a black silk ribbon through the ring of gold and pinned it to the front of her camisole right over her heart.

John had ridden his horse at a fast clip over to Lost Creek. The job was his if he wanted it, and he did. Always frugal, John had saved money from every job he'd ever had, from his young days grubbing sassafras root for old man Smithers to the good pay from his days scrubbing decks on a merchant ship.

Now it looked as if it might all be worth it. Copper was home. She was all he ever wanted.

Chapter 3

Saturday night, there stood John on Copper's front porch, holding his hat, his hair slicked behind his ears. A smile spread across his expectant face when she answered the door.

"These are for you," he said, withdrawing a bunch of wildflowers from behind his back and handing them to Copper.

"Come in." Copper opened the screen door. "We missed you at supper."

"Figured I'd eat at the schoolhouse. They'll have a big spread."

After setting the flowers on the table, Copper fussed about in the pantry, looking for a container to put them in. How dare he knock at her door on his way to somewhere else. A flush of anger heated her cheeks. Did he think a bunch of flowers would sway her mind about the dance? Did he think he could so easily take her for granted? She spied an empty jar on the back of the top shelf and stretched to reach it. A can of hominy went crashing to the floor followed by assorted other jars. What a mess!

Instantly, John was beside her, swooping her off the floor and depositing her in a kitchen chair. "Darcy," he said to the girl when she walked in, "fetch a pan of water."

"Surely," Darcy said and headed to the pantry.

"Forevermore, John." Copper drew herself up straight in the chair and tucked a strand of hair behind her ear. "What are you going on about?"

"You've cut yourself." He knelt before her, examining her bare feet. "There's blood everywhere."

Indeed, a river of red snaked out across the floor from behind the curtained pantry. She felt as if she might swoon. "Is it bad?" she asked, afraid to look. Funny, she never had a problem looking at anybody else's wounds.

He sat back on his heels. "No cuts on your feet. Raise your skirts."

"John Pelfrey! I will not."

"Don't be foolish. I've got to see where all that blood came from."

"Darcy can help me. You wait on the porch."

His hand lingered on her knee, but he got to his feet. "Darcy, can you come help Mrs. Corbett?"

"Just let me clean up this mess of beets first," Darcy said from the pantry. "They'll stain the floor sure as anything."

Copper tried to hold back her laughter, but John started first and released hers from her chest. Before she could protest, he grabbed a towel and dried her beet-stained feet. Every time they quieted, one would look at the other and start up again.

"We'll wake Lilly," Copper said finally.

"I reckon I can't take you to the dance like this."

"I wasn't going anyway, John."

Darcy watched, holding a pan of broken glass mixed with hominy and beets. "You could go, Miz Copper. I'll watch Lilly Gray."

"You know what, Darcy," John said, "dances are for young folks. Why don't you and Dimmert go on over to the schoolhouse? Me and Mrs. Corbett are going to set on the porch a spell."

"You mean it?" Darcy whipped her apron off and grabbed her shoes.

"Wait." Copper chose a wild rose from John's bouquet and put it in Darcy's hair. "There. You look pretty."

Darcy pounded across the porch. "Dimmert, get the horse. We're heading to a party."

Copper couldn't remember when she'd last felt such contentment. Her porch rocker creaked a welcome rhythm while Lilly Gray lay sleeping in her arms. She watched as the edge of the forest disappeared and dusky dark crept across the yard.

"There," John said. "There's one."

"Where?" she answered. "I don't see . . ."

"Right over there by the well house. There's another."

"Oh yes. I see now."

As if on cue, hundreds of fireflies rose from the grass, signaling with tiny flashes of brilliance until the whole yard was awash in fairy light.

"I wish Miss Lilly here were awake to see," Copper said.

"Wake her."

"She'd be cranky as an old bear. Lilly doesn't like her sleep disturbed."

John stood and leaned over them. "Would you like me to put her to bed?"

"No, she's fine. It feels good to hold her." Copper's chair picked up speed with the discomfort John's nearness caused. She needed the barrier her sleeping daughter provided.

He sat back down. His long legs stretched to the edge of the porch. The other rocker barely contained his wide shoulders. Against all reason, she wished he'd slide his chair closer to hers.

"You don't have to sit here with us," she said. "You must have things to do."

John didn't move his head, just kept it straight as if looking out to the yard filled with lightning bugs, but still she felt his eyes on her. She knew his sideways stare. "There's nothing in the world I'd rather be doing."

"You must have seen some beautiful things while you were sailing round the world."

"Yes. You wouldn't believe God's design, Copper. I surely wouldn't have until I saw it for myself."

"Tell me the most beautiful thing you saw."

"I'm looking at it now."

Her heart took a misstep and shuddered in her chest. *This*

isn't right, she thought, *sitting with Simon's baby in my lap and all the while inviting another man's attention.* Her rocker stopped. "I'd best get in and put Lilly down."

He turned her way. "Can I come again?"

Copper hefted Lilly, tucking the baby's head over her shoulder, preparing to stand. "Of course. You know you're welcome anytime."

"I don't mean anytime. I mean like this. You and me and Lilly taking in the night air together." Across the distance his hand reached out and covered hers. "Remember years ago when I asked your daddy if I could come calling? Well, now I'm asking you."

Glad for the darkness that covered her distress, Copper answered, "I don't think I'm ready. I couldn't offer you much."

"All I'm asking is to sit on the porch with you."

She stood with her daughter and walked away. "We'll see."

John opened the door for her before he slapped his hat on and turned to go. "Well, all righty then."

Through the open window as she laid Lilly in her crib, as she sat down on her bed, as she removed her dress and then the wedding ring from her camisole, all that time Copper could hear John's whistling tune until it faded into the darkness across the creek.

Her shoulders shook as tears streamed down her cheeks. What was happening to her? How could she even think of another man while she was still married in her heart? Kneeling, her head in her hands, she prayed for God's guidance and for Simon's forgiveness.

Surprisingly, her sleep was deep and hard. She hadn't woken when Darcy came in, so around 1 a.m., when necessity roused her, she tiptoed to her charge's bedroom door. Moonlight streamed through the window and illuminated Darcy's face, the rose still tucked in her hair.

After easing Darcy's door closed, Copper grabbed a quilt from her bed and went outside. Her chair sat where she'd left it, and John's was angled toward it. As always, Dimmert had filled the water bucket before he went to bed. Copper poured a cup with the granite dipper and settled down for a spell. She'd become used to these late night forays into reflection and enjoyed them until she let her guard down and her true feelings came tumbling out.

What would Simon think? Would he like the fact that she was back in her home place, back where she started? Or would he be disappointed that she had left the safety and security of their home in the city? The work was good for her; she knew that. Hard work soothed the soul and let her sleep at night. Well, most nights anyway.

And then there were all the lessons she had learned at her doctor husband's side. It seemed the bone setting and baby birthing and poultice applying among others had all fallen by the wayside since she came back. She was turning into a ninny. Why, she hadn't even been able to look at her own feet when she'd been bleeding beet juice.

Something on the windowsill caught her eye. She laid her quilt aside and got up to look. A glass canning jar beckoned her with faint light. Turning it in her hands, she smiled. It was full of grass and lightning bugs. The lid had been punctured with air holes. John remembered that as children when they caught fireflies for fun she'd never been able to let the bugs die in the jar. She'd always fed them stalks of grass and made sure they could breathe in their captivity. John was so thoughtful. A warm feeling settled in her chest, along with something she hadn't felt for a long, long time: a little leap of joy.

Settling in with the jar of light, her quilt, and her cup of water, she prayed for God's guidance as the rocker sang its squeaky song. *Lord,* she petitioned, *use me in whatever way pleases You. Help me set aside my petty worries and be the person You want me to be.*

Before long, after the comfort that prayer always gave her, she unscrewed the jar lid and let the insects stagger out, free to entertain another night. Soon she was back in bed, fast asleep. Her baby slept beside her. Darcy snored lightly in her room.

Way over yonder up the tangled holler where the sturdy cabin sat bathed in moonlight, Dance Shelton dared to crack open the door. The screen was still intact over the turtle prison. But what if it bumped against the porch? What if it reached up its beaked mouth and bit her through the screen? Fear gnawed at her belly. But Ace had been gone for two days and two nights, and hunger had sharpened her mind. She reasoned the turtle was as trapped as she. Maybe, just maybe, if she took a giant step she could clear the trap. *Don't look down.* Freedom lay on the other side. *Just don't look down.*

Ragged breaths shook her body as she teetered in the doorframe. "Go on," she urged herself. "Just take one step."

Then she did. She cleared the turtle hole easily enough, and the next thing she knew she was standing on the porch steps. "Which way is Mammaw's?" Her voice sounded rusty to her ears. "Which way?" she asked again, waiting for her own direction. Fancying she could smell a drift of chimney smoke from over the far ridge, she thought she'd set out that way. Dance gathered her long skirt in her hand and took a step toward freedom.

And then the hooting started. Soon the forest round the cabin was alive with screaming whoos.

Tripping over her skirt, she scrambled back up the steps and flung herself through the door, then slammed it shut. As her heart hammered in her chest, she wedged a straight-backed chair under the knob. Then, pulling the bedcovers over her head, she waited for her heart to settle.

After a while, as she was nearing sleep, she thought to pull the chair away from the door. Ace wouldn't like it the least bit if he thought she'd shut him out of his own house. At least she knew what to expect from him . . . better than the dark outside. Who knew what waited there?

CHAPTER 4

Dimmert was hauling water in buckets from the creek so Copper and Darcy could keep the garden from drying up. They ladled two dippers for each tepee of runner beans and three for the tomato plants. The luscious beans had already provided several suppers, but hard, green knobs clung tenaciously to the itchy stalks of tomatoes.

Another week, Copper thought, rubbing the rash on her arms. Even the long sleeves of her housedress didn't prevent the itch caused by tomato leaves. The July sun beat down on the black bonnet Mam had left behind. She should have grabbed a light-colored one, but force of habit chose Mam's. It was a comfort somehow.

But now the heat made her swimmy headed. Her dipper fell as fireflies pricked a closing darkness.

Strong arms broke her fall and led her to the shade tree where Lilly slept in her wagon. Soon Darcy had her bonnet off. Looking through a kaleidoscope of color, Copper thought she might be sick.

"Keep your eyes shut," Darcy said. "You just got a tad too hot."

As if from a distance, she could hear Dimmert coming through the garden. Each brush against tomato bush, bean tepee, or potato hill was as loud as buckshot. Copper wondered if she was dying. What would happen to Lilly Gray?

Water splashed as if from the pretty waterfall she and Lilly had found, cool trickles ran under her chin and down her arms, and dippers full cooled her feet and ankles.

"Thank ye, Dimm," she heard Darcy say. "Maybe you should go for help."

"No," Copper protested weakly. "Help me sit up. I'm already better."

Dimmert lifted her to lean against the shade tree. With a pillow from Lilly's wagon, he padded her back and shoulders.

She opened her eyes, and colors pulled together as her head cleared. Darcy handed her the dipper, and she took a long pull. Water never tasted so good. Sister and brother stood back a ways, giving her air, concern on their faces.

"My goodness," Copper said. "I'm sorry to be such a bother."

Darcy crouched beside her. "Did you eat this morning?"

"I think so. . . . Yes, a biscuit and apple butter and some coffee."

"We'd best get you to the house. Do you think you can walk?"

Before she could answer, Dimmert lifted her in his arms and

in a few dozen strides had her out of the garden and into the rocker on the porch. Darcy led Lilly Gray, looking a little peevish after being woken up, over to Copper. Lilly popped her thumb in and out of her mouth.

"Thumb out," Copper tried to say, but her words jumbled on her tongue.

"Dimmert," Darcy said, "go fetch Mammaw."

Dimmert pointed across the creek. "Mr. John?"

"Mr. John wouldn't know what to do," Darcy replied. "Men never do. 'Sides, he probably ain't home. We need Mammaw."

It felt strange to be in bed in the middle of the day, stranger still to have Darcy hovering about, stirring the air around Copper's face with a church fan. The bedroom window was propped open, and a little breeze joined with Darcy's fan. A wet rag lay across her forehead and one on Lilly Gray's. Lilly had pulled off her own dress and now lay, an invalid, beside her mother.

"Ain't you a sight, Lilly Corbett," Darcy teased. "We'll have to give you some of Mammaw's tonic."

Lilly frowned and burrowed closer to Copper. Her little body gave off unneeded heat, but Copper was glad for her presence. What might have happened if not for Darcy and Dimmert? Her mind spun with terrible possibilities. Lilly Gray could have toddled off and fallen in the creek or been bitten by the copperhead they had yet to find. Copper caught Darcy's arm. "You're a blessing in my life."

"Mammaw says God plants you where you're most needed." Darcy leaned closer with the fan.

Copper could feel tendrils of hair whipping round her face. She reached up shakily to tuck them behind her ears. "Well, God knows Lilly and I needed you and Dimmert, but how did your mammaw know to send you here?"

"Mr. John come by one night. Set on the porch for a spell. He's sure handsome, ain't he?"

Copper thought that was a question she shouldn't answer. John had been sitting on her porch most every night for two weeks now, but would she say he was handsome? She tried so hard not to compare him to Simon. It was unfair because they were so different. Simon had been dark haired and dark eyed, just a few inches taller than her, with an economy of movement, always aware of his surroundings. John was tall, broad shouldered, and a little clumsy, always tipping something over.

Just the night before when they'd gone for a walk across the creek, he'd tried to take her hand and nearly knocked her off the footbridge instead. But to be fair, that was probably her fault. As soon as he reached for her, she'd jerked away. He should have known she wasn't ready for hand holding. Walks and porch sitting were enough for now. Still she couldn't help but imagine what her hand in his would feel like. It would feel good, she figured. She wondered if he'd ever work up the courage to kiss her. Flushing scarlet, she shifted in the bed.

Lilly sat up, and the wet rag slid down her face. "Oh."

Copper laughed and drew the light cotton quilt up over Lilly's shoulders. "Darcy, I feel better. I think I'll get up and break some beans for supper."

"What if I bring them in here? We can break them while we wait on Mammaw."

Green beans with new potatoes and ham hock were simmering on the cookstove before Fairy Mae and her entourage arrived. Copper was up, if still a little shaky, when she saw Dimmert's horse pull a wagon full of young'uns into the yard. "We'd better make another round of corn bread, Darcy," she said.

The children scrambled out of the wagon and piled onto the porch. Lilly Gray was delighted; she finally had playmates.

Fairy Mae Whitt was considerably slower. It was quite a process getting the little woman out of the wagon. As wide as she was tall, with the shortest legs Copper had ever seen on a grown woman, she sort of trundled into the kitchen. Backing up, she plopped into the chair Darcy had waiting, her thick legs sticking out as stiff as kindling. Darcy slid another chair under them for support.

"Give your mammaw some sugar, Darcy," Fairy Mae said, her black eyes twinkling.

Darcy did as she was bid, bussing her grandmother on both cheeks and patting her face before going to the screen door and calling out, "Dory, mind Lilly Gray. Don't let her off the porch."

"Ain't she the best hand with young'uns?" Fairy Mae asked Copper. "Darcy's the best of the lot."

Darcy grinned. "Mammaw, you say that about all us kids."

"I owe you so much, Fairy Mae," Copper replied. "Darcy and Dimmert have been an answer to prayer."

"Well, their pa would be glad to hear that. He's a circuit rider, preaches anywhere there's a need, even as far as Tennessee." Her sharp eyes took Copper in. She pointed at another chair. "Come set with me a spell. Tell me what's ailing you."

Tapping a wooden spoon on the rim of the bean pot, Copper secured the lid before taking the chair Darcy pulled out. "I just had a sinking spell. I feel much better now."

"Don't look better." Fairy Mae leaned forward and pulled one of Copper's eyelids down, then lifted her upper lip to reveal her gum. "Close that door, Darcy."

The murmur of children's voices faded. "Can you pull off your shirtwaist, girl?" Fairy Mae asked.

Copper suddenly felt faint again and very frightened. Her fingers fumbled at her blouse as she followed directions.

Fairy Mae probed and prodded, sure as if Copper's body was a map and she a traveler. "You still nursing that baby girl?"

"She's not two yet," Copper replied, her head clearing.

Fairy Mae slid her arm around Copper's shoulders and pulled her head to the crook of her neck. "You cain't bear to give it up, can you, darlin'?"

"She's my only baby. I may never get to do this again."

Her gentle hands stroked Copper's tear-stained cheeks. "I know, lovey. It's a hard thing, but everything has an ending. Remember your Bible verse that says every thing has its season?"

"Is nursing all that's wrong with me?" Copper sat up and began to button her shirtwaist.

"I'd bet the devil. You don't weigh a hundred pounds, and most of that's bone. Buttermilk six times a day and put your wee one on the cup. You'll soon be right as rain."

Copper sighed. "Lilly Gray will not be happy."

"I'll leave Dilly with you for a spell. She's just the right age for Lilly Gray to want to shadow. Dilly will keep her too busy to know what she's missing."

Copper wanted to crawl up in Fairy Mae's lap and be rocked in her soft arms. It felt so good to be cared for.

"You come along next week when Dimmert brings Dilly home. It will do you good to get off this place, and I'll give you some flower slips. As I recall, Grace Brown always had flower beds."

"Yes, she did." Copper smiled at the happy memory. "Mam had a way with flowers."

Dilly Whitt was a five-year-old firecracker. Her hair was as red as Copper's, and she had the temperament to boot. From morning to night it was mud pie–making, egg-gathering, cat-wallowing, and firefly-chasing mayhem.

Her time with Lilly Gray was fun for the two little girls but melancholy for Copper. It was as Fairy Mae predicted: Lilly wore herself out keeping up with Dilly. Now she babbled constantly, always used the potty, and turned away from her mother. Only at night did Copper have her baby back, and then Lilly tumbled into sleep as fast as a rock down the mountainside. Copper bound her breasts as tight as she could bear to ease the physical pain.

In the evenings Copper and John would sit on the porch and watch all four children play Mother, may I? or freeze tag. Even Dimmert turned into a boy again with his littlest sister around. He was amazingly patient with the two little ones, carrying Lilly on his shoulders while he scissor-stepped or teasing Dilly out of a temper fit. Even though he didn't say much, he laughed a lot.

"Have you ever heard that boy talk?" John asked Copper one night as they sat companionably in the porch rockers.

"He talks when he needs to, but he is painfully shy. He does have some odd ways, though."

"Like what?"

"Well, for one thing he never comes in the house; he even eats outside. And for another, have you noticed he always keeps his horse in sight? No matter if he is hauling water or hoeing corn, Star is where Dimmert can see him."

"Good-looking horse," John said over the squeaking rocker. "This thing needs oiling."

"Never mind. I like the sound."

Too soon it was time to take Dilly home. Copper had grown fond of the little girl, and Lilly Gray was sure to pitch a fit when they left her at Fairy Mae's. It would be sad for Darcy and Dimmert too. Copper thought of John as the wagon taking Dilly home lurched along rutted roads. It felt right to be with him. Her foolish heart was yearning toward his. She dared to imagine children of their own playing in the yard someday.

Lilly Gray leaned against her, yawning, lulled by the wagon's sway. Copper pulled Lilly's thumb from her mouth. The little girl didn't protest, just nestled against her mother. Life was indeed worth living.

It was a relief when the wagon pulled up in front of Fairy

Mae's house. Bottoms numb and teeth jarred, everyone was ready for a break, and it was good to have friends to greet you at the end of a journey. Darcy jumped down with Lilly, and Dimmert swung the laughing Dilly over the side before he helped Copper down.

The cabin was pretty. It sat back in a grove of pines, but the front yard was bathed in sunlight. Flowers of many colors brightened the stepping-stone path where butterflies slowly winged their way along. Two hummingbirds darted in and out of a red geranium the size of a bushel basket. Lilly stopped and pointed, delighted by the humming sound of their tiny bodies.

Copper lifted Lilly to sit astride her hip. She bent down and cupped a bright yellow bloom. "This flower is a lily. Isn't it beautiful? Just like you."

Lilly pulled the head off. Sticking her nose deep in the blossom, she sneezed. "Boo-full."

"Come on up," Fairy Mae called from her chair on the porch, "and let me hug your neck."

Soon Copper was seated beside Fairy Mae. A bowl of soup beans with chopped onion and crumbled corn bread and a mug of sweet sassafras tea rested on the wide arm of her chair. The children, little and big, were in the kitchen, where Darcy and her sister Dawn supervised the noon meal. Dimmert took his bowl and hunkered down under a shade tree to eat with his brother Ezra. Star grazed nearby, pulling up little patches of grass with his long, yellow teeth.

"Fairy Mae," Copper said, "you have a beautiful home. I could sit here all day."

"That's mostly all I do now: sit."

"Do you hurt?"

"Not so much, just stiff as a dead cat. Rheumatiz, I reckon. I mix a little sulphur with cream of tartar when I ache. Sure tastes bad, though."

"Try adding a little licorice. You won't have that aftertaste."

"Hadn't thought of that. I'll sure enough try it." Fairy Mae looked her over. "You've fattened up some."

"Thanks to you." Copper patted Fairy Mae's soft arm. "I feel like you saved me."

"Honey, it's the same with women everywhere, especially mothers. We're always running our wagons off in the ditch."

Peals of childish laughter rang from the kitchen.

"This is a happy house. It's how I hope to raise Lilly."

"Love them and feed them in equal measure. That's the secret."

"May I ask about Dimmert? I worry that he talks so little." Copper said around a spoonful of beans.

"Dimmert keeps his own counsel, sure enough. He's good as gold, that boy is. Takes after his ma, I reckon. That woman hardly spoke all the time I knew her. Then she up and died taking all them unsaid words to the grave. I always figured it was because she married a preacher. Poor thing couldn't get a word in edgewise."

"What happened to her?"

"Early this year she come down with a fever on Tuesday and died on Thursday. God rest her soul. My preacher son delivered this pack of young'uns that next Monday. I ain't seen him since."

One of the young girls took the empty bowls and spoons, and then another girl brought out slices of rhubarb pie.

"Mammaw, you know I don't like rhubarb," Darcy said from the open door.

"There's a piece of peach waiting for you in the warming oven, sugar."

"How do you manage all this by yourself?" Copper asked.

"Their pa sends money, and Dimmert brings the wages you give him and Darcy. I didn't expect money. Feeding them is pay enough."

"Believe me, they earn it. I don't know what I'd do without their help."

They passed a pleasant afternoon talking and laughing, but soon it was time to head home. Darcy cut slips from all the flowers, then wrapped them in wet newsprint.

"Plant them as soon as you get home, and feed them dry chicken manure," Fairy Mae shouted as the wagon jolted away.

"Come back soon," the children yelled from the porch. Ezra ran alongside the wagon until they picked up speed.

Copper felt tears brewing. It was she who cried instead of Lilly Gray.

It was Fairy Mae's leftover soup beans and corn bread for supper that night, along with the squirrel meat John provided. While Copper fried the meat to crispy brown perfection, John milked Mazy. Copper's nose was out of joint. She preferred doing her own milking. It was one of the best parts of her day. She wiped her brow with the hem of her apron and wondered, not for the first time, how it was that women got stuck inside cooking and cleaning—those never-ending tasks—while men had the freedom to come and go as they pleased.

John brought in a jar of cream he'd skimmed from the milk bucket. Copper knew he wanted cream gravy made with the pan drippings. She browned a little flour and salt in the skillet, then reached for the cream.

"Hold still." John caught her apron strings and pulled her toward him.

"John! What are you doing?" She tried to pull away, but he was strong. "This will burn!"

"Won't take a second." He wiped her forehead with his thumb. "You've got flour all over."

It was true. Copper was not a neat cook. Darcy was just like Copper's stepmother had been. You could hardly tell she'd cooked a meal; the kitchen would be so orderly when she finished. But Copper was a different story. Bowls and pans, cups and spoons littered every surface, and her apron was a necessity, not a fashion. She needed a fresh one every day.

"I can wash my own face," she fussed at John.

"This is more fun, you have to admit."

"Call the others," she said, slowly pouring more cream into the skillet. "Supper's ready for the table."

Later, after everyone else was in bed for the night, after John had made his way across the creek, Copper sat on the porch and pondered her circumstances. She dared to think she might be happy again. Lilly, her home, her work, the friends she was making, all stitched together as cozy as a patchwork quilt. And John

. . . How did he fit in? She couldn't deny that the warmth of his touch lingered on her forehead.

Unbuttoning the top three buttons of her blouse, she slipped the straight pin from her camisole and withdrew the ring that rested over her heart. "I'm sorry, Simon," she whispered. It was time to put the ring away in her keepsake box, buried under quilts in the blanket chest, time to get on with the business of life.

CHAPTER 5

"Are we ever going to church?" Darcy asked one hot Sunday morning.

Busy brushing the tangles from Lilly's hair, Copper didn't pause. "You don't need my permission to go to service."

"No, ma'am, I know, but it don't seem right to go off and leave you and Lilly here by your lonesome. Besides, ain't it a law?"

"What do you mean?"

"Don't the Bible say to remember the Lord's Day? That's what Mammaw told me anyway."

Copper bent over her daughter's head. Darcy brought her to shame. The last time she had been to the little white church in the valley of the mountains was the day she married Simon. It would be too painful to go there again. Memories of that bright

June day streamed like silky ribbons in her mind: her dress, pretty as a layer cake, and the bouquet of summer roses and service berries. Just beyond stood her daddy with tears in his eyes. The door to the church opened wide, revealing her beloved standing at the end of the aisle ready to receive her.

The memory ribbons twirled and fluttered away like feathers in a breeze as recollections of darker days crept in to take their place: Simon's handsome face losing color, his lips as cold as death when she kissed him one last time, the weeping willow she'd had planted to keep watch over his grave, the tombstone that said nothing of their love.

Stop it, she chided herself. *I'm not the only person on earth to suffer a loss.*

"Ouch, Mama!" Lilly's complaint jerked Copper back to reality. She clutched the comb so hard it left tiny pricks across her palm.

"Sorry, baby." She swooped Lilly's black hair with its unusual streak of silver back with a green ribbon. "Would you like to go to church, Miss Priss?"

Lilly clapped. "Go bye-bye. Mama too? Darcy too? Dimm too?"

"Yes, Mama and Darcy and Dimmert if he wants. If we hurry we can still make Sunday school."

Copper couldn't say she was warmly greeted by the people she remembered so fondly as she walked across the churchyard with Lilly on her hip. Maybe it was her lavender watered-silk dress with a formfitting bodice set off by coffee-colored embroidered lace or the lavender hat with rosettes that matched her dress. It was the simplest Sunday dress she owned but still much too fancy. Watered-silk might be de rigueur in the big city of Lexington, but unadorned black dresses or simple cotton shifts were the style on Troublesome. She'd have to drag out Mam's old Singer before next Sunday.

The ladies couldn't resist Lilly Gray though, and once the ice thawed a little and the folks remembered who Copper had been instead of who they figured she was now, they began to sidle up, touching Lilly's foot or stroking her hand.

"Who's she favor?" one woman asked. "She don't look like a Brown."

"Don't you remember her pa?" Jean Foster interjected. "She looks just like Doc Corbett." Squeezing Copper's shoulders, she continued, "So sorry, honey, to hear of your loss. We're all so glad you're back. It ain't right for Will Brown's farm to fall fallow."

"Thank you," Copper said. Jean Foster, she recollected, was a straight-shooting woman, the truth her calling card. "I'm glad to be home."

"What marked that baby?" old Hezzy Krill mumbled around her snuff stick, one bony finger tracing the silver streak that shot through Lilly's black hair.

"Hezzy," Jean said sharply, "let Copper catch her breath before you start your devilment."

Thankfully, the church bell rang just then, calling the flock to worship. As was their custom on days of fair weather, people fell into place along the stone path that led to the open church door, two elders first, followed by several deacons, which took care of most of the men, with women and children last. In a custom Copper loved, Elder Foster's commanding voice led them in singing "Onward, Christian Soldiers" as they marched in to find their seats.

Copper hung back with Lilly and Darcy, not sure where she should sit. It wouldn't be good form to take someone else's pew. Tears filled her eyes when she saw the empty seats left for them—the very spot where her family had sat every Sunday for years. Indeed, watered-silk or not, she was home.

It seemed Copper hadn't been home from church twenty minutes, just enough time to take off her fancy dress and hang it in the chiffonier, before trouble came to call.

"Hello!" someone shouted from the barnyard. Then, "Hello!" again before she had a chance to slip on a day dress.

"I'll go, Miz Copper," Darcy called from the kitchen.

Peeking through the bedroom window as she tidied her hair, Copper saw a stranger astride a saddleless horse. Darcy tarried at the edge of the yard, listening to the man without going too close, holding tight to Lilly's hand. Dimmert stood back in the shadowy barn. Was that a rock clutched in his hand?

"Oh, forevermore," Copper said, turning back to her reflection in the wavy mirror of the wardrobe. "I'd better get out there before Dimm accidentally kills somebody." She tucked one more comb into the mass of her red hair, grabbed her shoes, and headed for the door.

The stranger was tall, and he didn't dismount. He seemed in a hurry to get somewhere else.

"Mister," Copper said, "light a spell and tell me what the matter is."

"Folks say you're a doctor. My brother's hurt real bad. Will you come?"

Why, the stranger wasn't a man at all but a big-boned, husky-voiced young woman clad in a pair of overalls and a man's long-sleeve shirt. A felt hat sat askew on her head.

"Of course," Copper replied without a second's thought. "I'm not a doctor, but I'll do what I can. Let me get my bag.

"You keep Lilly in the house until I get back, Darcy," Copper instructed as she readied her medical kit and grabbed her doctor's bag. "And don't light the stove. There's plenty to eat."

"Yes, ma'am. You know I'll mind the baby proper."

A kiss for Lilly Gray and one for Darcy before Copper fairly flew out the door. By the stranger's demeanor she could tell time was of the essence. "You ride and I'll lead," the young woman said as Copper approached.

But Dimmert was having none of it. He stood beside Star, his eye catching Copper's. "I'll take you," he said.

The ride was rough, and she held fast to Dimmert's shoulder as sure-footed Star maneuvered around rocks and trees, climbing ever higher behind the stranger. Envious, Copper noted the ease with which the young woman rode, while she struggled just to stay put, sitting sideways on Star. Dresses and petticoats sure got in the way sometimes.

Within the hour they came upon a clearing and a cabin that had seen better days. At least a dozen stair-step children and half as many dogs stood watching as they approached. Two boys ran over to take their mounts, but Dimmert didn't give Star up. After helping Copper down, he withdrew to a copse of trees, sitting on his haunches. Copper knew he would be watching. A little thrill of fear snaked up her backbone, but it wasn't because of these people. It was because she didn't know what waited on the other side of the cabin door.

The children closed in, silently ushering Copper to a set of rickety wooden steps leading to the porch. One small hand closed over her own as she clutched her doctor's bag, and others clung to her skirts. Just as she reached for the knob, the door swung open and an older version of the big-boned girl who'd come to fetch her stood trembling in its frame. Her skirts hung awry from angular hips, and her thin, graying hair was skinned back in a tight bun.

The woman's eyes met Copper's for a fleeting moment. Without a word she stepped back, her motion drawing Copper in. The woman turned to the bed that was pulled up in front of a roaring fire. Copper thought she might pass out—whether from fear or the heat in the room she didn't know.

Beside the bed a man stood and uttered the first words spoken: "Thank you for coming, Doc. Would you see if there's the least thing you can do for our boy Kenny?"

Opening her mouth to protest her lack of a medical degree, Copper sighed instead. As soon as she saw the boy, she knew it didn't matter. A dozen doctors couldn't save this one young life. The boy lay prostrate, white as bleached muslin, in the middle of the iron bedstead. Blood soaked his bedding and pooled on the floor beneath. A deep, dark wound slashed across his belly. His blue eyes were open and stared beseechingly at Copper as she bent over the bed and took his hand. He tried to sit, but Copper saw that he couldn't move his legs.

"Kenny, I'm Copper. I'm here to help."

His grip was surprisingly strong, as if he put whatever he had left into it. "Mommy told me not to go up there," he said between panting breaths. "I should have listened to her."

With a strangled sob the big-boned woman fled from the room. The man's shoulders slumped, but he stayed put. His lumpy, knuckled hand brushed hair as fine as corn silk from Kenny's forehead. Over and over he brushed as if that was all he knew to do.

"Can I have a drink of water, Daddy?" Kenny gasped.

The man looked at Copper for an answer.

"Sure," she said, knowing it mattered not if he ate or drank. She thought he wouldn't live to see the night.

"I'm going to draw ye some cold well water," his father said. "I could put another log on the fire if ye want, Doc."

"No, I believe we'll let it die down if that's okay."

Kenny's father shook his head. "I couldn't think of anything else to do for my boy except keep him warm."

After he left to get the water, the young woman who'd brought Copper took his place at the bedside. "I'm Cara Wilson. This here wart's my brother Kenny."

"Ain't a wart," Kenny denied as the ghost of a smile played on his face.

"Frog kisser." A fat teardrop slid down Cara's cheek.

"Cara, I need to talk to your mother and father. Would you stay here for a moment?"

"Guess I can give the little wart some time, though he's just trying to get out of chores."

"Am not," Kenny managed.

"Are too," Copper heard as she stepped out into fresh air. Mr. Wilson stood on the first step holding a bucket of water. Mrs. Wilson looked at Copper with such longing, such hope that Copper's heart squeezed tight with regret. All Kenny's brothers and sisters sat cross-legged on the porch, just waiting.

"I'm sorry," was all she had to offer . . . such puny words. "I'm so very sorry."

Mrs. Wilson gasped and fell to her knees, her hands clasped in prayer. "Oh, Lord, Kenny's only ten years old. Take me, Jesus, and leave my boy."

The dropped water bucket sloshed down the steps and rolled across the yard. Mr. Wilson grabbed his wife under the arms and hauled her up. "Hush, Miranda," he crooned as he rocked her. "Hush now."

One of the big boys dashed after the bucket and took off for the well. "I'll get Kenny's water."

"You won't leave us, will ye, Doc?" Mr. Wilson said over his wife's head. "You'll stay until it's over?"

"Of course. Let me speak to Dimmert there—" Copper looked to the tree line where he waited—"then I'll go back in."

CHAPTER 6

On a pad of paper from her doctor's kit, Copper scribbled a note to John. *Come to the Wilsons' on Little Fork near the old Smith place and bring the preacher.*

Dimmert didn't want to leave her; that was obvious.

"You have to go stay with the girls," she ordered. "I don't know how long this will take, Dimm. We can't leave them alone come dark. And you'll need to milk Mazy." He gave in, taking the square of paper she handed him. "Be sure this gets to Mr. Pelfrey, and thank you."

Mrs. Wilson stood slumped against her husband when Copper returned. A low moaning sound came from the room beyond the door. The children had moved off to the yard; one little girl covered her ears, one sobbed, and one boy lobbed green walnuts at a tree. The family's plight—Kenny's plight—made Copper appreciate all that Simon had taught her. Maybe she couldn't save the boy, but she could give him comfort and through that she could comfort the family.

"Stay here, Miranda." Mr. Wilson half carried his wife to a hickory chair. "I'm going to take Kenny a drink."

The boy struggled to raise his head as his father offered him a dipper gourd of well water. *Plop, plop, plop,* Copper heard.

"More," Kenny said. "So thirsty."

Copper looked under the bed. It may have been the saddest sight she'd ever seen, the water Kenny drank dripping out to mix with his blood in an ever-widening circle of loss.

"My belly pains me," he whimpered.

Mr. Wilson caught Copper's eye. "What can we do to help ye?"

Copper shook out the long white apron she carried in her bag and retrieved the white scarf she would tie her hair up in. "Pray. You'll see some visitors soon. I've sent for John Pelfrey and the preacher."

As she slipped the scarf on, Copper directed Cara to tear a clean sheet into the wide strips they would use to bind Kenny's wound.

Ever so thankful for the apothecary supplies in her doctor's kit, Copper removed a dark brown bottle of precious morphine. Her hand shook. Forcing herself to slow down, she took a deep breath before she applied a few drops to a lump of sugar. She could hear Simon's cautioning voice as if he stood beside her. Kenny was ten years old but small, so she must be very careful to give just enough medicine to quiet his pain without stilling his breath. With a prayer she put the lump of sugared medicine into Kenny's mouth.

When Kenny's moaning stopped and he appeared to be sleeping, she and Cara set about the task of bathing him and wrapping his belly with the cotton strips. After they freshened the bed, Cara scrubbed the floor while Copper monitored Kenny's heartbeat and his breathing pattern. He was slipping into a coma, and his blood loss was too great to sustain life much longer. She hoped the preacher made it in time.

As the fire died out in the fireplace, Copper raised the windows to catch a cooling breeze. Cara hung extra pieces of the old sheet over the windows to keep out flies and to darken the room.

While they worked, Cara recounted the accident that had caused such suffering. Kenny was a mischievous boy, as most boys tended to be. He was determined to go swimming that hot Sunday morning, but his mother was just as determined that he wouldn't. Rounding up a couple of his brothers, Kenny convinced them that their mother would never know they were gone if they left while she was frying the chicken for their noon meal.

At their favorite swimming hole, a thick twist of grapevine hung from the branch of a sycamore that leaned out over the water. Kenny grabbed hold of the vine and ran backward as far as he could, then forward in a dead run. In seconds he was airborne, flying out over the water before he dropped. Of course, he didn't see the broken wooden plank, probably washed downstream during the recent flooding, nor could he know it was lodged upright beneath the water. He didn't know until he sliced his stomach open and severed his spine. His brothers saved him and carried him home, and Copper knew the rest of the story.

"It wouldn't have happened," Cara related her mother saying, "if they had gone to church as they should. If they had gone to church, Kenny would have been in his Sunday school class instead of swinging on a grapevine rope.

"Now Mama will wear her grief across her shoulders for the rest of her days," Cara said.

"Well . . . ," Copper started but couldn't think what to say. Cara was right. A mother would never get over this grief, but accidents happened and boys got hurt. You couldn't wrap them in cotton batting and keep them in the closet. "I think we can let the children visit now," she finally said. Everything was in order.

The brothers and sisters filed in youngest to oldest. Mrs. Wilson knelt by the bed, her forehead resting on Kenny's chest. A little sister laid a bright cardinal's feather at her brother's feet. "Here, Kenny," she said, "I brung you a present." One by one they each had something to say or something to put on his bed. Soon Kenny had an assortment of gifts.

The preacher and John stepped quietly into the room. Copper had a few whispered words with them before Mr. Wilson's welcome. Mrs. Wilson took to crying silently, rivers of salty tears dripping off her chin.

Reverend Jasper opened his big black Bible and began to read the familiar words of Jesus from the book of John: "'Let not your heart be troubled: ye believe in God, believe also in me. In my Father's house are many mansions: if it were not so, I would have told you. I go to prepare a place for you. And if I go and prepare a place for you, I will come again, and receive you unto myself; that where I am, there ye may be also. And whither I go ye know, and the way ye know.'

"Let us pray," the preacher said, his arm stretched out over the dying boy. "Lord, we ask for grace and ease for Kenny Wilson's crossing. I remember well the day I baptized this boy in Your holy name. Now he's ready to meet You face-to-face. Give peace to his family and strength for the journey."

Even the smallest child joined in a chorus of amens.

Soon neighbors and friends of the family began assembling in the yard. Someone set up sawhorses and made a makeshift table to hold all the food that would be the family's supper. Only the closest came inside. The rest stood vigil outside.

Copper walked with John under the trees. His face was as troubled as her heart. "Poor little mite," he said.

"I feel like my heart's going to burst. I don't know if I can go back in there."

"Sure you can. It would be even worse for this family without you."

She wiped her tears on the skirt of her apron. "It might take a while. You should probably go on back."

"I went by and checked on the girls before I came. Dimmert's there to watch out for them, and I'm not leaving you."

Copper allowed herself a moment's weakness and leaned her head against his chest. "I'm so glad you're here."

It was dusky dark when Kenny Wilson's young soul slipped beyond the binds of his earthly home.

How glorious, Copper thought, *to be a part of this boy's passing.*

Pain free and awake at the end, Kenny looked straight into his mother's eyes and said, "Don't fret now, Mommy. It's beautiful where I'm going."

Copper's job was over. A couple of ladies came in to help Cara and Mrs. Wilson prepare the body. Quietly, Copper cautioned them not to remove the belly wrap, not to let his mother see that gaping wound again. But it was as it should be when a child was lost; the woman who gave him life would minister to his body in death.

It seemed a long way home. John's horse picked his way down the steep trail. Thankfully there was bright moonlight to show the way. Copper was silent, holding back sorrow, afraid if she let the dam burst she'd never stop crying. She was comforted, though, by John's presence. She felt safe with him.

"Listen," he said, reining in the horse.

Suddenly the night was alive with the hooting calls of owls. Such a sad night, but still the owls made her smile. She loved their questioning song. *What would you do,* she wondered as they rode along, *if you had no answers to the mystery of death?*

The Scripture Brother Jasper read came back to comfort her: *"In my Father's house are many mansions."* Somehow those words of hope released pent-up sorrow. Her tears wet the back of John's shirt, but she didn't turn her head.

They reached the barnyard and John dismounted. She knew what would happen before he even reached up to help her down. After sliding into his strong arms, she let him hold her. Then he kissed her gently there between her tears.

"I'm sorry you had to go through all that," he murmured.

She would have answered if she could. She would have told him that being with Kenny at the moment of his passing was worth every aching stitch in her heart. Instead, she sobbed as he led her across the yard to the light of the lamp Darcy had left burning in the window. At the door she leaned into his arms again, and when he kissed her, she welcomed him.

"Well, now." John stepped back. "I've been waiting for that all my life."

"I've got to go in. I'm longing to see my baby. We'll talk tomorrow."

"I'll be gone for a spell. I've got a job logging, and it's a far piece from here. I'll be staying there right on a week."

"That's good. It will give us time to think."

John dried her tears with his calloused palm. "I don't need time. This is what was supposed to happen."

Shaking her head, she stepped into the comforting light of the kitchen. *It's all right*, she reassured herself. It was time to let the past sleep and get on with life. She listened until John's whistle faded clean away before she lifted Lilly from her crib and snuggled beside her in the bed. More tears flowed then—cleansing tears of release.

CHAPTER 7

Copper moped through wash day, every thought turned toward the Wilsons. The heat and smoke from the fire under the wash-tub seemed to mix with her heavy sorrow, pushing it down around her shoulders. Copper patted her neck with a clean washrag. "It must be a hundred degrees today."

"At least the clothes are drying fast," Darcy said. "We'll be done by noon. We'll eat that wash-day cake Mammaw sent by Ezra."

"Did he get some milk to take home?" Copper asked.

"Yeah, and some of that butter." Darcy wrung rinse water from a pair of overalls. "Him and Dimmert was taking the rest over to the Wilsons' like you said."

"Good. Somehow I missed seeing Ezra."

"You was sorting clothes in the side yard. You looked like you was a million miles away."

Stooping, Copper fished a potato bug from Lilly's tight fist. "Easy, baby. You'll smush the little thing."

"Out," Lilly demanded, tired of the confines of her wagon.

"Looks like you're doing fine right there." Copper laughed as a black and yellow butterfly lit on Lilly's shoulder. "Just another minute and you can stretch your legs."

Copper poured a stream of water over the fire. It was too hot to let it burn itself out. "Which job do you want, Darcy?"

Darcy's face knit in puzzlement. "I'll do the outhouse today, and you can do the porch. Miss Lilly can go with me. It will be cool for her under the maple tree."

Copper hefted a bucket of soapy wash water and carried it to the necessary as Darcy pulled the wagon. "Watch her close. She's just itching to get out."

Lilly lay on her back in the bed of the wagon, her arms and legs stuck straight up. "Me be bug."

Copper tickled the small round belly. "Be good for Darcy while Mama scrubs the porch."

My, that child can talk, Copper thought as she carried water from the washtub to mop the kitchen floor and scrub the porch. *If she talks this much now, we're in for trouble when she turns two.* Truthfully, she loved Lilly's quickness and often wrote things Lilly said in a journal before she went to bed. Her mood lightened as she cleaned the house and porch. When she finished she filled a barrel with the rinse water. She saved every drop. It was good enough for cleaning and dish washing. And hot as it was, they might be in for a drought.

Her thoughts turned to John, and she wondered how he was doing working in such weather. He'd be clearing brush and dead trees, helping to make a trail for logging come late fall. Tracing her upper lip with her index finger brought his kiss back to mind. Oh, my, how quickly life could change with just one kiss.

Her stomach growled, reminding her of Fairy Mae's stack cake setting on the back of the stove. She'd slice a tomato and an onion, and she and the girls would have corn bread sandwiches before dessert.

By late afternoon the house was spick-and-span, and the laundry was folded and put away. Copper was sitting on the porch trying to catch a breeze. Tuesday's ironing was starched, sprinkled, rolled, and waiting under a damp towel in the wicker basket. Mam wouldn't like it if she knew how little ironing Copper did. Sheets and pillowcases went right from the line to the beds, and her tea towels never felt the touch of an iron. Still it was half a day's work to do everything else. She would start in the morning at six, right after milking, and not be done until one or two. A trick she had learned from her housekeeper in Lexington made the job much quicker. She kept two sadirons on the stove and switched them when one got cool. Thankfully, she had Darcy to keep Lilly out from underfoot.

A familiar clip-clop, clip-clop signaled the postman on his weekly rounds. Her heart beat fast. She must have mail, else Mr. Bradley wouldn't come this way. Maybe there would be a letter from Mam or one from Alice. Even better, maybe they had both written. How exciting the possibilities were. She poured a glass of water for Mr. Bradley, then went down the path to meet the mail.

Mr. Bradley handed her a fat package wrapped in familiar stenciled brown paper. "Looks like you got yourself something interesting."

"This paper is from Massey's Mercantile in Lexington," Copper replied, giving him the glass of water. "I'd know it anywhere."

"Need some help with that there twine?"

"No, thanks. I think I can get it."

"Well then, I'll just step down to the creek and water my horse before I finish my route," the postman said.

Halfway to the porch Copper called over her shoulder, "Thanks, Mr. Bradley." Why would she get a package from Massey's? What could it be?

"Darcy," she said quietly through the screen so as not to rouse Lilly from her nap, "come see what came in the mail."

Dusting flour from her hands, Darcy settled at Copper's feet. "My, that's sure pretty paper."

"Mr. Massey has rolls of it in his store in Lexington," Copper answered. "It's all stenciled with this print."

"What's it called?"

"Fleur-de-lis. I think it's French."

"What do you reckon is in there?"

Copper laughed. "I don't know. It seems too pretty to open."

"Want me to get the scissors?"

"If I can just get this one knot–" Copper tugged at the heavy white string that secured the package–"we can use this again. It would be a shame to cut it."

"Does that feller need something?" Darcy asked. "He's just standing there in the middle of the road."

"Goodness," Copper said, standing and laying the package aside. "Mr. Bradley, come on up and set a spell."

"Don't mind if I do." He quickly stepped onto the path that intersected the yard. "I'll have another glass of water if you don't mind."

Copper handed him a full glass. "You don't mind if I tend to this package while you rest, do you?"

"No, ma'am. You go on about your business."

The more she worked at the knot, the tighter it seemed to get.

Finally, Darcy could stand it no longer. "Let me try," she said and went at the knot with her teeth, like a terrier with a bone. Mr. Bradley was taking out the blade of his jackknife when the knot gave way. Reverently, Darcy laid the package back in Copper's lap.

With held breath, Copper unfolded the heavy brown wrapper. Like a jack-in-the-box, beautiful dress fabrics and shiny ribbons popped out of the package.

Darcy's eyes popped along with the package. "I got to wash up," she said, jumping up to go to the wash bench. After washing and drying her hands, she hung the linen towel on a nail. A length of red silk ribbon slicked through her fingers. "Ain't this the prettiest thing you ever saw in your life?"

Copper studied a bolt of brightly printed cotton. "Do you

think we could run up a couple of dresses before the quilting circle at Jean Foster's on Thursday?"

"You mean for me too?"

"Of course. You choose what you'd like."

"I'll have to think on it," Darcy responded. "It's a big decision."

"Who sent you them fotch-on pretties, Miz Corbett?" Mr. Bradley asked.

Copper nearly jumped out of her skin. She'd forgotten all about the mailman. She hadn't heard the term *fotch-on* since she was a girl. Her daddy used to say that when Mam would order anything from the city.

"My sister-in-law, Alice Corbett," she replied. "Such a kindness."

The fabric lay like a treasure in her lap. Except for the ribbon, there wasn't a fancy piece in the whole lot. She wouldn't have expected Alice to be so understanding. A spool of colored thread fell from the package. Old Tom batted it, playing like a kitten. "Do you have a favorite color, Mr. Bradley?"

"I've always favored blue."

"Might I borrow your knife?" Copper asked, unrolling a length of sky blue ribbon. Mr. Bradley handed it over, handle first, and Copper cut a long length of the ribbon. "Take this to your wife if you please," she said.

"Well, thank ye. Ain't that pretty?" He folded the knife against his leg. "I better shake a leg. I got a far piece to go yet."

"I've made up my mind," Darcy stated before Mr. Bradley was even off the porch. "I favor this." She held a length of dark green cotton splashed with red and yellow flowers.

"Perfect," Copper said. "Let's go oil Mam's old Singer. We'll haul it right out on the porch. . . . Um, Darcy, do you know how to sew?"

"Surely. My ma taught me."

"Good. I drove my mam to distraction when she tried to teach me."

"You can cut then, Miz Copper, and I'll do the stitchin'."

Copper and Darcy measured and cut and sewed that evening and the next day until the porch was littered with small pieces of leftover fabric.

"Looks like fall out here," Darcy observed as Copper hemmed a skirt. "Just like leaves off a tree."

"You could practice piecing with them," Copper said.

Darcy's eyes lit up, and she began gathering the scraps. "I'll take some pieces to Mrs. Foster when we go. She can help me get started."

Smiling, Copper stepped into the kitchen. Darcy's happiness was contagious. It was then the laundry basket caught her eye. Oh no! In her haste to make dresses she had forgotten the ironing. She'd let Tuesday slip away. She lifted the basket to the kitchen table. She could smell mildew already. Most of the laundered pieces were fine, but two of her shirtwaists, a camisole, two pairs of drawers, and Lilly Gray's best pinafore were sprayed with dots of black mold. What kind of homemaker was she that she'd let her laundry go to ruin? Maybe it wasn't too late.

"Darcy," she said, stepping onto the porch with the basket under her arm, "I forgot the ironing."

Darcy guided Lilly down the steps to the side yard and shook out the laundry while Copper rubbed the stains with soft soap mixed with salt. "Now, we'll just lay these over the bushes to catch the dew overnight," Copper instructed. "The early sun will finish the job."

"Wonder if it's legal to iron on Wednesday," Darcy teased.

"I guess we'll find out. I knew this day was too much fun. My mam always said, 'Laugh today and you'll cry tomorrow.' Reckon I'll be crying over that hot iron come morning."

"Them dresses we stitched might be worth a few tears."

Copper hugged Darcy. "I like your attitude, girl."

Lilly Gray came up between them. "Me, me!" she cried.

"There are hugs enough to go round, Lilly," Copper said, holding her daughter and Darcy. "The more love you give, the more God sends."

CHAPTER 8

"Miz Copper, did you see my fabric scraps?" Darcy asked from her bedroom door.

"Not since Tuesday. Where did you put them after you picked them up?"

Darcy frowned. "Right in the drawer of that little table by my bed. Pshaw, I wanted to show them to Mrs. Foster."

"Don't fret. There's sure to be plenty of scraps to share today. Now hurry and get your bonnet. We don't want to miss any of the quilting circle."

Several ladies were already seated at the quilting frame, needles and thimbles flashing in the midmorning light, when Copper arrived with Darcy and Lilly.

Jean Foster rose to greet them. "I'm so glad you could come, Copper," she said, her warm cheek pressing Copper's own. "We've decided to finish this quilt for Kenny Wilson's mother. Do you like the pattern?"

Overcome with emotion, Copper felt tears form. Graduating shades of yellow mixed with red and brown revealed an appealing Jacob's ladder. "It's beautiful. It's sure to bring comfort to Kenny's mother."

Hezzy Krill snorted. "If Miranda Wilson made them boys mind, she wouldn't have nothing to grieve about. Instead she leaves them run wild with no more manners than a pack of dogs. And what about that girl of hers? That Cara, dressing like a man!" She paused to pinch a bit of snuff from a small tin and worked it under her lip with a frayed-end stick. "Abomination, if ye ask me."

At a loss, Copper just stared at the mean old woman. How could she say such a thing after what happened to Kenny? And Cara was as sweet as could be.

"Now, Hezzy," Jean said, "I expect Miranda Wilson does the best she can, like we all hope to do. Copper, sit here beside me. Here's a needle already threaded."

Copper fished her mam's thimble from her pocket and began taking the tiny even stitches that bound cotton batting to the quilt top.

The ladies spoke of their children and their gardens, shared sorrows and blessings. Copper found she enjoyed their companionship, and Lilly was in heaven, playing under the quilting frame with Jean's five-year-old boy. Bubby stacked empty thread spools—he must have had twenty-five or more—then let Lilly knock them down, scattering the pieces all across the floor. Lilly laughed each time the little tower fell. Her joy was so contagious she soon had all the ladies laughing with her. All except Hezzy. It seemed as if her back was up since Jean's admonishment. But she could quilt; Copper had to give her that. There was music in her flying fingers.

All too soon, the party was over and the ladies began gathering up their things and making their way out. Copper was invited to join the ladies' quilting circle regularly at Jean's house.

"I would love to," Copper said. "And you all can tell by my crooked stitches that I need the practice."

Jean squeezed her hand. "Welcome home. You and John must join us for supper one evening."

Copper blushed. Did everyone know about her and John? Word sure traveled fast in the mountains. She couldn't help but smile. "Thank you. I'm sure John would like that."

As Hezzy hitched her way across the floor, her foot slid on an errant spool. Copper reached out to steady her. The old woman pushed her face in Copper's. The rank smell of tobacco issued from her mouth, and her eyes flared like struck flint.

Wary, hand to her heart, Copper stepped back.

But Hezzy pursued. "Too bad about John Pelfrey's wife. They never found her body, did they?"

John's wife? Surely she hadn't heard right. Copper felt the blood drain from her face. She had to get away from Hezzy. She stooped to pick up her daughter. "Lilly Gray, give Bubby his spool."

"Aw, let her keep it," he said. "I meant for Lilly to have it."

Copper reached out and ruffled the boy's blond curls, glad for the distraction. "Thank you, Bubby."

Jean touched Copper's arm. "Are you all right?"

If she could just get outside, away from all the stares, she would be. "Goodness, yes. I hope to see you all soon." As she walked across the yard with Darcy and Lilly, she forced her steps to be as steady and evenly paced as quilt stitching, though she wanted to run. She couldn't bear for her shame to show.

"Look, Miz Copper," Darcy chattered, holding out a stack of quilt pieces, each gathered into a round the size of a silver dollar. "I got a good start. Don't you think?"

"I do," she said as if her world were the same as when she had stepped up on Jean's porch that morning. "You'll have a full quilt in no time."

"And see," Darcy continued, "Mrs. Foster gave me these extras to make more."

Blessedly, they were soon on the path through the woods that led home.

It was midmorning the next day when Jean and Bubby came to call. "I hope you don't mind," she said, "us just showing up like this, but I had to see if you're okay."

Darcy took the children out to play under the apple tree in the front yard. "We'll catch jar flies and listen to them buzz."

Copper cut pieces of gingerbread and poured cups of coffee. Jean sliced through the moist cake, but she didn't take a bite.

Instead she laid her fork aside and reached across the table to Copper. "Honey, didn't you know?"

Copper dropped her head, squeezing her swollen eyelids shut. She'd cried all night with pain she'd never felt before. Tears of loss and longing and sorrow as dark as a moonless night were all too familiar to her heart, but she'd never cried from betrayal before. And to think it was John—*her* John—who had laid his lie before her.

She shook her head; her fingers tapped her lips. Finally she spoke. "I didn't. John never said a word in all this time. I feel like such a fool."

"I'm sure he never meant to hurt you. He just . . ."

"Just what? Just conveniently neglected to tell me he was married?" There, she'd said it. It was true. "Oh, Jean, forgive me. I don't mean to take my anger out on you."

"Anger's good. Don't hold it in, else it will fester like a boil."

"I've never been good at holding anything in. You should ask my mam."

"Do you want me to tell you what I know? Or would you rather wait and talk to John?"

Coffee sloshed from Copper's cup, and a wet, brown stain spread across her apron front. "Tell me," she whispered.

"I didn't know the woman he married," Jean started. "I don't think anyone did. I heard her family was gypsies, but I don't know if there's any truth to that. You know John was away for a while?"

Copper nodded. His leaving had been a burden on her for a very long time, for she knew that once she had broken his heart.

Now he had broken hers. "He left to work on a merchant ship when I was promised to Simon. He wanted to marry me way back then."

"I don't want to spread gossip, so take this with a grain of salt. All I can tell you was what was told to me. I heard that John's young wife died in an accident at Torrent Falls. They'd been married only a few days."

"That's dreadful." Wetting her finger, Copper captured a gingerbread crumb from her plate. "I must seem so selfish, only thinking of myself, not that poor girl nor John's sorrow."

"You have a right to your feelings, but perhaps you should withhold judgment until John has had a chance to explain himself."

Copper went to the door to check on Lilly. Darcy had spread an old quilt in the shade, and the children seemed quite content. A quick wind whipped the leaves of the apple tree; it seemed a storm was brewing. She felt Jean's touch on her shoulder. "I thank God that you are my friend, Jean Foster."

"Pray about this, dear, and don't be too hard on John. He really loves you."

"I cannot hold to a liar, but I'll always care for him."

Dance Shelton gripped her belly and gritted her teeth. Ace was gone again, and she was as alone as she would ever be. Water trickled down her leg and puddled on the floor. She began pacing. It wasn't so bad when she walked; the walls enclosed her pain. And with each step she prayed, *O Lord, please send help.*

Late that night, unable to rest, Copper slipped out to the porch. The storm that threatened earlier in the day had dissipated after only a little wind and a few hard drops of rain, and now a perfectly round moon cast a golden light across the parched yard. The flower slips from Fairy Mae that she'd planted looked listless in the moonlight. Grabbing the water bucket and dipper, she made her way to the small plot by the side of the steps. She'd give each lily and rose just a smidgen of the cool water. It was nice being out among the plants in the moonlight. Maybe she'd take up night gardening since she couldn't sleep anyway.

She'd just straightened up from smelling the one rose that had blossomed. Nothing had a better fragrance than roses. It was her favorite flower.

Suddenly, Dimm materialized out of the darkness, riding Star right up to the porch.

Copper gasped and covered her heart with her hand. "My, you gave me a fright, Dimmert. What are you doing out so late?"

He slid off the horse and made a quick motion with one hand as if to say, "Come."

Copper shook her head. "You'll have to use words if you need something."

"Dance," he managed, then closed his mouth.

"Dance? You want to dance?"

"My sister," he said and clutched his belly in a pantomime of pain.

"At Fairy Mae's?" Nothing was making sense or else she was dreaming.

"Dance," Dimmert tried again. Then a whole sentence stumbled out. "I . . . I . . . I been watching."

Copper finally understood. His sister Dance, who lived with her husband up a holler somewhere off Troublesome, must have taken ill. "Let me tell Darcy. I'll be right back."

After waking Darcy and telling her she'd be back shortly—no need to alarm the girl with news of her sister until morning—Copper fumbled around in her small apothecary. She grabbed castor oil and sweet tincture of rhubarb—sure cures for a belly-ache—and just in case, she took her entire medical kit.

The farther they traveled, the farther it seemed in remove. They were halfway to nowhere before they came to a clearing in a jumble of trees and vines. Obviously Dance and her husband didn't want folks just dropping by.

The place gave Copper chills. The cabin was eerily silent. The front door stood open to the night, but only a weak light wavered in one window. She could see a stooped figure leaning in the doorway. Dimmert helped her down, and she rushed up the steps and had started across the porch when he jerked her back.

"Watch out," he said, pointing to an odd opening in the floor.

Gingerly Copper stepped across the hole in the floor and over the threshold, though Dimm held back. "Dimmert?" she asked.

He pointed again. "There's a turtle."

If she had chills before, now she had the shivers. Something was very strange here. Something was very wrong.

Dance was in labor. It would be hard to mistake that particular kind of discomfort. She gave a low shuddering moan and clutched Copper's arm. "How'd ye find me?" she asked.

"Why, your brother brought me. Where's your husband?"

"Gone," she answered. "I'm caught up in this jail. He hit me with a poker."

Copper's blood went cold. "Oh, my word. When will he be back?"

Dance shrugged before sinking to her knees in distress. "It's my time."

Copper got Dance to the bed in the corner of the room, then turned up the lamp. After asking Dance about her predicament and doing a quick exam to see how far along she was, Copper called out to Dimmert, "I need wood for the fireplace, and please draw some water."

Soon she heard a clunk of wood against the floor as he tossed pieces across the threshold. He leaned far in with a bucket of water, set it inside the door, then disappeared again.

Curious, she went to the doorway. Dawn was breaking, turning the dark sky into shades of lavender gray and stirring the birds to sing. Dimmert had taken a seat on the top step; a little cache of rocks lay beside him. She guessed he was waiting for Ace Shelton, the man Dance had said was her husband. Copper tied the strings of her long, bibbed apron behind her neck and sighed. What was she to do with Dimmert? But what if he was right? What if Ace was a danger to them? After all, Dance was kept prisoner in her own home by nothing more than a trapped turtle. The man wielded great power over her.

"Dimmert, leave the rocks for a minute. I need you to come inside and build up the fire. I've got to get some water boiling."

The young man stood on one side of the hole while Copper stood at the other. In the faint light of morning she saw no more than a dishpan-size shell hiding what would be an ugly beaked head and short legs with clawed feet, but Dimm's face was blanched white with fear. She held out her hand, and Dimm clutched it like a lifeline. "The turtle can't hurt you. I promise," she said.

His love for his sister won out over his fear as he mustered his courage and stepped across the doorway. With that done, he wasted no time in building up the fire.

Soon Copper had a pot of water heating. Dance was making fast progress, but Copper was dismayed by the lack of preparation for the birth. No cloths had been torn, no clean newsprint lay stacked and waiting, but thankfully there was a short stack of fresh linen in the cupboard.

"Dance, why didn't you have Dimmert fetch your mammaw? I expect she would have liked to be here."

Dance grunted and started panting. "I didn't know Dimmert was hanging around out there," she gasped. "Ace wouldn't like that one little bit." She squeezed Copper's hands tightly. "Whoee, this hurts like the dickens."

When Dance relaxed her hold, Copper scurried to the fireplace and pulled scissors and two twisted cloth ties from the boiling water with tongs. "It won't be long now."

"Uh . . . uh . . . ," Dance replied.

"Don't push yet. Wait on me." Hurriedly Copper got her things assembled at the bedside before guiding her patient's hands into strips of stout cloth that had been looped and tied to the bedposts. "Okay, now push, Dance. Push!"

It was a first baby, so it would take a little while longer. Copper had Dance rest between efforts. She could see Dimmert through the window, walking up and down the yard. It seemed there was always an anxious man pacing during deliveries. Copper reckoned he had to do something to relieve his anxiety. She was very glad to have him and his stack of rocks out there, especially since she'd seen for herself the scabbed-over burn on Dance's arm. She'd sure like to know more about this husband of Dance's.

Dance was snorting and blowing and grunting, pulling with all her might on the handholds Copper had fashioned. Her face was as red as boiled beets and contorted with pain.

"Push!" Copper shouted as if the louder she called, the harder Dance would work.

Dance pushed mightily, then fell back against the bed.

Copper wiped Dance's face with a cool, wet cloth and brushed strands of sweat-soaked hair out of her face. "You're doing good."

Dance answered with a long and heavy sigh. "This ain't fun."

Copper rubbed Dance's weary shoulders. "That's why they call it labor."

Midmorning, as the day heated up and a nice breeze sailed in through the open door, Dance's healthy baby boy was born. He was cheesy and slippery wet. His little head peaked into a long cone, and his eyes were mere creases in his wrinkled face.

"Ah," Copper said and meant it, "you have a beautiful boy, Dance."

"Jay," Dance said, her tired voice a whisper. "Ace wants to name him Jay."

Once mother and baby were cleaned up and settled, an hour-long task, Copper began to take stock of the situation. She couldn't leave the two of them here, and she couldn't stay herself. With each passing hour she felt more at risk. Darcy didn't really know where they were, and she'd be worried to death. Plus, she had to get Dimmert out of here. Good as he was with rocks, he'd be no match for a man with a gun. And Copper suspected Ace knew how to use one.

First things first though. Copper took off her dirty apron and put on a clean one. Dance had to eat–had to have some nourishment before she could be moved. Copper surveyed the larder. Some milk, some withered potatoes, some flour and salt–no eggs, no meat. Ah, but there was a perfectly good turtle right outside the door.

"Dimm," she said tapping her shoe beside the turtle hole. "Get out your pocketknife and pry this screen up."

Leaving his lookout spot on the step, Dimm swallowed hard but crouched down beside the trap. Soon tacks were flying in all directions.

"You know how to clean a turtle?" she asked.

"Watched some," Dimmert managed to stutter out. "Never did my own self."

"Well," Copper said, steeling her voice, "now's the time. Your sister's hungry. I'll help, but you and I've got to cook this turtle. It makes a good, rich soup for convalescents."

By noon they'd all been fed, and Copper was anxious to leave. She put the dishes to soak but she'd not take the time to wash them. The soiled linens were stuffed in a pillowcase to take along. She'd leave them with Dance at Fairy Mae's. The girls could do them up. For all she knew, Ace Shelton was mean as a striped snake, but still, she didn't want him walking into a house stained with blood. Her scalp prickled with fear at the thought of him.

"It's time to go," she said, bundling the baby and helping Dance to her feet. "Dimmert, bring the horse around."

CHAPTER 9

Fifteen minutes later and they'd have been gone. Dance was on the horse with the baby in her arms when her husband made his appearance, shouting curses and threats their way. Taking offense, Dimmert wound up like a baseball player and clocked Ace Shelton on the forehead with a carefully aimed missile. Ace went down like a felled tree.

"Goodness, Dimmert, you might have killed him!" Copper cried.

Truthfully, Copper wavered there on the path between safety and a man who could be dying. "Go on, Dimmert. I'll catch up." He hesitated. "Go!" she demanded, scared witless.

She found a steady pulse under Ace's scraggly beard. There

was a trickle of blood from where the rock had found its target but not enough to worry about. He would be fine.

She'd just straightened up from her examination of his wound when his fingers circled her ankle.

"Mister," she said, "you'd best let go."

"You've got no right to take my wife," he sniveled.

"Doesn't look like Dimmert agrees," Copper said. "I'd stay away from those Whitts if I were you."

He sat up. "I ain't afraid of them."

"Then be afraid of this. I'd bet you've got a moonshine still hidden somewhere up this holler. Dance told me about your treks in and out by way of the creek bed. I can't think of any other reason you'd want so badly to hide your trail. Am I right?"

He didn't answer, but his eyes told his story.

"You leave Dance alone and I won't tell a soul. You have my word."

"What about that brother of hers? You can't make a promise for him."

"Dimmert just wants to take care of his sister. He won't tell on you."

It was nearing suppertime when Copper and Dimmert got home. They'd left Dance and her baby at Fairy Mae's, safe at last. It did Copper's heart good to see their joyful reunion, but she'd never felt so weary. All she wanted was a hot bath and a soft bed.

Dimmert had just helped her down and turned to give Star a well-deserved drink from the watering trough when out of nowhere John appeared. In a flash he had Dimmert up against the barn door, his forearm under Dimm's neck. Dimmert's eyes bulged as his dangling feet thrashed the air. "I ought to whip you good."

"John!" Copper grabbed his arm to no avail. He was too strong for her. "John," she repeated, afraid he would choke the boy to death, "let him go."

He backed off, and Dimmert slid silently to the ground. He made no move to stand.

"What are you doing?" Copper cried, aghast.

John stood over the trembling younger man. "Don't you ever take Copper off like that again without telling me your whereabouts!"

Dimmert scrambled to Star's side, where he hoisted himself up. Horse and rider disappeared around the side of the barn.

"Sweet girl," John said, all softness now, "when I came by and Darcy told me you and Dimmert left in the middle of the night, I was scared to death." He reached out for her. "Let me get you in the house."

She smacked his hand aside. "Don't you touch me, John Pelfrey. You've got no claim on me."

He threw up his arms and turned his back. She watched him take off his hat and run his fingers through his hair, calming himself before he faced her. "Where have you been all this time? And what gives you cause to be mad at me? I've been out of my mind with worry."

"I've been delivering Dance Shelton's baby boy." Copper moved away from him. "Are you proud of yourself? Treating Dimmert that way?"

"I'll make it up to him." John slapped his hat back on. "But somebody should have told me where you were going."

"You should have told somebody something too." She tapped her chest, right over her heart. "You should have told this somebody you were married."

If she'd have hit him in the gut with a hammer it wouldn't have made more of an impression. Her words hit their mark, and she had to steel herself against giving in to pity.

"Will you let me explain?" John asked.

"I'll have no truck with a liar," she said.

"Copper, just listen . . . please?"

"I don't want to hear anything you've got to say." Seeing him all sorrylike made her so angry she felt as if she might burst into flame. "Nothing you say will make this right." Righteously indignant, she gathered her pride and walked away, leaving him standing alone in the deepening dusk.

Inside her house Copper leaned against the closed door. Briefly Jean Foster's words came to her mind, but she didn't have the energy to care. Another chapter closed, she thought; all hope of a life with John was over.

Then Darcy came out of the bedroom with Lilly in her arms, and she knew it didn't matter. They'd be fine. She'd send Darcy to find Dimmert at first light, and her family would be complete. They really didn't need anyone else.

Feeling like a whipped dog, John walked back across the creek to his place. Man, he'd been such a fool. He should have come clean about his past the minute he laid eyes on Copper again. But the innocent way she looked at him, the washed-clean way she made him feel, always stopped him in his tracks. More than anything, he wanted to be that man he saw in her eyes, not the one he had become.

His hand rasped over his stubbly beard, and he took his hat off. He was wrong, but she could have listened at least. Didn't she owe him anything?

In the barn he stopped to study the situation. Maybe he'd go visit his folks, bide his time, and let Copper cool down. She'd come around eventually, given some time. He began to saddle his horse. He'd stop by Elder Foster's on his way over the mountain. He'd take his hound Faithful along. She was the only girl he wanted to see for a while.

CHAPTER 10

September came in with torrents of rain. Mold formed in the strangest places, and mushrooms sprouted by the dozens under trees. They hadn't been able to do a decent wash for two weeks, making do with a scrub board and lye soap. Clothes hung drying over makeshift lines in the kitchen.

"Mercy," Copper said after nearly hanging herself on a line of baby clothes, "I hope the sun pops out soon." She folded several little undershirts and set them aside for ironing. Sad to say, no matter what the weather, a person could always iron. "I've got to go check on the chickens, Darcy. Will you get Lilly down for her nap?"

Throwing an old slicker over her head, Copper made a dash across the barnyard. The hens had gone stir-crazy, cooped up as they were, and had started eating their own eggs. Carefully,

Copper placed a doctored egg in the middle of the floor, pointed end up to keep from spilling the contents. Last night she had poked a hole in the shell with a darning needle, let out the contents, beat the yolk with a dash of strong mustard and a sprinkle of black pepper, and refilled the shell. The fabric patch she fashioned probably wouldn't last long once the guilty hen started in with her strong beak. Thankfully, chickens weren't very smart. Once they tasted mustard, they'd think all the eggs were the same. Copper had seen her daddy use this never-fail remedy on chickens and egg-sucking dogs alike.

"Oh, dear, what's wrong, Penny?" It looked like her favorite of all the laying hens, big-bottomed Penny, had the gapes. Backing Penny into a corner, Copper caught her and tucked the hapless hen under her arm. With luck, only one chicken was infected. Hopefully, it wasn't too late to save her. Gapes could kill every chicken in the house if Penny had spread it.

In the barn, way back under a bench, Copper found a divided wooden box and a twist of cured tobacco. She stripped off some burley and put it in the box along with the hen and carried them to the house. Darcy held the chicken while Copper stacked a few hot coals in a small iron skillet. The skillet she put in one side of the box, the hen she put in the other, and the tobacco she tore into fine pieces, sprinkling it over the coals in the skillet. The old slicker she wore was fine to cover the box with.

"Now," she explained to Darcy, "we'll smoke this hen until she's drunk."

Darcy's eyes widened. "Are we going to eat Penny?"

Copper had been squatting by the box, fooling with the

chicken, but now she fell back on the floor, holding her belly, laughing until tears streamed down her face. "Darcy," she sputtered, "haven't you ever seen a chicken with the gapes before?"

"No, ma'am, I don't reckon I have, but it looks mighty like you got the gapes your own self."

Copper squealed with laughter. Foolishly, she lifted the edge of the slicker and took a long draw of tobacco smoke. "I'm cured." Light-headed, she lay there enjoying the moment.

Darcy shook her head. "I think you've gone round the bend."

"It's this weather. I need some sunshine."

"It'll be Indian summer soon." Darcy peeked in on Penny. "That makes the prettiest days of the season."

Copper thought about that later when she took Penny to the barn and closed her up in a pasteboard box. "Sorry, Penny, but you're quarantined for a while. I can't afford to lose the rest of the chickens." Taking an ear of corn, Copper popped all the kernels in one line down the cob with her thumb. The rest came off easily when she rubbed the cob with the heel of her hand. "Here's some supper." She sprinkled a few kernels in the cage. "Don't tell the other girls I'm treating you special or they'll be so jealous they'll go on strike."

Penny didn't look so good. It wasn't often you could see a chicken's tongue, and hers lolled out the side of her mouth. Copper stroked her feathers. "It might be a kindness if I put you down." Funny, sometimes if she had a chicken who wasn't producing, all she had to do was walk around the henhouse saying, "Looks like I'll have chicken and dumplings for supper," and it would shock the hen right into business. Sadly, Copper thought Penny might be beyond that. "Rest now. I'll check on you later."

Rain drummed on the roof as she scrubbed the watering trays. The hens fussed about, scratching the floor and clucking. It was hard getting anything done with them gathered around. Usually she swept and cleaned while they were out in their fenced yard. Oh, she wished the dreary weather would let up. She wondered what John was up to. Hard as she tried, she couldn't stop her thoughts of him. He'd been gone for more than a month, but Dimmert had told her that he was back home. She hadn't seen him since that awful night they'd argued.

She mixed a couple of teaspoons of camphor spirits to each quart of the fresh water she used to fill the clean trays. Daddy used to massage a pea-size bit of camphor gum down the chickens' throats if the gapes got real bad. Copper hoped spiking the drinking water worked. That was a whole lot easier.

"I should have given John a chance to explain," she told the hens who murmured in sympathy. "I always rush to judgment." One chicken took advantage of their hen party and pecked hard at a button on Copper's shoe. "Here," she said, scattering the rest of the corn from her pocket. "Lay some eggs."

John stared hard out the window at the rain. He'd been home a week and still had not dared to go across the creek. The only thing that drew him back to this hardscrabble farm was the thought of Copper. It was what had kept him here all along, even before she came back from Lexington. All the time she'd lived away, the memory of her had been enough. If he could only walk where they'd walked as children, when life was full of promise, then he had been content. He'd never faulted the stranger who'd come and stolen her away, and he never faulted her for breaking his heart. Why didn't she love him the same way? He didn't know which way to turn. He reckoned he had to make her hear him out. It was the only chance he had.

But, Lord, why did my doing a good deed turn out to be so bad? I purely thought I was in Your will. Please help me understand.

John was not a man for self-examination. If he figured out the sad turn his life had taken, it would have to be through God's guidance. He took up his Bible. Closing his eyes, he let it fall open and traced a finger blindly down a page. He'd watched his ma search the Scripture the very same way when times were hard. Wherever your finger stopped was God's answer.

Isaiah 54:10 was what his index finger pointed out. John sat at the kitchen table and read, *"For the mountains shall depart, and the hills be removed; but my kindness shall not depart from thee, neither shall the covenant of my peace be removed, saith the Lord that hath mercy on thee."*

Frowning, he studied on the verse. He wished he could ask his ma what it meant. She was a good one to figure the Bible sayings. The mercy part he understood, for it was mercy he needed. Mercy and forgiveness.

He sank to his knees and bowed his head. *Oops, sorry, Lord.* Chagrined, he removed his hat. He was turning into an old hermit, wearing his hat in the house. Ma would have cuffed his ears.

I reckon I need You to give me some of that mercy and a little of that peace that passes understanding, for to be real honest with You, Lord, my heart is plumb broke in two. I'm just about to grieve myself to death, and it's all because of my own foolish pride. I ask Your forgiveness for not being up-front with Copper. Even though I was never married in my heart, still a piece of paper said I was. I guess this lie of mine is a hill that needs to be removed before she will give me another chance, and my pride is a mountain that has to depart. John closed the Good Book and laid it on the mantel.

He wished he'd never met that odd woman, that Remy Riddle–God rest her soul–much less married her. But she'd seemed so desperate when she'd showed up at his door all that time ago. And she missed Copper almost as much as he did. Missing Copper was the only thing they ever had in common.

He'd just knifed open a tin of beans, crumbled some stale corn bread into a glass of buttermilk, and sat down to his supper when a familiar sound caught his attention–snorts and grunts so loud they drowned out the pouring rain. "Old Hitch. Finally." Pushing back his chair, John grabbed his loaded gun and settled his hat on his head. It sounded like the wild boar that had nearly ruined his corn crop and eaten half a dozen of Fairy Mae Whitt's laying hens was back.

All summer long he had tracked the beast over many days and many miles, sometimes taking Ezra Whitt along, teaching the boy what he knew of tracking. The hog's hoofprints reminded him of the fluting his ma used to make with a fork around the edges of her pies. Funny that a thing so ugly could leave such a pretty sign. Sometimes, they noted, the hog left only three marks as if he favored his left hind foot. "He's got a hitch in his giddyup," Ezra'd said.

John knew the feral hog's favorite wallowing hole, and he'd seen places where the animal rooted, often leaving holes three or four feet deep in the choppy ground. Ezra had nearly snapped his ankle when he stumbled into one unawares. They actually set eyes on the ugly thing once. The hog stared at them from the edge of a forest as calm as you please, his ugly snout spread in a catch-me-if-you-can grin. But before John could raise his gun, the animal had melded with the trees. His snorting laugh teased them along as they thrashed through the woods in hot pursuit, but they never saw Old Hitch again.

"That's all right, you old devil," John said to the empty room. "I've got you now."

He cracked the door open and eased out onto the porch. The squealing of the hog and the baying of Faithful mixed in a cacophony of sound. Man, that hog was loud. Then Old Hitch grew silent, and John smiled. "Caught him!"

His smile never had a chance to stretch from ear to ear, however, and his time of self-congratulation ended abruptly when Faithful was flung halfway across the yard. Landing on her side, she slid to a stop at his feet. Not easily deterred, Faithful shook herself and streaked back toward the pig trap.

"Faithful!" he yelled. "Heel!"

The dog did as he bade though he knew she didn't want to. She would have fought to the end, but he wasn't about to let that nasty pig kill his favorite coon dog. He cocked his gun. The rain pelted him, narrowing his vision. Cautiously, he approached the snare he'd set with field corn and rotted meat.

"I don't believe it!" The wire pen was trampled to the ground, and Old Hitch was gone. All he'd managed to do with his trap was provide the rangy boar an easy meal. Angry, John whipped off his hat and threw it to the ground. Faithful cowered, whimpering behind him. "Sorry, girl. It ain't your fault. That pig's just smarter than me, I reckon. For instance–" he palmed rivulets of rain from his face–"Old Hitch would have had more sense than to throw his hat on the ground during a driving rain."

Faithful's long tail beat a drumroll against his leg. She was itching for a fight.

"We'll track the thing come morning." John held the cabin door open, and Faithful trotted in. With a soft woof she settled on the hearth. The fire popped and cracked a cozy sound that kept out the damp and the coming dark. Holding his can of beans, John settled down beside her. He'd finish his supper, then clean his rifle. They'd get Old Hitch tomorrow for sure.

CHAPTER 11

Copper didn't know quite what to do with her unexpected freedom. Darcy and Dimmert had gone to visit their mammaw, and Copper let Lilly Gray go along. It was against her better judgment, but Darcy pleaded, and while Copper put up arguments against it, Lilly ran to the bedroom and came out with her little bonnet on backward, the ties streaming down her back. "Bye-bye," she said and stomped her foot.

Copper stood on the porch in the early morning sunshine and reveled in the quiet. She couldn't remember when she'd last been alone. Probably before Simon came to claim her, that autumn when she'd roamed the mountains unsure of her future and doubting her past.

It was a pretty day. All up the mountain, trees revealed their colors, and there was that fall smell in the air. Closing her eyes, she breathed in the heady scent of dying leaves, fallen apples, and damp clay, all mixed with a whisper of coal smoke. She wished she could bottle that smell and bring it out come winter on one of those days when she began to doubt it would ever be warm again.

"What should I do with this lovely day?" she asked the cat.

As if her question offended his dignity, Tom stalked away, the tip of his tail twitching like a worm on a fish hook. A patch of golden sunshine on the bottom step met his particular requirement, and he stretched out, soaking up the warmth.

Copper sat beside him, resting her hand ever so lightly on the cat's bony spine. The steady vibrations from his purr tickled her. Sometimes she wished she were a cat. All play and no work. "You're so right, Tom. It's much too pretty to stay indoors."

After fetching her walking stick, a linen sack, and her slingshot in case of trouble, Copper set off. A walk was what she needed. She could check on the pear orchard she and Lilly had discovered a few months ago. The skirt of her brown and white checked gingham dress swayed as she marched across the barnyard, and the brim of her matching bonnet cast a shadow on her face. She'd piled her thick red hair on top of her head and secured it with combs, but still she could feel tendrils escape the bonnet. She might as well give up on taming that mass of curls and just keep it braided as other mountain women did.

It was an easy climb up the steep trail without Lilly Gray on her back, but Copper missed the baby who was as much a part of her as her right arm. She knew Darcy would take good care of Lilly. Still she wished she had not let her go to Fairy Mae's. Her baby was becoming a little girl, and Copper was not sure she was ready for the coming independence. She laughed at herself. *I'm going to give myself the vapors if I keep this up. It's way too pretty today to spend my time fretting.*

The ground was slippery mud from the rain, so she watched her step, but her troubles fell away as she climbed. A crow cawed in a tall pine, and somewhere far off a cow's bell tinkled. The only other sound was the even, calming resonance of God's creation: branches sighing in a sudden breeze, leaves falling delicately to carpet the forest floor, small creatures scampering away from a hawk or snake, her own breath mingling in perfect timbre. She drank it in like fresh cold milk, a sweet taste on her tongue.

The meadow was as she remembered, except she hadn't noticed a deserted cabin at the edge of the field before. Nearly hidden by tangles of honeysuckle, blackberry, and wild rose, it listed to one side. The pears were past their prime, most already fallen, but she gathered some up anyway; they would make a few pints of pear butter.

Copper hung her linen sack and her bonnet over a low branch before plucking a piece of yellow-brown fruit and settling in the doorway. Oddly, what she could see of the yard–the part that was not covered in purple thistle and jimsonweed–was chopped up like frozen ground, and a pool of mud as thick as pudding looked like a wallowing hole for something big. Probably a bear on its way up the mountain looking for a cave to hibernate in come winter. Bears wouldn't stay this far down for long. Interesting. She'd have to remember to tell Dimm about it.

Idly, she wondered if the house had never had a porch or if it had just rotted away. Entertaining herself for a moment, she thought of the family who might have lived here, conjuring up a tall father and a slight mother as three little girls in airy muslin slips ran through the rooms of her imagination. Fruit juice trickled down her chin, and she barely caught it before it stained her collar.

The inside of the cabin beckoned her, and she left the sunny doorway for its shadowed interior. The floor was hard-packed dirt, and hunks of chinking lay scattered along the bottom of the walls. Sunlight filtered in through the missing mortar and laid a game board at her feet. Delighted, she danced a crooked hopscotch on its surface. In one corner stood a rusted bedstead with a ticking mattress pocked with holes. Across the room, a wardrobe's door hung ajar, begging examination. Not wanting to come upon a snake unaware, she found a stick and poked inside. But nothing rustled or threatened, so she rummaged the shelves and found a long cotton nightdress and a tiny infant gown.

Her mind filled with questions. What had happened to this woman, and why did she leave behind her bed and nightgown, not to mention the cabin and pear orchard? It was a puzzle as strange as the riddles Daddy teased her with when she was a girl. "Round as an apple, flat as a plane, hole in my pocket, beggar again." She remembered that one and her favorite: "I found a thing good to eat, white and smooth and ever so neat, neither flesh, nor fish, nor bone, in three weeks it ran alone." Daddy gave her a penny for her pocket when she guessed the first one, but the second had her stumped for days until he took her to the chicken house and they watched a doodle peck its way out of a smooth, white shell.

Copper folded the musty nightgown carefully, as if the lady of the house might return anytime, then laid it and the baby's gown on the shelf and closed the crooked door.

Suddenly, an odor as evil as death filled the room, and she sensed a dark presence behind her. Alarm pricked up her spine.

Daring a glance, her mouth went dry at what she saw. A huge hog sized her up with narrowed piggy eyes. Where was her sling-shot? Her heart did a double beat when she remembered hanging it on the pear tree in her linen sack. She had made a terrible mistake. In seconds that seemed like hours, she remembered every story she'd ever heard about the wild boars roaming the mountains, killing indiscriminately. Legend was they'd eat skin and bone, leaving nothing behind.

Holding her breath, Copper turned to face her fear. At least two hundred pounds of meanness blocked the doorway. Unlike the pigs in her pen at home, this boar was tall and rangy with a narrow build. Bristly hairs stood up along his spine, which ended in a long, straight tail. One yellowed tusk was broken and jagged, and the other projected from his mouth like a dagger. Grunting with pleasure, the hog scratched himself against the doorway, dislodging clods of dirt. A fine gray dust rose off his body and danced in the streams of sunlight that made the hop-scotch board. Slowly, he lifted his ugly snout and blew dirt bullets across the room.

Copper's mind screamed, *Run!* But there was nowhere to go. She opened her mouth to yell at him, to show him she was not afraid, to maybe buy herself a little time, but her tongue stuck to the roof of her mouth and only a whimper issued forth.

The hog eyed Copper's discarded pear. He slurped it up before turning his attention back to her. He clicked his teeth, a strange warning, as his calloused snout dipped and twitched, scenting his prey.

Copper took the only chance she'd probably get; she dropped and scrambled under the bedstead. Her hair caught painfully on the strung rope that held the bed together, trapping her with her feet sticking out. The hog nosed her ankle, the touch of his breath as hot as sin. Screaming, she yanked free and gathered herself into a ball, willing herself to silence. Maybe he would forget she was here.

Instead the boar charged the bed. From her hideout, Copper watched his hooves retreat, then pound forward like a bull seeing red, bent on destruction. The bed shuddered and creaked with each assault until finally it collapsed. Copper covered herself with the feather bed, but the enraged hog hooked it with his tusks and flung it away. Feathers shot high in the air, then fell like snowflakes as the mattress ruptured.

Copper closed her eyes; she couldn't bear to see what happened next. *Lord,* she prayed, *help me.*

Angels come in many forms, and Copper's guardian was in the shape of a coon dog named Faithful. Copper dared to look when she heard the hound's baying bark. Incredibly, the feral hog was cornered by the dog's quick countermoves when he tried to dodge away. It would have been a show to watch if her life was not at stake. Ready to flee, she cowered instead when the sound of gunshot filled the room. It was over. The hog was dead, and she was safe.

Her legs wouldn't support her when she tried to stand. But there was no need, for John lifted her up and carried her out into the sunshine. It seemed she would never stop trembling as she sat there under the pear tree in the circle of his arms.

"You're safe now," he kept saying, giving her sips of water from his canteen and wiping her face with his wet handkerchief.

"Faithful?" she managed to ask.

"Aw, she's okay. She won't leave the boar until I release her."

Taking out his knife, he peeled a pear, cut it in small pieces, and fed her. "You need some strength."

"How did you find me?"

"We've been tracking Old Hitch for weeks. Today was our lucky day."

Copper shuddered. "I think this was God's mercy instead of luck. You and Faithful saved my life."

He laid his hat aside and turned his face toward hers. "Does this mean we're on speaking terms again?"

She couldn't help but laugh. "John Pelfrey, you're a sight."

"Speaking of sights . . ."

Her fingers searched through her tumbled hair as she tried to find her pins. "I lost my combs."

"You're the prettiest thing I ever saw just as you are."

Tears filled her eyes, and she leaned her head on her bent knees. "John, we can't just go back to the way we were as if nothing happened."

"I'm ready to tell you the whole story," he said in his earnest way. "I never meant to keep it from you."

Copper wiped pools of tears from under her eyes with the tips of her fingers. "Then why did you?"

Shrugging, he said, "It never came up, and when it did, you wouldn't let me."

Copper felt sick and shaky and tired. When she thought about it, she realized John had lost someone too. She didn't have a lock on sorrow. "Well, call Faithful out first. I can't bear to think of her in there with that . . . that thing."

One sharp whistle and John's hound ran out of the dilapidated cabin. Then she settled under the pear tree at their feet.

Copper opened her mouth to speak. Now that she had agreed to listen, a dozen questions arose in her mind.

But John shushed her. "Just listen," he said, turning her in his arms so she couldn't see his face.

Giving in, she settled her head in the curve of his shoulder and listened. . . .

There was a freezing rain that January day, John recollected. He was sitting by the roaring fireplace mending a harness when Faithful left the hearth and set to barking. The door was frozen shut, and ice shattered around him as he jerked it open. He didn't see anything at first, only drifts of crusted snow and shimmering, ice-covered trees.

Faithful bounded out, skittering across the porch to a body collapsed on the ground beside the porch steps. John joined his dog and feared the worst as he hauled whoever it was into the house.

Finally the lump thawed, revealing the strangest-looking person John ever hoped to see. She was as colorless as the snow outside, and her eyes were pale blue and pink-rimmed like a rabbit's ear. It took him a while to make out her age, for her hair was as white as a granny's and her voice was as old as time. Not that she said much. She just sat there on his hearth, her sky blue shawl dripping dirty water on the floor.

He rustled around in an old trunk and found some clothes he thought would do. After stacking them beside her, he shrugged on his coat and trekked out into the cold. He guessed he'd have to feed the woman; then he'd take her to Jean Foster's. Jean would know what to do. They'd have to walk, because a horse would break a leg on this ice.

He felt better for having a plan, and after an hour he opened the cabin door feeling like a stranger in his own house. The woman was dry at least, and the boots he'd laid out seemed to fit. The clothes she'd changed out of steamed on the hearth, and her shawl hung across the rocking chair.

John took out a bowl and filled it with brown beans and fatback from the pot on the cookstove. He wiped the rim of a drinking glass with his shirttail, poured cold buttermilk to the top, set the food on the table, and pulled out a chair for her.

Grabbing the spoon, she wolfed down the food, then licked the bowl.

He stood back, dumbfounded. No matter how much ice and snow, he couldn't wait to get her out of his cabin and safe in Jean's.

But when he told her of his plans, she swelled up like a bull-frog and said, "Mister, I ain't going."

"Well," he answered, standing foolishly by the door, his galoshes on his feet, "what's your plan? You can't stay here."

The woman looked somewhere over his shoulder, her strange eyes never meeting his. "Humph. Right now I ain't got no plan."

John didn't take his overshoes off. "You can see the problem," he pleaded. "There's no missus here, and I can't have you staying here–with me–alone."

"I ain't afeered."

"No need for you to be, but Jean Foster's close by. She'll make you welcome."

The woman just sat there, turning his words away. "I'm so hungry my belly's eating my backbone."

John clomped across the floor, piled more beans in her bowl, and slapped it back on the table.

Attacking the beans with one hand, she handed him her empty milk glass with the other. Revulsion mixed with intrigue as he watched her gulp her meal. Bean juice and milk trailed down her chin when she pushed the empty bowl away. Who was she? What was she doing in his kitchen?

John felt her watching as he took off his boots and hung his coat on a peg. He'd sit with her and talk reasonable to get her away from his table and out the door. Might as well start with the obvious. "Why'd you come here?"

"Yore Purty's friend." Her voice was as thick as molasses, mesmerizing him.

"Purty?"

"I heered *you* call her Pest."

His heart hammered against his rib cage. This was Copper's fey friend Remy Riddle. Once he and Copper had searched for her in vain; he remembered Copper's tears.

This changed everything. He'd put her up for the night like Copper would expect him to, though he'd probably freeze to death in the barn, grown accustomed as he was now to the easy life.

And he had. He had nearly frozen to death, or it felt like it anyway. He and Faithful had taken refuge in the stripping room. His acre of tobacco was long since stripped and tied in hands, but the small stove he used to cure the burley would do for the night, he reckoned. But it didn't put off much heat. He was grateful for the warmth from the sleeping dog.

After another day and one more night in the stripping room, he decided to talk straight to Remy. He'd had enough of her. "I'm going to fetch Jean and her husband to take you to their place."

He couldn't believe her answer. "Mister, mind yore own business."

"This is my business!" he exploded, throwing his hat to the floor. "Ain't them my biscuits you're eating and ain't that my coffee in my cup?"

Remy didn't even wince, just squinted at him and stuck one foot out from under the table. "I figure I need a week."

Then he saw her ankle puffed like rising bread over the top of her unlaced boot. Anyone else sitting at his table and he would have knelt to take the foot to assess the damage, but he couldn't bring himself to touch Remy, and he sensed she wouldn't let him anyway.

"Who are you running from?" he asked instead. "What brought you out in such weather?"

She barked a dismissive laugh. "You don't rightly want to know."

"Try me," he said, pouring two mugs of coffee and taking a chair across from her. "I figure you owe me as much."

Sleet beat against the windows with icy fingers, and a log in the fireplace burned through, sending a shower of sparks shooting up the chimney. Faithful leaned against his knee and yawned until John said, "Lie down." He could see she was grateful as she curled up by the fire.

"My pap was in the pen a long time but not near as long as we'd thought he'd be." The sluggish voice started in the middle of the story, John supposed.

"You mean jail?" he asked.

"Thing is Ma died whilst he was gone. My brothers and sisters is scattered all over, living with this'n and that'n." Remy broke a piece of biscuit and dunked it in her coffee.

"Why was your pap in prison?"

"Collarmoggis."

John tugged at his shirt collar. "Pardon?" Suddenly the room seemed very small and very hot.

"It's what took Ma."

"Cholera morbus?"

"Ain't that what I just said?"

John got up and cracked the door. "I'm sorry about your ma."

The sting of sleet felt good against his face. The world beyond the cabin was starkly beautiful. Snow piled in drifts against fence rows, and trees reached gray skeletal arms to the pewter-colored sky. Maybe he'd just whistle to Faithful and walk out across the barren fields—walk and walk until he never had to face the unwelcome person who had taken root in his house. Instead he took a draft of clean, cold air to clear his mind and sharpen his senses before he shut the door.

He twirled a straight chair and straddled it, facing her, his arms resting across the back. Might as well be comfortable; getting the truth from Remy might take a right smart while. He rested his chin on the backs of his hands. "Tell me. I'll set here all night if that's what it takes."

"He cain't make me."

John never spoke, just sat there astraddle the chair staring at her. Her gaze slid all around the room, never lighting, never meeting his.

He knew he was making her uncomfortable, and he knew she was cracking, thawing toward him like she'd thawed the day Faithful found her, in little drips and drabs.

"Pap says I have to marry up with Quick Hopper," she finally explained. "But I ain't jumping no broom with that smarmy old man. Pap's blinded by Quick's gold. He won't never let up."

John guessed that Remy was a little off-kilter—tetched in the head. "So what are you aiming to do?"

Her eyes met his. "Soon as I can hobble, I'm going to fling myself over Torrent Falls."

He felt like he'd been sucker punched. "It's a far piece to Torrent Falls," he said stupidly.

She shrugged as if the distance was of no consequence, of no more consequence than her life. "It's a purty place and peaceable. They's angels living there."

"Listen—" his mind scrambled for purchase—"we can figure this out. You don't want to harm yourself."

"See, I ain't hitching up with Quick Hopper, and ain't nobody gonna hit me again."

John flinched at her words. A fading bruise on her right cheek bore witness to her suffering.

Outside his snug cabin, the dark sky hunkered down for the night. Wind whistled down the chimney and fanned the fireplace flames. Faithful woofed in her sleep—chasing rabbits, no doubt. John loved Copper with all his being; there'd be no one else for him. And Copper had loved the desperate girl sitting across from him, loved her like a sister. She would expect him to take care of Remy Riddle, distasteful to him though she was.

"I'll give you my name," he said. "That way your pap won't have no claim on you. You can live here until your pap sees it's legal; then you'll be free to go wherever you want."

She laid her head on the table, the first sign of weakness he'd seen. "Why would you do something like that for me?"

"Because of Copper. She'd expect me to take care of you."

"We ain't never gonna—"

"No!" He heard his own voice, too forceful. "No. I'll live across the creek in the Browns' empty house. Nobody ever has to know our deal but us."

The very next day, with Brother Jasper and his wife sworn to secrecy, John had married Remy Riddle. Faithful and the preacher's wife stood attendance. They had the paper to prove it when Remy's father came pounding on the door nearly a week later.

Rastus was a mean little man and as dangerous as a cocked gun; John could see it in his black eyes. He'd thrown a right smart fit before John tossed him off the porch.

Rastus cursed as he tumbled across the frozen ground. "You'll live to rue the day you took to interfering with me and my brood."

Less than a week later, one early morning when John forded the creek to check on Remy, she was gone . . . along with his plowing mule and the thin gold wedding band that had once belonged to John's great-grandmother Pelfrey. He reckoned she took the mule to carry her to Torrent Falls and his grandmother's ring because she wanted to hold on to something pure, something that held meaning. His heart turned over in pity to think a person was so desperate she'd take her own life. Seemed he should have been able to stop her.

As he had supposed, he found his mule at Torrent Falls, but there was no sign of Remy Riddle. For two days John and Brother Jasper scouted the banks of the creek below the falls, swollen with snowmelt, looking for Remy's body. Miles downstream, they found her blue mantle and one boot with John's great-grandmother Pelfrey's ring knotted in the lace. Figuring she had died in a plunge over the falls, they buried the shawl and the boot at Torrent Falls. John left the ring knotted in the lace. He figured it was the least he could do.

Copper was in tears before John finished his sad story. "I can't believe it. I can't believe Remy is dead."

"I'm sorry. I feel like it's all my fault—like I should have saved her." John rooted in his pocket for a handkerchief and handed it to Copper.

She mopped her face. "I can remember feeling the same way about Remy. Her life was so hard compared to mine." Folding the handkerchief into a rectangle, Copper pressed it to her swollen eyes. Guilt stabbed like sharp needles at her heart. She'd hardly thought of Remy in years. "When we were girls, I used to beg her to come and live with my family, but she wouldn't listen. Poor little Remy." Fresh tears came, leading to sobs that shook her body. "It seems so unfair, John."

"I know," he said, patting her shoulder. "I know."

Faithful stood and stretched, then loped back to the old cabin. She looked back at John as she stood in the open doorway.

"I guess we'd best get you home," he said, standing and helping Copper up.

Copper swayed against him.

He caught her with one strong arm. "What do we do now?" he asked.

"I love you all the more for what you did for Remy," Copper replied. "We have time; don't you think? Time to let our love grow and see where it leads?"

Copper's house never had looked so good when they got back. John wanted to come in, but she shooed him away. She needed time alone. After heating a pot of water, she stripped off her ruined dress and took a pan bath, washing away the scent of hog with rose-scented soap, a gift from her sister-in-law.

When she'd dressed and tidied her hair with the combs John found, she sipped a cup of chamomile tea to quiet her stomach. It made her nauseous to think of what almost happened to her and what did happen to her friend. Every time she closed her eyes, she saw Remy tumbling over the falls. Life was a beautiful gift but so fragile. Here one moment and in heaven the next. And she was sure that Remy was in heaven. They had talked, and she knew Remy believed in her own backward and curious way.

Sinking to her knees, Copper thanked God for sparing her life today, saving her from that feral hog, letting her live to raise her daughter. And she thanked Him for Remy and the short time she'd had with her. Doubled over, her face to her knees, she cried again for the loss of her friend.

Out in the barnyard Mazy bawled. Copper got to her feet. It would soon be time to milk, time to gather eggs, time to start some supper before the children came home. She was a mother with a daughter to raise. It was time to get back to work.

CHAPTER 12

Sunday after church service, there would be dinner on the grounds. Copper was still sore, bruised from her encounter with Old Hitch, but there was lots to do. All day Saturday, Darcy ruled the kitchen. Anyone who ventured as close as the porch was given a job. Copper was churning butter for a pound cake. Dimmert stood at the wash bench peeling a huge green and white cushaw for Darcy to bake with butter and brown sugar. John, who'd come innocently for breakfast, sliced apples for the four pie shells waiting to be filled. Lilly was in the yard, playing dolly with one of the small cushaws from the garden. Its long, crooked neck fit perfectly over her shoulder. Copper smiled to see her pat its back, crooning to her pretty squash baby.

Finished with his task, John took the apples to the kitchen.

Although John had apologized to him, Dimmert flinched as he walked past, drawing his neck into his shoulders. He reminded Copper of the turtle they'd had for supper the night his sister Dance delivered her baby.

John reached for the hat that rested by the apple-peeling chair. "Dimmert, let's leave these women to their work. What say we rustle up some fat and tasty rabbit for Miss Darcy to fix for tomorrow?"

"What about my cushaw?" Darcy asked, eyeing John.

"I'm thinking your fried rabbit is every bit as good as Ma Hawkins's fried chicken. Why, if we could get a platter of your rabbit on the table tomorrow, folks will be knocking elbows to get a piece."

Darcy's eyes widened. Ma Hawkins's fried chicken was legendary.

Dimmert's Adam's apple bobbed as he shot a look from John to Darcy. He had half a cushaw to go.

"What if you was to help Dimmert?" Darcy countered. "Then I could get that cushaw on the stove."

Copper caught John's slow wink and his smile. He threw up his hands. "I give up, Darcy Whitt."

Soon the pale yellow meat of cushaw overflowed the gray granite cooker.

"Ready, Dimmert?" John said as he started down the steps.

"Get three," Darcy called after them, wiping her floured hands on the front of her apron. "No, four. I'll need four if you really think my fried rabbit is better'n Ma Hawkins's chicken."

"Four it will be," John answered with a backward wave. "Get the skillet ready."

Dimmert walked at least six paces behind John. Once he glanced back at Copper, and she gave him a smile. Poor thing was probably afraid John was going to shoot him out there in the woods. John was making amends the best he could, and it would be good for Dimmert to spend some time with him.

Finished with the butter, Copper sat Lilly on her hip and carried her to the cellar. She needed to bring up some canned green beans.

The cellar had been built years ago by Copper's daddy's daddy. He'd dug a big hole in the side of a hill and installed free-standing shelves. The walls were lined with flat rock, and the floor was hard-packed dirt like the cabin in the meadow. The wooden door with heavy crosspieces was cumbersome to open, an attempt to deter thieves. "Some folks would steal the dimes off a dead man's eyes," her daddy liked to say.

She was just about to set Lilly down and tackle the cellar door when something off-kilter caught her eye.

"Pretty," Lilly said.

"For goodness sake, what's this doing out here?" Copper admired a string of quilt pieces threaded together on a length of green ribbon and tacked over the cellar door, small circles of color dancing in the doorway.

"Mine?" Lilly asked, smacking her fingers against her palms.

"I think this is Darcy's." Copper recognized the scraps of material and the silk ribbon. "We'll look at it later."

"Mine!" Lilly shrieked and drummed her feet against Copper's legs.

"Lilly Gray Corbett, behave yourself." Flustered, she sat her daughter on the stone step behind her and wrestled the door open. When Copper turned around, the pretty trifle was torn loose and flung away. On hands and knees, Lilly started up the stairs.

One swat to Lilly Gray's little bottom was all it took to deter her. "Now sit there and mind me!"

By the time Copper had put two half-gallon jars of green beans in her basket and closed the door, Lilly was in a full-blown tantrum. With the basket on one arm and her daughter hanging like a sack of potatoes from the other, Copper trudged back to the porch.

On Sunday morning John came around with a buggy to take them to church, all except Dimmert. He was off somewhere on Star. Copper didn't monitor his comings and goings. As long as he did his work and minded his manners around the house, she figured he was capable of making his own decisions. He would soon be eighteen, after all.

Between running back and forth from the kitchen to pack all the food she and Darcy had fixed—pound cake, apple pies, green beans, two rounds of corn bread, and four fried rabbits—and dealing with Lilly Gray's bad mood, Copper thought they'd never leave the yard. They'd have to eat right there in the buggy.

Finally, everyone was ready and they were off just like a regular family. Copper hoped her riding to church with John didn't cause tongues to wag more than they already were. Funny how folks liked to mind other people's business.

Lilly and Darcy looked like sisters in matching blue floral-print cotton dresses. Darcy's was trimmed with rickrack at the hem and sleeves, while Lilly's was smocked across the top. Jean had patiently taught Copper the intricate smocking stitch, and Copper couldn't wait for her to see it. They wouldn't make any new frocks for a while, however. Copper didn't want folks to think she was showing out. It was best to not lord it over anyone if she wanted to make any more friends than Jean, who seemed to be without judgment. Copper admired the older woman tremendously and hoped someday to be as kind as Jean was.

The novelty of riding in a horse and buggy delighted Lilly Gray, and soon she was sitting on John's knee and helping hold the reins, her bad mood forgotten for a moment.

Copper had shed a few tears last night when she'd tucked the sleepy baby in bed and kissed her rosy cheek. How could she have spanked her precious child? Even though it had been just one light swat, Copper felt the sting of recrimination.

As if she sensed her mother's guilt, Lilly Gray let go of the reins and hung over the seat back, whining and reaching for Darcy. My, it was hard to be a mother.

"Penny for your thoughts," John said.

"I was just thinking what a sassy child I was and how often Mam had to discipline me."

"You, sassy? Imagine that," John teased. "Your mam was awful hard on you."

"Mam's willow switch taught me some valuable lessons, and I needed every one of them when I lived in the city."

"Still," John said, "my ma raised thirteen young'uns and never raised her voice, much less a stick."

Copper laughed. "Your ma is the most patient person God ever put on this earth. If I had thirteen children, I'd go insane."

John turned her way, letting the horse find the familiar path to church. His hair fell across his eyes, and he swiped it back with his palm. His eyes were as green as her own, and she couldn't look away from their directness. "How many kids you reckon on before you'd go crazy?"

Copper rolled her eyes toward the backseat of the buggy, where Darcy was entertaining Lilly Gray with a fuzzy black and brown woolly worm. "Little pitchers have big ears," she reminded. And then quietly, for him alone, "I'm not doing so well with one."

John took control of the horse with one tug on the reins, and he took control of her with just the touch of his hand on hers. She kept still, not even caring if Darcy saw, for his touch felt so right and she was ever so tired of being alone. Her heart wished for a life with John.

The church service was a little too long considering what waited outside on sawhorse tables: Ma Hawkins's fried chicken, Jean Foster's potato salad, and Mrs. Mullins's dried-apple pies. Singing all seven verses of "The Sheep of Christ" was tedious. Brother Jasper's long-winded sermon took its toll on people's patience. Stomachs growled as men shuffled on the hard wooden pews, older women fanned themselves, and young mothers chastened squirming children.

They'd harmonized the beautiful, calming words of the doxology, always the end of their service, when Opal Smithers declared she had backslid for the umpteenth time.

Some folks couldn't suppress groans as Opal stood and declared this week's stumbling block: the dandelion wine her husband brewed last spring. "Just a tad," she whispered. It seemed Opal was determined to enter heaven without a single jot by her name.

In her seat by a window, Copper noticed a group of boys dart out of the woods and grab food from the table.

Elder Foster, from his stance in the open doorway, also noticed and ran out. "You boys! You'll be in the back of the line."

That's all it took. The pews emptied out as women took their serving positions behind the tables and Brother Jasper took his rightful place at the head of the line. Even he couldn't resist the tempting sights and smells of so much food. His blessing was short.

Copper stood between Jean Foster and Ma Hawkins, remembering—just yesterday, it seemed—when she would have been with the children, jostling for position behind the elders and deacons. Now she ladled food, filled glasses, and sliced desserts. Darcy came through the line holding Lilly and leading Bubby, who waved a drumstick at Copper.

Elder Foster punished the mischievous boys, one his own son Dylan, by making them wait until the ladies had finished serving and filled their own plates. Truly, there wasn't much left but bony chicken backs and gristly necks. Dylan kicked up a fuss until his father raised his hand. Copper saw Jean wrap her piece of chicken in a napkin and set it aside. Copper knew Jean had a soft spot for her oldest son.

After dinner the children paired off for games of tag and hide-and-seek. The men pitched horseshoes, and the women visited among themselves. It was a great gift to sit with friends in the churchyard on such a beautiful day.

"Has anyone called on the Wilsons lately?" Copper asked.

Hezzy's eyes lit up, but she didn't open her mouth. Even she wouldn't gossip in the shadow of the church.

"My husband went up there yesterday," Jean replied. "He wanted to remind them about dinner on the grounds."

"How is Mrs. Wilson holding up?" Fairy Mae asked.

"As well as can be expected, I guess," Jean responded.

As if nobody knew what she was doing, Hezzy hid behind her apron and poked snuff between her cheek and gum. "Humph," she snorted.

Copper determined to make a call on the Wilsons. She shouldn't have put it off so long. Lifting Lilly from her lap, she shifted her to the blue and white double wedding ring quilt she'd spread under the shade trees. Surrounding her blanket were other mothers whose babies slept beside them. Copper wished she could fly to the top of the highest tree and look down on the quilt of souls God had designed. *It must be a perfect picture to His eyes*, she thought. *All His children stitched together for an afternoon of harmony.*

Hezzy spat into a patch of weeds. Copper looked at her.

Where did her mean spirit fit into God's design? An image of the quilting circle at Jean's house came to mind. Of course, Hezzy was the crooked stitch. Maybe not so pretty as the precise stitches of a seasoned seamstress, but a crooked stitch held the quilt together just the same.

At Mammaw Whitt's cozy cabin, Dance Shelton walked the front yard with her fussy baby. Nothing satisfied him this morning. Nothing satisfied Dance either. Mammaw had tried to get her to go to church and dinner on the grounds, but Dance craved solitude.

Back and forth Dance trekked, jouncing her baby on her shoulder. She'd dreamed last night of Ace and wakened with a sensation that he was near. If he was coming, she hoped he was smart enough to come while Mammaw and Ezra were gone. She was ready to go home, for she couldn't stand the way everyone–Mammaw and her brothers and sisters, even the baby–clutched at her here.

Jay broke out crying. She carried him into the house and put him on his belly in the dresser drawer where he slept. His screams followed her to the porch, and she covered her ears. The cabin up the holler where she'd lived with Ace seemed a tranquil place now. Ace wasn't so bad, just that one time with the poker. She couldn't exactly remember what happened with that.

Dance sat on a step, gathering her skirts and tucking them under her knees. She hankered for a smoke to settle her nerves, but Mammaw didn't keep tobacco about. A movement in a copse of trees caught her eye, and she strained to see what was coming. . . . Just a deer. He was sure a pretty thing, standing at attention at the edge of the trees, his ears flicking, his antlers like a coatrack on his head.

She dared to uncover her ears, testing the air for danger like the buck did. The baby was quiet, finally sleeping. Dance crossed her arms on her knees and rested her head there. What must it be like to be a deer, so beautiful and so free? Dance wished she was pretty like that woman who'd come like an angel in the night to deliver the baby. She had red hair and green eyes, Dance recollected, and her hands were kind.

"If wishes were horses, then beggars would ride," Mammaw always said.

Dance felt like a lump of leftover clay. She'd never felt desirable, never thought she'd catch a husband until Ace came courting, and for a while she was as pretty as any other girl.

Dance's nerves jangled like a bird on a wire. She wondered how she was going to stand another day. She wondered if Ace was ever going to come for her.

Jay woke. His mewling cry was pitiful enough to break a heart, but it did not move his mother. She did not wonder why she didn't love her baby.

CHAPTER 13

Winter was coming; Copper could feel the change of season, the mornings no longer warm, night falling earlier and earlier. She had begun lighting the fireplace each evening to ward off the chill. Last night, after Dimmert brought a scuttle of coal to the door, she'd lugged it inside and laid a fire. How much easier her life had been in the city, where a furnace in the basement worked like a slave tending to her needs. Coal was delivered through a chute directly to the basement under their house. Her house-keeper's husband kept the furnace stoked.

Searcy and Reuben had been her servants, though she never thought of them that way. When she left Lexington, all she would have had to do was ask and Searcy and Reuben would have come to the mountains with her. But she could never have been that selfish, uprooting the elderly couple from the only home they'd ever known. Instead she'd put money in the bank for them, ensuring they'd never have to be servants again. My, she missed them.

Drawing her apron up over her arms, Copper looked to the hills. Early morning mist clung to ghostly bare trees, and the air she breathed was damp. A familiar Scripture, learned at her father's knee, tripped off her tongue: "'Even them will I bring to my holy mountain, and make them joyful in my house of prayer.'" She'd gladly trade all the niceties of Lexington, even the furnace in the cellar, for the privilege of standing in the shadow of the mountains.

A little banty rooster crowed from the open door of the hayloft in the barn. The big red barnyard rooster had announced sunrise from his perch on the fence many minutes before, but the banty thought his duty was to remind. He puffed his tiny chest out and tipped back his head. Copper thought he might throw himself off his feet, his call was so joyful. "Praise the Lord," she fancied he sang. "Praise the Lord!"

The screen door squeaked, interrupting her reverie. Barefoot, her blanket trailing behind her, Lilly Gray held her arms out to Copper. "Benny wake me."

"That's Benny's job. See him there in the hayloft?"

Lilly crowed.

Darcy came up beside them. "Mammaw says a whistling woman and a crowing hen always come to a very bad end. Are you a crowing hen, Lilly Gray?"

She crowed again.

Copper nuzzled her daughter's sweet-smelling neck. "Let's get you dressed, little banty rooster, so we can go milk Mazy."

Lilly leaned against her mother's knee as Copper milked Mazy. The milk pinged against the sides of the bucket. "Me milk," Lilly said.

Copper drew Lilly's small hand beneath her own and let the child feel the rhythmic pull and tug of her fingers. "You can milk enough for Tom and the kitties; then you need to let Mama finish."

When they were done, the barn cats were fed and Mazy was turned out to begin her morning trek up the mountain. Copper carried the full bucket of milk to the springhouse. Lilly Gray followed, the handle of a small tin berry bucket clutched importantly in her hand. Old Tom trailed Lilly, winding around her legs, watching for a spill.

"Stay right here, Lilly," Copper said as she stepped into the cool springhouse. "Stay with Tom."

Lilly squatted by the battered pie pan they kept there for the cat's dish. Tom waited.

Copper carried the heavy bucket to the cream separator and slowly poured the milk in. For only a moment her back was to Lilly Gray. The picture of her daughter bent over the pie pan, pouring creamy milk from her little bucket was etched in her mind. But when she turned, her baby was gone.

She's just out of sight, Copper thought. "Lilly! Come where Mama can see you."

Just that quickly, dread took her breath away. The bucket

missed the shelf and clanged loudly to the stone floor as she ran, calling, "Lilly? Lilly Gray!"

Darting this way and that, she scanned the yard; Lilly was not there. Maybe she had taken her little bucket back to the barn. Maybe she wanted to give more milk to the mother cat and her kittens.

Dimmert appeared in the barn door, a pitchfork full of straw in his hands. "Baby?" he managed to say.

"Oh, help me. Lilly was at the springhouse and now she's gone."

His arm swept the air behind him. "Not here." He flung the pitchfork aside as he ran toward the springhouse.

Copper saw Darcy walk out onto the porch. She was holding a pan of biscuits for their breakfast. Lilly loved biscuits. *Maybe she's in the house. She probably wants to show Darcy her pail.* Copper ran, sure of it.

Darcy met her halfway. Biscuits rolled like wheels across the ground. "She ain't in the house, Miz Copper."

The world shifted. Every object in the barnyard took on a silvery sheen; even an errant biscuit shot off sparks as it came to a stop at her feet. Copper fell to her knees. *Lord,* she prayed, *please . . .*

Darcy knelt in front of her, her forehead touching Copper's. "She'll be all right. God won't let nothing happen to our baby."

Copper clung to those simple words, and they became a mantra while they searched every nook and cranny of the barn, the house, the yard.

Hours passed and still no Lilly Gray. Copper's heart felt as heavy as lead. "We need to walk the creek, Dimmert. Get some tobacco sticks."

They waded into the clear waters of Troublesome. Thankfully, it was a gentle stream today and not flooded. She went downstream and Dimmert went up. Darcy stayed at the house keeping watch.

Within a short time, Copper came to the swimming hole where she'd played so often as a child. A crow called a mournful song, and the branches of an ancient sycamore clacked in a sudden gust of wind. Leaves as big as dinner plates swirled on the surface of the dark water.

This was a place she'd bring Lilly to when she was older. Here she would learn to swim and hear the Bible story of Zacchaeus, the tax collector. It was the mighty sycamore tree Zacchaeus climbed to better see the Savior when he traveled through Jericho. Jesus noticed what the little man had done and went home with him and gave salvation to his house.

Would Copper ever tell that story to Lilly? Would she bring her to this tree and act out Zacchaeus climbing the tree as her father had done for her? Fighting her fear, she used the slender tobacco stick to probe the water, poking under riffles and gnarled roots. She gigged a frog and he jumped on the bank, his mighty legs like springs. *Please, Lord. Please, Lord.*

Suddenly a dark knowledge caught her breath—a memory she'd buried in the depths of her mind. This was the creek in which her natural mother had drowned when Copper was just an infant. She stood still as the cold water crept up under her arms. Then she had a fleeting but terrible thought: if Lilly had joined her mother, then Copper might as well also. The beating wings of dark angels surrounded her. Lucifer and his crew, beckoning for her soul.

But Copper's faith was as old as the hills. Tried and true, passed down through generations, solid as her great-grandmother's blanket chest. She'd taken leave of her senses for a moment, but now she climbed out of the creek bed. This was not the way to go. *"God won't let nothing happen to our baby."* She needed to get back to the house and find Lilly Gray.

Standing by the footbridge, she hollered for Dimmert. She shouldn't have sent him on this foolish errand. He would stay in the creek until the cows came home; he'd die an old man before he'd return without Lilly. She'd have to ring the dinner bell to bring him in.

The dinner bell! Why hadn't she thought of that before? Lilly Gray loved to ring that bell. They didn't use it often, for everyone in her household knew when it was time to eat. Wet and bedraggled, Copper hurried to the side yard where the black iron bell sat atop a tall pole. With a hard yank to the knotted rope, she set the bell to ringing.

A faint rustle from the edge of the garden where the dry cornstalks stood signaled something traveling low to the ground. Copper trembled with relief when she saw her baby. Lilly still carried the tin berry bucket.

Overwhelmed, Copper didn't know what to do with the rush of emotion flooding her. She wanted to cry and shout. She wanted to kiss her baby all over, and she wanted to shake Lilly Gray for not minding, for walking away when she was supposed to stay.

Instead she sat on the ground and drew Lilly onto her lap. With her thumb in her mouth, Lilly curled up like a puppy in the crook of Copper's arm. Copper held her daughter close, stroking the silver streak in Lilly's dark hair and trailing her fingers down Lilly's cheek. "Where have you been?"

Lilly popped her thumb out of her mouth. "Me walking."

Darcy came with a cup of milk. "Praise the Lord."

Copper held Lilly as the toddler drained the cup. "How did you get lost? Tell Mama and Darcy."

"Tom bite mousey."

"He did?" Darcy said. "That bad cat."

Lilly opened her arms wide. "Mousey runned away."

"And Lilly chased the mouse," Copper finished.

"Yup."

A louder noise came from the cornfield this time as Dimmert crashed out. His face was a mask of fear.

"Dimm!" Lilly invited him to the party.

Copper's eyes filled when she saw the wet streaks on Dimmert's dirty face. "Kneel with us, Dimmert. We need to thank God for this bountiful blessing."

It was an odd little family that held hands and praised the Father at the edge of the dying cornfield, but a family just the same.

"Food's on the table," Darcy announced.

Copper's walk was as wobbly as a table with one short leg. "Let's eat. I'm starving."

CHAPTER 14

The day was nearing an end, and Copper was glad to see it go. She thought she'd had hard times before. She'd grieved when she learned that her precious daddy had consumption. And she'd spent months in the valley of the shadow when her husband died. But nothing touched the fear of losing her daughter, a fear that left her weak and trembling for hours. She was sure she'd aged ten years this morning.

Now she just felt grateful as she sat with John at the kitchen table eating blackberry cobbler with nutmeg cream. Darcy had lain down with Lilly–like Copper, she couldn't get her fill of the baby–and they both slept.

Copper shared the day's happening with John, but like a hiccup the episode repeated jerkily in her mind. "Her dress was soaked," she said, licking her spoon. "I think she fell in the creek."

John took his coffee to the hearth and stirred the fire with a poker. He bent to pick up Lilly's wet shoes stuffed with newsprint, then sat down. "I think you're right. But the creek banks are awful steep there by the cornfield. How'd she get out?"

"It's the strangest thing. While I was bathing her, I asked, 'Lilly, were you in the creek?' And she said, 'Yup. Lady help.'"

"What does that mean?"

"I don't have the foggiest notion." Copper poured water in the granite dishpan from the kettle on the stove. "But sometimes I feel like someone is watching from the trees." She stuck the bar of lye soap to her nose before she dropped it in the pan. It was the cleanest smell, but it tickled her nose and she sneezed.

"God bless," John said. "Someone watching?"

Copper shook her head. "This is crazy, but it puts me in mind of Remy."

John choked on his coffee, sucking in air and coughing. Copper slapped his back, leaving wet handprints on his blue work shirt.

"Goodness," she said. "Are you all right?"

"I don't think it's good for you to conjure up visions of Remy that way," he said when he stopped choking.

He reached out his hand, and she let him pull her onto his lap. She was sure it wasn't right to be this close when they weren't truly promised, but she had a sense it wouldn't be long until he asked for her hand. She was willing to wait until the time was right.

"I know," she said. "But I can't help but think about her."

John shifted in the chair, and she tucked her head in the curve of his neck. "Kindly leave me out of hearing about that kind of daydreaming," he replied sharply.

Stung by his words, Copper moved away from him and stared out the window into the night. "I don't want to just forget about her."

"Fine for you," he said, "but I do."

"John . . . ," she started but stopped when he reached for his hat and headed for the door. "Why are you mad at me?"

"I'm not," he said, his hand on the doorknob. "But can't you see that woman nearly ruined my life? Can't you see Remy Riddle was a manipulator and a common thief?"

"Remy was only trying to save herself the best she could, John. Forevermore! I thought you understood that."

"Huh," he snorted. "If not for Remy we'd be planning a wedding instead of arguing about her."

Copper's anger flared. "Who says we'd be planning a wedding, John Pelfrey?" She flounced to the table and began to gather up dessert bowls and spoons. Oh, he made her so mad sometimes.

It seemed his anger matched hers as a frown knit his brow. Faithful stood between them looking first one way then the other.

"I say it." John strode to face her. Carefully he took the bowl from her hands and set it on the table before he pulled her into his arms. "I say let's plan a wedding."

"Funny," Copper teased, looking up at him, "I don't remember a proposal."

"Will you?" His voice was husky when he asked, his arms tightening their hold, lifting her up. "Copper Brown Corbett, will you marry me and make me the happiest man in the world?"

In the circle of his strong arms, she was home. He was her rock and her comfort. "I will, John Pelfrey," she replied with strong conviction. "I will."

Like Lilly would do to her, Copper trailed John out the door and across the porch and watched as the dark swallowed first him and then Faithful, leaving only the trace of his whistled tune.

Old Tom wound himself around her ankles. She picked the cat up and rocked him in her arms until he protested. He was old, and rheumatism stiffened his joints. Holding the door, she let him into the warm house. He could sleep at the foot of the bed tonight.

She dumped Old Tom on the bed where Darcy still slept with her arms around Lilly. Copper fetched an extra quilt from the blanket chest under the window and covered them against the night's chill. Tom circled their feet before he too curled up for the night. His rich purr warmed Copper's heart.

A few dishes waited. The water was cold, and the bar of soap had turned to mush. Fishing out what she could, she saved it on a saucer. Her heart beat fast when she thought of John's proposal. Maybe next spring they'd marry—they really should wait a little while. By rote, she washed the cups and the bowls and the spoons until they squeaked cleanly under her hands.

If she could just come to terms with Remy's terrible demise.

She couldn't help but feel guilty. There must have been something she could have said all those years ago when they were friends–something to teach Remy there was always hope. Her mind took its own ride on a merry-go-round of memory carrying her backward into another space and time. . . .

Mam had threatened Copper that summer of her fifteenth year. Leastways it felt like a threat to Copper–talk of boarding school and making her into a lady. With John's help, Copper planned to run away. She would live in a cave on the mountain. Mam would never find her.

The fall weather was so beautiful, and the air was crisp and smelled of apples. She had gone to the cave to find herself, to find a way out of her stepmother's restraint and had found a friend instead–Remy Riddle, the girl John had married.

Remy of the pale skin, wild white hair, and deep voice. Remy had been running too, and her plight made Copper's seem childish, because she was fleeing a father who cared so little he could discard Remy like a broken wheel or a give-down mule.

Then winter had come, and it was Remy who lived in the cave. Copper helped out as much as Remy would allow, for the girl was overly proud. Each time Copper mentioned seeking advice from Mam or Daddy, Remy would threaten to run even farther. So the two girls had compromised. Copper didn't ask questions, and Remy started to eat the food and wear the clothing Copper left for her to stumble upon, for Remy had made it clear that Riddles didn't take handouts.

Over that long and bitter winter they shared more than cast-off clothing. A bond was formed, one that Copper thought would never be broken.

The teakettle on the stove whistled urgently. Copper started, confused for a moment to find herself standing in what used to be her stepmother's kitchen, her hands as wrinkled as prunes in the cold dishwater.

She rinsed the dishes, then poured water for tea. The clock on the mantel struck one time. My goodness, it was after midnight, but she was not the least bit sleepy. Her tongue caught a salty tear. Her friend was dead. How could that be? Dear little Remy was gone. Surely if Copper went back to the cave, she would find Remy there, fey as ever with a red foxtail fixed to the back of her dress.

There was too much to think on. Copper slipped a shawl around her shoulders, then took her tea and stepped out the door. The shadow of a man startled her. Dimmert sat slumped on a porch step, fast asleep. Star stood just beyond, ever patient.

She whispered, "What are you doing here?"

He started violently at the sound of her voice and leaped up.

"I'm sorry. I didn't mean to scare you, Dimmert, but you need to go to bed."

Even in the scant moonlight she could see his Adam's apple bobbing, trying to come up with a word. "B-baby," he stuttered. "Watch baby."

"Oh, Dimm." He must have been watching for John to leave so he could take up his vigil. Copper would have liked to gather the young man in her arms and comfort him, but she settled for patting his arm. "Lilly's fine. Darcy's with her."

Nodding, he gave a funny little wave, almost a salute, before he turned and started toward his room in the barn. Star followed.

Taking the seat Dimmert vacated, Copper sipped the cooling tea and thought of John's story—John and Remy's.

CHAPTER 15

The rooster crowed and Copper startled from sleep, jerking her hand and splashing tepid tea down her skirt. Cold and stiff, she stood and set the cup aside. She'd slept, what part of the night she slept at all, leaning against the porch railing. She could feel its imprint on her shoulder.

Another day, she thought, as mist rose off the yard and Benny scratched about in the loft. There was breakfast to cook and Mazy to milk and a basket of shucky beans waited to be strung, but she needed a moment with the memory of her friend Remy. Pans rattled in the kitchen. Darcy was making biscuits. Leaning in the door, Copper asked, "Can you keep an eye on Lilly? I want to walk a ways."

"'Course I will. See what I come up with." Darcy showed

Copper a long knitted string. "I'm going to tie Lilly to me until she learns not to wander."

"I don't know if Miss Priss will cotton to being a puppy on a leash."

"Maybe not, but I don't cotton to going through what happened yesterday again neither."

"Nor do I." Reaching around the door, Copper fetched her walking stick. "I'll be back directly."

She wished for time to hike to the cave where she'd first met Remy, but she had to settle for the place where she'd last seen her. Copper's life had been so busy after she left the mountains for the city that she had not given much thought to her fey friend. It made her heart sore to think of how easily she'd left the very memory of Remy behind.

The creek followed a dip and bend before Copper reached her destination. *Right here*, she thought, pushing aside dry weed stalks with her walking stick. *I said good-bye to Remy right here.* She could almost see Remy that long-ago day, one fist tapping her chest to remind Copper that the heart doesn't forget.

Cold air nipped at Copper's nose, and she rubbed her hands together as she stood lost in reflection. She wished there were a proper grave to visit, but John had said they'd found very little left of Remy Riddle.

A chill shook Copper. John said they'd buried Remy's sky blue shawl with gold stars around the border. If Copper closed her eyes, she could almost see Remy's delighted face when she found the shawl that Christmas so long ago—found it where

Copper had left it for her to stumble upon. Things always had to be done Remy's way.

"I'm so sorry," Copper said. "I'm sorry I lost you, Remy. I'm sorry I wasn't here when you needed my help."

Copper gathered a fistful of leaves and stepped down the bank to the edge of the creek. One by one she released the orange and gold and red leaves, watching them swirl through eddies and bump over rocks. "'A friend loveth at all times,'" she whispered, her throat raw with unshed tears, "'and a brother is born for adversity.'" She tapped her chest in the place right over her heart. "I'll always love you, Remy. We'll always be sisters."

In the spring she'd come back to this spot and plant a willow for her lost friend and maybe someday eye blossoms to choke out the thistles and weeds. She'd have Dimm make a small bench where she could rest and visit with Remy from time to time. It was little, she knew, but it was all she had to offer.

CHAPTER 16

Copper was lost in thought as the big wooden wheels of the surrey turned faster and faster. With her permission, Dimmert had repaired the light buggy, greasing the wheels and oiling the leather fabric until it was restored to its former glory. Now she sat clutching the bench to keep from being flung over the side as Star pulled them to Fairy Mae's.

"Dilly," Lilly called from the backseat. "See Dilly, Mama?"

"Yes, baby. Dilly is waiting with her mammaw."

"Now?"

"Soon, Lilly Gray. Very soon." The carriage bumped over a rock in the road, snapping Copper's mouth shut like a coiled spring. "You sure this buggy can stand the trip, Dimmert?"

Dimmert just ducked his head and pulled the reins, slowing Star to a trot.

"Why, Mama?"

Knowing better, Copper answered anyway. "Why what, baby?"

"Why Star slow?"

"So we won't bounce so much."

"Why?"

Copper rested her pounding head against the leather seat back. "Enough questions. Say your ABC's."

Truth be told, Copper was as anxious to get to Fairy Mae's as Lilly was. Dimmert had come back from one of his jaunts last evening with news that his sister Dance had left the safety of her mammaw's to return to her husband's house. Fairy Mae told Dimmert that Dance went willingly. She had a right, Copper supposed. She was a grown woman and could make her own decisions. But why?

Lord, she prayed, *please help me figure this out.*

"A B, A B," Lilly warbled from the back. "A B, one two free, A B C!" Then blessed silence, for a moment anyway, until, "Why, Mama?"

"Why what?"

"Why Benny crow? Why kitty say meow?"

"That's just how God made them, Lilly. That was God's plan."

Copper could hear the pop of Lilly's thumb before she answered, "Oh."

Copper had to admit that sometimes she was very glad Lilly sucked her thumb. It seemed like the only time she was quiet. At two years old she was a precocious child who questioned everything.

Even without the pretty summer flowers, the Whitts' cabin was a warm and welcoming place, buzzing with children's laughter and Fairy Mae's pleasant countenance. Copper didn't know how she could keep her humor this time, however; for Dance had left her infant son in her arthritic grandmother's care.

"How could she?" Copper asked. "I could have sworn Dance would never willingly lay eyes on Ace Shelton again."

"Honey," Fairy Mae replied, "I cain't figure them two out. Dance has always been that way about Ace. The day they was to marry I warned her she was crossing hell on a rotten rail, but she didn't pay me no mind." The old woman held her great-grandbaby over her shoulder and patted his back until she was rewarded with a loud burp.

"He must have threatened her," Copper said.

"No, he didn't. She set up nights waiting for him. I caught her at the window many a time."

Copper took Jay to change his wet nappy. After cleansing, she patted his bottom with a fine talcum. "Why?" she asked, sounding for all the world like Lilly Gray. "Why would she leave her baby?"

Copper was sorry the moment the words left her mouth, for Fairy Mae's sunny smile trembled. "Poor Dance. Her nerves have always been strung tight. That's why she's lived with me since she was just a tad. Dance does the best she can, I reckon." Taking the clean and dry baby, she upended the glass bottle and stuck the India-rubber teat in his mouth.

Copper was glad to see the vigor with which baby Jay went after the bottle. If he didn't get diarrhea from the cow's milk, he stood a good chance of living.

Taking in the room crowded with children with a sweep of her arm, Copper asked, "How are you going to manage, Fairy Mae?"

"The good Lord provides." Her face crinkled in a smile of certainty. "We'll make do."

"I can take Jay if you need me to," Copper offered.

"Bless your heart," Fairy Mae said. "But we're all right for now. The young'uns do all the work. And it feels good to have a baby in these old arms again."

Copper knelt by the stool Fairy Mae's feet were propped up on. She took a tube of sweet-smelling salve from her dress pocket and began to massage the crippled feet.

Fairy Mae sighed. "That feels so good."

Copper had to give voice to her worry. "You know, Dance will have another baby way too soon now that she's stopped nursing."

Fairy Mae laid her veined hand on Copper's head. "Babies are God's smiles. I reckon you cain't get too many."

"I hope I can grow as strong in my faith as you."

"All you have to do is trust in His providence, child."

"Reckon Ace would shoot me if I go to check on Dance?"

"If he was going to shoot you, he would have done it already," Fairy Mae said. "He might sick that snapping turtle on you though."

Copper laughed. "Depends on how much he likes turtle soup."

It had rained during the night and turned colder. Copper could see her breath as she talked to Dimmert. He was comfortable enough now to talk to her, but it still seemed an ordeal for him to pull his words out of storage. "I wonder if Ace will be home this time of day," she said.

"Umm," came from Dimmert, then a cough followed by, "Ain't . . . umm . . . often there mornings."

"That's what I thought. I figured he'd be off tending his still this early."

Star skittered on the trail made treacherous by slick leaves and mushy walnut hulls. High overhead, squirrels peeled the round green nuts, letting the hulls fall where they may. Squirrels were good farmers, eating some of the nuts and burying others to keep for the coming winter. Their nests looked like bad house-keeping, just piles of leaves stuck in the tops of barren trees. The overlooked walnuts, acorns, and hickory nuts planted here and there by squirrels would sprout as new trees in the spring.

"I should have brought a gun," Copper said. "There's our supper overhead."

As if in answer, a gray squirrel chattered threats, snapping his tail repeatedly like a tiny whip. When that didn't scare Copper and Dimmert off, he bounced from limb to limb, then tree to tree before disappearing.

In truth they probably should have brought a gun. Who knew what Ace would do? But Copper felt guns would only worsen the tension between Dance's husband and them. Hopefully she and Dimmert would come and go before Ace even knew they'd been there. They might be bringing Dance with them. It was up to her.

No such luck. They caught Ace right in the middle of the

yard. Or he caught them, depending on which way you looked at it. He stared and drew his neck down in his shoulders.

"Mr. Shelton," Copper hollered from the edge of the forest, "we want to visit with Dance. We don't mean any harm."

The door of the cabin opened, and Dance peeked out. Ace stood in the yard for the longest time. His hand slipped in and out of his pocket. Copper wondered if he had a pistol. Likely so.

"We don't have any weapons," she yelled. Unless you counted rocks. Dimm had so many in his pockets that he'd drown if he fell in the creek.

The cabin door closed. Dance would be no help.

Ace planted his feet and withdrew the pistol Copper rightly guessed he had. He didn't aim it their way but made a show of spinning it on his forefinger.

Dimmert reached into his own pocket. Ace should remember that deadly aim. He'd have Ace out cold before he could point his gun.

"No, Dimm," she whispered. Cupping her hands, she used them as a megaphone. "I have news of the baby."

The cabin door opened again and Dance stepped out.

Ace dropped the pistol back in his overalls. He took a step their way and motioned for them to come.

Dimmert slid down from Star and looped the reins over a tree branch before he helped Copper dismount.

Ace met them midway through the yard. "If you got bad news, don't take it to the porch. Dance cain't take no bad news."

"Your son is fine," Copper replied. "He misses his mama though."

"Don't be telling her that," Ace said. "Like I said, she cain't take no bad news."

Over Ace's shoulder, Copper could see Dance pacing the porch, front to back instead of side to side, and every time she approached the door, she reached out and touched the knob.

"I guess you took out the turtle trap," Copper said.

Ace removed his greasy felt hat. His black hair spilled down over his eyes, and he shook it back with a practiced gesture. "I'll talk to you but not in front of him."

"Dimmert, why don't you go visit with your sister?"

Dimmert didn't budge but stood as straight as a sentry beside her. Why did men act so possessively? Not a one she ever knew, save her father, thought she could fend for herself.

"Perhaps, Mr. Shelton, if you'd put down your gun . . ."

Ace walked to the barn and disappeared into its shadowed depths. He came back with his pockets inside out.

"Dimm?" she asked. She felt his hand meet hers as he slid a rock the size of a small potato into her palm. "All right then," she said. "You can watch from the porch."

"Walk a ways with me," Ace said.

"Dimmert won't like it if he can't see me," Copper responded.

"I cain't figure why everybody's got me pegged for the devil," Ace said, waving his arms around.

"I'm willing to listen." Copper walked with him toward the barn.

"You all come in here and took my wife and stole my baby, and nobody give a thought to me." Ace sounded angry, but he kept his voice down, reminding Copper of the first quiet whir from a rattlesnake. "I ain't even held my baby. I only seen him once, and I had to spy to do that."

"Your son is fine, Mr. Shelton. He—"

"Mr. Shelton," Ace mocked. "What are you, a schoolteacher? Cain't you talk like other folks?"

Copper held her tongue, turned in her tracks, and started back the way they had come.

He grabbed her shoulder. "I didn't mean no disrespect."

A stone pinged off the barn door directly over his head. A warning from Dimmert.

Ace put up his hands in surrender. "But I ain't a cur you can just kick out of the way. I got a right to my family."

Copper faced him. "Mr. Shelton . . . Ace, I only did what I thought was right for Dance and the baby."

"Why'd you think you needed to haul my wife off to her mammaw's?" His face was a study in self-pity. "You didn't got to do that."

Copper shook her head. The man was as dense as mud. "When Dimmert brought me here to deliver your wife's baby, I found her hungry. Hungry! And stuck in your house like a prisoner of war with a turtle for a guard. I believe it was the most inhumane—pardon me—meanest thing I've ever seen."

Ace tossed his head. His hair took flight, then settled on his head. "The turtle was to keep her safe. She wouldn't go out as long as it was in its hidey-hole. Truly, I never meant to leave her alone that long."

"Then why did you?"

"Ain't no reason to lie to you. Some lowlife found my moonshine, and it took me a time and a half to haul my still to a safer place. Seems like nobody respects nothing no more."

"I still don't understand why you needed to keep Dance locked up that way."

"Seems to me that's better'n letting her fall off a cliff or get lost back in the woods. Dance is . . . well, she's peculiar. Takes these notions to wander, and then she cain't find her way home. At night she has nightmares and walks in her sleep, but she don't go far after dark, for she's more scared of hoot owls than turtles, if you can believe that. I was trying to protect her, if anybody bothered to ask."

"That doesn't make it right. You can't treat a person that way."

"What's a body supposed to do? I had to work. She went with me until she got too big to climb the mountain."

Copper tightened her shawl around her shoulders. The weather was taking a mean turn. They'd have snow by morning. "You should have asked her family for help."

"I ain't never relied on strangers."

"They're your family too. There's not a better person in the world than Fairy Mae Whitt." Copper stomped her feet and rubbed her hands together. "Might we go in the house for a spell? I'm freezing."

"Surely," he said.

She kept pace with him, only stopping when they got to the porch. Dimm waited in the doorway. "There's something else," she said. "Dance said you burned her with the fireplace poker."

Ace shook his head as if he couldn't believe she still questioned him. "I got up to stir the fire one night. It had been raining for days, and the house was damp and chilly. I was certain she'd take a cold, so I kept the fire going. She sneaked up behind me and hit me with the soup pot." He rubbed the back of his head. "I whirled around and struck out with the poker. I never thought it was her. Tell you what, I took the knives out of the house after that."

Once inside, Copper sat for a while and took coffee with Dance and Ace. She wasn't sure what to make of Ace's strange story. Should she believe him or what she had seen with her own eyes? And did it matter what she thought? Dance had put herself back in this place of her own accord.

Ace asked and so she told them about Jay, how he was eating well and growing bigger every day.

A tear slid down Ace's cheek, and he hid his face in the crook of his arm. "You reckon I could see the boy?"

Pity stirred Copper's heart. One thing she'd learned in the city as she worked alongside her husband with all manner of people who had all manner of needs was that everyone had a story. Even a pancake has two sides.

Dance sat silently. She seemed to have no will of her own.

Copper touched her arm. "Would you like that? Would you like to see your baby?"

Dance sighed. "It don't matter. Whatever you want."

Copper stood and gathered her shawl and her bonnet. "We'll stop by Fairy Mae's on our way home. I'll tell your mammaw you'll be coming soon to see your son."

Ace walked her to the porch.

"Fairy Mae will welcome you," Copper told him. "There's no reason you can't take Dance for visits."

"Do you reckon I can ever bring him home?" he asked.

"Talk to her family," Copper said. "Maybe you all can work something out. Might be one of Dance's sisters could come and help."

Dimmert was waiting with Star. He had just reached down to pull Copper up behind him when Ace yelled as he headed toward the barn, "Hold up. I got something for you."

They waited until he came over with a gunnysack tied up with a piece of twine. "Here's supper. And I thank you kindly for stopping by."

Farther down the road, Copper dismounted by the creek and let the turtle go. She wasn't partial to turtle meat—give her a rabbit or squirrel anytime—but Ace must be quite the connoisseur. They waited until the snapper pushed his feet and his head out of the shell before they started off once more. Dimm shivered, but Copper reckoned it was good he faced his fear. They watched the turtle trundle down the bank. He was safe until Ace caught him again. She hoped Ace wouldn't know they didn't have turtle for supper.

CHAPTER 17

Winter came in with a vengeance. It snowed and snowed and snowed. By mid-December Copper was pretty much tired of shoveling paths between the barn and the cabin, tired of dirty snowmelt on her kitchen floor, tired of the isolation. Each day she counted the blessing of Dimmert, who worked right alongside her, feeding the animals and keeping the woodpile on the front porch stocked and the coal buckets full. The house was always cold in spite of their efforts. And try as she might, Copper couldn't get Dimm to move into the house. He could have slept in the open loft over the sitting area, but he wouldn't leave Star alone in the barn.

Christmas gave a reprieve. Snow still covered the ground and it was too much effort to go anywhere, but they'd celebrate Jesus' birthday just the same. John came over every evening the week before the big day and cracked black walnuts for the jam cake and fudge and divinity she and Darcy made and stored in tins on the top shelf of the pantry. Dimmert waded through waist-high drifts to find the perfect lopsided cedar tree. He cut it to size and nailed a crisscross of boards to its trunk. Now it rested on the porch just waiting for Christmas Eve. Every time the door was opened, the fresh smell of Christmas caused Lilly to jump up and down in excitement.

A package arrived from Massey's Mercantile, and John picked it up at the post office. He conspired with Copper to hide it until Santa came. Seemed everyone was conspiring. Dimmert was forever hammering on something in the barn, and Darcy picked up her sewing each day when Lilly went down for her nap.

Copper was as bad as the young ones. She could hardly sleep she was so excited. Early on the morning of Christmas Eve, she crept out of bed before her little family awoke and settled on the hearth with a cup of tea and a pilfered bit of black-walnut fudge. Her mind swirled with anticipation as she thought of the gifts from Santa that would appear under the tree tonight. Lilly was to have a real doll with black hair like her own. Darcy would receive a locket on a fine gold chain, and Dimmert—oh, Copper couldn't wait to see his face. In Massey's catalog she'd found the perfect gift for him. John thought it was extravagant, but it was her choice.

She traipsed to the window and pulled back the curtain. Thankfully it had stopped snowing. High white ridges of white sparkled under moonlight so bright it hurt her eyes. Or maybe it was the sudden tears that hurt. Back at the fireside she sat and pulled her cold feet up under her long flannel nightgown. Fudge melted on her tongue, and her teeth crunched black walnuts as the fire warmed her back. Grateful tears flowed; she didn't try to stop them. "I am so blessed," she whispered and sipped her tea. "So blessed. Thank You, Lord."

Copper missed her dog, Paw-paw. In years past, the old hound would have kept vigil with her. He loved nothing better than a warm hearth on a chilly night. She could almost feel his silky ears under her hand, the knobby ridge of his backbone. She wondered if the lilac bush she'd buried him under back in Lexington gave his old bones comfort and if his bones would rise on Resurrection Day. She thought they would. Wouldn't it be just like the Lord to give His children such a gift—to be reunited with their pets?

A shriek of wind tore around the corner of the house and rattled the windowpane. She put a lump of coal on the fire and poked hot coals around it. Maybe come spring she'd see about getting a dog. Truly, a house wasn't a home without a dog. But then, by spring Faithful should be sitting on Copper's hearth.

She took it for granted they'd live on this side of the creek. Her house was bigger than John's and had an extra bedroom. It went without saying that Darcy and Dimmert would stay on. Goodness how her life had taken on new meaning in such a short time. Her marriage to Simon seemed like a dream sometimes, Lilly Gray her only reminder of that precious time.

Enough of that. I don't want to entertain sorrow this morning. There will be nothing but happy thoughts in this house today. She stood and stretched, kneading the small of her back with her fists.

Might as well get started, Copper thought. She parted the curtains that closed off the pantry and retrieved the bread bowl. She cut a lump of lard into the flour and seasonings already in the bowl, then added a splash of cold milk. After dusting the table with flour, she dumped the dough out and patted it into a thick round. Mam's old tin biscuit cutter hung on a nail just inside the pantry, always ready for duty.

Soon two dozen biscuits, sides touching, waited in pie tins to be baked. She refreshed the flour, baking powder, and salt, then put the bread bowl back in its place.

She dressed quietly in the cold bedroom, pulling on long knit underwear and extra socks. Leaving her hair in its thick braid, she coiled it at the nape of her neck and secured it with pins. Back in the kitchen she scrubbed her teeth with a mixture of baking soda and salt, enjoying the fresh clean taste it left. It paid to be prepared. John might steal another kiss.

Her lips tingled when she remembered last night. He was preparing to leave for home and already had his hat on. Faithful waited by the door. Copper went to peck his cheek with a little good-bye kiss when he turned his head, and she met his mouth instead. Mmm, that was an early Christmas gift.

Her hat and coat, with gloves in the pockets, hung on the back of the door. She put them on and then struggled to pull Daddy's old galoshes over her work boots. Finally, she was ready to meet the day. The too-big galoshes marked her way on the packed snow. She was glad to find that it was a little warmer this morning.

Dawn broke. The barnyard rooster crowed. Benny echoed. Rays of morning's first light cast a beautiful picture for her eyes alone. Puffs of snow like cotton batting clung to each tree branch, and high drifts nestled along the fence rows and sculpted white ridges against the stark gray siding of the barn. She startled a rabbit, and it hopped away, leaving footprints as delicate as a chain of daisies.

So pretty, she thought, her gaze following the tracks. And what was this beside the barn? She followed the rabbit for a closer look. A row of perfect snow angels lay in the drifted snow. When had Darcy been out to make them? Copper couldn't help herself. First at one end of the snow angels and then at the other, she flung herself backward. Moving her arms and legs with abandon, she left her own angelic likeness in the drift.

Mazy mooed from her stall in the barn. Copper needed to quit playing and get busy, but first she took a minute to enjoy the gift of angels. Hers were taller and thinner than the others. It seemed as if they were holding hands, making friends on Christmas Eve morning.

Mazy bawled, demanding a rasher of hay and some feed. Copper hurried into the barn to the waiting cow. After she milked, she mucked out Mazy's stall. It was too cold to turn the cow out for the day, so she forked extra hay from the manger into Mazy's feed box.

Star stuck his long neck over his stall door and nickered a greeting. She scrubbed at the place between his eyes with her knuckles. He rested his head against her shoulder in delight. Star really was the most beautiful horse she'd ever seen. She fished a summer apple from her coat pocket and fed him his treat. Dimmert had already seen to Star's stall, and Copper knew he would also slop the pigs and feed the chickens.

She could have stayed in the barn all day. It seemed appropriate to be in a stable with the animals on Christmas Eve, but there was a ham to roast, a tree to decorate, and a little girl who waited for Santa. She finished her chores and rushed to the house, the snow angels all but forgotten.

Remy Riddle hid herself behind the barn, where there were no windows or doors for a body to spy her from. A copse of thorny locusts and overgrown cedar edged close to the barn, giving her the perfect escape if need be. She'd nearly been caught, though, when Purty veered off the path to the barn after she spied the snow angels.

She shouldn't have been so foolish as to make the angels, but it was a gift she couldn't resist leaving, a Christmas present to the only true friend she'd ever had . . . if she discounted the man who'd taken her in that season two winters back. But she counted no man as a friend, not even John Pelfrey. She didn't like to think on him. Ever since she relied on him that winter when her ankle was busted, she had an uneasy feeling when he came to mind. Thoughts of him made her heart feel hollowed out like her belly did when it was empty—as if she had something to be sorry for. She'd only wanted to get in out of the cold long enough for her ankle to mend, never intended for things to go as far as they did. But she'd learned from a master to get along by hook or by crook and not to count the misdeeds along the way. Her pap would say a body dumb enough to be made a fool of by a Riddle deserved their fate. And she reckoned her actions had made a right fool of John.

The rooster crowed again. Streams of gold pierced the heavy shadows of Remy's hiding place. She'd better get going. A cedar branch broom erased her footprints until she was far from Purty's house. She didn't mean to be caught.

Near dark that evening, Dimmert forced the Christmas tree through the kitchen door. Clumps of snow littered the floor, but the tree was so fresh that not a single needle fell. "Where?" he asked.

Of course there was only one place for the magnificent, raggedy cedar to sit: right where all the Christmas trees of Copper's past had been—there under the sitting room window. "Not too close to the fire," Copper said as he moved the tree this way and that. "Right there." He stopped, then twirled the tree so she could see each side. "Turn it just a hair more toward your left. . . . Yes, that's perfect."

Darcy bustled about, sweeping up the melting snow. "Law, Dimm. You could have knocked your boots against the doorjamb before you clomped across my clean floor."

Hanging his head, Dimmert started for the door.

"Don't leave," Copper said. "Stay and help decorate before Lilly wakes up from her nap. I shouldn't have let her sleep so late, but I wanted to surprise her with the tree." They'd strung popcorn the night before, and Copper handed Dimmert the first string. "You're the only one tall enough to do the top."

Copper watched Dimmert and Darcy trim the tree as she stood at the cookstove stirring cocoa powder into a pot of sweetened milk. She and Darcy had collected all manner of pretties that struck their fancy over the year—feathers, pinecones, various grasses (which they gathered into small bundles with scrap ribbon), and pressed leaves. Dimmert was awkward at the task—it seemed every trinket he hung fell off the minute he picked up another—but Darcy had a natural touch.

Soon the pasteboard box of decorations was empty, and they stood back to admire their handiwork. Copper knew from what Fairy Mae told her that the Whitt children had never had Christmas trees and gifts. As Copper set mugs of cocoa and a tray of cookies on the table, she wondered how Fairy Mae was doing with her brood. Copper knew the day would be filled with joy. Fairy Mae would see to that, and there would be presents under their tree thanks to Massey's Mercantile and John. He'd secretly delivered what Copper had ordered for Fairy Mae's grandchildren.

And then he'd snowshoed up the mountain to the Wilsons'. John told Copper that Cara had met him as he came into the yard with the burlap bag slung over his shoulder. Tears had streamed down her face as she took the pack, promising to hide it from her brothers and sisters until Christmas morning. John wiped a tear of his own when he told Copper there really was a Santa Claus.

"Sit a minute," Copper told Dimmert and Darcy, "and enjoy your cocoa and cookies. Then we'll wake up Lilly Gray."

"Oh, I can't wait to see her face," Darcy replied as Dimmert took a seat. "I'll drink my chocolate later."

Darcy scurried away. Copper could hear her gentle voice awaking Lilly Gray, whose eyes widened in wonder when Darcy carried her into the kitchen-sitting room. "Crip muss tree!" she announced, wiggling free from Darcy's arms. She ran up to the decorated cedar with her little arms flung wide. "How'd tree get here?"

"Santa's elves brought it while you were sleeping," Copper said with a wink to Dimmert.

Lilly walked backward, keeping the tree in sight, until she bumped against Dimmert's knees. "Huh," she said, turning to Dimmert. "Did you catched one?"

"No," Dimmert said, lifting Lilly onto his knee. "Too slick."

Copper laughed at Lilly's question and Dimm's response. "That's just what my brother Willy would have said. Once he made plans to capture Santa and his pack." Memories of Christmases long past flooded Copper's mind. It was as if she could reach out and touch Mam and Daddy, Willy and Daniel; their presence in the room was so strong. Now they were celebrating Christmas and a new way of life in Philadelphia while Copper did her best to celebrate as she always had in her precious mountain home.

Dimmert handed Lilly a cookie and let her sip from his cup before she danced away—right back to the tree. She knelt and stuck her head under the cedar boughs. "Where's my dolly?"

"Santa brings gifts to good little girls tonight, Lilly Gray, while they are sleeping."

Lilly's eyes widened again. "Me good, Mama?"

Copper swung her up and held her tight, breathing in the sweet, innocent smell of her. "The best. You're Mama's very best girl. Now we need the finishing touch." She carried Lilly to the pie safe and took out a small, tattered box. Setting it on the table, Copper removed the lid and unfolded crinkled tissue paper revealing a blown-glass star. "This belonged to your grandmother Corbett. Her name was Lilly too."

Copper settled into the rocker by the hearth with Lilly in her lap. Darcy sat at her feet, and Dimm perched on the edge of the hearth. He looked for all the world like a great blue heron, ready to fly away if startled.

"I want to read to you about the star before we put ours on the tree," Copper said.

"Pretty." Lilly turned the dark blue ornament etched with gold over and over in her chubby hands. It sparkled like diamonds in the firelight.

Thumbing through the familiar Scriptures, Copper came to the second chapter of Matthew. She cleared her throat and read: "'Now when Jesus was born in Bethlehem of Judaea in the days of Herod the king, behold, there came wise men from the east to Jerusalem, saying, Where is he that is born King of the Jews? for we have seen his star in the east, and are come to worship him.

"'When Herod the king had heard these things, he was troubled, and all Jerusalem with him. And when he had gathered all the chief priests and scribes of the people together, he demanded of them where Christ should be born. And they said unto him,

In Bethlehem of Judaea: for thus it is written by the prophet, And thou Bethlehem in the land of Juda, art not the least among the princes of Juda: for out of thee shall come a Governor, that shall rule my people Israel.

"'Then Herod, when he had privily called the wise men, enquired of them diligently what time the star appeared. And he sent them to Bethlehem, and said, Go and search diligently for the young child; and when ye have found him, bring me word again, that I may come and worship him also.'"

Lilly Gray wriggled on Copper's lap. The fragile glass ornament tumbled from her grasp, falling with a bounce to Darcy's lap.

"Careful," Darcy said. "We don't want to break baby Jesus' star."

"That's right," Copper added. "This is like the star that led the wise men to the manger where baby Jesus was born."

"Where baby's mama?" Lilly asked.

"Baby Jesus' mama was Mary, and she was there in the stable with him," Copper said.

"Where daddy?"

"His name was Joseph, and he was taking care of Mary and her baby."

"Where Lilly's daddy?"

Copper was taken aback. She was not ready for that question yet. "Sit still and let me finish the Bible story." She found her place and continued. "'When they had heard the king, they departed; and, lo, the star, which they saw in the east, went before them, till it came and stood over where the young child was. When they saw the star, they rejoiced with exceeding great joy. And when they were come into the house, they saw the young child with

Mary his mother, and fell down, and worshipped him: and when they had opened their treasures, they presented unto him gifts; gold, and frankincense and myrrh.

"'And being warned of God in a dream that they should not return to Herod, they departed into their own country another way.'"

"That was beautiful, Miz Copper," Darcy said. "I love the sound of your voice when you read."

Copper closed the Bible. "Why, thank you, but it is the story that's important."

"Yes, ma'am, I know. My daddy is a preacher, you recollect. All us kids have been saved."

"That is the most wonderful gift you'll ever receive," Copper replied.

Dimmert unfolded himself from the hearth. Copper had never seen him sit so long.

"Let's bundle up," Copper said. "We'll go find the eastern star and follow it like the wise men did; then we'll put our star atop the tree."

Everyone's hats, coats, and mittens on, they followed Dimmert out into the night. Moonlight glittered on the snow and outlined the dark stable, where the animals slept.

"There." Copper pointed to the place over the stable where she knew she'd find the star. Family lore was that her great-grandfather had positioned the barn in just such a way that the wise men's star would beam from that direction every December 24. Though, of course, that was not the actual date the men had found Jesus, her family always celebrated their trek that night just the same. It was a part of their Christmas tradition.

Copper drew Lilly Gray even closer in her arms as they gazed at the star. Had there ever been a woman more blessed than she? Here she stood with her baby girl in the very same spot her ancestors had stood, looking at the very same star that God had used to guide the wise men. All the gold and frankincense and myrrh in the world couldn't take the place of the riches she had received from her Savior's blessed birth.

Darcy held the blown-glass ornament up high as if to catch some star shine. Lilly reached for it.

"No, Lilly," Copper said. "Let Darcy carry it."

Copper could have stood there all night just drinking in blessings, but Lilly's patience was thin, so she led them back into the house. Dimm stretched as far as he could, but he still couldn't touch the top of the cedar. Darcy dragged a straight-backed chair over and gave him the star. Lilly tried to climb onto the chair with him.

"Here," Darcy said as she lifted Lilly to Dimmert, "you can help."

With a little bossing from Darcy, Dimmert slid the hollow stem of the star onto the cedar's pointed topmost branch, then handed Lilly back to Darcy.

"Pretty," Lilly said and clapped.

"Beautiful," Copper agreed. Soon everyone joined Lilly's clapping.

"Just one more thing," Copper said as she took another box from the pie safe. "A tree has to have a bird's nest or it's not complete." The robin's nest she retrieved was old but still in one piece. She couldn't remember a Christmas tree on Troublesome Creek that hadn't held this nest tenderly in its branches. She placed it far back in the tree, then stepped away and admired the cedar. "There. Now it's finished."

CHAPTER 18

It was nearly midnight on Christmas Eve before they finally got Lilly to bed. Her late nap combined with the tree trimming and sugar cookies had her wound as tight as an eight-day clock. Darcy had lain down with her in Copper's bed, and now they both slept, for which Copper was thankful.

Truthfully, Copper was wound a little tight herself. And it didn't help that she couldn't keep herself from pacing from the Christmas tree to the kitchen window, looking out for John. She was acting right silly, she knew, like a lovesick schoolgirl.

She traced the outline of her mouth, where she could still feel his last kiss. She hadn't been exactly sure what a kiss from him would feel like, but she had imagined it would be as sweet as John himself, just a light lingering of lips with no demands.

It would be pleasant being married to her best friend, she'd thought—pleasant and safe. But he had changed since they'd left Troublesome Creek, she for Lexington and her doctor husband, he for a merchant ship and travels far away.

She reheated what was left in the chocolate pot and poured herself a cup. Once more she found herself at the window, drawing back the curtains. *What's keeping John?* He was bringing Santa Claus with him, and Copper was anxious to see the gifts underneath the tree. Funny how people changed once they grew up. Now what used to be a day of receiving was instead a time of joyous giving. Lilly had turned two in November and was old enough to understand Christmas and get caught up in the excitement. And Dimm was going to be so surprised at what Santa left under the tree for him. That was, if Santa ever came.

Her mind wandered back to John. Her strong feelings for him frightened her. She'd married Simon impetuously, without a thought to what marriage meant. But she was a widow; she'd tasted passion and its wild result, and she had hoped to never feel that way again. Great love brought greater pain when it was lost, much too high a price to pay. Ah, well, it seemed her love for John had done taken over her heart. She'd just have to trust things would go well.

A light thump at the door caused her to rush to open it. There stood John with a sack over his shoulder and a big, lumpy package at his feet. "Does that boy never sleep?" he asked with a nod toward the barn. "I've been hiding out for an hour waiting for Dimmert to put out his lantern." He stomped his boots free of snow. "I thought I'd freeze to death."

Copper laughed and took the sack as he grabbed the package. "Come on in, Santa, and I'll make you some hot cocoa. That will warm you right up."

"I can think of something better to warm me up," John replied, hanging his coat behind the door.

Copper pretended she didn't hear as she busied herself at the stove. "Do you want cookies or jam cake with this?"

"Does the cake have them black walnuts I cracked?"

"Yes–" she pried the lid from the round tin–"and caramel icing."

"If this is the same recipe your mam used to make, then cut me two pieces." He stood in front of the fire, soaking up the warmth.

Copper could feel his eyes on her while she cut the cake, poured the chocolate in an ironstone mug, and sealed the lid on the cake tin. Finally, she looked up from her task and met his gaze. "Two pieces? You're so greedy."

"Come over here," he said.

"Just a minute. Let me put the cake back in the pie safe."

He crooked his finger, beckoning her. "Please?" was all he needed to say before she was in his arms accepting the meeting she was so afraid of. His kisses started as warm as sunlight on a clear day. Butterflies caressed her eyelids, her cheekbones. Then he found her mouth and claimed her. Every feeling she'd kept at bay for so long swirled as swift as floodwaters until she was drowning in her own desire.

"John," she gasped, "let me go. I can't breathe."

He didn't let her go, but his arms loosed their tight grip, and he gently lowered her to sit beside him on the hearth.

Resting her arms on her knees, she hid her face there. "Are you all right?" she heard from a distance, as if he stood across the creek. Her heart was pounding nearly out of her chest, and bright spots danced before her eyes. She took a deep breath and turned his way. "Promise you won't do that again."

John knelt on the floor in front of her and tenderly raised her head until she had to look at him straight on. "Are you saying you don't favor my kisses?"

She shook her head. Tears trickled down her cheeks. "Oh, John." She sighed. "I'm saying I like them too much."

He rubbed her cheeks with his thumbs, catching her tears. "Then I can't promise." He leaned in, kissing her again, easy this time. "That's near as much fun as coon hunting," he teased. Settling back down on the hearth, he put his arm around her shoulders and drew her close. "You reckon we need to set a date?"

She couldn't help but laugh. My, she loved him. "I reckon we do. I was thinking of a spring wedding. I'd like to wait until the apple and pear trees bloom so we can have sweet-smelling flowers. But let's not decide tonight. Tonight you're Santa, so unload that pack."

Soon shiny packages peeked out from under the Christmas tree. Everyone had wrapped gifts except Lilly, whose gifts from Santa—a dolly and a doll-size buggy—sat by the tree. Copper's parents had always set Santa's gifts apart from the others. She guessed it was so grownups could see Christmas through a child's eyes, see that first delight when a little one spied Santa's gifts. Copper wanted to carry on all the old traditions. It made up a little for not having her family here.

"Can you shove Dimmert's present back a little? Even wrapped it's too easy to tell what he's getting."

John toed the bulky package toward the wall. "You don't think you went a little overboard with this?"

Copper, holding Lilly's doll in her arms, looked up at him. "Dimmert has been so good to me. I couldn't resist." She undid the doll's braided hair and combed it with her fingers until it fell down her back in dark waves, just like Lilly's. When she laid the dolly in the buggy, the glass eyes closed in her china face. "Does it bother you that I spent so much money on Dimm?"

He pulled a tiny coverlet over the doll's shoulders. "You need to know a true thing, Copper. Nothing you could do bothers me. Even that time you broke my heart clean in two, I understood your reason." The buggy squeaked when he pushed it back and forth.

John sat down, cupped her chin, and looked into her eyes. "It's just that you're so good—so pure in your caring about other folks, I feel like I have to protect you, maybe even from myself."

Copper got on her knees and took his face in her hands. "John Pelfrey, I love you. Let's never go away from each other again." And then she kissed him.

This time it was John who said he saw stars. He stood and pulled her up. "I'd better get out of here or else we'll have to send for the preacher tonight."

The weather was warming ever so slightly, and outside Copper's cozy cabin, Remy was snug as a bug in the fur-lined boots and mittens she'd made herself. Earlier she'd watched from the woods, a keen eye on John as he hid behind the barn. She wondered what he carried in his pack. Remy knew he waited for Purty's hired hand to go to bed. She'd done that often enough herself so she could sneak up on the porch and spy.

Crouching, she peered into the house through a slit in the drawn curtains. John and Purty were kissing. A feeling of satisfaction warmed Remy's little knot of a heart. Then John was pulling on his hat. She'd better make her getaway.

The night sky was brighter than usual as Remy trekked up the mountainside. *It's that star,* she thought, remembering the Christmas story Purty had told her many years ago about shepherds and smart men and a baby boy in a manger. Purty had said this star was the same one that shone on that night so many years ago.

Halfway home she froze in her tracks. Her nose twitched, sniffing the air. Something familiar was following her. On her way to Purty's house she had taken the liberty of visiting Hezzy Krill's chicken coop, and now she slipped off her mitten and dug in her coat pocket for one of the smooth brown eggs secreted there. With her teeth she chipped a piece of shell from the pointed end and shook it until a bit of its contents leaked out.

Remy waited while the creature watched her and waited also. Finally, she could hear the calloused pads of its four feet creeping up behind her making the barest *whisk, whisk* sound. She wished she was light on her feet like that, but try as she might to eat as little as possible, her boots broke through the firm crust, each step sinking like a stone.

"*Tch, tch, tch.*" She clicked her tongue against the roof of her mouth, calling the animal closer until its long pointed nose grazed her bare hand. Out of respect, she kept her back to the red fox, slowly maneuvering the egg until the sticky end faced her forest friend. Remy could feel the lap of the fox's tongue before it snatched the treat. Only then did she turn to watch as the animal loped gracefully away. "Huh." That was as good as any gift she could ever get. Well, nearly as good, for she most treasured the necklace Purty had left for her to find . . . again.

Remy crawled into the snug opening of the cave that served her well as home and haven. The fire she'd left untended still burned. She held a stub of candle to the flame. When it lit, she sat it on a small, table-shaped rock. She took the Bible Purty had given her when she was a girl from its hiding place under a ledge, then traced the shape of the book before she opened it. Sometimes her eyes crossed she strained so hard to decipher the words, but she could make out only one.

The pages were slick and fragile. Remy had about worn out the ones with His name, but she was drawn to them. Whenever she found that word, she said it aloud. . . . *Jesus . . . Jesus . . . Jesus.* He was her rock, Purty had said, her rock and her salvation. Remy was surrounded by rock in her homey cave. She stood on it and leaned on it and slept on it. The only place she liked better was Torrent Falls. When she was just a girl visiting the falls with her brother Riser, she'd seen angels in the sunlit spray from the tumbling water.

Laying her head on the Bible, she curled up next to the fire. Sleep came easy to Remy, for though her heart was as hard as a pine knot, it was pure in her mind. She never did anything without the very best of intentions.

CHAPTER 19

It was early Christmas morning, and Copper hurried to the spring-house with a fresh bucket of milk. She was afraid Lilly would wake before she finished the chore. Mazy had been out of sorts when Copper milked her an hour too early—whoever heard of milking before the rooster crowed?—but it couldn't be helped today. After pouring the milk in a crock, she scrubbed the bucket before hanging it on a peg to dry.

The weather had warmed during the night, and the yard was a mess of slushy snow and mud. Rushing around the corner of the cabin, she nearly collided with Dimm, who startled like a timid rabbit. "Merry Christmas," she said.

"Merry Christmas," Dimm replied.

Copper put her hand on his arm. "Will you stay and eat with us?"

He ducked his head. "Reckon."

Copper grinned. Generally, he'd only come in the house long enough to fill his plate. They were making progress. "Wonder if Santa has come," she said, pulling open the door.

Indeed he had. Darcy had lit the few candles Copper would allow on the tree, and it glowed with promise and filled the house with its scent. Darcy handed each of them a mug of fresh-brewed coffee. Dimm stood by the door with his, but Copper carried hers to the hearth, where she warmed herself. Lilly Gray still slept.

"Is Mr. John coming for breakfast?" Darcy asked.

Before Copper could answer, he was walking through the door. Her heart leaped at the sight of him—so tall, so handsome, so hers.

Darcy handed him his coffee.

"Why's everyone standing around?" John asked. "Don't you want to know what Santa had in that pack of his?"

"The baby's still sleeping," Darcy replied.

John strode to the open bedroom door. "Ho! Ho! Ho!"

They all gathered behind him, peeping around to watch Lilly.

First she popped her thumb from her mouth, then scrubbed her eyes with her fists. "Crip muss?"

Copper asked the others to wait while she dressed Lilly in the dearest little robe and slippers Alice had sent. "Santa came while you were sleeping," she said as she brushed her daughter's hair and tied it back with a green and red plaid ribbon.

Lilly squirmed out of her lap and ran through the door to the Christmas tree. "My dolly!" She was so excited she held the doll upside down, its tiny soft shoes under her chin, its long dark tresses sweeping the floor. "Santa bringed my dolly."

Everyone laughed.

Darcy pulled a pan of biscuits from the oven before cracking brown-shell eggs into the cast-iron skillet. "We should eat before everything gets cold."

Copper agreed. "We'll eat before we see what else Santa left under our tree. John, would you say grace?"

They held hands around the table: John, Copper, Lilly, Dimm, and Darcy, a perfect circle. "Heavenly Father," John began.

"Stop!" Lilly cried.

Copper looked up, one finger to her lips. "Lilly Gray," she chastised.

"Heavenly Father," John said.

"Dolly," Lilly said.

Copper sighed. She didn't want to remove her daughter from the table on Christmas morning, but Lilly knew better than to interrupt prayers. "What is it, Lilly? What do you want?"

Lilly held out her doll's arm. "Dimm?"

A new pattern of held hands formed. Copper glanced at John. She could see a smile play around his lips as Dimm took the doll's pale porcelain fingers in his work-roughened paw.

"Heavenly Father," John prayed, "we come with humble hearts to kindly thank You for sending Your Son, a newborn babe, to save us from our shortcomings. Bless this food and bless each one gathered here. Amen." Finished, he picked up his fork. "Darcy, pass the biscuits."

After breakfast, they settled around the tree. Copper sat on the floor with Lilly in her lap. "Seems like I saw something with your name on it, Darcy. Here it is." She handed her a small, gaily wrapped box.

Darcy gave the gift back to Copper. "This can't be mine, Miz Copper. There's been some mistake."

"Hmm," Copper said, eyeing the card strung through the gift's red ribbon. "It has your name on it. See?"

Darcy knelt beside her. "Show me."

"'To Darcy. From Santa,'" Copper read. "There's no mistake. Why don't you see what's inside?"

"Can I wait? I want to make this last."

"Me open," Lilly said, leaving Copper's lap to plop down in Darcy's.

Darcy helped Lilly untie the ribbon and peel off the paper to reveal a red velvet jewelry casket. Lilly clapped. "Oh, pretty."

Trembling, Darcy opened the small case and pulled out a heart-shaped locket on a fine gold chain. "This is the prettiest thing I ever saw."

"Let Dolly wear," Lilly said.

Copper reached around Darcy and took the chain. "No, Lilly, this is Darcy's." Unhooking the minute clasp, Copper fastened it around the girl's bent neck, then straightened the locket on its chain.

"Boo-tee-ful." Lilly clapped again. "Darcy's boo-tee-ful."

One by one the remaining gifts were opened. Darcy had knit a muffler for each person. Dimm had constructed a wee wooden bed for Lilly's doll and made a pair of chestnut wood candlesticks for Copper.

John made them all laugh when he put his gifts from Copper on: leather gloves and a leather cap with ear flaps. He anchored the cap in such a way that his ears stuck out like a mule's.

Copper stood and repositioned the hat, tucking his ears under the fur-lined flaps. "Now you won't get frostbite."

"Mistletoe!" Darcy exclaimed. "Mr. John, kiss her under the mistletoe!"

John maneuvered Copper until she was directly under the doorway where Darcy had hung the evergreen ball. Copper ducked and weaved, teasing, so he couldn't plant his lips until he caught her face in his gloved hands and kissed her lightly on the cheek. Tiptoeing, Copper returned the gesture, liking the feel of his warm cheek against her mouth. Nobody noticed that Dimm was making his way to the door until a blast of cold air sailed into the room.

"Wait," Copper said. "Where are you going?"

"Work. See to the animals."

"But you haven't seen what Santa left you," Copper said.

He stopped and stood in the doorway. "Me?"

"Yes, you. For pity's sake, close the door and come here a minute."

John wrestled the awkwardly wrapped present from behind the cedar tree. "Looks like this is for you, Dimm."

It was easy to make out what the wrapping hid. Folds of

bright paper did nothing to disguise the saddle, but Dimm unwrapped it tenderly. When he finished, he stroked the girthed and padded leather seat and unbuckled the saddlebag, then buckled it back. His face flushed as bright as firelight, and his Adam's apple bobbed in its familiar way. Sitting back on his haunches, he looked up at John. "I ain't sure."

"It can be tricky," John replied. "But you'll soon get the hang of it. We'll have to go slow breaking Star, since he's never been saddled."

Copper had to turn her face to hide her tears. Every work-packed minute leading up to Christmas was worth it for this moment alone. To see the young man looking to John for help made her heart sing, and John's response made her love him all the more. She was sure there wasn't a happier family anywhere on Troublesome.

Once the fellows lugged the saddle outside, she and Darcy set about putting the house in order. Copper heated the sadiron until it was just barely warm before she pressed the used sheets of wrapping paper and folded them for another time. The ribbon was ironed also and wound on a spool except for the piece Lilly insisted on tying in her dolly's hair. Copper was pleased to see how tender Lilly was with her baby.

"What's your baby's name?" Darcy asked as she wiped the kitchen table, letting the debris fall into a crumb catcher.

"Dolly," Lilly said. "Dolly Gray Corbett."

Copper managed to stifle a laugh, for Lilly was all business, rolling the buggy around the room while she hummed a lullaby. "Dolly's crying. Her wants a ba-ba."

"Ba-ba?" Copper asked, bending down to Lilly.

"Like baby Jay. Her hungry."

The last time they had visited with Fairy Mae, Jay was still there. Although Dance and Ace visited frequently, Dance was not up to caring for the baby alone. She was making progress though, Copper could tell, for she held Jay close to her and even smiled once in a while. Lilly had watched Dance feed her baby boy. He had taken to the bottle like a porker and was as fat as one too.

Taking a key from her doctor's kit, Copper unlocked the top section of the corner cupboard where she kept a limited apothecary. She found a clean brown bottle and fitted it with a medicine dropper. The rubber bulb would make a handy nipple for feeding Lilly's doll.

Lilly settled like a mother hen on the hearth, her baby in her lap. "Here you go, Dolly. Eat up."

The day sped by. Just past the winter solstice, it was dark before Copper finished with the milking. She had just pulled the T-shaped wooden stool from underneath her when Dimm approached. "Trouble," he said and pointed to the open barn door.

Cara Wilson stood there, her face drawn in worry. "Can you come, Miz Copper? It's Mama's time."

"Of course. I'll be ready in a minute." Copper turned to Dimm. "You stay here and watch out for the girls. I'll be fine with Cara."

Already dressed for the weather, all Copper had to do was grab her obstetric supplies and her medical kit from the house. Her heart beat fast. Next to being a mother, birthing babies was her favorite thing. And she was good at it. Simon had taught her well, and before she left Lexington, she'd delivered more than a dozen babies on her own. All of her babies were healthy, and she'd never lost a mother. Simon said she was a natural.

Climbing up on the horse behind Cara, she held on tight. Cara was a good horseman, and she egged the horse ever faster until it seemed as if they flew through the dark night. The trail was slick with snow and mud. Copper feared the horse would stumble and fling them over the side of the mountain, but Cara's mount was as sure as Cara herself.

"How is your mother?" Copper asked over the rushing wind.

"I thought I could do it without any help except Daddy's," Cara shouted, "but it's taking too long. Mama dropped the others easy as pie, but this'n seems hooked on something." She shuddered. "I'm right scared, Miz Copper."

A trill of fear snaked up Copper's backbone at Cara's words. What if this trip turned out as bad as the last time Cara came for her? "Let's pray. Pray that God will be with your mother and the baby." *And me*, Copper petitioned silently. *Please, Lord, help me know what to do for Mrs. Wilson.*

CHAPTER 20

Where were the children? Copper wondered when she entered the Wilsons' cabin. Sent to the neighbors perhaps or waiting outdoors in the cold barn. She stood by the bed for a moment, the same one that had once held Kenny.

Cara received her coat and her hat. Mr. Wilson thanked her for coming. Miranda Wilson lay on her back. Although she seemed calm, her face was moist and flushed from exertion. She raised herself a little ways and tried to smile, but her head fell back against the pillow. *Not good*, Copper thought. *She's exhausted already.*

A wash pot full of water boiled over the fire in the fireplace. Clean linen was stacked on a chair. A pair of scissors and two long strings of tying worsted lay on a cloth-lined tray by the bedside. Copper was glad to see Cara knew what she was doing. After rolling up her sleeves, Copper scrubbed past her forearms with lye soap. Mr. Wilson stepped outside, and Cara was busy filling another basin, but Copper felt as if she was being watched. Glancing up, she saw many eyes peering down from the loft.

Cara saw too. "Do you want me to get Daddy?" she said.

A scurry of feet told them the children returned to their beds.

Who can blame them for wanting to see what is going on, Copper thought. *They must be scared to death.* It made her think of the big homes in Lexington where she'd attended many of her patients—imposing homes where labor and delivery were confined to a separate part of the house, where everything was neat and tidy . . . and secret. She rinsed the lye soap and reached for a towel. *At least these children will know where babies come from, unlike myself when I got married, seventeen and still an ignorant girl.*

"Help me, Cara," Copper said. "Let's see what this baby is up to."

Her patient was dilated and fully effaced. This baby should have been delivered long ago. Was Miranda just too worn-out to make the effort?

As if in response to an unvoiced question, Miranda groaned and grabbed her knees, red in the face with the exertion of bearing down.

"Push!" Cara coached. "Push! Push! Push!"

"Mercy, that push should have delivered a watermelon." Then Copper's fingers found the problem. It was not the baby's bony skull plate she felt but soft flesh. The presenting part was wrong. Only once before had this happened. It was during her very first delivery, and the infant was a footling breech. She didn't feel a foot or buttocks, though, but more likely a side or even the back. Copper's mouth went dry. *Lord,* she prayed, *I don't know what to do.*

Mrs. Wilson struggled to push again as Cara helped her assume the delivery position.

"Don't push!" Copper exclaimed. "Whatever you do, Miranda, don't push!"

"Help me," Miranda gasped between moans. Reaching out, she clutched Copper's shoulder with the last of her strength. "Please do whatever you got to. I can't leave the young'uns God's already give me."

The room spun. Copper closed her eyes. Horrible pictures from Simon's medical texts—of death and destruction, of tiny disjointed limbs and decapitated heads—played like a slide show behind her lids. It was the other side of childbirth, the side gone terribly awry. Could she take a baby's life to save the mother's?

Copper stepped back from the bed. She heard every sound with sharp clarity: the children's soft breathing, the pop of the fire, Cara's pleading prayer, snowmelt dripping from the eaves outside. She strode purposefully across the room and jerked open the door. Mr. Wilson stood hunched against the cold. "Come in," Copper said. "We need you."

Stumbling, he followed her. Copper knew he expected the worst.

"Pray, Mr. Wilson," Copper said. "Pray out loud. Pray hard." She called up to the loft, "Children, get on your knees and pray."

Bending over Miranda's swollen belly, she traced the

mound of the confined infant. Then she traced another. Twins! Forevermore. She showed Cara what she felt and told her what to do. Prayer covered them from above and every side as Mr. Wilson paced a circle around the bed, beseeching God with every step.

Copper worked and prayed over Miranda's swollen belly. She'd watched Simon successfully turn a breech baby once, and she attempted the same with one of the twins. After minutes that seemed like hours, one infant turned, and baby boy Wilson made his way down the birth canal. With strength only God could give, Miranda labored and pushed again and again until baby girl Wilson followed her brother into the light.

Copper and Cara each took a baby, tied and cut their navel cords, and dried them with warmed flannel receivers. Copper's baby cried immediately, but Cara's only gasped, her face a sickly gray. "Rub hard, Cara."

But Cara handled the puny baby as if she were a china doll and easily broken.

"Here–" Copper held forth the boy–"trade me." Kneeling at the foot of the bed, she grabbed another receiver and scrubbed the floppy body and wiped gunk from the tiny mouth until the infant took her first life-giving breath and mewled with protest.

"Praise the Lord," Mr. Wilson said.

"Praise the Lord," the children echoed from the loft.

Copper wanted to lie right down on the floor and cry too; she was so relieved to see color flooding the baby's face. Instead, she handed baby number two to Mr. Wilson and set about attending to Miranda.

Later, after the babies were cleaned with warmed olive oil, after the belly binders were applied, after Miranda was bathed and comfortable, after the soiled sheets from the lying-in bed were put to soak in a tub of cold water, Copper took a minute for herself. She stepped out the door, tightening the shawl around her shoulders. The night air was much warmer than it had been over the past weeks. She filled her lungs with the crisp, clean air.

It was very late. She had successfully delivered her first set of twins. More than likely both would have died along with Mrs. Wilson if she had not been here. The weight of her talent settled heavily on her shoulders as tears streamed down her cheeks. Falling to her knees, she held her hands out to God. *What a gift You have given me, Father. Help me to be worthy. Thank You for Your intervention tonight. Bless these babies and their mother. Bless this family.*

She sat back on her heels. Truthfully, she was too exhausted to rise. Maybe she'd just crawl to the door. Her mind cast a picture of crawling across the porch, and she laughed at herself—at her frailty. "'The Lord is my strength,'" she quoted and was not surprised when strong arms helped her to her feet.

"Are you all right?" John asked. "How is Mrs. Wilson?"

"Just let me stand here for a second," she replied, soaking up his warmth. Quietly, while resting in the circle of his arms, she told him what had just transpired and how the Lord had saved Miranda and the babies. She could feel the scrape of his chin against the top of her head.

"It scares me for you, Copper."

She leaned back so she could see his shadowy face. "What do you mean?"

"You know that Scripture your mam used to say? Went something like when God gives a lot He expects a lot? I was never quite sure what that meant, but I was always afraid He would ask more than I could do. But you? Now that's a different story."

"How so?"

"You give your all. You never jump back from a challenge."

"I almost did tonight. I asked myself a very hard question, and I didn't rightly know the answer. I wanted to throw up my hands."

"But, see, that's how you're different from most folks. You didn't throw up your hands."

"Know what I did instead?" she whispered against his chest.

His arms tightened their hold. "What?"

"I had a prayer service. Praise His name, God heard our petitions."

"He surely did," John replied. "Are you ready to go home now?"

"No. Not for a while." She stepped out of the comfort of his arms, gazing out into the dark yard. "I'll have to stay until I know the babies will eat and until Miranda is past any danger of hemorrhage."

"How long might that be?"

"Just a couple of days. Cara is quite capable of tending to her mother and the twins. I'm really impressed by her."

"I'd say you're not the only one. Dimmert nearly swallowed his Adam's apple when he told me Cara came by for you."

"Oh, John, they hardly know each other," Copper said.

"Dimm goes out wandering a lot; wouldn't surprise me if this is where he disappears to."

"Cara never said a word." Copper touched John's arm. "What if he likes her, but she doesn't have the same feelings for him? I wouldn't like to see Dimm hurt."

"Love will find a way," John said. "All it takes is one little spark to set the whole barn afire."

With a smile Copper agreed. "I'd better get inside, and you need to go home and get some sleep."

John scrubbed his face with his palms. "You've got that right. I'll be back later to check on you."

Hand on the doorknob, Copper looked over her shoulder. "Better yet, send Dimmert with a ham from the smokehouse and some canned goods from the cellar."

"You aren't fixing to meddle, are you?"

"Of course not. I just want to see if there's any danger of the barn burning down."

John came for Copper bright and early Wednesday morning, and he brought a small surprise. Lilly Gray ran straight into her mother's arms when Cara answered John's knock at the door. "Mama!" she exclaimed. "Where you go to?"

"Lilly Gray—" Copper squeezed her tightly—"Mama's missed you so much."

Lilly snuggled against Copper's shoulder. "You been helping babies?"

"Two babies, a boy and a girl."

Lilly kept her head tucked close to her mother. Copper realized Lilly had met none of the Wilsons, and there were many to meet. The room was full of stair-step children.

"Want to see my twirling top?" one of the boys asked Lilly.

"No, come and draw a picture with me," one of the girls pleaded as she tugged at Lilly's shoe. "You can have a piece of paper from my tablet and use my fat pencil."

Their Santa gifts were greatly prized, and it touched Copper to see how they wanted to share.

When it was time for Copper to leave, John brought the two horses up to the cabin. Copper settled on one with Lilly in her lap. The cold winter air was welcome to her. It was so good to be outside after two days of confinement in the Wilsons' stuffy cabin. She was so tired that her bones ached and her mind was frazzled. Most of the snow was gone, but skims of ice on puddles shattered under the horses' hooves. Up and down the mountain, trees glimmered with feathery white spicules of hoarfrost. It was a beautiful picture.

"I wish I were an artist," she said. "I'd put this scene on canvas."

John stopped his mount beside hers. "I hear tell they'll make a small camera that anybody can carry around to capture pictures with."

"I wouldn't get a lick of work done if I had a contraption like that. I'd be outdoors every minute."

John laughed and guided his horse ahead of hers on the narrow, twisting lane. "Follow me. I've got something to show you."

After a few miles, he crossed Troublesome Creek onto his own property. The creek angled away as they continued up a wooded cliff. Copper recognized bare-limbed pawpaws, tulip poplars, and rhododendron before a valley of several acres spread out before them. A tumble of creek rock was piled near the center of the plot. John stopped there. "Want to stretch your legs a minute?" he asked.

When Copper dismounted, she could see the foundation of a house parceled out in stacking rock on the brown winter grass. "Did someone once live here?"

"Hopefully someone will," he replied.

"Well," she said, shifting Lilly on her hip, "it's sure a pretty place, but they won't be able to see the creek."

"I reckon I'll have to reroute the creek, bring it right on up the cliff, and run it past the kitchen window."

Copper set Lilly down and turned to John. "You can't mean . . ."

"Honey girl, it's yours if you want it."

Her hands flew to her cheeks. "Show me," she said, dancing away from him.

Carrying Lilly, he caught up and took Copper's hand. "I figured we'd have a porch around all sides so you can watch the seasons change from every angle. This here's the kitchen. I'll put one of those fancy cookstoves in this corner, and the pantry will be close by." He dropped her hand, then mimed opening and closing a door. "The parlor sits through here. It will have a wall of windows so you'll never feel closed in."

She stood in the spot he showed her and gazed out across

the valley, already imagining what it would look like through window glass. "I'm not hanging curtains. They'd only spoil this view."

"We'll have a Warm Morning stove for heat and a fireplace for enjoying," John continued, painting another sort of picture.

Copper couldn't resist. With a twist of her wrist, she turned an imaginary knob and stepped across a marked threshold. "What might this room be?"

John was not easily discomfited, but his face reddened. He cleared his throat. "I thought this could be our room. There will be windows here, but I reckon you'll want curtains."

Lilly ended her mother's teasing. "Where Lilly sleeping?" she asked. "Where Darcy?"

John swung Lilly up in the air. She shrieked with laughter. "Miss Lilly can sleep anywhere she wants. You can have your own room."

"No. Lilly sleeps with Mama."

Copper hid a smile behind her gloved hand. There could be trouble brewing. "Why didn't you show me this place before?"

"I was saving it for Christmas," he said.

"Well, it's the best gift ever." Copper cocked her head. "Listen. You can still hear the creek. We're going to be very happy here."

CHAPTER 21

Remy watched from the ridge high above Copper and John and looked on with satisfaction. She'd prowled all over this area once she saw John hauling sleds full of rock this way. She knew where the spring was and could see in her mind's eye Copper coming there to a springhouse with a bucket of milk. Using a divining rod, she'd found the best spot for a well and paced the number of steps it took to get to the front porch. It'd be easy enough for Copper to keep a water bucket filled.

Beside her a red fox sat quietly, its white-tipped tail tucked neatly around its body, keeping Remy company. It was the best sort of companion, she figured. It didn't ask anything from her but spent its time hunting for each day's measure. Like Remy, the fox took only what it needed to keep a body going, never laying up stores for the morrow. Remy had known this fox's ma.

Rarely did Remy let her mind wander, for a wandering mind was not alert to danger, but now she thought back to the time when she was a girl of twelve, back to the time when she had come upon the body of a trapped fox. Poor thing had dragged the heavy steel trap halfway up a hill before it came to the end of its tether; then it gnawed its foot to the bone in a desperate bid to escape. Remy understood hunters; she was one herself. But the cruelty of traps was beyond her ken. Squatting, she'd sprung the trap and lifted the still-warm body to her chest. She'd find a loamy area and give the animal a decent burial—seemed the least she could do.

It was obvious the fox had given birth recently. Something must have happened to her mate. Usually the vixen stayed with her little ones while her partner scouted for food. It saddened Remy to think the babies waited to be fed. Maybe she could find them. It was worth a try. Before she buried the fox, she freed the bushy tail and fastened it to the back of her skirt. By scent and look, she'd fool the kits.

With a hunter's patience she waited. It was a fine spring evening, not yet dark, and the forest was alive with the thrumming sound of insects ushering the rise of the moon. Bloodthirsty mosquitoes buzzed in her ears and bumped her nose until she hunkered down with her face in her lap.

Finally she heard the high-pitched yelps of hungry pups. It was easy to follow the cries to a cliff overhanging the creek. A den was dug in the bank, and she knew she'd find the babies there. She crawled under the cliff and into the hollowed dirt cave. The four round-bellied kits tumbled over each other to get to her. When she held out her hands, fragrant with the smell of their mother, they suckled her fingers.

Remy laughed, a slow, thick trickle of sound, and nuzzled a kit against her cheek. "Getting used to me already, ain't ye?" The little foxes put her in mind of her brothers and sisters, everybody grabbing at the stewpot at the same time, one shoving another away in order to get more for hisself. She wondered if they missed her.

"I'll go back," she told the kits, "as soon as Pap forgets what he's hepped up over." The kit lapped at her face. "I ain't standing still for no man to slap me around. I can take care of my own self."

Remy needed to move the babies for their safety, but they had to be fed first. She'd scouted the farms up and down this valley when first she'd come down the mountain. There were chicken coops and smokehouses galore.

Two places were easy pickings for a hunter such as Remy in those days. Number one was the Browns' springhouse—it always had so much milk and cheese that nobody'd miss what little she took. Second was Hezzy Krill's chicken coop. Remy didn't know what Hezzy fed those hens, but they laid the biggest brown eggs she'd ever found. At first when she visited, Remy had to be extra careful, for both cabins had dogs. But the Browns' old hound was so friendly he greeted Remy, and Hezzy's dog was so lazy he wouldn't rouse himself to bark.

The night Remy found the kits she made herself at home in both places. She carried a Mason jar full of blue-John from the springhouse. She'd pondered on whether to snatch full milk instead, but she figured the thin watery milk leftover from the cream separator might set better on the babies' stomachs.

At Hezzy's she took a minute just inside the chicken coop to let her eyes adjust to the dark, thankful for the moonlight that spilled in through the open door. The hens were so used to her they slept on. She'd pocketed half a dozen brown shells when the hens spooked and set up a squawking ruckus. Suddenly the air was alive with flapping wings.

Remy inhaled dust and pin feathers. Her sneeze was so hard, so unexpected that she bit her tongue and tasted blood. But that was not the worst of it. The lantern light she could see through the henhouse window bobbed across Hezzy's yard. The only door and the window led that way. The fat was in the fire.

Remy scrambled under the wide wooden shelf that held the chickens' nest boxes. Something else had beat her there, however. A fat possum grinned at her, his teeth flashing white in the moonlight.

That's why the chickens got all feisty! Well, I ain't afraid of no possum. No, siree. I might be scared of that shotgun Hezzy's surely packing, but I ain't feared of no possum.

Before Remy could make her move, Mr. Possum rolled over, dead as a doorknob.

"Surely ye don't think I'm falling for that old trick," Remy whispered. Grabbing the possum's long, hairless tail, she jerked him up and flung him out the open door.

A gun exploded into the night. Ears ringing, the smell of gunpowder tickling her nose, Remy clambered back under the shelf, playing possum herself.

Hezzy hop-stepped into the little house. Her stiff leg

impeded her progress, but she was taking her time. "Thieving varmints," Remy heard her say. The lantern swung in front of Remy's eyes, and Hezzy swept the barrel of the shotgun under the nests. "Are you girls all right?" she asked the chickens that scratched around her feet. "I shouldn't have left the eggs go all day, but my leg was aching something fierce."

Stupid birds, Remy thought. *They've forgot all about the possum. They're looking for corn.*

Hezzy complied and broadcast kernels. Some bounced off the dirt floor and pinged Remy's way. One hen pecked corn from Remy's lap, then stretched and pecked her nose. *Fair enough*, Remy reckoned, holding her breath.

Seemingly satisfied, Hezzy went back outside. Remy could hear the click of the latch sliding into place. "Must be sprung, else it wouldn't have popped open," Hezzy said. "I'll send for that Pelfrey boy. He'll mend it for me." She kept talking as she walked off, her words fading away.

Must be hard getting old, Remy thought, *legs rusting and all.* Maybe she should leave Hezzy's chickens alone. But it was obvious she had plenty—enough to let them go ungathered— easy pickings for Remy and the possums.

Remy found a small stick and slid it between the door and the frame. After popping the latch, she eased her way out, half a dozen brown shells nestled in her pocket. Her found babies would eat well tonight.

The kits had flourished under Remy's care that time five years ago, lapping up the blue-John mixed with egg yolks. She'd moved them to her temporary home, a clean, dry cave, and stayed with them all summer. It was that fall when she'd first met Purty. Her one true friend.

Now Remy sat with the fox and watched her friend's dreams coming true. Purty would soon have her very own place on Troublesome Creek, just like she'd always wanted. And it was meant to be that she would marry John. He was a good feller. Remy could trust her friend to him. A little fissure of guilt cracked the merest corner of Remy's heart as she looked at John Pelfrey far below. She couldn't remember ever apologizing to a single soul for nary a thing she'd ever done—not thieving, not twisting the truth, not nothing. But if she wasn't playing dead as a puff adder, she might just say a few *I'm sorry*s to John.

"I should go across the mountains and never come back," she said to the fox. "It wouldn't do for me to get caught. It would be the ruination of Purty's plans."

She watched as Purty mounted the horse and then saw John swing Purty's little girl up to her. Lucky she'd come across Lilly that day in the creek.

Remy fingered the tiny walnut basket that hung around her neck on a leather thong. Once before when they were girls, Remy had borrowed this selfsame trinket from Copper's bedside table. That time she'd gifted the necklace back to Copper. Now she'd found it again plus a fine gold ring in the blanket chest that set under an open window in Purty's house. All she'd had to do was reach in and help herself. She'd threaded the ring and the one John Pelfrey had given her on the leather thong with the little basket. (She'd watched John and the preacher bury his ring at Torrent Falls, still knotted on the lace of her old boot.)

Since then she wore both of them all the time. Just a touch of her fingers on the necklace or the rings comforted her. John Pelfrey had given her the one ring, and as far as the other ring and the necklace, Copper would want her to have them. She used to leave things for Remy to find all the time. Just like the fine blue mantle with the little stars knit into its border. She'd found it with her boot and ring, but it was ruined, so she'd buried it again and shed a few tears in the process.

It wasn't bad being dead, especially since it got her pap off her trail and released John from his promise. She'd never meant to harm herself in the first place, but John took her ramblings to heart and offered an answer to her dilemma. Looked like things had worked out all right in the long run though. John and Purty were happy, and she owed nobody nothing. She was a free woman.

Remy scanned the valley below. She liked John's plan for the house. It would be as purty as Purty herself. She rested her head on her knees and looked sideways at the fox. It was preening, wiping its whiskers with its paw, enjoying the visit. "I'll stay just a little longer. I'd like to see Purty wed before I go." The fox turned its catlike amber eyes her way. She knew it understood.

After all, if everyone thought Remy Riddle was dead, it wouldn't hurt to linger as long as she was careful. To Remy these mountains were like that place Purty told her about. That place called heaven, where the lion would lie down with the calf. Thinking about heaven put her in mind of milk and honey, and she wondered if Purty had any of the long sweetening left in their cellar.

CHAPTER 22

January passed slowly, each day as dull as dishwater. Just-laundered clothes froze on the line as soon as Copper hung them there, and every Monday evening she hauled shirts and overalls, skirts and shirtwaists, linens and long drawers into the house and stacked them like kindling beside the cookstove to thaw.

Darcy fetched jar after jar of green beans, corn, and tomatoes from the cellar. She kept blackberry jam or apple butter on the table at all times. One morning she brought up pear butter, and Copper recounted the day she'd found the ripe pears and how John had saved her from the feral hog. Darcy never tired of the story. Sitting at the kitchen table, spreading pear butter on her biscuit, Copper ate that summer day and licked her lips.

When they tired of cured pork, Dimmert and John went hunting. Fried squirrel in gravy and crispy brown rabbit tasted extra good on cold days. On special occasions, Copper made chicken and dumplings; it was Lilly's favorite. Copper's also, but she daren't take many hens for the stewpot. Eggs were too valuable. And then there was Mazy's creamy milk to round out their menu.

One memorable morning, Darcy brought in a whole hog's head and some sausage that Dimmert had traded a basket of potatoes for. It was late for killing hogs, but the neighbor who traded for the potatoes didn't have a choice. The hog had managed to strangle itself trying to reach an ear of corn dropped outside its pen. Copper doubted he'd get the hams and shoulders to cure, but Darcy was pleased to get the head. She was determined to pickle the ears and turn the rest into mincemeat. Copper was not fond of either, but if Darcy hankered for pickled pig's ears and mincemeat pie, she was game.

Lilly Gray stood on a chair at the kitchen table watching as Darcy lifted the lid from a large blue-speckled pan. The hog grinned hazily from under a length of cheesecloth. Lilly stared, then screamed. Copper barely caught the chair as it fell backward. Lilly screamed again, jumped to the floor, and ran from the room, shutting the bedroom door behind her.

Looking stunned, Darcy covered up the lolling head. With a flick of her wrist, Copper indicated for Darcy to remove it. Following Lilly, she knelt on the floor and peered under the bed. She was under there along with her dolly. "Lilly, come on out."

"No! Piggy eat Dolly!"

"Piggy's gone, baby. He can't hurt you." Copper stretched out to grab Lilly's arm.

Lilly was faster and scooted to the far corner. Her little chin trembled as she clutched her doll tight. "Bad, bad piggy."

Copper slid under the bed to comfort her. "Honey, don't you know Mama would never let anything hurt you or Dolly?"

Lilly was not mollified. "Dolly wants Dimm."

"But he's working."

If there had been more room under the bed, Lilly would have let go in a full-blown tantrum. Her face threatened like a quickly brewing summer storm, and she opened her mouth to scream.

Copper covered Lilly's mouth. "Don't," she said.

Then she wished she hadn't, for instead of screaming, Lilly sobbed, big sobs that turned to hiccups. "Dimm," she said when she could catch her breath. "Dimm make bad piggy go away."

"Want me to get him, Miz Copper?" Darcy asked.

Now there were three of them under the bed. Copper would have laughed if she hadn't been so aggravated and jealous. She wanted to be the one to comfort her daughter. "Please. I think he was clearing brush behind the barn."

When Darcy left, Copper cuddled Lilly as best she could in the tight space. "Mama's sorry. I'm so sorry you got scared."

"Bad piggy," Lilly said again.

"Yes, he is a very bad piggy for scaring you that way. Want to hear a story?"

"No piggies."

"Oh, but this is about three good little pigs. Once upon a time there were three little pigs. . . ."

Lilly quieted and curled against her mother. Copper soothed her with the story, and Lilly laughed when Copper huffed and puffed to blow a house down. By the time they could see Dimm's knees bent on the floor, Lilly was nearly asleep. But she scrambled over Copper and into Dimm's arms when he said her name.

"Dimm!" she said as if surprised by an unexpected visit. "Wanna story? Once a day free piggies . . ."

Inching out from under the bed, Copper sat cross-legged on the floor beside Dimmert and Darcy as Lilly, snuggled in Dimm's lap, huffed and puffed and laughed again. Ashamed, Copper prayed for forgiveness for her selfishness. Using her fingers as a comb, she pulled dust balls from Lilly's hair and thanked the Lord for all the people who loved her daughter.

It was late that night before Darcy brought the covered pan in again. And the banty rooster crowed his salute to the sun before the hog's head was nothing but jars of pulled meat for mince-meat pie.

Darcy didn't save the ears. She told Copper she was afraid of what Lilly would think if she caught her eating them. Besides, she could always sneak off to the cellar and help herself to last fall's pickled pig's feet.

⚜

It was a great relief the following morning when Copper carried the milk bucket to the barn. She'd rested some during the night with her head on crossed arms at the kitchen table, while waiting for the hog to cook or the jars to boil, and now fresh cold air revived her. It was good to be out of the house. The dried cornstalks that Dimmert had scattered over the muddy barn lot were frozen, and they crunched under her boots. The door was unlatched, so she elbowed it open.

Mazy was not in her stall but stood in the open barn looking miserable.

Dimmert pitched forkfuls of bedding into a wheelbarrow. "Scours," he said when he saw Copper.

Copper held her nose as the mess of diarrhea-soaked straw piled up. "This is not good."

"Reckon," the man of few words replied.

Copper found a burlap bag and used it to wipe Mazy as clean as a cow with the scours could be; at least she was dry. She fetched a couple more bags and covered Mazy's bony back. Usually skittish and prone to kick, Mazy stood quietly, her big square head hanging to her knees as Copper drew the milk stool up to her side.

While she milked, she sorted through all the remedies she'd ever heard for scours. Daddy always said it was a sign of too little salt in the diet, and she remembered John's father dosed his cattle with watery wheat paste at the first sign of the runs. What was it Reuben did in Lexington? It was just at the edge of her consciousness. Reuben was the best with any animal. Sometimes she missed him and Searcy so bad it brought tears to her eyes.

Let's see. Surely I can remember, though it happened only one time. Searcy was cooking up a mess of something for Reuben to use. Potatoes!

That's it. Three pecks of boiled potatoes chased with flaxseed tea divided in doses.

Glad to have a plan, Copper led Mazy to the clean stall Dimmert had prepared for her. Mazy balked at the door; it was not her usual stall. Dimm came up behind her and pushed on her rump as Copper pulled on her lead. "Mazy," she said, "you're the most exasperating animal I ever saw!" She stepped out and fastened the door. "Don't feed her, Dimm. I'm going to cook something special."

On the other side of the barn, Star stuck his head out over his stall door and nickered. They used to keep a pair of work horses on the farm, but now Copper borrowed John's mule whenever she needed to plow or haul something. So far, Star was mainly just for show.

"That's all right, Star," Copper said as she rubbed his long nose, then fed him the piece of apple she'd brought. "You earn your keep by being pleasing to the eye."

Beside the stable at the pigpen, Copper poured the warm milk into a long wooden trough. Two porkers came running and squealing like they'd won a prize. She hated to lose the milk, but she was afraid to serve it to her family with Mazy being sick and all. They'd have no more fresh milk for a couple of days, and that was if potatoes cured the runs.

Another night in a straight-backed chair, but it couldn't be helped. Every couple of hours Copper roused herself from fitful slumber and trudged across the barnyard to check on Mazy. It wasn't so bad being the only one awake—such a peaceful time.

At the barn, she reached around the door and lifted the lantern off the hook. Stepping back outside, she sheltered the flame of a match and lit the wick. She'd learned from her father to never strike a match in the barn. She'd made an exception for the small stove in the room where Dimm lived.

Dimmert met her before she had a chance to knock at the tack room door. Copper bet he hadn't slept at all. "Time for more warm potato soup and tea," she said.

It was a two-man chore. Dimm held Mazy in position, her head back and jaw open, while Copper poured the curative down the cow's throat, stroking her neck to get her to swallow.

"What do you think?" she asked.

Not trusting what the eye could see in the glow from the lantern, Dimmert grabbed the pitchfork and turned some bedding over. "Better."

A bit of soup sloshed in the bottom of the bucket. "There's some left. You want it?"

When Dimm took a step backward, she was sorry for her teasing. "I was just funning you," she said. He let his shoulders drop and smiled. Why hadn't she noticed the change in him? At what point had he trusted her enough to smile? He was still bony—she supposed he would always be thin—but he ate well at her table. His shoulders had broadened, and his face had filled out. Why, he was handsome in the light from the coal-oil lamp.

"All right then," she said. "Good work."

Back in her chair in the kitchen, Copper nursed a cup of tea and thought of Dimmert. Was John right about him and Cara Wilson? And if so, would Cara break Dimm's heart? She shook her head. They were both so young—seventeen, the same age as when she left the mountains as a newlywed. How would two young people without a pot or a pan to call their own possibly make a life together? *Ah, well,* she figured, *love would find a way.*

CHAPTER 23

Late in March, after several days of springlike weather, Copper heard the first serenade from the tiny knee-deeps. One evening she led Lilly Gray through a wooded area and down to the creek, where she bade her listen. Not an easy task, for Lilly was rarely quiet. It was cold there by the water; Copper wrapped her shawl around Lilly and drew her close.

Yeep, they heard as the lavender twilight turned just this side of purple, then *yeep, yeep, yeep*.

Lilly's mouth made a perfect circle. "Doodles."

"You're so smart," Copper said. "They do sound like the baby chicks in the brooder house." The postman had delivered four cartons of the bits of fluff last week, and Lilly was enthralled with them. "But these aren't chickens. Just listen."

It seemed the woodland around them exploded in sound.

Lilly smiled and covered her ears. "What's that?"

"They're tiny frogs singing to each other. They're called peepers."

"What they doing here, Mama?"

Copper knew they were coming in from the woods to find a mate. The males, who made all the bragging noise, of course, would congregate in a boggy place and wait for the egg-laying females. They would sing their happy song, and soon there would be tadpoles in abundance. "They want to make friends," she told Lilly.

Lilly shivered. "Peepers get cold."

"If it gets too cold, they snuggle down in the mud by the creek. The mud is just like a warm blanket."

"Get one peeper."

"It's too dark to see them, but we'll come back another night with a lantern." She held Lilly's hand as they walked back to the house. "Your papaw says when he was a boy the peepers were knee-deep in the springtime."

"When's Papaw coming?" Lilly asked the same question a dozen times a day.

Copper gave the same answer each time. "In May, remember? When John and I get married."

"Yup," Lilly said, "John will be Lilly's daddy. . . . Darcy's daddy too?"

"No, just yours. Darcy already has a daddy."

"Okay." Lilly stopped on the porch steps. They could still hear the tree frogs yeeping. "Get the lantern, Mama."

"Another time, my little peeper." Copper gathered her daughter up and carried her into the warmth of the house. "You have to go to bed now. Tomorrow we're going quilting at Mrs. Foster's."

The trip to Jean Foster's was a delight to the eye and a balm to Copper's winter-weary soul. There had been no quilting circles and few church services in cold, snowy January or in muddy, dismal February. Copper was hungry to see Jean and the other ladies. They had each been working on squares to combine into a friendship quilt. Copper embroidered a bluebird of happiness on hers, and now she spied that very bird clinging upside down from the branches of a serviceberry. While other trees stood wintry bare, the flowers of the serviceberry warmed the forest with spring charm, shouting, "Winter is over!"

Copper plucked a cluster of white blossoms with reddish bracts. From a distance the flowering trees looked like peaked meringue scattered up and down the mountains. In early summer the trees' purple berries would provide a feast for blue jays, catbirds, and the like.

Lilly reached for the flower. Copper lifted her instead and let her pluck her own blossom, then helped her fasten the pretty flower into Dolly's hair. Back on the ground, Lilly ran ahead on the familiar path.

"Don't run out of my sight," Copper called.

But she did and soon Copper was hurrying to catch up. She was just around the bend in the lane, Copper was sure, but when she turned the corner, there was no Lilly to be seen. Except for the tiny pair of black high-tops peeking out from under a bushy cedar. Copper took note but kept walking. Out of sight she stopped and waited.

"Mama!" Lilly shrieked, pounding up the lane until she found Copper. "You lost me." Her dark gray eyes welled up, and her chin trembled.

Copper hugged herself to keep from hugging Lilly. "Hiding from your mama is not a good game."

Lilly ducked her head. "Sorry, Mama."

"All right then, shall we go to Mrs. Foster's or should we go home?"

"No home," Lilly replied. "Carry Dolly."

"No, Lilly, remember when Mama said to leave Dolly behind? You said you'd carry her if she came."

Lilly slumped her shoulders, and tiny sparkly tears appeared again. "I tired."

Copper lifted Lilly and sat her astride one hip. "What if Mama carries her baby and you carry yours?"

"Okay," Lilly said.

Copper used every opportunity for teaching Lilly, so she had tarried on the trail, pointing out various birds and trees. She was late. The other ladies were already seated, needles flying. She was glad Darcy had come earlier to help Jean set up the bulky quilting frame. Lilly found Bubby Foster in his usual place under the frame, and Copper could hear her showing off her doll to her playmate.

She stopped to admire little Jay Shelton, nestled in a basket beside Fairy Mae. "He soon won't fit in there," Copper said.

The only empty space on the benches was on the far end next to Hezzy Krill. *That's what I deserve for being late*, Copper chided herself. As she took a needle and a length of thread from her sewing box, a newcomer caught her eye. A young woman, her bibbed feed-sack apron starched and ironed to a fare-thee-well, sat across from Hezzy, head bent to her task. Why hadn't anyone introduced her to Copper? Beautiful stitches flowed as she worked. She looked up and smiled.

"Why, good morning, Cara." Copper almost hadn't recognized the young woman what with her hair pulled into a bun and a dress on under her apron instead of overalls. "How good to see you here."

Jean rested her hands on Cara's shoulders. "I thought it was time Cara joined our circle."

"I wanted to help with your quilt, Miz Copper." Cara pointed to one of her squares: dark blue with a spray of serviceberries and her initials, C. W.

"It's beautiful." Copper looked about the frame. All the ladies were busy with the task of making a quilt for Copper's wedding gift. Each woman's personal selection was pieced into a background of blue and brown print and had her name or initials embroidered in a corner. It would cover her with their love every time she used it. Tears came to her eyes. "I don't know how to thank you. It means so much. . . ."

The ladies tsk-tsked, as if their work was of no import.

Copper laughed, lightening the moment. "Why, this makes getting married worth it."

That set the ladies loose. Each had a story to tell of her

own wedding and married life. Hezzy told of getting married at fourteen to a man whose wife had died leaving him with four children. She still lived in the house she'd set up housekeeping in with all five of them. She'd been a widow nigh on twenty years now.

"Do you still miss him?" Jean asked.

"Not so much," Hezzy replied. "The first ten years was the hardest. Now I miss him when I got to chop wood or some such manly thing."

"You shouldn't be chopping wood at your age. You'll hurt yourself," Jean responded, her face stern.

Hezzy spit tobacco juice in the jar she carried and wiped her chin. "I don't do much with this bad leg, just whack a little kindling now and then. John Pelfrey comes by pert near weekly to see if I got any needs. He's been doing for me since he was a just a sprite. Them Pelfreys is good folks."

A bevy of bobbing heads agreed with Hezzy. Copper loved hearing stories about John.

Hezzy paused in her stitching and turned to face Copper. "Reminds me. Tell John the rope on my well bucket is near wore out. That is, if you see him before I do." She cackled and winked.

Copper was embarrassed but not much. These were her friends after all. She joined in their laughter. "How is your mother, Cara? And the twins?"

"You wouldn't believe how fat the babies are. Baby Kenny never cries, and Kenneta never stops. And now Mama smiles again."

The ladies had heard the story of the night the twins were

born, and they bested each other with tales of their own pro-
longed labors and pain so bad it would tear you in two.

Jean interrupted the chatter with a chocolate cake topped
with whipped cream. "Let's end this tattle before we scare Darcy
and Cara to death."

As Copper left Jean's with Darcy and Lilly, Cara approached her.
"Mind if I walk your way?" she asked.

"Goodness, no. I always love your company."

"Is Dimmert at home today?"

"I believe he was thinking of plowing the garden, although I
told him it is a little early." Copper stopped in her tracks. "Cara
Wilson, do you have something to tell me?"

Cara's face turned as red as a cardinal's feathers. "We've been
sparking. Dimmert Whitt and me."

Darcy whirled around on the path ahead. "You and Dimm?
Sparking? How'd he sneak that by me?"

Cara's face fell. "You're not mad, are you?"

"'Course not." Darcy grabbed Cara's hands. "Are you getting
hitched?"

"Darcy," Copper chided, "for goodness sake. They're just
courting."

"Well, actually, Miz Copper," Cara said. "We've wanted to
talk to you and Mr. John."

CHAPTER 24

Dimmert had the mule at the end of a row when they got back to the house. Several furrows made a pretty sight in the garden plot. Copper stooped to grab a handful of the rich, dark loam. When she squeezed, it packed but not too much. Last fall Dimm had hitched up the mule and hauled a load of sand to amend the clay soil. It looked as if he knew what he was doing.

Cara stepped across the rows as daintily as a girl not given to dainty steps could. When Dimm saw her coming, he took a red bandanna from his overalls pocket and mopped his brow. Leaning on the plow, he gave her a crooked smile. Cara touched his arm, and he took her hand.

Copper was enthralled. *They make the perfect couple. To think these two young people found each other against many odds. God surely works wonders.*

Dimmert unhitched the mule and turned him loose to nibble at the grass and weeds in the unplowed portion of the garden. Star was doing the same, never straying from Dimm's sight.

Star is better behaved than my daughter, Copper couldn't help but think as Lilly tugged on her skirt demanding a can for the earthworms that wriggled out of the broken ground. Lilly already had a fistful of the long brown worms.

"Lilly Gray, whatever will you do with those?" Copper asked.

"Feed the doodles."

Indeed, the hens that had been let out of their fenced yard to forage zeroed in on the hapless worms, pecking with their sharp yellow beaks and tugging them out of the ground.

"I think the baby chicks are too little to eat worms. They have to eat their oats just like you do."

Lilly's face tightened in concentration. Copper could almost see the little wheels turning. "Feed the peepers!" Lilly said.

Copper couldn't hold back her laughter. Neither could Darcy. The poor worms in Lilly's hand squeezed through her fingers like bread dough. Copper loosened Lilly's grip.

"Let me take her fishing," Darcy said.

"Yup," Lilly said as if that is what she had planned all along. "Feed the fishes."

"Let me get a coffee can and a pole," Copper replied. "You can go for a little while, but I doubt they're biting yet."

"Then we'll just feed the fishes," Darcy said.

Copper watched as Darcy and Lilly disappeared over the ridge toward the fishing hole. Darcy carried the pole Copper had fetched from the barn, and Lilly clutched the tin can full of worms.

The sun warmed Copper's head, so she loosed her bonnet and let it hang down her back, reveling in the warm weather. But March was deceiving, she knew. Although butter yellow daffodils bloomed on the creek bank and chickens feasted on worms from tilled ground, there would be more cold weather to come. It gave her hope, however, of sunny days ahead. Copper always thought of the Resurrection in the springtime. Jesus' triumph over the grave, the greatest hope ever given.

Now where had Dimmert and Cara gone? Then she saw Star standing patiently a little ways down the creek bank. There were their heads leaned together.

Copper could hear them talking, so she walked away from their voices to the porch and sat on the top step. Sweethearts needed privacy. Old Tom circled her ankles until she stroked his ears. He leaped to her lap and circled round until satisfied; then he plopped down, purring.

She wished John were here, not off working. Picking up a small, sharp stick, she began to clean the garden dirt from under her nails. He'd show up for supper, she expected. She couldn't wait to tell him of Hezzy's demands and to see his face when Dimmert and Cara shared their plans. Contentment settled in her heart like warm sunshine on her shoulders. Life was good indeed.

As if wishes made dreams come true, John's voice startled her from her reverie. "So why's the mule standing in the garden by his lonesome?"

Shading her eyes, she looked into his handsome face. "What are you doing here?"

"Just like a woman to answer a question with another question," he teased.

"John Pelfrey, just what do you know about women?"

He slapped his hat against his thigh. "Truthfully, not much. Scoot over."

Faithful ambled closer, looking for the pat on the head Copper always gave her. Old Tom took offense and leaped down hissing and spitting. The hound backed up, eyeing the cat from a safe distance.

"Just a minute," Copper said. "I'll be right back."

On the back of the stove, she found the pork-chop bone she'd saved. She took it and a tiny scrap of meat outside. After settling down beside John, she pitched the bone to Faithful and coaxed Tom back on her lap with the scrap meat. The cat nosed her offering as cats do before they eat, while Faithful, with a low growl, chewed on the bone.

"Where is everybody?" John asked.

"The girls are fishing, and Dimmert has a visitor."

"Oh yeah?" John moved so close she nearly tumbled off the side of the step. Tom held on, sinking his claws into her skirts. John's arm circled her shoulders, pulling her back. "Reckon I could steal a kiss seeing how we're alone and all?"

"I'll have to think on it." Copper's heart beat a tattoo against her rib cage.

He didn't wait for an answer but tipped her chin with his thumb and kissed her slowly on the mouth. Chagrined, she pulled away.

"Why is it we have to wait until May?" he asked.

"You leave me wondering myself. You know I love you."

"I know you do," he said, the bulk of him blocking the sun from her eyes. She could see her own reflection in his. "But not near as much as I love you."

"We could argue that," she said, playing with the hair that tumbled over his shirt collar. "You need a haircut."

"I need to finish plowing the garden if Dimmert's given it up. Who's he talking to, anyway?"

"Cara Wilson came home with me from the quilting circle, and she's got Dimm down by the creek. You were right all along."

"Told you."

Rising, she upended Old Tom. The cat stalked down the steps and took a swipe at Faithful just for the fun of it. "Grab that stool," Copper said. "I'm going to get the scissors."

John sat on the low seat with a towel around his shoulders while Copper cut his unruly hair. "For pity's sake," she said as wheat-colored hair fell to the porch floor, "you've got more cowlicks than a salt block."

"It's a sign."

She stepped back and cocked her head. "A sign of what, pray tell?"

John tapped his forehead. "Means there's a lot going on. Why, my brain's so busy my hair don't have time to lie down."

Copper lifted the hair at the nape of his neck and snipped a straight line before ruffling his hair and combing it in place. "There. That's much better. Now you'll look handsome for Hezzy Krill."

John gave her a quizzical look.

"Mrs. Krill wants you to visit," she teased. "I hear you're at her beck and call."

"Sometimes it feels like it. What's Hezzy need now?"

Copper told him about the well bucket and the rope. In truth she was proud he was so good to Hezzy.

"Here come the lovebirds," John said.

Copper followed his gaze and saw Cara and Dimmert coming around the barn. "I don't know how you knew when I didn't."

"It was a while back. When you went up there to tend Kenny. I was out in the yard with Dimmert when Cara stepped out on the porch. Dimmert lit up like a Christmas tree."

"Wonder how they'll make it."

John pulled the towel from around his neck and shook it over the edge of the porch. Bits of fluff caught on currents of air and swirled away. She stood beside him as the young people approached. "Love finds a way," he replied.

"Mr. John . . . Miz Copper," Cara said, clinging to Dimmert's hand. "We've come to ask you something." Dimm stood stiffly beside her. Copper couldn't tell if he was even breathing. Cara nudged him sharply with her elbow. "Dimm?"

His Adam's apple could have been the bobber on the end of a fishing line. "Cara and me—we're getting married," Dimmert choked out.

"Why, congratulations," John said. "What's your folks say, Cara?"

"They really like Dimmert. They won't stand in our way.

That is, as long as we can make our way. That's what we wanted to talk to you about." She poked Dimm again.

Dimmert was so nervous he jumped like a gigged frog. "Need a hired hand?" he said when he landed.

John rubbed his jaw. "There's plenty to be had here and more come May when we combine these two farms. What do you say, Copper?"

Copper dabbed at tears. Rushing down the steps, she hugged Cara, then Dimmert. "I say I couldn't be happier. How about a double wedding?"

"Good idea," John seconded. "Then we'll only have to pay the preacher once."

A week later Copper found Dimmert in the barn next to Star's empty stall. He'd hung the saddle over a rail and was polishing it with an old rag. "Where's Star?" she asked.

His shoulders slumped, and she thought she saw a glisten of tears in his eyes. "Sold."

Copper was poleaxed. She couldn't take it in. "Sold?"

"Sold," Dimmert repeated, rubbing the shiny leather round and round.

"What for?"

Tears streamed down his cheeks, but he stood as proud as a soldier. "I needed money to start a life with Cara."

She had a million questions and a million answers. Why hadn't he come to her? She would have bought Star, and then he could stay with Dimm. Why didn't he sell the saddle and keep his horse?

Or why didn't he ask for a loan? She would have given him the money. She wanted to tell Dimm she'd buy Star back, fix it for him, but his look held her back. She mustn't treat him like a child.

"I'm sure Star will be fine," was all she offered, turning her attention to Mazy, but a big lump formed in her throat. It was all she could do to keep from bawling.

It wasn't until later that evening that Copper got mad. John came by, and they were walking to the apple orchard. John wanted to check for blight. She was telling him about Dimm and Star when he said, "I know."

Her heart leaped with joy. Of course, Dimmert had gone to John.

But his next words dashed that hope. "Dimm made a down payment on a few acres next to the creek with the money. I told him he and Cara could live in my cabin until he could build one of his own."

"You mean you didn't buy Star?"

"Well, no, I don't need another horse."

She could feel her face heat up. "John Pelfrey, how could you let this happen? Star belongs with Dimmert!"

"How'd this get to be my fault?"

"You could have fixed it and you didn't. Don't you see?"

"Life's about making choices," he said, taking her hand. "Dimmert chose Cara, a person, over Star, a horse. Nobody gets to have everything."

Copper pulled away. "Why not? For once in his life why can't Dimm have everything?"

John reached for her, but she hid her hands behind her back. "Don't you know, sweet girl, when Dimm has Cara he has everything he ever needs?"

Sorrow as sad as a mourning dove's song blurred her vision. "But what about Star?"

"Believe me, Star will be fine. The man who bought him doesn't mistreat his stock. You'd approve of Star's new home."

"That makes me feel a little better." But in her heart a picture formed of the beautiful Star looking over his stable door for Dimmert. She hoped his new owner had apples.

CHAPTER 25

The third Thursday in May dawned sunny and warm. Copper was in a tizzy. A little more than a week before the wedding and her house was inside-out. The quilting ladies had shown up on her porch right after breakfast with mops and brooms and bars of lye soap. Now mattresses lay outdoors to bake in the sun, rugs hung over the clothesline, and windowpanes gleamed as Jean polished the winter grime away. Balls of damp newsprint gathered at her feet until Bubby started lobbing them at Lilly Gray, who giggled and threw them back.

Fairy Mae and Hezzy sat on the porch, hemming the two wedding dresses: Copper's pale green silk shantung and Cara's creamy white taffeta. Copper had ordered a short white veil for Cara and for herself a hat the color of her dress, trimmed with matching netting and a nosegay of artificial violets. Lilly would wear a dotted swiss pinafore over a lavender frock with a dropped waistline. Jean made a darling handkerchief-linen bonnet with long lavender ribbon ties that Lilly was already begging to wear. Copper had to hide it in a hatbox on top of the chiffonier.

Copper stood at the stove stirring chicken soup for the noon meal. She'd stayed up until nearly midnight making yeast rolls from Searcy's recipe. She was sure some of the ladies had never tasted light bread, and she wanted to give them a treat. Copper mopped her brow with the hem of her apron. She didn't remember it being so much trouble the first time she got married.

It was the letter the postman brought last week that had her frazzled. Otherwise, spring cleaning could have waited until September, as busy as she was with other things. But Alice was coming! Yes, she had invited her, and she would be happy to see her, but who would have expected Alice Upchurch to come all the way to Troublesome Creek, even for Copper's wedding?

A knock on the kitchen window made her jump. She dropped the spoon, and it slid down her clean apron before bouncing on the floor. Old Tom pounced, licking the savory broth. She thought she might just pull her hair out, but she smiled and turned toward the window.

"Is this inside or out?" Jean asked, pecking at a smear on the glass.

Copper squinted. With her dish towel, she rubbed until the streak gave way. "In."

Copper set the round oak table with the twelve place settings of fine china that Alice had sent along with her letter.

Miraculously not a piece of china was broken when Copper unpacked the barrel stuffed with wood shavings. A vase of wild-flowers made a pretty centerpiece.

"When's your folks get here?" Hezzy asked after everyone had settled at the table and Jean said grace.

"Next Friday," Copper said, passing the basket of bread.

"And your sister-in-law?" Jean asked.

"Oh, my," Copper said, "less than a week now." Just saying it made her stomach knot. Her late husband's sister was what these women would call stuck-up. She lived in Lexington in a big house full of servants, and her husband was a banker. What was Copper going to do with her? Mam and Daddy and the boys would stay at John's, but Alice and her daughter, Dodie, would sleep in Darcy's room. Thus the mattresses in the sun and the shiny windowpanes.

"This must be what heaven tastes like," one of the ladies said, buttered yeast roll in hand.

"Try it with some of this honey," Fairy Mae said, offering a bit to baby Jay. "You'll think you've died and gone on for sure."

"You all make me so thankful," Copper told them. "How would I have gotten everything done without your help?"

"Oh, we just come to see what that pretty quilt looks like on your bed," Fairy Mae laughed.

Hezzy gave Copper a sly look. "Just don't be trying it out before ye dance down the aisle."

"Hezzy!" Jean exclaimed.

Fairy Mae couldn't hold back a giggle, and soon all the ladies were laughing.

"Sounds like a hen party in here," John said from the other side of the screen door.

Well, that did it. Copper laughed until her sides ached, and every time she calmed down, Hezzy would snort or Jean would giggle and she'd start in again. It was just the tonic she needed for her jittery nerves. *Thank You, Lord, for friends and laughter.*

As Wednesdays tend to do, this one came and with it, Alice. Copper paced the porch until she saw the carriage far off in the distance. When it pulled into the barnyard, she was there to meet it. "Alice," she cried. "Oh, Alice."

All her fretting fell away as soon as her sister-in-law stepped down from the buggy. It was so good to see her.

Alice had changed not a whit and stood regally in Copper's embrace. "So this is Troublesome Creek," she said with a little frown.

"I can't believe you're here." Copper pulled Alice along to the porch. "And, Dodie, you're such a big girl now."

"Where's Lilly?" Dodie asked, taking in the rooster who chased a hen across their path.

Copper lifted Dodie into her arms and nuzzled her neck. "She'll be up from her nap directly. Oh, she'll be so glad to see you."

Two men carried a large trunk from the carriage to the porch. "Where do you want this, ma'am?"

Darcy opened the screen door. "Bring it on in here." When they had hefted the trunk through the door, she poked her head back out. "Should I feed these two fellers, Miz Copper? It's right on noon."

"Yes, Darcy. They're probably starved."

"My word, Laura Grace," Alice said, "are you sure that's the proper thing to do?"

No one had called her by her given name since she left Lexington, Copper realized. *Laura Grace* sounded strange, as though it belonged to someone else. "In the mountains we never let a stranger go away hungry. There's always a pot of beans simmering on the stove and a round of corn bread in the warming oven."

The screen door squeaked in welcome. "Here," Copper said, "let me show you and Dodie to your room. I know you'll want to change into something more comfortable and maybe rest a spell after your long journey."

Entertaining Alice was not as hard as Copper had imagined, for all she wanted to do was sit and hold Lilly Gray. When Copper first saw Alice with Lilly, it caused a bit of a shock. From Lilly's stormy eyes to her black hair with its streak of silver, not to mention finely arched eyebrows, Lilly Gray was the spitting image of Alice Corbett Upchurch. *I'm in trouble,* Copper thought, *if Alice's exacting personality goes along with that handed-down beauty.*

Later, after supper—when Alice met John for the first time—and after the little girls were tucked in for the night, Copper had a chance to talk with Alice.

They sat on the porch, rockers side by side, sipping from cups of chamomile tea, taking in the pleasant evening air. Copper reached out and patted Alice's free hand. "I still can't believe you came all this way to see me get married."

"Contrary to what I once would have believed," Alice said, "I've missed you terribly."

Copper thought back to their strained relationship after she'd married Simon and gone to live in the city. Alice had given her nightmares then. "And I have missed you. Tell me, have you heard anything from Marydell? And how is Andy?"

Marydell and Andy were brother and sister to Alice's adopted daughter, Dodie. In Lexington, Copper had discovered the children living in dire straits. She had befriended them and continued to pray for them daily.

"I hear from Marydell's grandmother on occasion," Alice said. "Marydell is well and attending school. Andy continues to live at Mrs. Archesson's boardinghouse, but he takes supper with us once in a while. I think it is his way of staying close to Dodie."

"And Searcy and Reuben? Are they well?"

"She keeps her little house tidy and leads a Bible study for her acquaintances. He has a garden and the cow you left with them, so he is happy." Alice patted her hair as if it had come out of its pins. "Dodie and I visit with them every week. They are like grandparents to her."

Alice Upchurch calling on a housekeeper? Copper was amazed. *Will wonders never cease?*

A little wind blew fast around them, whipping their skirts. The leaves of the apple tree in the side yard whispered against each other. The air darkened with an approaching storm, and lightning cracked the sky.

"We'd best go in," Alice said.

"Just one more question." Copper stacked Alice's cup and saucer with her own and nested the spoons inside, afraid of the answer. "What do you think of John?"

"May I say I am pleasantly surprised?" Alice's voice softened. Copper held her breath. "He is quite rough but charming nonetheless. I'm sure you can smooth his rough edges."

Copper inhaled. "Thank you. That means so much to me."

"I ask only one thing, Laura Grace," Alice said, turning her sharp eyes on Copper.

Copper held her breath again.

"I intend to be a part of Lilly Gray's life. I will come for visits until she is older, and then I want you to bring her to me on occasion."

"Fair enough," Copper replied as rain moved in and thunder rolled. She rushed to hold the door for Alice. "I'm so glad you're here."

"Surely you didn't expect that I wouldn't come. I had to see about Lilly Gray, after all."

Ah, Copper thought, smiling, *Lilly is her soft spot. And why shouldn't she be? The child is all she has left of Simon.*

CHAPTER 26

On the Friday night before the Sunday wedding, Copper and John had a shindig for everyone who lived within shouting distance and some who didn't. Copper was afraid they'd turn it into a shivaree, with wild tricks and lots of noise. It was the custom, but John said he'd put a stop to that foolishness. He didn't fancy riding a rail down to the creek for a dunking. Instead they'd keep everyone busy eating and dancing. Elder Foster brought his banjo, and his son Dylan played the mouth harp.

Darcy borrowed lanterns from anyone who had an extra, and Dimmert hung them from the branches of trees. The yard glowed with soft yellow light while children chased fireflies and men swapped stories. Copper's lady friends sliced ham and dished up fried chicken and potato salad. Fairy Mae brought coconut cake, and Cara's mother, Miranda, brought a four-layer chocolate cake with caramel icing. There was coffee, cold sweet tea, and milk to drink. But Copper suspected some of the men behind the barn were sipping something stronger. Ace Shelton had probably brought it. She tried to catch John's eye to send him around there to check, but he was picking and singing a ballad with Elder Foster and Dylan.

A chill ran up Copper's spine. "Barbara Allen" was so plaintive a song to sing on such a pretty night. She rubbed her arms and shivered; a goose must be walking on her grave.

"Are you all right, Laura Grace?" Mam asked, dropping a shawl over Copper's shoulders.

"Oh, this feels good. It's just the song they're singing. 'Barbara Allen' always makes me lonesome." Knotting the shawl at her waist, Copper looked around. "Where's Daddy?"

"I sent Will out to the barn. I don't like the looks of what's going on behind there. Daniel," she called.

"Yes, ma'am." Copper's little brother stopped running wild long enough to answer.

"Ask the fellows to sing something happy," Mam said.

Soon "Oh, Susannah" had folks clapping and singing along.

"Look, Mam," Copper said, pointing at Hezzy and Fairy Mae tapping their feet on the porch floor. "Did you know you could clog sitting down?"

Then John was pulling Copper off the porch and she was looking up into his beaming face as the little band played a couple's waltz. She couldn't say who looked prouder, John or Dimmert, who did a quick slide step with Cara.

Copper's moment of melancholy drifted away as she let the music soothe her. She was in her beloved's arms. Her family and friends surrounded her. It was a time for happiness.

Remy slipped away from her hideout in the trees behind the barn. She was aggravated, for she enjoyed watching, but some men were lifting jugs of white mule. Remy knew from experience how things could turn ugly when that mule kicked. Her pap was the meekest of men, wouldn't step on his own shadow, 'til he got a taste of corn liquor. Which, come to think on it, he generally tasted all day long. No matter, she hadn't seen his sorry hide since before she fell over Torrent Falls.

The spring night was warm, and a high silvery moon made her hike through the forest easy. Not that it mattered; Remy had eyes like a cat. The slip of feet on new grass let her know she was not alone. "Hello there, Foxy," she whispered.

The fox padded behind, never going ahead, trailing her right side. Remy stopped for a moment, her hand hung loosely. The vixen nuzzled her palm.

"I ain't got nothing for ye. I was eyeing some potato salad, but they was too many folks about."

Remy sat on a rock and waited, giving time and space. She didn't turn around. Foxes didn't like to meet her eyes, she knew. They liked to keep their secrets to theirselves. Soon she could feel Foxy's presence just a couple of feet behind her. Remy could feel her hunger.

"What say we visit old lady Krill's henhouse?" She scooted off her rock seat and started down the hill.

⁕

The party was over; everyone said their good-byes as women gathered children and men fetched wagons and horses.

"It ain't too late, John," one man called.

"Yeah," another shot back. "Run for the hills while you still can."

John stood laughing, his arm around Copper. "Bring me a broom and a preacher, and I'll jump it right now. How about you, Dimmert?"

Dimmert didn't say a word, just grabbed the broom from a corner and handed it to John.

Everyone fell out laughing, even Alice. Copper couldn't believe it. Dimmert bested John. How funny.

Finally everyone was gone, and her family was sleeping. Copper waited on the porch, knowing her father would come to sit awhile with her.

"Daddy," she said when he wrapped her in a bear hug. Trying to hold back tears, she gave in instead and cried against his chest.

"Whoa, Daughter," he said, his voice like music to her ears. "This is not a time for tears."

"I know." She sobbed, taking his handkerchief and wiping her tears. "I don't know what's gotten into me. I guess seeing you and Mam and the boys has got me missing you even though you're here."

"You've got the high lonesomes. You've given too many pieces of your heart away."

The rockers on their chairs squeaked in rhythm. "Is there a cure for the high lonesomes?" she asked.

"No. You don't want to be cured of missing the folks you love, but loving more folks makes it tolerable."

She took his calloused hand and held it tightly. "I am happy, Daddy. I love John so much."

"Well, that's good, because John acts like he fell in a barrel of long sweetening when he's around you."

"Are you glad for me?"

"A father wouldn't want any more for his daughter than what John will give you, Copper." He folded his handkerchief and stuck it in his pocket. "Now go get my grandbaby. I aim to set here with her all night."

⁂

Across the creek and up Krill holler, Remy congratulated her lucky self. There were eggs aplenty in the chicken coop she pilfered. She was extra careful, for the old woman had been up late tonight. She eased out the door with a pocket full of hen fruit and secured the latch. She held her breath and started up the path. Over her shoulder, she kept an eye on Hezzy's house, where a lamp still shone in the window.

The necklace of rings and a tiny walnut basket swung against her chest, then gave way and fell to the ground. As she stooped to search for it in the tall grass, Hezzy's door swung open and she hitched outside. Then her shotgun blasted the warm night. "I've got you now, you nasty varmint."

Where was that necklace? Remy wasn't about to leave without it. There—her fingers closed over her treasures. She stayed crouched and scuttled away, hardly feeling the bullet that shattered her long leg bone. She heard more than felt the assault, like the fearsome shriek of a shovel striking rock. Someone was digging her grave. *Whomp*, she hit the ground. A roar, not unpleasant, filled her ears.

Torrent Falls—they's angels there, Remy thought as darkness closed her eyes.

The rooster didn't have to wake Copper the next morning. She couldn't wait to see the dawn. Sometime during the night, Daddy had wakened her when he brought the sleeping Lilly Gray back to bed, and now Lilly lay curled on her side with her thumb in her mouth.

Copper pulled on a dress and carried her shoes to the porch. Stretching and yawning, she made her way to a chair. Morning damp seeped into the back of her dress, but she didn't mind. All she could think was, *Tomorrow I'll marry my sweetheart.* Her heart gave a little leap, and a smile curled her lips. The unease of the night before was gone. The days of her life spread out before her as sweet as clover honey.

A favorite Scripture came to mind: *"Even them will I bring to my holy mountain, and make them joyful in my house of prayer."* Behind closed eyes, the faces of family and friends shimmered, one replacing another—Daddy, Mam, Willy and Daniel, Lilly, Darcy, Dimmert, Alice, and a host of others. Then John, with his unruly hair and his teasing green eyes, smiled and beckoned her to come away with him. She opened her eyes and shook her head. Sometimes a body had more joy than she knew what to do with.

The sun had just started its familiar route when Copper strode across the barnyard. The rooster atop the fence post shook out his feathers and threw back his head. Little Benny waited his turn in the hayloft. It seemed the sunrise mimicked her like Benny copied the big rooster—she was sure the color of her joy was reflected there.

It was cold where Remy lay—cold and dark. Her mind was play- ing tricks. Was that her ma calling, "Remy, come in. Supper's ready"? And there was her brother Riser with a dipper gourd full of water. She tried to hold on to them, her ma and Riser, but the roar of Torrent Falls caught her unawares. . . .

It was snowing the day she took the mule to ride to the falls. John Pelfrey's cabin and his understanding ways were closing in on her; she had to clear her mind. It was a tedious journey, what with the slick of mud underneath the slushy snow.

Once she made her way to Torrent Falls, she slid down from the mule's bony back, kicked snow from a clump of grass, and left him eating near a copse of trees. Full of snowmelt as it was, Remy could hear the awesome plunge of the water before she saw it. Her ankle was still swollen, but she ignored the lingering pain as she hurried to the water's edge. She was desperate to see the angels; maybe that would make her feel better.

Mulling over her plight, she could come to no conclusion other than that she had used Purty's friend John in a devious way. Now devious ways had never bothered any of the Riddle clan, and Remy was surely one of them. Devious was how they managed to survive in a world full of folks who kept their good fortune locked up tight in cellars and smokehouses as if only they had a right to the land's bounty. So, Remy wondered, why did it feel so wrong now? Who was John Pelfrey that she should care?

Had she meant it when she told John she was going to throw herself over the falls? Not really, but she was so tired that day—tired of running from Pap and that awful Quick Hopper, tired of being hungry, tired of hurting. And then John had come up with the answer to her problem. What did it matter really if a piece of paper fooled her pap and set her free? She didn't mean it when she put a squiggle on the license after all.

Standing so close to the falls she could feel its icy, needle-sharp spray, and pulling her sky blue mantle tight around her arms, Remy looked for the angels in the shimmering water, but they did not appear.

Maybe she should say some Scripture to make them feel at home. Purty taught her a verse one time, but she couldn't rightly recollect it—something about friends sticking closer than brothers. If she hurt John, then had she in some way hurt Purty?

Her stomach was all strange again, and her heart felt sore and tired. She could pray although she only knew the one prayer that Purty had taught her years ago. Kneeling and folding her hands, she said, "Now I lay me down to sleep. I pray the Lord my soul to keep. If I should die before I wake, I pray the Lord my soul to take."

Remy wondered if God would let her come to heaven some-day. Probably. Purty said He loved everybody the same.

Her knees were cold, near frozen, so she stood and, unde-terred by danger, crept close to the plunging edge. The rock was as slick as wet moss. Next thing she knew she was falling–kicking and flailing and screaming. Then in midair she stopped. Just like that: one minute falling, the next hanging, her mantle snagged on a jutting tree limb. *A purty predicament, halfway between heaven and hell.* The rush of angels' wings surrounded her then. They were louder than hard rain on a tin roof, louder even than the falls.

Suddenly, she was on the bank. But she found nary a bruise nor a broken bone. Her shawl hung halfway up the falls, whip-ping about in the wind. She'd lost one boot and John's great-grandmother's ring. She was sorry about that.

Remy dragged herself away from the water and found a hunter's winter lean-to well hidden in the forest. Wet and shiver-ing, her teeth clattering, she cracked the door and crept inside. There was a stack of firewood and a stash of jerky. It didn't seem possible she was alive, but here she was and she was ever so thankful.

Remy was scouting around a couple of days later when she heard John and the preacher talking about her demise. She was above the falls looking down on them as John shoveled a deep hole and planted her mantle and her lost boot. The preacher said a few words, then patted John on the shoulder. "Her body's been washed away," the preacher said, "or some animal got the remains."

Remy saw John shudder at that remark, but then the men walked away, leading the mule, leaving the little grave to molder on the bank of Torrent Falls. And just like that, Remy had the solution to her problem and John's. Guilt fluttered from her heart like moths from a wool sweater, leaving her feeling light and free.

A jolt of pain brought Remy back from memory to the present. The falls were gone, her ma and her brother just imagination. Nothing was real but the hurt in her leg and the thirst in her throat. She whimpered, and there was Foxy's head in a ring of light. With great effort, Remy patted the sides of the trap she seemed to be in—a hollow log. Now she remembered crawling up the hill to safety. Surely if she crawled in the log she could crawl out, but her leg wouldn't mind and her hands lay weakly at her sides.

She raised her head. "Is there any angels out there?"

Foxy stuck her long nose in the log, giving what comfort she could. For the moment it was all Remy needed.

CHAPTER 27

If Copper could have lived any way she wanted, it would have always been like the Saturday morning before her wedding. There were so many people at her noontime table that they'd had to pull the benches in from the porch for seating. It had been a harried morning: Alice and the little girls picking flowers for bouquets tied up with ribbon; Mam baking a cake; Daddy searching his Bible to find the perfect blessing for the ceremony; Willy and Daniel sweeping the porches and the front yard; Darcy frying chicken; Dimmert, nearly comatose with nerves, stumbling over his vows, saying "I do" over and over again until Copper sent him to the barn to pitch hay or clean stalls—whatever would take his mind off the next day.

Now her family gathered at the round oak table. Two leaves

stretched its seating capacity, but still Dodie had to sit on her lap. The child had barely left her side since she'd alighted from the carriage. It did Copper's heart good to see how the little girl abandoned by her mother had prospered under Alice's watchful eye. Really, if Copper didn't know the story of her rescue, she would think Alice had birthed her.

Lilly didn't seem to mind a bit that her mother held another child. She sat in her high chair next to John's empty place and waved her fried chicken leg while she jabbered a long story. Where was John? The potatoes were getting cold while everyone waited.

"Let's eat," Copper said. "I'm sure John'll be here directly. Daddy, will you say grace?"

The screen door squeaked on "amen," and there John was, kissing the top of Lilly's head and winking at Copper. "Sorry I'm late," he said, spreading butter on his corn bread. "One of the preacher's kids came by with a need just as I was leaving."

"What did he want?" Copper asked.

"Hezzy sent him to get me. You know she always wants something." He forked two green beans and put them on Lilly's tray. "Trouble is, she thinks nobody can do for her but me."

"That's because she's sweet on you," Copper teased. "You sure it's me you're getting hitched to tomorrow?"

Everyone was laughing, enjoying the moment, but when John looked at her, it was as if no one else were there. "Honey girl, I'm not dancing down that aisle for anyone but you."

She could feel the blush that rose from her chest and crept up to her cheeks. What would happen if she just leaned across the table and kissed him? Instead she asked, "What does Hezzy need this time?"

"Seems there's a fox hanging around on the hillside in front of her house. It was stealing eggs last night. She thought she'd shot it, but it never left."

"That's not normal acting for sure," Will said. "It's a little early in the season for rabies."

Willy bounced on his seat. "Can me and Daniel go with you, John?"

"Certainly not," Mam said. "You'll both wind up with lockjaw."

"Please, Mam," Willy pleaded. "Please? Pretty please with sugar on top."

"Finish eating, boys," Daddy said, "and we'll all go."

Copper saw the look that passed between Mam and Daddy— confidence in Daddy's and relief in Mam's. She couldn't wait to share those looks, those moments, with John.

Soon all the fellows were on their way, leaving the ladies to a moment's peace. Copper shooed Mam and Alice to the porch while she and Darcy cleaned up the kitchen. Then she filled the kettle again. "Let's wash our hair while we've got a little privacy."

She stood in her camisole and slip, bent over the wash pan while Darcy poured warm water over her head. Then she did the same for Darcy, followed by a rinse of rainwater from the barrel under the eave.

"Did you remember the vinegar?" Mam called from her rocker.

Copper held her nose and looked at Darcy. "Oh, Mam, we'll smell like pickles."

Mam laughed. "That brings back memories. You said that same thing every time I washed your hair."

"And you always answered, 'The smell will go away as soon as your hair dries.'" She wore her towel turban style outside. Handing a comb to Mam, Copper sat on the floor in front of her chair.

"Come here, Darcy, and I'll do yours," Alice said.

Copper couldn't believe her ears. Alice was sure different than she used to be.

It was restful, Copper thought, sitting here while Mam combed her hair. The sun was warm, and the scent of roses from the wild bush in the side yard sweetened the air. Two house wrens chattered in the morning glory vine that screened one end of the porch with abundant green leaves and purple trumpets. Dodie and Lilly played paper dolls on the porch steps.

Darcy's straight brown hair hung halfway down her back. "Why you reckon men would druther shoot a mad dog than sit here peaceable like this?"

"It's the thrill of the chase," Alice replied. "When it's your turn, young lady, be very careful who catches you."

Alice's words of wisdom made Copper reflect on what she knew of her sister-in-law's marriage to a wealthy but abusive man. Lord forgive her, she hadn't even asked how that was going. She'd been so busy with her own selfish needs since Alice arrived. But Alice seemed all right, and Dodie was obviously thriving. Things must be okay. Copper made a mental note to find some time to spend with Alice before she left for Lexington. Or maybe she'd just keep Alice here. She could be quite the grande dame. A chuckle slipped out at the thought of Alice holding court on Troublesome Creek.

"What's so funny?" Darcy asked.

"Oh," Copper said, "just thinking about the fellows dancing to Hezzy's jig."

"Poor fox, I say." Darcy hung her towel over the porch rail to dry and reached for Copper's. "Who wants a cup of tea?"

The men gathered behind the chicken coop at Hezzy's place. Just as the old woman had said, a red fox sat by a felled log quite a distance up the hill.

"Odd," Will said. "Animals with rabies don't sit still like that."

"Reckon it has something trapped in that log?" John asked.

"Could be," Will answered, stroking his white beard. "Maybe a rabbit hiding in there."

"Humph," Hezzy snorted. "It's acting strange. A fox don't sit around making itself a target. I drew a bead on him, but he's too far away."

"I'll go take a look," John said, holding his gun so the barrel pointed toward the ground. "I hate to shoot it if there's no need."

"No need?" Hezzy cast an exasperated look at John. "That varmint's been stealing eggs. If you don't kill him, he'll be right back tonight."

"You're right," John replied. "I'll take care of it."

"I'll go with you." Willy stepped up beside John. His eleven-year-old face set in concentration. "Daddy, can I borrow your gun?"

"Willy Brown, you know better," Will said. "Take one step forward and I'll send you to the porch."

"Shucks," Willy said. "I don't ever get to do anything fun."

"Just watch, boy," Will said. "Watch and learn. That will be fun enough."

⁂

Remy heard voices. She tried to raise her head and peer through a knothole, but it seemed too heavy to lift. She'd drifted all night on a sea of memory. Mostly she liked to think on the times she'd spent with Purty, her one true friend.

They'd first met in Remy's hidey-hole, a cave set way back in a warren of caves up in the mountains. Purty's old hound Paw-paw had managed to get himself trapped in there. Remy took care of him until Purty came back to claim her pet. Remy knew Purty was scared of her—her looks put folks off sometimes. But she'd gotten over it soon enough and they'd been friends, although on Remy's terms.

At first Purty tried to change her—folks always did. It seemed she couldn't accept that Remy was tickled to live as she did. Her pap always said he wouldn't trade his freedom for a farm in Georgia, and Remy agreed. Purty thought Remy needed a soft pillow for her head and a warm bath once a week. Huh, there was always a trade-off for that kind of easy life. She'd heard tell that folks who lived down mountain had to pay tithes to the government or they'd take over your property. Riddles didn't truck with that nonsense. Better not to ever have a deed or a title than to give it to the law.

Pain shot up Remy's leg, and she knew she might not make it this time. But she was all right whatever befell. She'd rather die in a hollow log than be buried in an oak-board coffin. This seemed fitting somehow.

The voices sounded agitated now. Men were gathering; she could sense it. She tried to call out to Foxy. "Run," she wanted to say, but her dry tongue stuck to the roof of her mouth.

⚜

Copper's hair was dry and Mam was playing with it, trying to decide how to arrange it for the wedding. "What do you think, Alice? An upsweep like this or a chignon at the back?"

"Most definitely the upsweep. I saw a style just so in this month's *Woman's Home Companion*." Alice came close for an inspection. "Oh yes, with my pearl combs."

"Let's play dress-up," Darcy said. "Let's try on our dresses and practice walking in our high-heeled slippers."

"Good idea," Copper replied. "I want Mam to check my hem one more time. It still seems a little long."

"Hurry up then," Mam said. "The men will be back soon, and we don't want John seeing you in your dress before tomorrow."

"Surely you don't believe in that old superstition," Copper said, then felt sorry when she saw Mam wince. She gave her stepmother a quick hug. "Don't worry. Nothing can go wrong now. Tomorrow will be perfect."

CHAPTER 28

Warmth surrounded Remy. The brightest sun she ever saw poured in from the end of the hollow log. Foxy shimmered in the light. A halo rested just over her black-tipped pointy ears. She turned her head and smiled at Remy with her white teeth. *Why*, Remy thought, *Foxy has turned into an angel.*

John pulled the hammer back on his gun and sighted down the barrel, but he couldn't bring himself to squeeze the trigger. He'd always been partial to the pretty animals and didn't like to kill them. Why didn't the fool fox run? He couldn't rightly scare it off with everyone watching him from the shade of the henhouse. Hezzy'd never let him live it down.

One thing for sure: this fox didn't have mad dog; for whatever reason it seemed to be protecting the log. Maybe it had had a litter in there, unusual but not unheard of. Foxes preferred to raise their young in dens stolen from groundhogs or some such thing.

He walked up the hill. A glint of gold caught his eye, and he stooped to see what it was. The thin gold band he retrieved from the grass caught his breath. How in the world . . . ? His great-grandmother's ring lay as true as sunrise in his palm. Suddenly he knew what was in the hollow log. He knew what the fox protected.

Each step up that hill seemed mired in thick molasses. His heart hurt like the dickens, and he breathed in ragged gulps. Then he was kneeling, and there was Remy. "Don't let me be too late," he whispered as he turned toward his comrades waiting below. "Help," he called. "I need some help here."

Copper's wedding dress slid in place over her spiral wire bustle.

"You couldn't have picked a better color," Mam said from her seat on the bed.

"It brings out the green in your eyes," Alice agreed, handing her the matching hat. "Let's see this too."

"This isn't going to work," Copper said. "It will ruin my hair and hide your pretty combs, Alice."

"You're right," Mam said, "but you have to have something on your head for the church service."

"That's easy enough." Alice snipped at the hat with a pair of scissors and removed the netting veil and the nosegay of artificial posies.

"Just the netting, I think," Mam said. Arranging it in a circle, she secured the soft crown to Copper's hair.

"Just the right touch." Alice held the nosegay to the side of Copper's head. "What do you think?"

"Too fussy," Mam said.

"I could carry them in my teeth." Copper admired her reflection in the chiffonier's wavy looking glass.

"No, mine hat, Auntie Alice." Lilly thrust her new bonnet at Alice.

"Lilly . . . ," Copper warned.

"I have a splendid idea," Alice said. "Let's put some of these flowers on your bonnet, Lilly, and some on Dodie's."

"Yup," Lilly replied. "Pended idea."

"What about the length?" Copper asked, twirling her skirt.

"Seems just right to me," Mam said. "Now if you'll slip out of your dress, I'll press it one more time."

"Look at you, Darcy," Copper said. "Come see yourself in the mirror."

Darcy's cheeks turned the same color as her pink mull frock. White satin epaulet bows adorned her shoulders. "I look like one of them ladies in your fashion magazines, Miz Copper."

"Oh no," Copper said. "You're much prettier than they."

"Wonder if Cara's trying on her dress today," Darcy said.

"I can't wait to see her all dressed up tomorrow," Copper answered, removing the netting from her hair.

"I'm going to the porch, where I can see to thread a needle."

Alice carried the little girls' hats. "Dodie, Lilly, you two come with me."

Copper marveled to see the way Lilly minded Alice. There'd be no back talk to her auntie.

The looking glass revealed a funny sight. Darcy stood in front of Copper, who stood in front of Mam. Mam unfastened the first few in the long row of tiny buttons up the back of Copper's dress, and Copper did the same for Darcy.

"Stop wiggling, Darcy," Copper said. "You'll make me pull a button off."

"I can't help it. You're tickling me."

"You'd best hurry up," Alice called through the open window. "I see the men coming."

Mam pulled back the curtain for a look. Copper saw Mam's face lose its color before her hand flew to her throat.

"What is it?"

"Someone's hurt."

Copper joined Mam at the window. John was cradling a body in his arms. Willy? Daniel? But no . . . both boys hung back with Daddy, who supported Hezzy. And there was Dimmert rushing forward as if parting the waters.

She heard the screen door squeak, and suddenly John was filling up her bedroom door. "Copper, Lord help us," he said, "it's Remy."

Her mind stuttered. Remy? Remy was dead.

Mam pulled back the bedcovers, and John gently laid the small body down. "She's been shot," he said.

"I didn't mean it," Hezzy cried from the vicinity of the

kitchen. "I thought she was a fox. I never would have pulled the trigger if I knew it was a human."

Copper could barely hear Remy's panting moans over Hezzy's carrying on. Tears ran unbidden down her cheeks as she took Remy's wrist, searching for a pulse. "Oh, my little lost friend," she said, sinking to her knees. "Someone get my doctor's bag and someone go for the preacher."

It was hours later before Copper had hope that Remy would live. The good news was the bullet went straight through the leg, leaving a ragged wound but no projectile to fish around for. But there was much blood loss and, Copper was certain, a fractured thighbone. There were the telltale signs: loss of mobility in the limb, swelling and distortion, and a grating sensation–crepitus, Simon had taught her to call it–when she placed her hand on the injured part.

Remy was not an easy patient. Though feeble and in considerable pain, she thrashed about like a feral cat whenever anyone, save Copper or John, came near. Even the preacher couldn't come close enough to lay hands on Remy to anoint her with oil. So he prayed and quoted Scripture at the kitchen table. Copper was calmed by his healing words.

She could have cared for Remy alone except for the setting of the broken bone. For modesty's sake John couldn't help her with that. Darcy was willing, but Remy wouldn't stand for it. Copper pleaded and soothed, but still Remy flung herself about, nearly falling off the bed. Copper was glad Mam and Daddy had taken Lilly and Dodie to John's house for the night. Remy's fits would have scared the little girls to death.

Copper was at her wit's end before things finally settled down. In the middle of one of Remy's tantrums, Alice marched into the room, walked over to the bed, cupped Remy's chin in her hand, looked her straight in the eyes, and said, "That is quite enough, young lady. Stop this silly carrying on."

Remy's eyes rolled in fear. She tried to jerk her chin from Alice's grip, but Alice held firm. Remy gave up and lay still. Despite morphine, she moaned in pain as Copper and Darcy manipulated the ends of the broken bone into their natural position. Alice stood at the foot of the bed, ready to fetch supplies or lend a hand.

Dimmert fashioned long splints from thin, firm boards as Copper asked. Once the bone was set, she and Darcy fastened the splints to either side of Remy's leg with soft flannel. When that was finished, Copper looked the job over. It would have to do until she could send for plaster of paris powder and loosely woven lint bandages. The hard part would be keeping the leg fully extended.

The clock over the mantel struck three times; Copper woke with a start. Evidently she had fallen asleep at the bedside. Someone had stuck a pillow under her head and covered her where she knelt at Remy's side. Now she had a crick in her neck, and her legs were so stiff she could barely hobble.

Alice sat in a straight chair. A kerosene lamp turned low illuminated the Bible in her lap.

"How long have I been asleep?" Copper asked.

"A couple of hours," Alice said. "I've been keeping watch."

Copper felt Remy's pulse and listened to her heartbeat through Simon's stethoscope. She pulled back the cover and checked the dressings on her leg. Alice brought the lamp closer, and Copper felt Remy's warm toes, a sign of good circulation. "If we can keep her wound from getting infected, I think she has a good chance."

"She's awfully pale," Alice said.

Remy's face framed by her wild white hair was the same color as the pillowcase her head rested on.

"She never has much color. Even in the summer she stays bleached out like this." Copper patted Alice's arm. "Why don't you go to bed now?"

"You take a break and then I shall. There's hot water on the stove for tea."

Copper stretched and yawned. "Thanks. Tea sounds good. I won't be long."

As she poured water from the cast-iron kettle over sassafras shavings, she inhaled the fragrant steam. It was too hot to drink, so she carried it outside, stirring the tea with a spoon. John sat there on the steps. She suspected he had been there all night. "Take this," she said, handing him the cup. "I'll make another."

When she came back, he had scooted over, making room for her.

"How is she?" he asked.

"Sleeping," Copper said. "I'm worried about infection, of course, and she's lost so much blood . . . but if anyone can survive this it's Remy."

"I was never so surprised to find her in that log. I thought sure she was dead." He shook his head. "'Course I thought that once before."

"But you never found her. Seems like we would have suspected."

John turned to her, and she could hear the anger in his voice. "I searched for days, figuring her body would bob up somewhere along the banks. I think she was hiding out all along watching me, else she would never have found the ring I buried. What makes a body act like that—like they have no feelings for anyone but themselves?"

"Remy's just different. You know how hard her life was, John. Her family was always fleeing from the law because of her father. I guess she did the best she could."

"By wrecking other people's lives?" His voice shook. "Today was supposed to be our wedding day, but now . . ." His shoulders slumped. "What are we going to do?"

She steadied herself by clutching the warm teacup. In her joy at having Remy alive, she hadn't thought about this day at all. Setting the cup aside, she smoothed the skirt of her wedding dress, now stained with Remy's blood. She was tired, so very tired. "I don't know."

"Listen, we can marry anyway. Everyone who matters knows I was never truly wed to Remy Riddle. Nobody would hold that against us."

"John . . ."

"We'll go away. Me and you and Lilly. Anywhere you want, just name it."

"Surely you wouldn't ask me to live in adultery." It was surreal, sitting here on the porch, her shoulder touching his, all their plans falling away like petals from a discarded daisy.

"Don't you see? It was all a mistake. God wouldn't hold us to it."

Copper didn't like the way John pleaded. It made her want to turn away from him. She didn't want to see his weakness. It fell on her. She'd have to be strong enough for both of them. Lifting her cup, she took a swallow. "She is your legal wife. I won't break the law of man, much less the law of the Lord."

"You always do the right thing, but ain't you even tempted? I am."

She fought every instinct to take him in her arms. Instead she sat and gathered her faith. "God will not suffer us to be tempted above that we are able," she remarked, feeling much too prim and proper.

John didn't answer, just stood and walked away, leaving her sitting there in her ruined wedding dress, a cup of cold sassafras tea in her hands.

Daddy came by while Copper was doing the milking. It was so good to have him here. She needed the wise counsel she knew he would give. "How's the patient?" he asked.

"She spiked a fever this morning. Alice is giving her an alcohol rub, and then I'll check her leg again." She leaned her head against Mazy's warm flank. "It's so funny to see Alice taking care of Remy. Remy doesn't dare to sass her like she does me."

"Let me finish this," Daddy said.

"I need to be milking. It makes me feel normal."

Her father squatted beside her. "I talked to John," he said.

"Tell me I'm doing the right thing," she whispered, knowing that he would.

"As far as we know now, John's marriage to Remy is legal and binding. You're doing what God would have you do, and I am proud to call you daughter."

Mazy was empty and so was Copper. Daddy stood and helped her up. "It's not easy," she said, leaning against him.

"It's not supposed to be." He took the milk bucket from her. "What do you want to do about today?"

"It's still Dimmert and Cara's wedding day. I'd like you and Mam to make sure they have the wonderful ceremony we planned."

"They're waiting on the porch to talk to you. I think they want to postpone it."

She wished she had changed her blood-spattered dress when she saw the young folks waiting for her. Cara's cheeks were tear stained, and Dimmert looked like he did the day he sold Star. "Now listen," Copper said as she stepped up on the porch, "I'll have no talk of postponed weddings."

"But, Miz Copper," Cara replied, "we can't be all happy if you and Mr. John won't be there with us."

"Sure you can. Why, look at the beautiful day God has given you. We prayed for just such weather. You can't deny folks the pleasure of seeing you two wed. You know everyone who comes to church and Sunday school will be staying."

"I'm sad for you," Cara said.

Copper took Cara's hand and held it to her cheek. "Don't be. Do you know what I would like from the two of you?"

"Anything," Cara said.

"Come by after the ceremony. I want to see you in all your finery."

Dimmert swallowed. "My overalls won't bend."

Copper laughed. "That's to keep you from keeling over during the service. We found the stiffest new overalls we could for you. By the way, did someone iron your white shirt and press your jacket, and did John show you how to tie your tie?"

"Everything's taken care of," Cara said. "Don't you be worrying about us. Sounds like you've got your hands full already."

"It's a job worth doing. Have everyone at church pray for Remy today. Ask for God's blessing and for healing."

"We will," Cara said as Dimm helped her down the steps. It made Copper smile to see Cara handled like a fine piece of china. At the edge of the yard the couple paused.

"See you later," Dimm said with a wave.

"That was good, Dimmert," Cara said. "I'm right proud of you."

Thank You, Lord, for the blessings Dimmert and Cara have brought into my life, Copper prayed. *Please take good care of them. Let them grow old together and let them always be as content with each other as they are right now.*

CHAPTER 29

The house was full of hustle and bustle. Alice and Mam had the little girls dressed and ready to go to the wedding. Willy and Daniel stood handsome and proud in their Sunday suits. Darcy was pretty as a picture in her pink frock. She was sure to catch some young man's eye.

When they were ready, Daddy brought the buggy around and fitted everyone inside except the boys, who were content to hang on the outside of the buggy.

"Not so fast, Will," Copper heard Mam call as they drove away. "You'll fling the boys off."

Mam was such a worrier, Copper mused. My, she wished they wouldn't go back to Philadelphia. But she knew they must. The boys couldn't miss much more school.

Remy was sleeping, so Copper took advantage of the privacy. She closed the kitchen door and pulled all the curtains before she attempted to take off the dress she'd worn since last afternoon. It was no use. She couldn't contort herself enough to reach the row of buttons up the back.

Standing in front of the mirror over the washstand, she appraised herself. "You would have been a beautiful bride," she said. One tear was followed by another as she resolutely took up the scissors and cut her dress away. She never wanted to see it again.

After heating water, Copper filled a washbasin and bathed. She brushed her teeth and combed her hair, coiled it at the back of her head and fastened it with tortoiseshell combs. She must remember to give Alice back the pearl ones she'd lent her. Copper put on one of her prettier day dresses, then filled the kettle again and made preparations to bathe Remy.

With one palm she touched Remy's forehead, still warm but not as hot as earlier. A bath should help. The temperature rise could as easily be from blood loss as from infection. Washing Remy was like bathing a child—she was so slight she barely made a dent in the mattress.

At least this time she put up no fuss. Her eyes were half open but so cloudy Copper wasn't sure she could see. Copper found herself singing lullabies and making soothing motherly sounds as she rubbed Remy's arms and one good leg with the soapy flannel cloth. Her heart might be broken, but still she was glad to have Remy back. "Once you were lost," she said as Remy blinked back to sleep, "but now you are found."

Finished, Copper took the bathwater outside and scoured the porch with it. She shouldn't be doing such tasks on Sunday morning, but she couldn't stand still. If she didn't stay busy, she'd unravel like a poorly knit sweater. From down the creek, she heard someone working. It sounded like a sledgehammer meeting rock. She knew it was John. It appeared she wasn't the only one with an ox in the ditch this morning. *Lord, forgive us.*

Back in the kitchen, Copper busied herself making broth for Remy. Once the chicken was stewed and the broth strained, she took it to the bedside. Slipping one arm behind Remy, she lifted her head and shoulders. Remy didn't open her mouth.

"Please try a bit of soup," Copper said. "You have to have some nourishment or else you'll never heal."

Like a baby bird Remy opened wide. Copper dribbled broth with a dropper and Remy swallowed.

Copper was overjoyed. "That's so good. Just a little more."

After no more than a couple of tablespoons, Remy turned her face away.

"All right." Copper held an invalid straw to Remy's mouth. "Just one sip of water and I'll leave you be."

Remy gripped Copper's wrist with surprising strength. "I'm sorry, Purty," she gasped. "I ruint your special day."

"Oh, my friend, don't you know how glad I am to have you here?"

Remy didn't answer. She seemed too puny to try.

"Do you remember the Scripture we shared, Remy? the one I said was just for us? Let me find my Bible, and I'll read it to you."

The Bible was in the kitchen on the washstand, tied round

with a green silk ribbon to match her wedding dress. She'd left it there yesterday so she wouldn't forget to take it to the church. With trembling hands she discarded the ribbon and carried her Bible to the bedroom.

Pulling a chair near the bed, Copper sat and thumbed the gilt-edged pages. "I know it's in Proverbs. You'll remember when you hear it." Leaning forward, she smoothed Remy's tangled hair from her forehead. "Are you awake?"

Remy nodded. "Read it to me," she whispered.

"Let's see. Proverbs 17:17: 'A friend loveth at all times.' No that's not the one. . . . Oh, here it is. Chapter 18, verse 24: 'A man that hath friends must shew himself friendly: and there is a friend that sticketh closer than a brother.' Remember that day by the creek—it seems so long ago now—when we declared we would always be sisters?"

Remy lay as still as death, her eyes closed, her blue-rimmed lips the only color to her face.

Copper put two fingers to the side of Remy's throat, searching for a heartbeat. Nothing, then a tiny flutter. "Remy, please don't leave me!"

"Can ye hear the falls, Purty? see the angel wings in the water spray?" Remy's voice was soft and sweet, childlike.

Copper had closed the window to the sickroom, but from the corner of her eye she fancied she saw the curtains stir. Dread raked icy fingers up her spine. Why had she sent everyone to the wedding? Why had she stayed home alone? She clutched her Bible to her chest. "Oh, Lord," she pleaded prayerfully. "Please. Please. Please."

On down Troublesome, John was doing the only thing he knew to do. Each whack with sledgehammer on rock caused a grunt of satisfaction. Each slam of pickax to rock crevice lessened his anger. And who was he mad at exactly? Copper for standing firm on her convictions? Or that poor wretch, Remy Riddle, who deserved life every bit as much as he deserved his one true love? Or maybe God? It seemed too close to blasphemy for him to toy with that. Guess he'd have to be mad at himself.

"Fool!" he cursed every time he swung. "How could I have been so stupid?"

The mule hitched to the sled cowered in its harness. Faithful dropped her ears and tucked her tail. His anger had such power that he was surprised the creek didn't run backward. Sweat ran down his back and dripped off his forehead. His daddy always said hard work never killed anyone. *Too bad*, he thought.

John stopped and wiped his face on his shirtsleeve, then took a long draft of water from the Mason jar. Pouring a little in his cupped palm, he offered it to Faithful. She lapped a drop or two as if afraid to deny him. He sat down on the creek bank and settled back on his elbows. "Sorry, girl."

"*Woof.*" He knew Faithful meant, "You're not the only one with problems."

He slid her silky ears through his fingers. "You're right as usual. Let's get this rock hauled to the new house. If we get enough, I can start on the chimney."

⚜

"Remy! Remy!" Copper shook Remy's shoulders until her eyes rolled back and forth like marbles. Everything Copper knew about medicine fled her brain. She was powerless in the face of death. Jumping up, she ran to the kitchen door. Surely there was someone about. *Help me, Lord*, she prayed. *I can't do this alone.*

She could just make out John's old mule harnessed to a sled, poking along across the creek. "John!" she screamed, running pell-mell across the yard, waving her arms like a crazy woman.

He looked her way, and then he was running too. As soon as she knew he saw, she sprinted back to the house.

He caught up with her in the kitchen. "What?"

Copper clutched the front of his blue work shirt in both hands. "Remy. Help her."

She could tell by his eyes when he saw Remy that he didn't hold any hope. "Maybe she choked. Let's turn her on her side."

"But she was talking. . . . I don't think . . ."

"Won't hurt to try."

John held the splinted limb steady, while Copper slid one arm under Remy's shoulders and one under her hips. Gingerly, they moved her.

Remy coughed and moaned. Mucus streaked with rust-colored blood spilled from her mouth.

Once again, Copper sought the beat of Remy's heart. Weak and thready, it tapped against her fingertips. Fumbling for the stethoscope she'd left on the bed, Copper stuck the tips in her ears and listened to Remy's lungs. "Full. Sounds like pneumonia."

She shook her head. "I shouldn't have let her lay flat so long. I know better."

John's face was as white as Remy's. "I thought she was gone for sure."

"Just a minute." Copper ran through the house grabbing every pillow she could find. She packed them all around Remy, fixing her position. "She'll have to be turned every two hours regardless of what it does to her leg." She looked at her patient and sighed. "I focused on one thing and nearly let her die of another."

"What do we do now?" he asked.

"I need a minute to study up on pneumonia. My brain's so foggy I can't think straight."

Suddenly, her knees buckled. If John hadn't caught her, she would have collapsed.

"When did you last eat?"

"I don't rightly remember," Copper said, leaning against him. "Yesterday noon, I think."

He helped her to the chair by the bedside. "Don't move. I'll go fix you something."

"But Remy . . ."

"You ain't no good to Remy if you're passed out on the floor," John said, a stern note to his voice. "You can rest and still watch her." He took a pillow that had fallen to the floor and tucked it behind Copper's shoulders, then lifted her feet and rested them on the side of the bed. "There, now. I'll just be in the next room."

"Would you please bring me *Dr. Chase's Medical Receipt Book* from the top of the bookcase first? I'll study while I sit."

The saucer of chicken and biscuit he brought her was the

best thing she'd ever tasted. And the strong, sweet tea restored her strength. "Thank you," she said when she finished. "I don't know what I would have done if you hadn't been across the creek, John."

"You'd have figured something out." He glanced at Remy. "She sure looks pitiful."

"She's breathing much better, though." Copper handed him her plate and picked up her book. "Dr. Chase has many remedies in here. I've got to settle on what I want to try with Remy."

"I'm going to get the mule out of his harness," John said, "but I won't go far."

CHAPTER 30

It was a sad day when Mam and Daddy went home. They'd stayed a week past their original plans, yet Copper wasn't ready to see them go. On the morning of their leave-taking, she put on a brave face and hid her tears behind a smile. Trunks and hatboxes piled up on the porch before being transferred to the hired carriage that would take them to the nearest train station.

Mam and Lilly were in tears. "Don't go, Granny." Lilly wrapped her arms around Mam's knees. "Don't leave Lilly Gray."

Daddy and the boys were waiting in the carriage. Copper knew Daddy couldn't stand to see Lilly's tears. Mam cast a pleading look Copper's way, so she extricated Lilly and gave her stepmother one last buss on the cheek.

"Come back soon," Copper called as the buggy bumped across the rutted barnyard.

Lilly bawled and drummed her feet against Copper's legs. For once, she was thankful for Lilly's tantrum. It hid her own sorrow and fear.

"Let me take her," Alice said. "Lilly Gray," she soothed as Copper gratefully handed her over, "let's take a walk with Dodie."

"Do you want to take a walk with Alice and the girls?" Copper asked Darcy through the screen door.

"I don't think so. I'm making pies for supper tonight. Do you think Mr. John might be coming? He dearly loves my apple pie."

Copper went in and picked up the paring knife. "Probably not, but then again he might since the newlyweds will be here." A perfect, unbroken peel of apple joined with Darcy's in a yellow-ware bowl. Two unbaked pie shells in fluted pie tins waited to be filled.

"If you're going to pare the apples," Darcy said, "then I'll make my lattice for the tops."

Copper peeled and sliced while Darcy dusted the rolling pin with flour. "You make that look so easy," Copper said as Darcy cut strips of dough from two circles of pastry.

"Easy as pie," Darcy said and laughed. "Don't the house seem too quiet?"

"Sure does. I miss my folks already."

"I won't mind getting my bed back though." Darcy laced lattice strips across the top of one pie, then sealed the edge with a fork dipped in flour.

Copper had loved having the house jam-packed. Once

Dimmert and Cara were wed, they took over John's house, so Copper's folks stayed with her. Daddy and the boys slept on the short-legged bed in the loft, while Mam took one bed in Darcy's room. Alice had the other. Darcy and Dodie slept on pallets on the floor in front of the fireplace. Lilly had her crib, and Copper fashioned a bed of sorts from four straight-backed chairs pushed together. Remy, of course, had Copper's bed.

She didn't know where John slept. That wasn't hers to ask. She'd hardly seen him since the Sunday morning he helped her with Remy. He was keeping his distance and rightfully so.

Darcy slid the pies in the oven. "I'll save these scraps of dough for the girls to play with."

"Do you have time to help me with Remy?" Copper asked. "I need to bathe her and change the bed linens."

"I'll just wipe off the table first," Darcy said. "Then I'll be there."

Copper took a stack of sheets, pillowcases, and towels from the press and laid them at the foot of the bed. "Look, Remy. These pillow slips have daisies and bluebirds embroidered on them. Aren't they pretty?"

"Does she ever answer you?" Darcy said as she set a pan of water on the bedside table.

"She hasn't said the first word since that day she choked," Copper said. "But I know she hears me. It's important to talk to her."

"Then I'll tell her about baking pies." Darcy prattled on in a comforting way as they bathed and powdered Remy, braided her hair, and cleaned her teeth with the end of a washrag dipped in baking soda and salt.

"Funny she can swallow," Darcy said. "You'd think if she knows that, she'd know how to talk, poor thing."

Copper rolled Remy's body to one side of the bed while Darcy undid the sheets on the other side. "I miss the sound of her voice. Remy and I used to talk about everything."

Darcy rolled Remy her way as Copper removed the soiled linen from her side of the bed. "It will be fun to see Dimmert and Cara tonight."

"Yes, it will," Copper said, tucking the end of a sheet under the mattress. "I'm so happy for them."

Darcy held a pillow under her chin and slid a clean case over it. When the bed was finished, they propped Remy's head and shoulders up on her clean pillows. Copper held the invalid straw to Remy's mouth, and she took a sip. It reminded Copper of feeding an elderly patient of Simon's who had had a stroke. That woman remained bedfast the rest of her days.

"I'm going to take a scrub board to these bedsheets, Miz Copper. Else we'll never get done washing come Monday."

Alice wanted to set the table with Copper's good china and silver. She insisted on ironed linens, so Copper spent the afternoon heating the sadiron and pressing a tablecloth and nearly a dozen napkins. *The table looks pretty*, Copper thought as she laid the last napkin in place. And it was a nice way to honor the newlyweds, plus the Fosters were coming and bringing Hezzy with them.

Copper hoped she didn't fall asleep over her supper plate. What with the cooking, the ironing, seeing to Remy, and keeping Lilly Gray out of trouble, she was exhausted. She took a clean dress from the chiffonier, then sat at her dressing table to arrange her hair. All the while she could see Remy's reflection in the mirror. Pulling a brush through her tangled red locks, she pondered Remy's situation. Copper longed for just one word from her friend, just a sign that she was doing the right thing for Remy.

Mam would say, "'A wicked and adulterous generation seeketh after a sign.'" Mam knew her Bible. She would also say "Where there is life there is hope." Though that wasn't from the Bible, it was true. Look how good Daddy was doing. He'd been very ill when they moved to Philadelphia, and now he was much better. Of course he'd had to give up his pipe, and he couldn't work in the mines anymore. He said it was a small price to pay.

Copper laid the brush aside, then buried her face in her hands. *Give me strength for the journey, Lord*, she prayed. Seeing her own pale face in the mirror, she pinched her cheeks until they were rosy. "Oh, Remy, I don't know who looks worse, you or me."

"I brought some daffodils for the sickroom," Alice said, interrupting Copper's reverie. Marching in, she put the pretty yellow blooms in a china vase.

Copper pulled a flower from the bunch and held it to Remy's nose. "Doesn't this smell good? Don't daffodils make you think of spring?"

Remy twitched her nose, but she didn't open her eyes or utter a word.

"There's only one thing to do, Laura Grace," Alice said.

Copper put the flower on Remy's pillow, next to her nose. "About what?"

Alice swept her arms wide. "This situation of course."

"Let's talk on the porch. We should have a few minutes before everyone gets here."

They settled side by side in the rocking chairs. Copper folded her hands in her lap and waited, sure she wouldn't like what was coming.

"I'm not one to interfere. . . ."

Had those words really come from Alice's mouth? *Just listen*, Copper thought. *Listen and don't judge.*

"But it's obvious this is too much for you," Alice continued. "I propose to take Lilly Gray home with me for a few weeks to help you out."

Copper clinched her lips. Is this why Alice came after all? Not to see Copper happily wed but to find a reason to take her daughter away from her? Anger as hot as pepper burned her innards. "Thank you for your concern." She minded her words. "But that can never be. Lilly Gray belongs with her mother."

"Now don't get miffed. I'm only trying to help. Surely you will admit you have too much on your plate to care for Lilly properly."

"Alice, this is really none of your business." There, she'd done it—said what she'd wanted to say since the first day she'd met Alice Upchurch.

"Ah, but you're wrong, my dear," Alice said. "Lilly Gray is very much my business."

Copper sighed. How could you argue with a woman who was never wrong? "I'm sorry. Of course she is, and I'm thankful for that, but she won't be going home with you."

"Then tell me how you will do all this alone: the garden, the animals, this inconvenient house . . . not to mention all these people you collect. . . ." Alice fixed her with a familiar steely glare. "How do you propose to do all this and take proper care of my niece?"

For a moment Copper didn't know what to say. How was she going to cope? She was so weary she had to fight the tears that threatened. The last thing she needed was to show Alice her weakness.

Then there they were: her answers. As if on command, the Fosters' buggy drew up. Hezzy Krill leaned out the open window, and Dimmert and Cara walked around the side of the barn.

"I'll have plenty of help, Alice. All I need to do is ask."

Copper's chair moved in cadence with her aggravation, while Alice sat primly, her back never touching the chair. "Consider what I have offered at least," Alice said. "You must admit Lilly Gray has been getting short shrift."

Copper took a deep breath. What she needed to consider was how good Alice had been to her. She patted Alice's hand. "Thank you for caring so much. Now, if you'll go pour the tea, I'll greet our guests."

Hezzy mumbled and grumbled all the time Elder Foster worked to extricate her from the buggy.

"Do you need some help?" Copper asked.

"What I need is two good legs," Hezzy replied before Elder Foster could get a word out.

Jean Foster rolled her eyes and pointed out a dilapidated carpetbag sitting on the ground by her husband's feet. "I'm sorry," she mouthed to Copper.

Sweat broke out on Elder Foster's forehead. He handed his hat to Jean, then went around to the other side of the buggy. "Dimmert," he said as the young couple approached, "lend a hand."

Soon Elder Foster was behind Hezzy on the buggy seat while Dimmert stood in front of her. "Now, Dimmert," Elder Foster said, "you pull and I'll push."

Hezzy popped from the buggy like a piece of corn from a hot pan. If Cara hadn't been steadying Dimmert from behind, he would have fallen under the weight of Hezzy.

"She's doing poorly," Jean whispered in Copper's ear. "We like to have never got her in the buggy."

Dimmert and Cara assisted Hezzy as she limped across the yard. "Thank ye for your help," Hezzy said.

Copper linked arms with Jean and followed them. "Please don't tell me that carpetbag means she's staying."

"I am so sorry. She had her bag packed and sitting on the porch when we drove up." Jean squeezed Copper's arm. "Truly, I tried to dissuade her."

"But why?" Copper asked.

"She feels so guilty over the accident she wants to help you; I guess she wants to salve her conscience." Jean shook her head. "We've been sending our eldest over to check on her every morning; she needs the help and Dylan needs the discipline. He says Hezzy sends him up to the hollow log to put out eggs to feed that fox. Sure is strange."

Copper stopped their walk and leaned her head against Jean's. "I wouldn't admit this to anyone but you, but I don't know if I can take care of one more burdened soul."

"My husband told Hezzy he would be back to pick her up next week, Copper. Can you hold up that long?"

"I reckon so," Copper said, "but I'll need lots of prayer."

"Every day," Jean replied. "I pray for you every day."

CHAPTER 31

Yesterday's sunshine was gone. Dreary, drizzling rain tapped its dance on the tin roof, making Copper shiver despite the cup of tea she held. As she stood at the kitchen window, she watched a hapless chicken skirt a puddle while dashing toward the barn. It looked like Penny, though from this distance she couldn't be sure. Darcy had dubbed her Smoked Penny after they saved her from the gapes. She should go out and shoo her back to the chicken coop, but she didn't have the heart.

Behind her, Lilly Gray whined over her oatmeal. She heard Darcy scrape the last of the brown sugar from the bowl and knew it was going on Lilly's breakfast cereal. She should go to the pantry and refill the bowl from the brown paper sack tied up with string. But the sugar was sure to be as hard as a rock. She'd have to chip it with a hammer and soften it in the oven.

Last evening, her kitchen had been full of light and laughter. Even Alice joined in the fun, surprising Copper as much as seeing John's head bent toward Alice's on the porch after supper. Copper had peeked through the same window that was now streaked with rain, wishing she could hear why Alice looked so determined and why John looked so hopeful. Alice and Dodie had left for Lexington before daybreak. John had picked them up. How could Copper miss someone who irritated her as much as Alice did? But she did.

John had come into the kitchen this morning. She hadn't expected him to. She thought he would wait in the carriage. But in he came as if he were home, catching her in her nightdress, her hair in a long braid down the middle of her back. "Hey, Pocahontas," he'd teased as though it was any other day.

She needed to think about John, needed to come to terms with him acting like they were just friends again. Maybe that worked for him, but seeing him still made her catch her breath. And her foolish heart still did a double beat; it didn't realize he was no longer hers. Later. She'd think about that later.

Taking Lilly from her high chair, Copper took off her daughter's bib and cleaned the oatmeal from her face.

"Me tired," Lilly said.

"Why, Miss Lilly Gray, what makes you so tired?"

Lilly tucked her head in the nook of Copper's shoulder. "Want Dodie. Want Granny."

Copper could feel her baby's soft breath tickling her neck. "Oh, that's not tired. That's lonesome."

"Fix it, Mama."

Copper wrenched the door open—damp weather always made it stick—and carried Lilly out. "See the rain?"

"Yup."

"Do you know what comes after the rain, Lilly Gray?"

"Mud puddles."

"Yes, mud puddles and sunshine. Lonesome feels like rain," Copper said, "but then God sends sunshine to cheer us up."

"Yup. Rock me."

Copper dragged a rocking chair as far under the porch's tin roof as she could. "Sit here, baby. Mama will be right back." She hurried to the bedroom to fetch a quilt. Hezzy snored softly in the chair by Remy's bed. Remy looked peaceful. Back on the porch, Copper wrapped herself and Lilly in a warm cocoon and commenced rocking.

Soon Lilly slept, but Copper rocked on. The rainy day felt different from when she'd watched it through the window. She laughed when the fat hen chanced the barnyard again only to flee back to the barn. "Silly thing," she said as it shook the damp from its feathers, as if it was surprised that rain made feathers wet. "You should never have left the chicken coop; that's where your friends are."

I'm like that, she thought, *running around like a chicken with its head cut off, when all along my friends are waiting to help me, to keep me dry during the rain.* She rested her head on the back of the chair and closed her eyes. The faces of Fairy Mae, Dance Shelton, and Miranda Wilson flitted across her eyelids. *While Hezzy is here to care for Remy, I'll go check on them. Maybe that will get me over the doldrums.*

Who would have thought Hezzy Krill would be a blessing in her life? *A little rain, a little sunshine*, Copper thought before she nodded off.

Copper was making a fresh mustard plaster for Remy when Dimmert brought John's mule the next morning. He tapped on the door to announce his presence.

"Come on in, Dimmert," she called out. "I can't leave this poultice."

Dimmert merely opened the screen door and stuck his head in. "Ride's here."

Copper stirred equal parts of linseed meal and dry mustard into a bowl of boiling water. "Just hitch him to the rail, please. Will Cara be over later?"

"Later," Dimmert replied, already backing off the porch.

Copper was happy to see his clean overalls and ironed work shirt. It looked like Cara was taking good care of him.

After spreading the poultice on brown paper, Copper hurried to Remy's side. Hezzy had her ready for the treatment. "This seems to be helping," Copper said. "Her lungs were clearer this morning."

"I've seen bread poultice work." Hezzy helped Copper cover the paper vest with muslin. "Although it don't hold heat as good as mustard."

"Hmm. I've never heard of that."

"Years ago you couldn't hardly get linseed meal. My mammy always stirred stale bread crumbs in water, then set it to heat in the fireplace. You have to pour the water off a couple of times before it's ready to spread," Hezzy said around a chaw of cured tobacco. "Works good on children and ain't as likely to blister."

Copper peeled back a corner of the paper vest. The skin of Remy's chest was nicely pink. "Don't you think she's better?"

"Her eyes were bright this morning," Hezzy said. "I think she knew somebody different was feeding her. Scared her right back to sleep. Probably thought I was going to shoot her again."

"Now, Hezzy," Copper said, "nobody blames you. It was an accident."

Hezzy spit a stream of pungent tobacco juice into an old tin can. "Don't matter," she said, wiping her chin on a well-used man's handkerchief. "I blame myself."

Sitting on the edge of Remy's freshly made bed, Copper put her hand on Hezzy's knee. "Have you prayed about this? God will give you the forgiveness you need."

Hezzy's old rheumy eyes met Copper's. "I reckon I've got to do some works afore I petition the good Lord for anything. I got to show I'm purely sorry for what I done."

"Well, you're a big help to me, Hezzy Krill. I'm sure glad you were willing to extend your visit." Copper peeked under the vest again. "This is cool now. Let's take it off."

"Mama!" Lilly's excited voice could be heard from the kitchen. "Cow in the house!"

"You go on," Hezzy said. "I'll take care of this."

"How in the world!" Copper exclaimed before she burst into laughter. It wasn't really funny–Dimm would have to repair the screen—but John's old mule had poked his whole long head through the screen door.

Lilly jumped around, squealing with delight, while Darcy ineffectively flapped her apron in the direction of the door, saying, "Shoo. Shoo."

"Maybe he wants a cup of coffee," Copper said between gasps. She laughed so hard her sides ached. "Come on, Mule Head." She pushed on its forehead to extricate the animal from the screen and led him down the steps. After tightening the reins around the porch railing, she patted the mule's rump. "Stay out of trouble."

It was pleasant to be riding the mule up the mountain to Ace Shelton's place. Mule Head went at his own slow pace. Copper didn't mind; she didn't want to rush. For the first time in weeks she had time to gather her thoughts. She'd toyed with the idea of bringing Lilly along but thought better of it. Dance's mood was unpredictable like a toss of dice, not a good thing for Lilly to witness.

Ace and Dance had taken baby Jay home with them after the party at her house. She'd pondered whether to invite them, but how could she ask everyone else and leave them out? Besides, she wanted to win Dance over—she wanted Dance to know she had an ally. Sometimes women resisted going to their family when they were troubled. False pride, Copper reckoned.

Ace's cabin was tricky to find, but Copper thought she remembered the way. Mule Head picked his way along until he grew stubborn and stopped. Copper rocked on the mule's bony back and kicked his sides, but he wouldn't budge. She dismounted and sweet-talked him for a while. Finally, with a great bray, he gave in and allowed her to pull him along.

She'd made a misstep somewhere. Instead of the weed-choked path she remembered, she was in a shadowy cathedral of soaring spruce and fir trees. Here and there soft beams of sunlight spotlighted the mossy forest floor. Resurrection and maidenhair fern leaflets waved delicately as she brushed past. Birdcalls and squirrels' chatter seemed far off, muffled. The hush was intense, reverential. Goose bumps raised on Copper's arms. *Lord,* she prayed, *I feel Your presence. I praise Your name for the beauty of this place.*

Her innate sense of direction guided them along. Daddy always said she was born with a compass in her brain. She was never really lost.

She led the mule out of the forest right behind Ace's barn. Dance was in the garden hoeing weeds. "Hello," Copper called.

Startled, Dance dropped her hoe and raised her hand to shade her eyes.

"Mind if I visit for a spell?" Copper asked.

Dance tucked a strand of wispy brown hair behind her ear and smoothed her skirts with her palms. "Reckon not."

Copper stepped forward to meet her. "Your garden's looking good."

"Taters," Dance said, pointing, "maters, beans, squash."

"I brought you something from my garden." Copper fetched two packets made of newsprint from her linen sack. The unfolded envelopes revealed marigold and zinnia seed. "Flower seed. Want me to help you plant them?"

Dance stepped on the business end of her discarded hoe. The handle slapped against her waiting palm. "Here," she said, marking a shallow row with the pointed edge of the tool.

Copper knelt. "Zinnias or marigolds?"

Dance looked around as if she was waiting for someone to make the decision for her. Copper waited. Dance scraped the row a little deeper. "Here," she repeated.

"All right. Let's plant the zinnia seeds first. Then maybe you'd like a row of marigolds in front."

Dance settled on her knees. Copper sprinkled the tiny seeds while Dance covered them with a fine layer of soil. At the end of the row, Copper upended the packet and let the last of the zinnias fall willy-nilly.

Dance reached for the folded paper square. Carefully she picked each tiny seed from the soil and put them back in the envelope, then stuck it in her skirt pocket. "Keep some for the porch," she said.

Properly chastised, Copper repented of her wastefulness. Just because she had plenty didn't mean Dance did. "Good idea. We'll put aside some of the marigold too."

All the while they worked, Copper listened for a cry. Dance's baby must be sleeping. When the rows were finished, she walked with Dance to the house. There was neither welcoming chair nor humble bench on the Sheltons' front porch. A straw broom worn down to a nub and a wasp's nest in the corner of the window were the only decorations.

Dance handed Copper a dipper of water. It was stale but served the purpose of slaking her thirst. After pouring water into the washbasin, Dance stood back indicating for her guest to go first. The cool water felt good as Copper scrubbed her hands before drying them on a rough feed-sack towel.

Dance knit her fingers together under the water, twisting them like a wet dishrag, over and over. A red wasp circled over their heads. Finished, Dance turned and with swift motion hurled the water from the basin toward the window. "Hate them things," she said. The water-soaked wasp nest hung from a tiny stem, limp as crepe paper. The wasp buzzed off, his day's work ruined.

Taking her time, Dance put the basin back on the wash shelf. She moved it a fraction of an inch in all directions before settling on the spot that pleased. The lye soap she put in the exact center of the granite dish that hung from a nail on a sturdy post. Seemingly satisfied, she left Copper standing and disappeared around the side of the cabin.

Dance doing what Dance does best, Copper mused, *walking away–disappearing, giving little thought to others.*

CHAPTER 32

Copper leaned against the Sheltons' porch rail and waited. If the baby cried, should she go get him? Seemed like Jay had been sleeping long enough. Besides, she was anxious to check him over. She remembered the wise counsel of her stepmother whenever Copper fretted like this: "It's not your kitchen, Daughter," she'd say. In other words, "Don't stick your nose where it doesn't belong."

At last Dance came back, carrying several empty tins. Walking past Copper, she headed back to the garden, where she filled the tins with dirt. Back on the porch, she put the tins beside the washbasin.

Copper helped her plant the rest of the seed in the cans and water them from the dipper. "These will be pretty when the flowers bloom."

As if the cans were the finest of cut glass, Dance arranged and rearranged them on the porch. First she set them on the windowsills. Unsatisfied, she moved them to the side of the door, then walked out in the yard, where she studied the placement. Finally, she put one on each wooden porch step.

"They'll catch the morning sun here," Copper said.

"Thank ye for the seed," Dance said, giving Copper a smidgen of satisfaction.

Copper wiped the sweat from her brow with the tail of her apron. "The day's sure heating up. I'll bet it's nice and cool inside."

With a show of reluctance, Dance opened the door. Copper stepped in ahead of her. The cabin was clean and quiet. The table was set for two, and on the stove something savory simmered. Ace must be coming in for his noon meal.

Copper bit her tongue, trying not to meddle, but she couldn't stop herself. "Is the baby sleeping?"

Dance pulled out a chair. It scraped against the floor, shattering the silence. She pulled out another.

Copper sat. "Dance?"

"Don't judge me," Dance said.

Her words took Copper aback. There was a big difference between honest observation and condemnation, and she often noted that the guiltiest are the first to decry judgment. It was as if they preferred to remain lost, unchallenged in their misdeeds, as if by doing so they could hide from God Himself. Dance had taken offense, and Copper needed to proceed carefully if she was to win Dance's trust.

"I'd like to be your friend, if you'll let me," Copper said. "I don't mean to seem judgmental."

Dance got up to stir the pot on the stove, her back to Copper. "I like my life the way it is. Me and Ace have worked things out."

Well, now, she can converse when she wants to, Copper thought. *But I'm in a fix. I've been dismissed, and I haven't seen the baby yet. What is Dance trying to hide?* "That's well and good, Dance, but I still want to know how the baby is."

"Ace will be home soon. You don't want to be here when he comes in."

Copper squared her shoulders. She could get her back up too. If Dance thought she was leaving without seeing little Jay, then she had another think coming. "You might as well set another plate on the table, because I'm staying."

Dance slapped a plate (good thing it was tin and not china) and a fork in front of Copper. "You're sticky as a burr and just as aggravating."

Copper laughed, her anger gone. "You're right about that. My problem is I care about you."

"Why?"

"We're sisters in Christ. I'm convicted to love you and help you in any way I can."

Dance hung her head. "What's my job?" she whispered.

"Your job is to let me."

"What if I don't want your help or need it?"

"I can respect that, but there are times in everyone's life when we need each other. God didn't mean for you to be so alone."

Dance twirled her tin plate. It danced like a top across the table, then fell with a jarring clatter. "That's how I feel when there's too much going on. My nerves get all jangled."

"Do I make you feel that way?" Copper asked.

For the first time Dance looked at Copper straight on. She had beautiful eyes, light brown with specks of gold, framed by finely arched eyebrows. Her mouth was a Cupid's bow naturally tinted pink. Copper thought it sad that Dance didn't seem to know how pretty she was.

"Not so much," Dance replied. "Your voice puts me in mind of rain falling on the roof, kind of makes me sleepy."

A commotion on the porch made them turn in unison; Ace ambled in. "Well, lookee here," he said, not bothering to remove his hat. "Trouble herself sitting at my dinner table."

"How are you, Ace?" Copper asked.

"Dry as a lizard on a log," he said as he plopped down. "Woman, pour me some buttermilk and take this young'un."

Dance took a pitcher from the milk cupboard and poured three glasses. "You want to keep him 'til I dish up the stew?" she asked Ace.

"May I?" Copper said, eyeing the child in the sling across Ace's chest. As soon as she stood to take him, baby Jay set to kicking and laughing. His little legs reminded Copper of a fat stewing hen's, and she had to stop herself from planting kisses on his dimpled knees. When he smiled, his eyes disappeared in crinkles. "My word," she said when he was released into her arms, "what are you feeding this bruiser?"

Ace tipped his chair, balancing on its back legs, considering her from under his hat. He reminded Copper of the banty that greeted her every morning, always trying to best the bigger barn-yard rooster, trying to be bigger than he was.

"What don't he eat? That's the question, right, Mommy?" Ace put a piece of potato and some peas from his plate on a saucer for Jay and moved it in front of the baby. "Ye got to let that cool," he instructed Copper.

She laughed as the baby smacked his mouth and strained toward the saucer. With a spoon she mashed a bit of the food, then blew on it. "Here, baby."

"He likes it better if ye call his name," Ace said. "Ain't that right, Jay?"

Dance didn't light long enough to eat a bite. She jumped up for salt, then for clean rags to use as napkins. She poured more milk and left the kitchen to go to the well for water.

"What are you here for?" Ace asked as soon as Dance left. "It will kill her if ye take this baby away."

"Why would I do that?" Copper scraped up bits of food with a teaspoon. Jay looked like a baby robin opening its mouth for a worm. "Obviously he's thriving."

Ace chucked his son under his double chin. The baby fell back against Copper, laughing.

"He is, ain't he?" Pride shone from Ace's coal black eyes. He took off his hat and hung it on his chair. "He goes to work with me near every morning; then after dinner I put him in his cot and he sleeps the afternoon away. Spares Dance some worry."

Copper stuck her finger in her glass of buttermilk and let the baby suck it off. "What causes her to fret so much?"

"Huh!" Ace grunted like surely Copper had the answer to her own question. "She's got a nervous disposition, and she's afraid people like you will say she's a bad mother."

Copper's face colored. Hadn't she come here to check up on Dance and Ace? Hadn't she been afraid for the baby's well-being? Wasn't that a judgment of sorts? "Well, people like me would be wrong."

"See, the thing is, Dance don't know that. Her own mommy sent her away to live with her mammaw when she was just a bitty girl. Good as Fairy Mae was to her, I reckon Dance never got over losing her mommy." Ace slapped his knees. The baby startled; he'd been nodding off in Copper's arms. "I see to my son and I see to my wife. Cain't nobody fault me."

His words gave Copper pause. Both she and Dance had lost their mothers at a young age. Copper's to death and Dance's to circumstance. In that way they were alike, but why had they turned out so differently? Neither Mam nor Fairy Mae could be faulted for the nurturing they provided, so it wasn't that, and they both knew the Lord. So what was it?

Copper could see Dance through the open door. She stood at the wash shelf pouring water over her hands.

"That's one of her habits," Ace said. "Keeps her calm."

Jay grew heavy with sleep. His little head lolled against Copper's shoulder. "Do you want me to put him in his cot?" she asked.

"Nah," Ace said, taking his son. "I've got to change him first. Finish your dinner." Baby in arms, he went to the door. "Dance, come on in here and sit a spell with your company."

What a good father Ace is turning out to be, Copper mused as she watched him care for the baby. *Who would have guessed it? Of course, that's the answer. I had a daddy who loved me like Ace loves Jay, but Dance did not.* Even now, Copper knew, none of the Whitts saw much of their father.

By the time Ace had the baby settled, Copper and Dance were through with their meals. Ace sat back down, draining his glass of buttermilk.

"Do you have time for a story?" Copper asked.

Ace laced his fingers behind his head, his elbows sticking out like wings. "Work ain't going nowhere. It will wait, I warrant."

"It was March of 1866," Copper related. "I was two days old when a terrible flash flood swept my mother away."

She told them of men searching up and down Troublesome Creek and how her mother was found too late. "My daddy was left to care for me alone. He used to pack me around tucked inside his shirt as he walked the mountains searching for peace."

"I've heard of that flood," Ace said. "My own pa was part of the group of men that looked for Julie Brown. Folks still speak of it, but I never realized you was that young'un."

Copper blotted her cheeks. She was never able to tell the story without tears. "When you came in with Jay in that sling, Ace, it put me in mind of my father and the tender care he took of me."

Dance hid her face behind the skirt of her apron. Her shoulders shook.

"I didn't mean to upset you," Copper told Dance. "I just wanted you to know I understand there is more than one way to raise a baby. I think you and Ace are doing very well."

"I ain't upset for me," Dance said from behind the apron. "It just makes me lonesomelike for you, losing your mommy that away."

Copper made her way home the lost way, back through the forest cathedral. She'd never have guessed there were so many shades of green: tops of evergreen trees black-green in shadow; bright green spongy mosses; yellow-green and gray-green trembling fern fronds; and brownish green pine needles as soft as carpet underfoot. They all blended together to paint a picture as pretty as a song. *Majesty*, she thought. *God's majesty bestowed on man.*

The time away was good for her. She dearly needed some wandering time to remember who she was—it was so easy to get lost in the demands of her busy days. "'He leadeth me beside the still waters,'" she said as Mule Head headed for home. "'He restoreth my soul.'" But now she was anxious to get home. It felt as if she'd been gone for days.

CHAPTER 33

Hezzy was catching a breeze when Copper got back from the Sheltons'. She sat on the porch stirring the air with a paper fan. "You caught me loafing," she said as Copper approached. "Them girls won't hardly let me do nothing."

"Good for them," Copper replied, dipping a cup of water. "Want some?"

"I've got me a cup," Hezzy said, holding it up. "Like I said, them girls is taking care of me."

"How is Remy this afternoon?"

"I'm not happy with what I'm seeing around her wound," Hezzy said, "and she spiked a fever about an hour ago. The girls give her an alcohol rub."

Hezzy accompanied Copper to the bedroom. When Cara drew back Remy's light cotton covering, Copper was surprised to see not much more than a pile of bones held together by tightly stretched skin the bluish color of skimmed milk. She looked like a baby bird fallen from the nest before its time. It took Copper's breath away. She had grown used to Remy's condition, but her brief respite revealed a truth she didn't want to acknowledge: Remy was slipping away.

"Take a gander." Hezzy pointed to Remy's thigh.

Copper gently removed the lint bandage. Sprinkles of charcoal powder clung to the lint. All this time the deep laceration had seemed to be healing. She knew from Simon's tutelage to permit it to heal from the inside out and so had packed it with sterile gauze, pulling a small amount out with boiled tweezers each day. But as she bent close, a putrid smell filled her nostrils, and the drainage had changed from watery to thick. The edges of the contusion weren't pink anymore but an awful, angry red with dark edges.

"It's setting up to mortify," Hezzy said.

Copper stepped back, her hand to her chin. "I pray not. If it gangrenes, we'll have to find a surgeon. This is not within my ability."

"She wouldn't survive having her leg cut off," Hezzy said. "They ain't enough of her left to put up a fight."

Remy flinched.

Everyone stared. "Did you see that?" Darcy asked.

Copper put a hand on either side of Remy's body and leaned over. "Remy, I won't let that happen. You hear me? I am going to fight for you. We all will fight this battle for you—Hezzy, Darcy, Cara, and me. We won't give up!"

Remy's emaciated hand crept across the bed and covered Copper's. One finger tapped against hers, a blessed message of hope. It was enough to set all the women in the room to crying. Lilly woke from her nap and joined the cacophony with loud wails of her own.

Darcy lifted Lilly from her bed and hugged her close. "These is happy tears, Miss Lilly Gray. We're happy because Remy's awake."

"Mama's dolly waked up?" Lilly asked.

Copper could hardly believe her ears. Mama's dolly? From the mouths of babes . . .

Lilly wriggled free of Darcy. She tugged on Copper's skirt. "Rock me."

A thousand needs tugged at Copper: Remy, supper, milking—had she fed the chickens today? But there was her baby, clinging to her dress, reminding Copper who came first. "Baby girl," she said, swinging Lilly up, "you're exactly what Mama needs. Let's go find the rocker."

"I'll sit with Remy," Hezzy said, "and I'll be careful of my words."

"Think I'll fry up some chicken and make a cobbler for supper," Darcy said. "We need a celebration."

"I'm staying," Cara replied. "Dimmert will find me easy enough. I'll go milk Mazy."

All Copper had to do was sit on the porch with Lilly and ponder what just happened. Truthfully, she hadn't thought she would ever see this day. She supposed Remy would lie up in bed like a baby for the rest of her earthly time, or worse yet like a dolly, a body without a brain. Mam always said there are things worse than death, and Copper knew it to be so. Still, like a mother clings to her stillborn baby, loving that shell of broken promise, Copper clung to her remembrance of her friend Remy. She wouldn't let her go. She couldn't let her go. But now, with just the tap of a finger, joy pierced her heart and soared higher and higher—to the very heavens.

Just as Mam always said, "Where there is life there is hope." Copper knew God was blessing her quest to save Remy. Now she had to figure out how to save Remy's leg. She'd tried every remedy she could think of—good ones from Simon's medical texts and old-timey ones she'd known herself: dusting the wound with burnt flour, feeding Remy onion juice with a medicine dropper to purify her blood. Neither seemed to be working.

She remembered a horrifying story her daddy told of the past war when soldiers' wounds were soldered with a hot poker. Copper shuddered. She could never bring herself to do that.

What she needed was an honest-to-goodness doctor, a man with a medical degree. Guilt, that old bugaboo, crept round her heart, threatening to strangle her with doubt. Well, it was too late now. In Remy's state she couldn't be carried off the mountain, and by the time they found a doctor willing to make a house call, her leg would gangrene for sure.

Copper prayed for God to send a way to bring Remy through the valley of death on her own two legs, a whole person. This might be too much for her, Copper Brown Corbett, but all things were possible with God. Copper claimed Matthew 7:7. *"Ask, and it shall be given you; seek, and ye shall find;*

knock, and it shall be opened unto you." Then she rocked her baby
and waited for supper.

John surveyed the new house. It was coming along nicely, and he
was rightly proud. He'd hired Ezra Whitt to work alongside him,
and Dimmert helped out when he wasn't busy tending Copper's
crops and animals. Those Whitt boys were worker bees. Ezra
helped John finish the chimney today.

At least with the one room done he had a place to sleep and
cook—or more likely open his canned beans. Mostly he took his
meals with Cara and Dimmert, though Cara was not the cook
Darcy was.

John slapped his hat against his thigh and whistled for
Faithful. They walked along in companionable silence. He was
settling, he knew, for breathing the same air as Copper. It was
not as he had wished, but it was all he had.

Maybe he should think on what Alice Upchurch had advised.
She'd surprised him right smart before she left for Lexington. He
couldn't remember her even speaking to him before, but on that
day she'd followed him across the yard. "A word," he remembered her saying in that haughty voice of hers. Well, he'd stopped
to listen. It wasn't as if a body could say no to Mrs. Upchurch.

But if he did what she counseled, he'd have to leave for
weeks, possibly months, with no assurance of success. He had
the funds, but it was a gamble at best. And John was not a gam-
bling man. No, he'd best stay put. At least this way he could
keep Copper safe and keep an eye on her. His biggest fear was

losing her in one way or another. Being friends was better than nothing. He was sure on that. Whoever heard tell of such a thing as annulment anyway?

Maybe he'd take supper at Copper's tonight. The thought lightened his mood. He whistled as he walked.

"Leeches," Hezzy'd said. "We need leeches."

So Copper was in the creek and it was nearly dark. Why hadn't Hezzy asked for leeches while it was still light out? She turned up the lantern, then set it and a Mason jar on the bank and commenced her search. She picked the nasty-looking creatures from the underside of rocks and dropped them into the jar. Yuck, she'd always hated the slimy things—hated the way they snuck up on you while you were swimming or wading and attached themselves to the tenderest skin. Water ticks, Daddy called them.

It was pleasant being in the creek at dusk—except for the leeches of course. When she and John were children, they used to sneak off and go swimming after dark. It was forbidden, but she did it anyway, chancing the sting of Mam's willow switch. That just made it all the more exciting.

Copper sighed. Seemed she couldn't keep her mind off John. He'd come by earlier and stayed for supper. Sitting right across the table from her, he talked crops with Dimmert, teased Darcy, and fed Lilly from his plate, as if life was as it had been. All the while, Copper hurt so bad she couldn't eat.

She waded out of the water and wiped her feet in the grass.

The leeches flipped this way and that in their creek-water bath. Copper wondered why they didn't suck each other's blood. Turning the lantern off, she headed home, finding her way easy enough in the dark.

The coal-oil lamp cast a golden glow over Remy's wound as Copper and Hezzy bent to their task. Copper pinched a leech from the jar.

"Find the head," Hezzy said.

Both ends looked the same to Copper. The vile thing squirmed between her forefinger and thumb.

Hezzy took it from her and wiped it with a soft cloth. "It's the smallest end." Holding the leech with the folded cloth, she placed it on Remy's wound, where it lay like a dead slug, paying no attention to the job at hand. "I need me some sweet milk."

Copper fetched a cup from the kitchen, then watched as Hezzy smeared the milk on Remy's wound. Once again, Hezzy directed the head to the festering sore. She did the same with two other parasites. Then she and Copper watched.

"Leeches work like buzzards," Hezzy said, "cleaning up."

The buzzard leeches siphoned blood. "Don't pull it off," Hezzy cautioned. "It'll fall off on its own when it's had its fill."

One by one the parasites detached, looking like overripe grapes against Remy's pale skin.

"These is good suckers," Hezzy said while she laid them on a saucer and sprinkled them with a little salt. The leeches disgorged Remy's blood. Red splotches stained the small white plate.

As if she did this every day, Hezzy washed the leeches and dropped them into a glass filled with fresh water. "These is keepers."

Copper bathed Remy's oozing wound and covered it with cotton wool. "What do we do now?"

"You go to bed and I'll keep watch. I'll catch me a nap after a while."

Copper straightened Remy's bedclothes and turned down the lamp wick. "I wish I hadn't let Lilly Gray go home with Cara."

"It was for the best," Hezzy said. "Ye didn't want the little thing to witness this."

"You're right. And Darcy's with her. She'll be fine, but I won't sleep a wink."

After prayers Copper crawled into Darcy's bed. Too tired to braid her hair, she fumbled with pins and combs and let it fall unfettered. She stretched her tired muscles, then plumped the bolster pillow under her head. Darcy must have just changed the pillow slip; it smelled of starch and lavender. This was the first time she'd slept in a bed since Remy got hurt. The curtains were open, and the window raised to catch the warm, early-summer breeze.

She turned on her side. "This feels so good," she said as Old Tom curled up in the crook of her knees. It was her last conscious thought before she fell into a dreamless slumber, welcome as sunshine in February—God's restorative gift to His children.

It was very late when Copper woke. Way past midnight. Her mouth felt as dry as a moth's wing. Reluctantly she pried herself from the bed. Tom meowed his protest but didn't stir. She grabbed her robe from the foot of the bed and tied the sash.

Hezzy's snores sounded like a rusty saw crossed with a donkey. *Scree-haw . . . scree-haw*, she heard. *My word, if that doesn't wake Remy from her lost state, nothing will.*

There was water in the bucket, but it was stale. She craved water from the well. Barefoot, she made her way to the well house and let down the rope. The wooden bucket fell with a rewarding splash. Hand over hand, she hauled it up. Copper groped in the dark until she found the dipper gourd hanging from a nail just inside the well-house door. She drank greedily. Cold water dripped from her chin and splashed the front of her robe.

Back in the house she checked on her patient. Remy's breaths were deep and regular, and her skin was cool to the touch. Though there wasn't much response to stimulation, Copper was pleased. If she had wakened once, surely she would again. She resisted the urge to check Remy's wound. Hezzy had said to leave it be until morning.

Hezzy slept in the chair, her head thrown back, her feet propped on the bed. She should switch places with Hezzy, take the second watch. Copper swayed on her feet. She could barely keep her eyes open. Darcy's bed beckoned. The bolster pillow called. Feeling selfish, she left Hezzy and Remy as they were. After crawling back in bed, she arranged the covers, the pillows, and the cat to her satisfaction.

Sleep didn't come. Her mind's switch was set to worry. Mentally she took stock. Hezzy was with Remy. Lilly was with

Darcy. Here was Old Tom purring up a storm beside her. She was sure she'd closed the well-house door.

Copper punched the pillow, straightened her gown, moved the cat several inches to the right, and closed her eyes. A sudden breeze stirred the curtains, bringing the smell of rain. She'd have to close the windows. With a heavy sigh she slipped from the bed.

In the sickroom she removed the screen that propped the window up and lowered it. Quietly she tiptoed out. Thankfully she hadn't wakened Hezzy. The kitchen window was a different story. The aggravating thing was stuck. Thunder rolled, and far off she saw lightning play across the night sky. With the side of her fist, she tapped the framework around the window, then pulled on the sash as it inched its way down. Damp air whooshed through. Her gown billowed out.

From across the yard a flicker of light caught her eye. What was Dimmert doing in the barn this time of night? What was it he had said at the supper table about Mazy? She was off her feed? She'd been so distracted with Lilly's demands, Remy's needs, and the leeches that she hadn't really paid attention. Some farmer she was. Poor Mazy. She hoped it wasn't the scours again.

She slipped on a dress, then ran across the yard. Just as she neared the barn door, the heavens opened, releasing a driving rain.

"Dimm?" she said, shaking rain from her skirts.

Holding up a lantern, a tall figure unfolded himself from a bench near Mazy's stall. "It's me," John said.

Copper blinked, adjusting her eyes to the dim light. "John? Forevermore, what are you doing here?"

"I've been here all night. Dimmert said Mazy was sick. I've been doctoring her."

"Oh no. What's the matter?"

John hung the lantern on a nail inside the cow's stall. "From the looks of things, she got in the feed bin and foundered herself."

"But I always keep the bin closed and latched. I'm very careful about that." The flush of shame heated her cheeks. She hadn't even looked in on Mazy since early yesterday morning, leaving the care of her cow to others. Foundered! If Mazy died, she would never forgive herself.

Copper peered around the stall door, afraid of what she'd find. Years ago, when she was just a girl, she'd come upon a foundered cow out in the field. It lay on its back with its legs stuck straight up like fence posts, its belly hugely swollen. Black flies swarmed the dead body like bees at a hive.

Unperturbed, Mazy stood chewing her cud, rolling her big brown eyes at Copper.

Relief flooded through her. She clutched John's arm. "What did you do?"

"Epsom salts," he said. "She'll need one more dose."

Watching where she stepped, Copper went to Mazy and scrubbed the spot between the cow's eyes with her knuckles. Mazy swung her big, square head in delight. "You aggravating thing," Copper said.

As naturally as if they were still children, Copper threw her arms around John's neck and hugged him close. "Thank you. You're the best friend a body could have."

He moaned. His arms tightened, claiming her before she remembered he was a married man.

What had she done? "John! Turn me loose!"

He buried his hands in her hair and tilted her chin. His mouth was so close. She was sorely tempted. "John . . . don't."

His arms dropped and his shoulders slumped as if he'd had the air knocked out of him. "I'm sorry." He turned away, then reached for his hat on the bench, slapped it on his head, and started for the door. "Mazy will need another dose about six. It's already mixed."

Copper followed him to the barn door. Rain drummed on the roof. Thunder shook the ground, and lightning bolted down with a tremendous flash. She saw it strike a towering tulip poplar, lighting the yard like the brightest sun. Dark clouds funneled high in the heavens. "Don't go out in this," she pleaded.

"Sweet girl," he said, "I can't stay here."

As she watched him walk away, her tears matched the torrent of rain falling from sodden skies, her heart split clean as the tulip poplar. She couldn't bear this. She simply couldn't. Seeking comfort, she went back to the stall, laid her head on Mazy's broad back, and sobbed. "Help me. What am I going to do?"

As if she endured such actions every day, Mazy stood stoically, swishing her tail and mooing softly, giving what comfort she could.

CHAPTER 34

Copper was glad to see the sun rise. Benny made the wake-up call from the hayloft as usual. Up to her ankles in muck, Copper swung the pitchfork with practiced aim. Behind her, Mazy bawled for food. Copper leaned on her pitchfork and wiped her brow with her forearm. Manure-soaked straw sucked at her boots, nearly tipping her over. "You're not getting a bite before evening," she said, exasperated, "unless you want some more Epsom salts. Truthfully, I could do without the results."

Trucking the heavy wheelbarrow behind the stable, she dumped it on the growing pile. After it aged, it would make fine fertilizer for the garden and the fields. Her back hurt and her eyes smarted from lack of sleep—or more likely the crying she'd done through the long night, her anguish harmonizing with the howling wind and the crashing thunder. Broken tree limbs and shredded leaves littered the ground, bearing witness to the storm's fury. Her heart bore witness of another kind.

Benny threw back his head and crowed again. Copper watched him in the open window and smiled. Sad as she was, she still appreciated his comical mimic. Funny though, it seemed she hadn't heard the big red barn rooster. Wonder where he'd got to.

Back in the barn, she wiped the pitchfork against the ground and hung it on the wall. She fetched a pail of water from the water trough in the barnyard and washed Mazy as best she could, paying careful attention to her hindquarters. Satisfied, she got fresh water, soft soap, and a clean rag and wiped down Mazy's udder and her teats. After scrubbing her hands and arms, she was ready for the good part of her morning.

Hungry, Mazy pulled hard against the rope fastened to her bell collar and attached to the scaffold girt above the feed box. She backed halfway across the stall before Copper jerked the rope more tightly. Pulling the little T-shaped stool up close to Mazy's flank, Copper began to milk. Stubborn as a mule, Mazy refused to let down. From the corner of her eye, Copper saw the flash of a cloven hoof. She tumbled backward off the stool. Sprawled in the clean bedding, she lay flat on her back. The barn cat took advantage, settling with a buzzing purr on her chest. "I'll bring you some milk from the springhouse." Copper scratched the cat behind its ears. "Mazy's too dry from being sick all night to make any."

Dust motes danced in sunbeams. The straw smelled like

summer. The purr of the cat was solace to her ears. A tiny sharp eye peered down on her from a knothole in the hayloft floor. She closed her eyes. "I'll rest just a minute," she told the happy cat on her chest, the hungry cow at the empty manger, and the ever watchful Benny in the hayloft above. "Just for a minute. . . ."

"Mama, Mama?" Her baby's words drew her out of a foggy sleep. She looked up to see Darcy with Lilly astride her hip and a rooster under her arm. "We bringed Rusty home," Lilly said.

Copper blinked and opened her eyes wide before blinking again. Something was off-kilter. Why was she lying in hay with a cat on her chest? Why was Darcy clutching a bedraggled red rooster? She must be dreaming still.

"You look a sight, Miz Copper," Darcy said.

"It was a long night," Copper said.

"So I gather." Darcy set Lilly down.

"Me help you up, Mama." Lilly nudged the cat. It yawned and delicately shook each foot, casting off sleep, before it walked away. "Upsy daisy."

Copper struggled to her feet. "Darcy, why do you have that rooster under your arm?"

"Dimmert found him in a tree outside Mr. John's house this morning. No doubt the storm blowed him clear across the creek."

"Are you sure he's our rooster?"

"Even with half his feathers gone, Lilly recognized him," Darcy said. "Ain't it cute she named him Rusty?"

Copper kneaded the kink in her lower back. "Well, are you going to hold him all day?"

Darcy leaned close and whispered, "I think he's hurt bad. I didn't want Lilly to see."

Copper took the dazed-looking bird from Darcy. "Lilly Gray, will you do Mama a favor?"

"Yup."

"Go up to the house and help Darcy carry in the washtub."

"Me go swimmin'?"

"Absolutely. You can go swimming before Mama takes a bath."

As soon as Darcy led Lilly out of the barn, Copper started for the henhouse. "How did you get out, anyway?" she asked before she saw the door standing open, its latch broken, too puny to withstand the storm's onslaught.

Thankfully, the hens were all accounted for. They pecked the floor and strolled around the coop, ignoring the open door. Copper gently set the rooster in their midst. He stood dazed for a minute, then lifted one clawed foot–testing. He listed to one side, but he was upright. The chickens stood back, paying homage to their king.

Copper took some oats from a bag in the corner and scattered them at his yellow clawed feet. He tried to peck, but the motion sent him tumbling. "Oh, dear. Poor Rusty, what's the problem?"

Copper returned to the barn for a hammer, nails, shears, and a pasteboard box. Back at the coop, she picked Rusty up. The feathers on one wing were badly twisted. The rooster didn't put up much of a fuss as she trimmed the twisted feathers on one wing and shaped the other wing to match. She set him in the box along with an upside-down Mason jar fitted with a glass ring for water and a scattering of oats. Expertly she folded the box flaps, imprisoning the hapless bird. She poked holes in various places in the pasteboard so he could get some air.

"There now. You'll be safe while you get your sea legs back."

The hens gathered near while she fixed the door.

"Go on out." Copper liked for them to range on pretty days. One fat hen teetered on the doorsill, undecided. Chickens were timid creatures, Copper knew, and her little world looked decidedly different this morning. "Good grief. It's just tree limbs. It's not going to eat you."

Obeying, the hen plopped down from the sill. The others followed.

"Off with you. Go find your breakfast." Her stomach rumbled. She needed a little something herself, but first she'd have a bath.

Bless Darcy's heart. The tub was already filled. Lilly Gray splashed water like a puppy in a puddle. Copper stuck her head in the sickroom. Hezzy was spooning tiny bites of thin gruel into Remy's mouth. "How are things this morning?" Copper asked.

"We're holding our own, I reckon," Hezzy replied.

"I'll be in to help you directly," Copper said, pulling bits of hay from her hair.

"No hurry. We ain't going nowhere fast."

After Lilly was bundled into a towel, Copper poured a kettle of boiling water into the tub. Behind the bath screen, she let her dirty clothing fall to the floor. Ah, luxury. She lathered a bar of Larkin's Old English Castile Soap, her favorite. Alice had brought a dozen bars. Sighing with pleasure, she scooted down as far as she could. Did anything in the world feel better to aching muscles than a hot bath? She might just sit here all day. Sick cows, squirmy leeches, and drunken roosters could wait for a while.

John stood with hands on hips and surveyed his broken dreams. He figured it to be straight winds rather than a twister that brought the house to the ground. The only thing left standing was the foundation. The Warm Morning stove, still in its shipping box, rested high in the limbs of a massive oak, as if a giant's hands had placed it so. It would take some doing to get it down.

He worked for a while piling rock from the tumbled fireplace. Keeping his hands busy steadied his mind. Last night had taught him something he'd tried hard to deny. He couldn't be Copper's friend and benefactor. It wasn't enough just breathing the same air she breathed—not enough to look on her from afar.

Rocks shifted, smashing his thumb. He swallowed a curse. He'd never been a cussing man. Lessons learned at his mother's knee stood the test of time. But didn't Jesus say that what you think is what you are? Man, he was in a heap of trouble.

With the mule, he hauled a downed tree from the space that was to be the many-windowed parlor. The walls had tipped over but were undamaged. It wouldn't be that much trouble to put them up again. He probably should have built the house of logs, but he wanted a city house, something better for Copper. He picked up a clod of dirt and let it fly, smashing it against the Warm Morning stove overhead. Truth be told, he wanted to smash everything—take the ax to the boards and the sledge-hammer to the rocks.

He squinted against the early morning sun shooting through the tattered leaves of the oak. Like a child turning his anger upon himself, he climbed the tree until he was seated on a sturdy limb just behind the crated stove. He'd gone all the way to Hazard to fetch that stove—a special gift for his bride. Many a time he'd pictured them sitting round its radiant heat on the coldest winter day, snug as bugs, sweet potatoes roasting on the stove's flat top, cups of strong coffee in their hands, little Lilly Gray playing at their feet.

With a snort of derisive laughter for his foolish dreams, John planted both feet against the crate and pushed. It seesawed on the branch, teetering against its fate, until he shoved it again. With a rewarding thud, it crashed upon the ground; the wooden crate peeled away like matchsticks spilling from a case. But the stove lay intact, unscathed by his imprudent act.

"Lord," he asked in awe, "are You trying to tell me something?"

Refreshed from her bath, Copper stepped out on the porch with a brush. The day threatened to be hot and humid. A mist shimmered up from the grass like steam. She'd chosen her airiest dress, a pale rose linen shift that fell straight from her shoulders and required no corset. Her spotless green and pink calico apron nipped the shift round her waist. Bending over, she brushed tiny twigs and pieces of hay from her wild mass of hair. *Such a mess,*

she thought. *Such a bother.* She had a mind to chop it off. But what would her daddy say? She'd received her nickname from him because of her hair, which he said shone like a newly minted penny.

Back in the house she smiled to find both Darcy and Lilly asleep on Darcy's bed. *Too big a night for my girls*, she thought. Quietly, she raised the window and slid in the fly screen. She eased the door closed when she left. *No harm in a little morning nap.*

"Should we apply the leeches again?" she asked in the sickroom.

"I done it already," Hezzy said, "off and on all night."

"So? Is it working?"

Hezzy pulled back a thin coverlet, exposing Remy's leg. "Look see."

Copper's hand splayed on her chest. "Well, I never."

The wound, an angry slash of corrupted flesh just the day before, was dewy pink, the edges knit together as fine as Hezzy's quilt stitching.

"I've heard tell, though I've never seed it with my own eyes afore now. Her fever's gone too," Hezzy related.

"Hezzy Krill, I could kiss you."

The old woman cocked her head. "Go ahead."

Copper planted a noisy buss on Hezzy's soft cheek spider-webbed with wrinkles. "God bless you."

"I reckon He's already done so," Hezzy replied. "I ain't been this needed in a month of Sundays. Makes a body feel right good."

Copper knelt by Hezzy's chair. "Will you teach me the old ways?"

"I could set down a history if you'd fetch me a tablet and a pen. I can read and write, you know."

From the top of the blanket chest, Copper retrieved her traveler's writing desk, a marvelous contraption with a hinged lid that revealed a tray for paper, envelopes, stamps, pens, nibs, and bottles of colored ink. "You're a woman of hidden talents," she said.

Hezzy fitted a nib onto a pen. "Thank ye. Most folks don't look close enough to see what's inside me."

Copper squeezed Hezzy's shoulder before she left the room. A board in the porch floor squeaked under her weight. A hummingbird darted in and out of the red trumpet vine at the end of the porch. Hezzy's words stung like salt in a wound, for she knew she was one of those folks. She hadn't bothered to see the real Hezzy Krill until she was forced to. How many others had she summarily dismissed?

Copper prayed for forgiveness as she walked. The grass felt as luxurious as the finest Turkish carpet beneath her bare feet. Soon she was at the bend in the creek where Remy's bench waited. It was very comfortable with a rush seat and a sturdy back. Leafy tree limbs and sturdy grapevines twined together overhead, providing a cool and quiet bower for her time of reflection. It put her in mind of a brush arbor meeting. She wished she'd brought her Bible.

Time stood still. It could have been as brief as minutes or as long as hours that Copper rested in that place of quiet beauty before she felt his eyes upon her.

"I'm sorry," John said from across the creek. "I don't mean to disturb. . . . I just want to say good-bye."

Her heart fluttered painfully. Good-bye? She wouldn't listen. She stood and turned her back, making ready to flee.

"Copper," he said simply.

As always, his need called her back, bound her like the grapevine bound the tree limbs. Her beloved, her reason, was just across Troublesome. She faced him across the burbling creek. Feeling a rush of emotion, she rested her hand on the rough bark of a hickory tree. A mockingbird trilled its dozen songs high overhead. Her eyes played tricks, for she saw John through shimmered light like the reflection from a streaky, silver-backed mirror.

"Sweet girl," he said but made no move to cross the creek.

"Ah, John." Her voice broke on his name. "Don't."

"I'm leaving. . . ."

"No. Please," she pleaded through streaming tears. "I won't let last night happen again." Her arms stretched out to him across the creek, and his responded, too far away for touch.

"The dishonor is not on you," he said.

Her arms fell, hanging limply at her sides. She felt she might pitch face-forward into Troublesome. "Couldn't we disavow the last few months?" Her voice sounded childish and petulant to her own ears, but she couldn't stop herself. "Can't we be friends again?"

John snorted, a derisive sound that would have hurt her feelings if she weren't already scraped raw. "You can't expect that from me," he said, angry. "I tried and it ain't working."

"When are you going?"

"In a couple of weeks, soon as I get things squared away here. You'll have Dimmert and Ezra if need be."

She sat down on the creek bank, gathered her skirt under her legs, and dangled her feet in the cold water. "Do you reckon a body can die of a broken heart?"

"Girl, I'm not afraid of you dying. I'm afraid your heart will mend itself before I even get off this mountain."

"Don't tease me."

"Sorry. But listen. I've got plans. Good plans. I'm going to–"

"John," she interrupted, "I don't want to know where you're going. I don't want to know your plans." With a little slide down the bank, she was in the cold water and crossing to stand below him, looking up into his eyes. "There is only one thing in the world I want from you now."

He dropped to his knees. "What's that, Copper?"

Her fists tightened in her apron pockets. One touch and she'd be lost. "Just tell me you'll be back."

CHAPTER 35

Early July brought a break in the weather. It had been so hot that the hens stopped foraging and instead spent their days under shade trees in the yard, their chicks gathered under their wings. It seemed to Copper that she spent half her time fetching clean water for her animals and the other half watering her pitiful garden. Most of June had been as hot as August normally was, too dry to make a morning's dew. The hard-packed dirt in the barnyard was cracked like an old china plate.

The Fourth of July was known as a day of storms, and this year was no exception. Thunder and lightning and hot winds ushered in great relief, and early on the fifth Copper gave thanks for the restoration of her garden. Dark clouds formed as she walked among the rows, searching for weeds.

Rusty, the lop-winged rooster, pecked at potato bugs and the fishing worms that made their way to the saturated surface. The rooster had an affinity for Copper since she'd doctored him and liked to follow her around. He would have lived on the porch if she'd let him, but she wasn't having that mess close to her house. Each night she had to carry him to the chicken coop or she'd find him crowing on her windowsill come morning. Lilly loved it of course. Rusty followed Copper, and Lilly followed Rusty.

Dimmert had fashioned a small hoe for Lilly Gray, and now she whacked at the potatoes.

"Don't dig up the hills," Copper said. "Come chop over here."

Inch-high ragweeds poked their heads through dirt that had been hard just the day before. *So surprising,* Copper thought, *how fast weeds grow.*

She was just thinking how pleasant it was in the garden, how cool and refreshing, how rewarding to see the tomatoes and beans flourishing after the rain when Rusty squawked and hopped straight up in the air. His too-short wings flapped as he jumped.

"Nake!" Lilly screamed and flung her hoe. "Dimmert! Nake!"

Copper picked her up. "We don't need Dimmert. The snake won't hurt you."

Lilly shivered. "Ugly, Mama."

"Yes, he is that, but he's just hunting for food. He isn't a bad snake."

Trapped between the trunk of a tree and the hostile rooster, the serpent coiled, flattened its head, and blew out its upturned snout. Rusty stood his ground, cackling and dancing. Giving in, the hognose snake thrashed about as if in agony, then twisted to its back. The snake's forked tongue hung lifeless from the corner of its mouth. Victorious, Rusty threw out his chest and strutted away, still king of all he surveyed.

"Oh," Lilly said. "Nake died."

Copper squatted among the potato hills with Lilly in her lap. "The snake's just playing possum—pretending he's dead. Be real quiet and watch what happens next."

The snake stayed on its back for nearly a minute, looking as dead as dead could look. Then with a quick flip, it righted itself and slithered into the tall weeds.

"Yay!" Lilly clapped. She left Copper's lap and found her little hoe. "Nake still ugly."

Lilly Gray amazed Copper. So astute, she definitely took after her father.

Thunder rumbled. Copper grabbed her daughter's hand. "Run, Lilly Gray, before we get soaked."

A sight for sore eyes awaited her on the porch. Remy sat like a queen on the little settee dragged out from the house. She was propped up by pillows, and her feet rested on an overturned bucket.

Copper stopped at the edge of the porch. A few fat rain-drops patterned the dusty ground behind her. The coming storm was taking its time. "What's this?" she asked.

"Surprise!" Darcy cried, fairly dancing with joy. "I carried her out."

"Hezzy?"

"She's taking in the air." Hezzy grinned like a possum caught in the light.

"Forevermore," Copper said, "she's holding her head up."

"When we brung her out, she kept her eyes open for the longest time," Darcy said.

Copper gave Remy's shoulder a little shake. "Remy, wake up."

Rusty the rooster stalked the settee. Without warning, he hopped on the arm, threw back his ruby-feathered throat, and crowed to wake the dead.

And wake the dead he did—the near dead anyway.

With a tremor that started in her toes, Remy Riddle woke up. Her eyes were crossed, but they were open. Her voice came out feeble, but she used it. "I fear I'm going to live."

"Praise the Lord," Copper shouted.

"Praise His name," Darcy added.

"God bless us all," Hezzy said.

Rusty flapped his stunted wings. Lilly Gray laughed. Remy sat staring, dazed but fully alive.

A gentle zephyr stirred the tops of the trees. Leaves clicked like tiny castanets, heralding the coming storm.

"We'd best get her inside," Copper said. "We'll put you by the window, Remy, and you can watch the rain."

John knew by the lay of the land that he was nearing the end of his journey. Mountains had given way to hills and hills to the beautiful rolling land of Fayette County. He'd taken his time and lost part of a day, but here he was. He hobbled his mount by a good-size creek and pulled off his saddlebags. He'd need to get cleaned up before he faced the likes of Alice Upchurch.

A little lunch, a washup, and a shave and he'd feel better, so he gathered wood, built a fire, and heated water. He propped his sliver of mirror in the branch of a tree, then lathered up and scraped his straight razor over his ragged beard. He'd brought polished boots and a worsted wool jacket, which he hung from the limb of a tree so the wrinkles could fall out. Once he found lodging and established himself, he'd buy ready-made clothes suitable for facing a judge. He could have brought his wedding suit, but that didn't seem right.

Over hot coffee and a stale ham biscuit he studied his Bible. He needed a Scripture to cover the next few weeks. It would have to be powerful; it would need to speak to his heart. Generally he favored the deceptively simple commands from the prophet Isaiah.

John was a far cry from being a Bible scholar. He'd never read the Bible through like Copper's father did every year, but he tried. Especially in times of trial he'd search for meaning and direction. Maybe he'd never be brave enough to walk naked in obedience for three years as Isaiah did, but still he believed. He figured that was good for something.

Last evening he'd stretched out by his campfire, his head resting on his saddlebags, and read until he came to Isaiah 14:3. How come he'd never recognized that particular Scripture before? Funny how the Lord revealed His word in just such a way to give solace or direction when needed.

Now, as he buttoned a clean shirt and shrugged into his

jacket, he repeated those words: "'And it shall come to pass in the day that the Lord shall give thee rest from thy sorrow, and from thy fear, and from the hard bondage wherein thou wast made to serve.'"

He knew his sorrow and his fear. Living without Copper and losing Copper, of course. And his bondage? Ah, that was easy enough. Being hitched to a creaky wagon like Remy Riddle was burden enough for a dozen stalwart men. And way too much for him—fool that he was. Yet he wanted the best for her. Didn't he? In his heart of hearts hadn't he wished her dead when he pulled her broken body from that hollow log? His prayer as he prepared for the end of his journey was unassuming: "Forgive me."

Breaking camp, he covered the fire, packed his coffeepot and cup, and picked up his Bible. He always packed it last so it would be easy to get to. An ornate piece of paper loosed from its pages, caught in a draft, and fluttered away.

"Oh no!" John yelled as he high-stepped down the creek bank. The paper flitted in the wind, teasing him. "No! No! Don't go in the water!" Just before the document landed, his hand shot out and grabbed it, creasing what had been perfectly kept.

His heart thumped as he scrambled up the steep cliff. "Man, that was close."

At the top he smoothed the license against his thigh. He'd never really looked at it and didn't care to now. That piece of paper held the biggest lie he'd ever told—a lie to wreck his life and Copper's, a lie that benefited no one but Remy Riddle. His gut clenched at the thought. He had some forgiving to do himself, he figured, before God was going to return the favor.

John found Alice Upchurch's house as imposing as the woman herself. He'd never want to live in a house like this, too big for itself. Even the entrance was pretentious, with double wide doors and huge brass knockers. Taking one in hand, he tapped it.

No one answered.

He tapped again—with authority this time—and was rewarded with a sweep of the opening door. A stately black man in some kind of uniform ushered him in. "May I ask who is calling?"

"Umm, John," he stammered. "John Pelfrey."

"May I have your calling card to present to Madam?"

For a moment John was at a loss, his brain searching for meaning. Calling card? Oh, right, those fancy little announcements. Kind of silly since he was standing here in person. "Mrs. Upchurch knows me."

The house servant stuck out his hand. John stuck his out too, but the man didn't take it. "Your hat," he said.

"Sure." John handed over his slouch-brimmed felt hat. "You're welcome to it."

John's belly felt as if he'd just made a meal of green apples as he watched the back of the servant disappear. He was of a mind to head back out the door and let this fellow keep his hat, though it surely wouldn't go with his strange attire. Instead he polished the toes of his boots on the back of his pants and straightened the sleeves of his jacket. Last evening he'd washed his extra pair of pants and hung them to dry with a crease down the legs. He'd thought he looked right presentable until he saw this fellow dressed in a starched white shirt with a stand-up collar and a long-tailed coat. It put John in mind of a penguin.

Before John could think what he was going to say, the fellow was back. "Mrs. Upchurch will receive you now."

John, as nervous as a schoolboy called before his marm, followed down a long hall.

Alice stood when he entered the parlor. Dressed in dove gray with a little frill of lace at the throat, she was a calming presence in the glitzy room. His eyes didn't know where to light because there was so much froufrou about, every surface covered with books and pictures and funny white figurines.

Alice offered her hand. "How was your journey?"

He kind of patted her hand between his two. It didn't seem right to shake it like she was a man. He felt like he should bow or something befitting a queen. But she was gracious and soon had him sitting in a comfortable chair, a cup of really good coffee at his side.

"Tell me everything that has happened since I left," she said.

So he did and there was a lot to relate. Alice listened to every word as if it was of great import. He noticed her eyes light up whenever he mentioned Lilly Gray. Of course they would, John realized. Lilly was her late brother's only child after all.

The gilded clock on the mantel ticked the afternoon away. At one point Mrs. Upchurch's daughter, Dodie, came in and played a song for him on a child-size violin. His heart seemed squeezed tight in his chest. He thought they'd never get to why he was here. It didn't seem proper for him to bring it up.

Finally all the niceties were over, all the proper etiquette of entertaining your dead brother's replacement had been met, John presumed, for Alice looked at him straight on and said, "I have taken the liberty of talking to my husband about your predicament. Benton is an attorney as well as a banker."

John leaned forward, his hands on his knees. He wanted to hurry her up, and at the same time he never wanted to hear her next words. It seemed to him his whole life lay in the balance.

"Benton is willing to petition the court on your behalf." Alice sniffed delicately behind a snowy white hanky. "He believes you stand a good chance of winning an annulment."

John stood. "Mrs. Upchurch, I can't thank you enough."

"I care very much for my niece and her mother, Mr. Pelfrey." Alice permitted him to take her hand before continuing. "If Laura Grace insists on raising my brother's child on that mountain, I like knowing you would be there to protect them both."

"With my life, ma'am," John replied. "With the last breath in my body."

CHAPTER 36

John found the livery station easily enough. He left his horse and then walked to the address Mrs. Upchurch had printed on the back of her cream-colored calling card. Strange the way they handled things in the city. Back home you could show up in anybody's yard, holler hello, and chances were they'd take you in for a night or a week. Here you had to have a special card, like a secret handshake, to gain admittance. He reckoned it was for safety—too many strangers lurked about.

Mrs. Archesson's boardinghouse was a white two-story with big round columns. Wrought-iron benches and pots of red geraniums adorned the veranda, making a body feel right at home.

The door opened before he could knock. A crippled fellow held out a twisted hand. "I'm Tommy Turner. Come on in."

John hardly had time to take off his hat before he was seated at the kitchen table with a glass of sweet tea and a piece of gingerbread. Mrs. Archesson was a tiny, frail-looking woman with an outlandish flower-bedecked hat on. John must have interrupted something. "Please don't let me keep you, Mrs. Archesson."

"Goodness me . . . goodness," Mrs. Archesson said, "I have not another thing to do . . . not another thing." She slid a second piece of warm cake on his saucer. "We're so glad you've chosen to abide with us."

A little one-armed boy sidled up and pinched a piece of his gingerbread while smiling disarmingly. It must have been the long trip from the mountains and the nights of poor sleep that made John feel as if he'd stepped inside a circus tent.

One by one a trio of elderly ladies inched to the table and creaked into chairs pulled out by Tommy. Clouds of talcum puffed out as they sat. The air smelled of faded roses. "Tell us about Copper," one said.

Another held a hearing aid to her ear; it looked like the horn of a phonograph, only smaller. "Yes, do tell," she echoed.

"No. No, mustn't tell yet," Mrs. Archesson trilled. "Wait for supper. Wait for supper and Andy."

"Yes, oh yes," the ladies murmured among themselves. "We'll wait for Andy."

The little boy made himself comfortable on John's knee and licked cake from John's plate.

It took John a minute to sort everyone out. He remembered the story Copper had told him about how she rescued Mary

Martha Archesson from a lunatic asylum and how ultimately the birdlike woman had opened a boardinghouse. The young boy must be Robert, the one Mrs. Archesson had adopted when he was an abandoned baby. And the Andy they mentioned had to be Andy Tolliver, Dodie's brother and a real friend to Copper when she lived here. Copper hadn't changed a bit; she still collected folks.

The upstairs room Tommy showed John to was neat as a pin. A large window overlooked the backyard, where John could see an old stone washhouse and a small apple orchard. A single tombstone sat inside a black iron fence. John wondered what import it had, what sad story lay there.

He pulled off his boots and set them side by side under the bed. Exhaustion overtook him. He wasn't the sort to laze about in the daylight, but that bed looked mighty comfortable. Opening his Bible, he checked to see that the marriage license was secure. Perhaps he'd close his eyes for just a minute.

Hours later Tommy and Robert woke him for supper.

A blind man could see that Mrs. Archesson doted on Andy Tolliver. The best piece of chicken and an extra large helping of peas and new potatoes went on his plate. John reckoned he deserved it. The twelve-year-old lad was as respectful as could be and by all accounts helped run Mrs. Archesson's boardinghouse business. Tommy told John that Andy did all the repairs in his spare time, and every Monday he did the whole wash with only the help of Tommy.

As soon as they were settled around the supper table, John was peppered with questions about Copper and Lilly Gray. He answered as best he could without letting his supper grow cold. Mrs. Archesson sure knew how to put a good meal on the table. Her fried chicken was nearly as good as Ma Hawkins's.

"My goodness," Mrs. Archesson said, "I'm so glad to hear news of Copper and the baby. Copper is the reason I have my own little boy, you know. She rescued me when I was very ill and not myself. No, not myself at all." Her words fluttered and stopped as she looked away.

Tommy jumped in and told a story much like Mrs. Archesson's. It was Copper's husband who had rescued him from unwarranted life in an insane asylum, but it was Copper who had made him feel welcome in her home and never seemed to notice his twisted body. He'd gotten his job helping out at Mrs. Archesson's boardinghouse because of Copper.

"Miz Copper's my best friend," Andy said quietly. Elbows on the table, he leaned forward. "She saved my whole family, and we didn't even know we needed saving. I expect me and my little sister Dodie would be in the orphanage if not for her. She was real good to my ma even though you could say Ma took advantage." He moved bits of food around on his plate. "Everything worked out for the best, though, I reckon." He cleared his throat. "Tommy here goes with me to visit Ma and my other sister, Marydell."

The room grew quiet. It seemed that no one knew what to say after hearing Andy's painful story.

"Tell us about your day, Andy," one of the powdered ladies said and patted Andy's cheek. "Did you work for the undertaker or at Massey's Mercantile?"

"Well," Andy said, forking a potato, "it's like this: I was on my way to Mr. Massey's to straighten up the display cases when Miz Battinger stepped out on her porch. You know Miz Battinger, right? She's the one's got all them cats."

The ladies nodded in unison while Tommy just smiled. Evidently, Andy told good stories.

Andy finished his mouthful and took a swig of tea. "Seems a kitty was missing—Pete, the number nine and newest cat, to be exact. Miz Battinger wondered could I help her find him. 'Well, sure,' says I. 'There ain't another thing I'd druther do than look for your number nine cat.'"

Mrs. Archesson slipped another piece of chicken on Andy's empty plate and one each on John's and Tommy's too. "Go on, Andy," she encouraged as she refilled his glass.

"Thing is," Andy continued, "I've been in Miz Battinger's house delivering groceries and such, and I know all her cats look the same, all got four legs and two ears. . . ."

One of the ladies tittered behind her frilly hanky as if she'd never heard anything so funny.

"Plus, they're all the same gray color. How could Miz B. know which one was Pete and which one was Harry or Tom? Anyways, I scooted under the porch and I beat the bushes and checked the carriage house, but Pete never showed as much as a whisker. By this time Miz B.'s crying and wringing her hands. 'Pete's never missed a meal before,' she says. 'I know something terrible has happened.'"

Andy started in on dessert, gingerbread with whipped cream. "I figure I got to do some fast thinking before something terrible really does happen . . . what with Miz B.'s bad heart and all."

"I didn't know she had a bad heart," one of the old ladies said.

"I didn't know either," said the second.

"Did you know, Emma?" the first lady hollered at the last one.

"Yes," she said with conviction, raising her ear trumpet. "I saw her stirring the batter." She held up her saucer. "I'll have another piece, please."

Mrs. Archesson sliced another piece of cake. "Please, Andy. Did you ever find Pete?"

Andy nodded. "Thankfully, I remembered seeing a gray cat behind the bank last evening when I was hauling the trash to the alley. 'Don't you worry,' I say to Miz B. 'I think I know where Pete has got to.' Then I hightailed it down to Mr. Upchurch's bank. Well, I pretty much knew that cat wasn't Pete because I'd seen him there lots of times, but a gray cat's a gray cat, ain't it?" He started scraping dishes, handing them off to Mrs. Archesson, who took them to the sink.

"Did Miz B. know the difference?" Tommy asked.

"I didn't think so. I carried the alley cat to her house, and she clutched it to her chest like it was a long-lost sweetheart. She tried to pay me a nickel, but I refused. 'This is not a sack of groceries,' I told her.

"Anyways," he continued, "to make a long story longer, I stopped by on my way home this evening–just to make sure everything was okay. Miz Battinger seen me coming up the walk and threw open the door before I even knocked. She said she was very happy with her number ten cat. Seems Pete number nine was watching the whole transaction from his perch up the sugar maple in the front yard. Miz B. said he come scattering down after I left the alley cat. Probably afraid number ten was his replacement."

After the laughter died down, Andy looked at John. "Your turn. We're all wondering why you're here."

John told them what he felt comfortable telling. Of course they wondered why he was here in Lexington, what had befallen him. He wondered himself. If things had worked out as he had planned all those years ago he surely wouldn't be sitting at the table eating gingerbread with folks he didn't even know.

Slowly the conversation changed. Miz Emma asked a question. Andy started another story. Thankfully the onus was off John. He picked at cake crumbs with his fork as his mind swirled away. . . .

Wasn't it just yesterday that he had fallen in love with Copper Brown? They were both children when he knew she was his one true love—his one and only. He claimed her like gardens claim rain, like trees claim mountains, like stars claim the night sky—elementally. He thought his right to her love was a given, like seasons or sunlight.

He was fifteen when he staked a claim on a piece of property up near Knobby Ridge. His pa lent him a hundred dollars. He'd paid back every cent. His boy's mind could see a little cabin there; his boy's heart was already promised. Copper would have come to love him too if it hadn't been for the copperheads.

It wasn't long after the brush arbor meeting, just a few days after Copper's family and John's attended to hear the enthralling fire-and-brimstone sermon and witness a fearless snake-handling preacher. Copper's little brother Daniel was enraptured by the whole event, though at the time no one thought a thing of it.

But as John's mother often said, "Boys will be boys," and in due time Daniel found himself a den of copperheads. Having much desire to be like the viper-loving parson but lacking the reverend's skill, Daniel suffered the serpent's revenge.

Then came the stranger, a doctor who saved Daniel's life and captured the heart of John's true love, Copper.

Now here John sat, a stranger in a strange land still in love with the girl of his youth.

"Mr. Pelfrey." Andy's voice pulled John from his reverie. "How about we go see the town? Me and Tommy will show you where Copper lived, and you'll want to meet Searcy and Reuben."

"Sure. I'd like that."

"I'll go get the buggy," Andy said. "Tommy here can't walk too far."

CHAPTER 37

The lethargy of long, hot August days took over Copper's household. Since Hezzy took Remy to her house, the urgency that had held Copper in its sway for weeks dissipated. She could hardly believe that Remy had chosen to live with Hezzy. But the bond that had developed between the two was as unexpected as it was beautiful, and Copper knew it was a good and true thing.

Since Copper no longer had to make every minute count for something, mornings she spent in the garden, afternoons she canned whatever was ripe, and after supper there was time for porch sitting and tea drinking.

John had been gone for nearly a month. He'd gotten off to a slow start, Dimmert relayed, for after one day's journey Faithful had caught up with him. Copper laughed every time she thought of John carrying the hound back to Troublesome. Dimmert brought the dog to Copper because Faithful wouldn't touch her food with John gone. Now she moped on the porch, but at least she ate. Copper knew just how she felt.

The post brought a letter from Alice, so she knew where John was and what he was about. Lawyers and judges and courts would decide their fate. What would be would be. Copper didn't fret, but she wished this summer would go on forever, this blissful time of dreams and hope against hope, for the coming fall might bring pronouncements she didn't want to hear.

One early Wednesday morning she was sitting outside braiding Lilly's thick black hair when a man she didn't know rode up in a cloud of dust. He was a big fellow and very handsome. Spurs jingled as he crossed the yard.

"Ma'am," he said with a sweep of his hat, "I'm Spears Russell. I've heard tell you're a baby catcher. I'm hoping you'll see fit to attend my missus."

Copper wrapped a red ribbon around the tail of Lilly's braid. "I'll help in any way I can. Let me get my things."

Soon she was bouncing along behind Mr. Russell. His horse was powerful and easily held them both. She would have liked to have her own mount, but Dimmert wasn't around to fetch one from John's place for her. And from what Mr. Russell relayed, they didn't have time to waste. It was his wife's third lying-in, and she was always quick to deliver. Mrs. Russell's sister had attended her other births, but she had recently married and moved away.

"Her mother's with her, but she's got a touch of nerves," Mr. Russell said. "Besides, I want the best for my Lolly, and I hear that's you."

Before they reached his home place, Copper and Spears were on a first-name basis. She found him to be a friendly, talkative man. He and his wife, Lolly, had bought the old Miller property over near Quicksand several years ago, and he bred and traded horses to make a living. His dream was to move his family to a place better suited for horses, somewhere out West. Spears had his heart set on being a cowboy.

The Russell place was blessed with many acres of flat-bottom land, which Spears had enclosed with whitewashed plank fencing. A horse-shaped weather vane graced the peaked roof of a large black stable. Copper was enthralled. It reminded her of Lexington. Horses whinnied greetings as they rode up. The grounds were as neat and clean as any she'd seen.

Lolly Russell paced the porch, her hands pressed against her back, her belly stuck out round as a pumpkin. Two little girls followed her like ducklings, matching each step. A frail-looking woman Copper took to be Lolly's mother rested on a bench.

The birth of the Russells' third girl was quick and easy. Within a couple of hours after Copper's arrival, the infant was nuzzling her mother's chest. Copper would stay through the night in case of emergency, then turn Lolly's care over to her mother.

After supper Spears showed Copper around the farm he proudly called a ranch. His oldest daughter sat on his shoulders and held tight to his ears as he walked and talked of the wide open spaces out West.

About a dozen horses followed inside the fence as they walked. A little white dog with brown-tipped ears and a smiling mouth ran laps around the large beasts.

"Mind the hooves, Maggie," Spears called out to the dog. "Maggie's smart as a whip and fearless, keeps the wolves and coyotes away."

"I'd be afraid a horse would kick her to kingdom come," Copper replied.

"Ah, they like her all right. She can be a right good companion."

"If she ever has puppies, I'd like to have one," Copper said. "My old dog died a few years back. I've missed him ever since."

"Way I see it, a house ain't a home without a dog," Spears said.

"I agree. I have an old tom, but cats don't replace dogs." Copper turned her back and leaned against the wooden fence. Dusky dark crept across the pasture. A gentle breeze cooled the air. There wasn't a weed to be seen or a piece of grass out of place. "You've sure got a nice spread here."

"Got to keep a nice place to raise my cowgirls." Spears lowered his daughter to the ground. "I can't thank you enough for taking care of Lolly. I'll pay for your service of course."

"I don't charge. It's my ministry."

She could see the protest form on his face. She started to deny him, but before she could say a word, a weight fell across her shoulder. A soft nicker blew against her neck. She laughed and reached up to stroke the horse's long nose. "This one's a friendly thing."

"I've never seen him act like this." Spears shook his head, obviously perplexed. "That horse don't like nobody, and he's as contrary as sin. I'd sell him in a heartbeat, but I don't want to foist his cantankerous ways on someone else."

The horse raised his head from Copper's neck and nuzzled her palm. Giggling, she turned to see his face, and her heart skipped a beat. "Star! Oh my goodness, it's Star."

"You know that ornery piece of horseflesh?"

"This horse means the world to me."

Spears pounded his fist against the rail like an auctioneer pounding a gavel. "Sold!" he exclaimed with a ready smile. "One good turn deserves another."

A light heart and a borrowed saddle accompanied Copper home the next day. She'd insisted she could find her own way back, but Spears being Spears insisted more strongly that he wouldn't hear of it, so she followed him on a docile Star.

Copper wasn't the least bit tired, though she'd spent the night through caring for Lolly and her infant. The Russells and their ranch had delighted her and lifted her spirits, not to mention the thrill finding Dimmert's horse had given her.

A few miles before Troublesome, she reined in her mount and called to Spears. He turned back and rode alongside. "Would you mind," she asked, shading her eyes against the sun, "if I go on alone? This is the perfect opportunity for me to call on a friend who is recovering from a long illness."

"Don't mind at all, little lady." He adjusted his wide-brimmed white hat, sitting tall in the saddle, a natural on a horse. "You need anything, you holler."

"But what about your saddle?"

"I'll pick it up one day—give Lolly and me a chance to visit."

Star neighed; his great head seemed to nod good-bye.

Spears's laughter boomed. "Tell you the truth, I'm glad to be shut of the prince there." Wheeling his horse, he lifted his hat in salute, then rode away.

It didn't take Copper long to find the path to Hezzy's cabin. Hezzy's old dog raised one rheumy eye when Copper slapped Star's reins over the porch rail. As she scooted the dog's rump away from the open door, she hollered, "Hezzy, it's me, Copper."

"Come on in here, girl," she heard Hezzy answer from somewhere in the house.

Copper squeezed past the sleeping dog into a narrow pathway. Buckets and barrels, chairs and feather beds, faded paintings of men and women in long-ago costume, yellowing newspapers, and, incongruously, a stuffed skunk threatened to topple over and smother her to death. A musty smell caused her to have a sneezing fit.

"Bless you," Hezzy called.

"Gracious goodness, what is all this stuff?" Copper asked when finally she spied the old woman sitting in a cavelike clearing with her foot propped up.

"Them's all recollections," Hezzy replied.

"Recollections?"

"Memories of my people and my late husband and his people. Seems the only family I got left is in them things."

Copper's heart softened. "Oh, Hezzy."

Hezzy worked a bit of snuff with a frayed-end stick. "Don't you go feeling sorry for me. Sometimes things is easier to deal with than family."

Copper nodded; as usual she'd overstepped her bounds. It was time to change the subject. "Where's Remy?"

"Off somewheres. Since she healed up, I cain't keep that girl to home."

Copper perched on the edge of an overstuffed chair. "How are you two getting along?"

Hezzy peered around her, making a shooing motion. "Charley! Mind yore manners."

A huge tiger-striped cat stretched against Copper's back, then padded over the chair arm and jumped down. A piece of stuffing clung to one foot. He stalked across the floor stiff legged, tail in the air, pausing now and then to shake his foot frantically as if it were being attacked by a fluffy, deranged mouse.

"Kitty, kitty," Hezzy said, patting her lap. "Kitty, kitty." Charley leaped up, and Hezzy freed the piece of cotton batting, tucking it up under the cuffed sleeve of her dress. "I might need this for something." Relieved, the cat curled around, instantly asleep on Hezzy's welcoming lap. "Now, what was it you asked? My mind ain't no better than a flour sifter—cain't keep nothing in it."

"I wondered how you and Remy are doing."

Hezzy shook her head. The furrows in her forehead deepened. "They's something wrong there. I cain't figure it, but something's worrying that child's head."

"Is she giving you trouble?"

"No." Hezzy paused. "I cain't say that and I'm glad for her company; that's why I brung her here, you know . . . for company and to make amends for shooting her in the first place."

"Now, Hezzy, we talked about that."

"I know, and I put a thumb card in my Bible to mark the verse you give me." Hezzy moved Charley aside and heaved herself upright. "Where'd I put it anyways?"

"Can I help you?"

"No, won't take but a minute. I just looked at it this morning." Hezzy rummaged around, dislodging a stack of papers and a book or two from a marble-topped table. "Here it is. Now where's my magnifier?"

"Just there." Copper pointed. "By that cast-iron skillet."

"Forevermore. I wondered where that skillet had got to." Hezzy carried her Bible and her tortoiseshell-handled magnifying glass back to the chair. She squeezed in beside Charley, then let the Good Book fall open. "'And be ye kind one to another, tenderhearted, forgiving one another, even as God for Christ's sake hath forgiven you.' Them's powerful words, ain't they?"

"Can you imagine a world without God's loving-kindness and forgiveness?" Copper asked.

"Be pretty bleak, I expect. I read some Scripture to Remy last evening. She's got some things to learn, else she's bound to get hurt again. I figure maybe that's why God sent her my way."

"Will you share with me?"

The magnifier crept up the page. "It's in this selfsame chapter," Hezzy said. "I come upon it by accident. 'Let him that stole steal no more: but rather let him labour, working with his hands the thing which is good, that he may have to give to him that needeth.'"

A thrill stirred Copper's soul. "That is amazing. I've read Ephesians many times, but I've never noticed that verse. May I?" She took the Bible from Hezzy and read the verse again. "It's as if it was written for Remy alone. I never was brave enough to address her thieving. I always figured God would forgive her in her innocence."

Hezzy stroked Charley's back with one knobby, blue-veined hand. The look she gave Copper was calculating, discerning. "Remy ain't so innocent anymore. She's going to have to account for herself just like the rest of us."

"I think I'll try and find her. Do you know which way she went?"

"Up the hill behind the henhouse. She's looking for that fox, I warrant."

"She can't be far," Copper said, "walking with a crutch."

Hezzy settled back in her chair with Charley and her Bible. "Easy to track anyways. Ain't too many three-legged creatures about."

Chapter 38

As Hezzy said, it was easy enough finding Remy. Her new gait was a step slide sort of pattern dragged through the tall grass of the hillside. She was crouching over something when Copper approached. "Hey, Purty," she said without turning her head.

"Remy Riddle, how'd you know it was me?"

Remy's laugh sounded like a cackling hen. "I smelled ye. Ye always put me in mind of honeysuckle vine. Plus, Foxy took off, so I knowed somebody was near about."

Copper knelt beside her. "What have you got there?"

"I found me a patch of sang. It will fetch a purty price when it gets some age."

"I remember Granny Pelfrey could always find ginseng," Copper said.

"It's hunted to death these days," Remy said, casting a sideways look at Copper. "Kinda like me and Foxy."

Gathering her skirts around her, Copper sat on the ground beside Remy, careful of the ginseng. "I hope you don't mind me coming to find you."

"Don't mind so much as just aggravated. Time was when I coulda been right beside ye and never been spotted." The crutch Dimmert made for her rested against a tree; she knocked it away. "Guess them days are over."

Copper brushed a strand of hair from Remy's eyes. Remy no longer flinched at the slightest touch, she noted. "I'm so sorry."

"I cain't stand me no sympathy." Remy settled down beside Copper, stretching out her legs, one obviously shorter than the other. "I'm lucky to be alive, even in plain sight. Though I didn't know I wanted to be in the midst of my pain—alive, that is."

"Do you know that now?"

Remy plucked a blade of sweetgrass and chewed it. "Somebody's got to appreciate all this." She opened her arms wide. "I reckon that's the job God give me."

Copper rested her chin on her knees. The hillside was abuzz with life: trees spreading restful shade, crickets chirping, an anthill being studiously constructed one grain of sand at a time, a box turtle bumbling across the path, a jaybird calling his raucous tune. "Seems like an important job to me."

Remy's voice fell to a hoarse whisper. "I ain't a good person. I figure God give me a second chance so's I can work my way into heaven. I dearly want to see my ma again someday." Her voice rose in timbre, and she laughed before she spoke. "Plus I want to live somewheres my pap ain't at."

"The things you say, Remy Riddle." Copper laughed in spite of herself.

"What can I do, Purty?" Remy said, now serious. "How can somebody as lost as me ever hope to get to live with the angels?"

"Do you know what mercy means?"

Remy pulled up her skirt tail, revealing her scarred leg, and rubbed her misshapen knee. "I reckon it's being found in a holler log and pulled out by somebody I done wrong. I reckon it's John Pelfrey carrying my sorry body to ye."

"That's right. God showed His mercy to you through John. Now He offers you grace."

Copper could see her face reflected in Remy's eyes as Remy studied her. "What's that mean?"

"You know how you said you need to work your way to heaven?"

"Yeah. I figure with this patch of sang I can pay back what I owe folks. God will like that, don't ye reckon? Maybe that will get me in the gate."

"We're all saved through grace, not works," Copper said. "Grace is Jesus dying on the cross to pay for our sinful ways. None of us would go to heaven if not for that."

"Hezzy read me the story of the cross. I cain't hardly stand to think on His suffering."

"You're a good and kind person, my dear friend."

"Nobody's ever told me that before." One fat tear trickled down Remy's cheek.

Copper took her small, rough hand. "Are you ready to accept

Jesus into your heart? You know He is God's only Son, and you know He came to save us from our sins."

"That's a heavy burden," Remy said as one tear followed the other.

A cooling breeze whipped around them and stirred up a dust devil. They watched the whirlwind full of grit and dead leaves dance over the box turtle; he never stopped.

"There's a verse that explains that burden, Remy. It's one you'll want to commit to memory—John 3:16. 'For God so loved the world, that he gave his only begotten Son, that whosoever believeth in him should not perish, but have everlasting life.'"

"That'd be mercy and grace, I warrant," Remy said.

"Do you believe?"

Remy caught hold of her crutch and maneuvered around until she was standing. She raised one hand to heaven. "I believe."

Unable to help herself, Copper jumped up and pulled Remy in a mighty embrace. "Oh, Remy, my heart is near to bursting."

"Now I get dunked?" Remy asked.

"Are you ready?"

Remy raised her thin shoulders, then let them fall. "I reckon I am."

"I'll send for Brother Jasper and Elder Foster as soon as I get home. They'll want to talk with you, and then we'll have the baptizing after church on Sunday."

"You'll have to come along, Purty, else I'll be afeered."

"Honey," Copper soothed, "we'll all be with you. Hezzy, Darcy, Cara, Lilly, and me. Don't you fret. A beating with a stick wouldn't keep us away."

CHAPTER 39

The city was bearing down on John, chipping away at his ease with each passing day. Lexington was noisy and nosey–everybody loudly stirring each other's pots, busy minding each other's business. He'd probably explained his predicament to a dozen folks, starting with Mrs. Upchurch and ending yesterday with a black-robed judge.

As he sat on the edge of the bed rubbing sleep from his eyes, he turned that meeting over in his mind. Judge Ledbetter was an imposing figure sitting up over the court like a king on his throne. John suffered through several cases before his turn came: men caught thieving and women caught doing worse. The judge liked to pound his gavel, John perceived, liked to watch the wretched souls before his judgment twitch like lizards on a hot rock.

John sat on a hard wooden bench between Benton and Alice Upchurch, trying not to sweat, trying to look collected. It was a funny feeling to know another man held his future in his hands. John had spent some time with Benton and his law books preparing for this very day in Judge Ledbetter's court. Hopefully it would be over soon; hopefully the judge would agree to hear their case. Today was only a preliminary hearing, but if Judge Ledbetter denied them, it was the same as over. Benton was confident that because the marriage was never consummated the judge would look on him with favor. It was a known legal reason for annulment.

John swallowed hard when his name was called. Alice gave his hand a squeeze before he and Benton approached the bench.

"Your Honor," Benton began. And then John's shameful story spilled out as dark as blood across the polished wood floors, staining the heavily plastered walls and splashing against the many-paned windows. John could hear the shift of bodies on the benches behind him, feel the watchers' lurid interest turn his way. Mortified, he kept his back straight but his eyes downcast, afraid of what he'd see in the judge's eyes.

His head felt full of mush, but snippets of Benton's fevered plea jumped out and clung to him like fleas off a dying dog: "Said party . . . fraud . . . ignorant . . . therefore . . . unconsummated." He'd *felt* like a fool before; he *was* one now.

"Mr. Pelfrey."

John heard the judge and raised his eyes, giving his full attention.

"I presume you signed a license," Judge Ledbetter intoned.

"Uh, yeah," John stammered. "It's in my Bible. I could fetch it for you."

For long moments the judge stared down from on high. Once he opened his arms and his robe spread out like black wings.

John met and held his gaze, but he saw no compassion there. His head was in the bear's mouth for sure.

"Do you aim to make a mockery of the court?" the judge asked as if incredulous. "Do you aim to challenge the sanctity of the marriage vow?"

John gathered his courage to answer, but beside him Benton shook his head ever so slightly; evidently he was not to speak. Suddenly, the collar of his starched white shirt tightened like a garrote. With one finger he loosed its hold a bit.

The judge's voice filled the room with import, each word as menacing as a rattlesnake's dry whir. Then, mercifully, John's verbal flogging was over. The gavel rose with authority and hammered down. "What God has joined together, let no man put asunder!" With a swish of black robe, the judge was gone, the court dismissed, and John remained a married man in the eyes of the law.

He thought he wouldn't sleep at all after that humiliating day. After listening to Benton's angry comments concerning Judge Ledbetter's pronouncement and suffering Alice's righteous indignation, he'd stumbled back to Mrs. Archesson's boarding-house intent on packing up to leave. Instead he'd stretched out on the bed, instantly lost down a tunnel of sleep.

Now he poured water from the blue willow pitcher into a

matching washbowl and picked up his razor. He smelled bacon frying and coffee perking; his belly growled. From somewhere a dog barked, a rooster crowed, a door squeaked open, and the contagious laughter of a child made him smile in spite of himself.

His lathered face glared back at him from the mirror. "Where are you going?" it seemed to say. That was the question he pondered as he stuck out his chin and worked his razor over the stubborn stubble. Pulling a thick, clean towel from the washstand, he dried his face, then scrubbed his teeth with tooth powder from a tin Mrs. Archesson supplied. Perhaps he'd stay right here. He was learning his way around easy enough. He could do worse. Plus he could keep tabs on Copper and Lilly Gray through Mrs. Upchurch. There was an ad posted at the livery station he'd noticed: *Need Help. Good Pay. Inquire Within.*

Head in hands, he sat on the unmade bed. He'd have to write to Copper before Alice did. He should be a man and go back to Troublesome Creek to tell her himself. Ah, but he *was* a man, and therein lay the problem. He simply couldn't trust himself to be around her. Not yet. Time would dull the pain, he knew. It had done so before. Eventually, he'd have to go back to make arrangements with Dimmert and Cara; they'd be good farm managers for him. He'd want to pack up some things and of course fetch Faithful . . . just not right now. His heart was way too sore.

He'd see to the letter tonight. There were a few pieces of tablet paper tucked away in his Bible, and he could buy an envelope today and a stamp. For now he'd content himself with hot coffee and Mrs. Archesson's breakfast.

Father, he prayed without kneeling, *I am so weak; I ask for*

*strength. I don't understand why this is happening; I ask for wisdom.
I am fearful, not for myself but for Copper and Lilly Gray. I ask for
protection for them. I am lost; I ask for direction. I thank You for the
courtesies of this day.*

"Breakfast," he heard Tommy call from the hallway.

John pulled suspenders over his shoulders and buttoned the
top button on his freshly ironed shirt. "I'm coming."

Copper let Star amble his way home from Hezzy's. Her heart
was full of gratitude and awe at God's blessing. How could it
be that after all this time Remy was ready to give her life to the
Lord? How could Hezzy bring about the miracle of Remy's salvation when Copper herself had tried so hard and failed?

Copper thought it might be because she was too tender with
Remy—so afraid of offending her that she let Remy continue in
sin rather than confront her. And it was sin that had kept Remy
from finding the Lord. Copper leaned forward in the saddle and
stroked Star's neck. It didn't matter a whit who brought this
miracle about, of course. She was just so grateful.

She and Remy had talked the afternoon away, and now the
edge of night darkened the sky. Tree frogs peeped in the near forest, and locusts burred in the long, swaying grasses bordering the
path that led home. Really, she should hurry. Her family might be
worried, but the things Remy had shared simmered like a watched
pot in her mind. It all finally made sense. Poor John—what he had
suffered, just because of his love for her and his misguided kindness to Remy. Poor Remy—she had acted out of desperation and

set about a chain of events that nearly cost her life and more than likely ended any hope of Copper having a future with John.

Copper sighed. What would she have done if she had been in Remy's shoes—destitute, injured, and hunted like an animal by her self-serving father? Would she have chosen any better? If she had lived Remy's life, probably not.

Copper cried buckets of tears as Remy related these events, but Remy shed not one—all cried out, Copper figured. When Remy finished her long story of her marriage to John and her feigned death, she asked Copper for forgiveness. They had knelt and prayed together. It was with a grateful heart that Copper headed home. She had her fey friend back. Whatever else happened was in God's hands. She could live with that.

Star picked up his pace. Home was in sight. He nickered as they came around the corner of the barn. Copper strained to see in the near darkness what perked Star's ears, and then there was Dimmert. For the longest time he stood stock-still, staring at Star in the waning daylight. He rubbed his eyes with his fists; then he ran to them, flinging his arms around Star's long and lovely neck.

Oh, what a glorious reunion. It was Christmas morning all over again. Cara with a lantern and Darcy with Lilly on her hip spilled out of the cabin door.

Dimmert helped Copper down and took the bit from Star's mouth and the saddle from his back. "Stand back," he warned.

They all laughed as Star did a funny bucking dance, shaking foreign dust from his heels. Faithful joined in the fun with baying barks that more than likely scared every coon on Troublesome up a tree.

"Apple," Lilly said. "Star wants apple."

Darcy carried her to the side yard. Copper could barely make Lilly out as she twisted a piece of the ripening fruit from the tree. But she could feel Dimm's joy as Star slurped the apple from Lilly's palm. They were all together again. Her family was complete save one. Her heart yearned toward John. She wondered if he was thinking of her.

John sat on the veranda of Mrs. Archesson's boardinghouse and listened to the evening sounds of the city: the clip-clop of horses' hooves, the low *ka-thump* of carriage wheels on cobblestone, the musical conversation of people out of view in buggies, the occasional sharp commands from coachmen, and the beat of his own lonely heart.

Though the porch lights were off to discourage moths and mosquitoes, light from lamps inside each long window spilled brilliance out into the night. John had carried his Bible and a pen to the porch. He pulled a chair close to a lighted window and sat, one foot resting over the opposite knee. He'd intended to write his letter out here in peace, but he couldn't sit still.

Laying his Bible aside, he walked a little ways out into the yard and looked back. Each window held a happy vignette: Tommy and Andy played chess in one. John could see the concentrated effort on Tommy's face—set to let the young lad win, which John knew the master chessman did on occasion. In another, the powdery old widows took turns with a double-eyeglass stereoscope, no doubt enjoying the slides one had received in the post from her son today.

Through Mrs. Archesson's bedroom window, John could see her head resting against the back of a rocking chair, her little boy lying in her arms.

Melancholy swept over him. Man, he wanted a house like that. Maybe he and an older Lilly Gray playing checkers in one window and in another, Copper rocking a newborn. He couldn't help but smile. But then his mind took a turn, and in the middle window was Remy laughing at him.

Resentment as bitter as a green persimmon replaced melancholy. He'd better walk awhile. At home when pure anger overtook him, he'd just go climb a mountain. The effort never ceased to serve. Here, the gently rolling land didn't seem to satisfy in the same way. Maybe he needed to walk harder, farther.

It never got really dark here in town, John noticed as he went from the glare of one gas lamp to another. He missed sitting on his porch, where the only light after the sun went down was that of flitting fireflies putting on their show. He missed a lot of things, truth be told. Could he really acclimate to living in all this hustle and bustle? That remained to be seen.

It was a pleasant night for walking once his anger gave way to common sense. He'd never been one to hold a grudge. He might as well get over being riled at Remy, but that judge . . . well, that was a different story. John couldn't figure why the man would use his power to humiliate just because he could.

With no thought to where he was going, John strolled down a familiar street and stopped in front of a familiar house. This was where Andy brought him to meet Copper's friends, once her servants, Reuben and Searcy. Too bad it was so late; he'd like to talk to them again.

"Who's there?" a melodious voice called. "Step closer."

"I'm sorry, ma'am," John replied. "I didn't mean to disturb."

"Ain't no disturbance, child. Searcy be out here watering her flowers. It just too hot earlier."

John doffed his hat. "They're mighty pretty."

"Reuben," Searcy said toward the open door, "Miz Copper's friend be here." She set her watering can down. "Be right back."

A moment later she was shaking her head when she came out of the small bungalow. "He's sound asleep."

"I'll be going," John said, sorry he'd interrupted the lady's evening.

Searcy walked closer and cocked her head, studying him in the shimmering gas light. "You be troubled. Sometimes talking helps."

John told the whole story right there in Searcy and Reuben's front yard. There was something about Copper's old friend that invited confidence, something nonjudgmental and wise. They stood several feet apart, him yakking like a gossipy woman, her listening without comment. John felt as if he'd lanced a boil–poison poured forth.

"What you gonna do now?" Searcy asked when he was finished.

"I thought to stay here–in Lexington, I mean. Get a job; keep busy. Try and forget."

Searcy folded her arms, her elbows resting in her hands, and shook her head. "Why you be wanting to forget Miz Copper?"

"Truth is, I can't live with that kind of hurt."

"Humph," Searcy said, working over her flowers in the near

dark, deadheading marigolds by feel, her gaze fixed on John. "Anything worth having is worth losing. Don't never get to keep nothing forever." The sweet, spicy smell of marigolds bathed the night air. "We all just traveling through this old valley," Searcy said as she gathered stems. "This ain't our resting place."

John felt like a boy at his mother's knee. "It's like I've lost my way."

Searcy handed him a bunch of flowers. "Take these here to Miz Mary Martha. And read your Bible. It will set your feet on the narrow path again."

Serenity as comforting as the fragrance of marigolds settled over John as he made his way back. Searcy was right. When had he stepped off the straight and narrow road onto the twisted path of his own desire? He was ready to give it all to God. He hurried on, picking up his pace. He couldn't wait to get hold of his Bible. The only direction he needed could be found there. It seemed so easy now.

He'd write that letter after church tomorrow, and come Monday he'd see about the job at the livery. And, he'd noticed, the old washhouse behind Mrs. Archesson's needed repair. That was something he could do to help her out. Perhaps she'd let him rent it; he could see bringing Faithful there.

He walked with purpose, his bitterness and anger culled like the heads of dead flowers, pitched away so new life could form. Lexington's city streets would be home for a couple of years; he figured it would take that long for his sore heart to heal. Then he'd head back to Troublesome.

CHAPTER 40

The first Sunday in September was a glory hallelujah day. People lined the creek banks, their bodies gathering up the last of summer's heat. Men hunkered down to wait, and women stood or sat, flapping pasteboard fans against the still air. Children leaned into their mothers or stood between their fathers' legs, waiting and watching, warned to be quiet.

The branches of an ancient sycamore overarched the deep baptismal pool. The dark water, as yet undisturbed, reflected the sycamore's large-leafed, mottled limbs and the puffy white clouds chasing endlessly across the sky. Yesterday Elder Foster and Dylan had scythed scrub willows and invasive false honeysuckle from the banks in preparation. Dimmert and Ezra had fashioned rough-hewn benches but obviously not enough. Who would have expected such a crowd?

The assembly stood as one, every eye turned to see Brother Jasper approaching. The water ringed in ever-widening circles as he broke its flat surface. He was knee-deep when he turned to assist Remy.

Remy was all in white. Her dress, layered for modesty and weighted with small, smooth stones tucked into the hem, had been sewn by the ladies of Copper's quilting circle. Her hair was covered by a long scarf that was intricately folded and tied at the nape of her neck. Her boots and her crutch waited on the creek bank. Cotton stockings covered her feet. Copper steadied her at the edge of the pool where grass gave way to the muddy bank. Remy paused and tightened her grip on Copper's arm.

"Don't be afraid. Jesus is with you," Copper murmured.

Brother Jasper stepped closer, lifting Remy down the bank. She was so tiny beside the big preacher it seemed she might float away. "Having repented of her sins," Brother Jasper addressed the church body, "Remy Riddle comes to be baptized this blessed Lord's Day. Sister, repeat after me: I believe that Jesus is the Christ, God's only begotten Son, my Lord and my Savior."

In a small but clear voice, Remy publicly confessed her commitment to Christ.

Brother Jasper raised one hand to heaven. "I baptize you in the name of the Father, the Son, and the Holy Ghost," he proclaimed before he lowered his arm. Remy held a man's white handkerchief to her mouth and nose. Brother Jasper placed one hand over hers, positioned his other hand on her upper back, and dunked her beneath the waters of Troublesome Creek.

Copper shivered in the presence of the Spirit as Remy came up from the water. Tears flowed as people gathered around Remy, praising God for her salvation. One of the women wrapped her in a quilt.

Brother Jasper was just about to step onto the bank when a voice called out, "Wait. Wait up." A man walked out of the woods and headed toward the preacher. He hesitated not but strode right into the water, hat, boots, and all. "I need me some baptizing."

"Ace," Copper gasped. She caught sight of Dance standing far back from the crowd, near the tree line. She was holding baby Jay.

"Well, now, Ace Shelton," Brother Jasper said, "I never figured on seeing you here today."

"I been convicted," Ace replied.

Like everyone else, Copper stepped closer. It was a wonder they didn't all fall in.

"Do you confess your sins?" the preacher asked.

"All of them," Ace said. "And they ain't many I ain't done. But I'm purely sorry."

Once again Brother Jasper asked for the good confession, and once again he plunged a sinner beneath the cleansing water.

Ace came up sputtering and coughing but free. His slouch hat floated downstream, and a young boy plunged into the water to catch it.

Elder Foster started singing, "'O how sweet to trust in Jesus, . . .'" His rich baritone reverberated up and down the hollow as everyone joined in the hymn: "Just to trust His cleansing blood, just in simple faith to plunge me 'neath the healing, cleansing flood!"

As they sang, half a dozen more folks, one the boy who'd fetched the hat, made their way into the water to be baptized, following the example of Jesus Himself. Copper hadn't been so moved since her own immersion years before in this very same place.

Many tears followed as people hugged each other and cried together. Seemed like no one wanted to leave.

Finally Brother Jasper, soaking wet and smiling from ear to ear, announced, "We're having dinner on the grounds, brothers and sisters. Let's go break bread together."

Back at the church, Copper wondered how she had ever left these people and this place. She sat eating a piece of Fairy Mae's peach pie. My, it was good. The fruit was tender and sweet, and the crust was so flaky it crumbled beneath her fork. Had she been alone, she would have licked the plate.

Hezzy and Remy shared her quilt spread upon the ground. On one side was part of Fairy Mae's brood, including Ace and Dance, and on the other side were Cara and Dimmert. Where was Lilly? Oh, just there, chasing around with Bubby Foster. "Lilly Gray," she called, "come have some pie with Mama."

Lilly ran up for the last bite. Her dark hair, so carefully combed that morning, was tumbling out of its ribbons. Her face was flushed from play. "I having fun," she said, plopping down on Copper's lap, such a big girl now.

Resting her cheek against the top of Lilly's head, Copper prayed a silent, simple prayer: *Give me strength.* She was either the most blessed woman here to have two men to miss—Simon and John—or the most cursed. A chuckle escaped her lips. Sometimes she was such a ninny she had to laugh at herself.

"Why you laughing?" Lilly asked.

"Because I'm happy. You make me happy."

"Yup," Lilly said, tossing her head and looking up at Copper with her big gray eyes. "More pie."

John walked home with Tommy from the small Baptist church on the corner. It was a warm day in early fall, and they took their time—partly because Tommy had only one speed and partly because folks John didn't even know stopped to say hello. Maybe people in Lexington weren't so different from those he was used to after all.

He could smell food cooking before they reached the porch.

"Roast beef and mashed potatoes every Sunday," Tommy said.

"Smells good," John replied.

Mrs. Archesson met them at the door with tall glasses of lemonade. "You men rest your bones. Dinner will be ready shortly."

Companionably, John and Tommy sat sipping their drinks, sharing the Sunday paper. When John finished a section, he made sure to fold it in a neat square for Tommy. That made it easier for him to hold. *Funny,* John mused, *how quick a body adjusts to new people, new surroundings.* It scared him a little how fast he was settling in here.

"Massey's has a sale on hammers and nails," he told Tommy.

"I could use a good hammer, and when I redo the floor in the washhouse, I'll need a pound of nails."

"Let's see," Tommy said. John handed him the advertisement. "That's a fair price all right."

Tommy's twisted hands jumped as he held the paper. John wondered how he could even read. "Think you could go along in the morning?" John asked. "I might need some help."

"Sure thing. Did you see this piece about the bull escaping from the stockyards?"

Andy stepped out the door. "Ah, we caught him easy enough. Can't believe it made the papers."

"I guess it was a slow news day," Tommy said. "How'd you happen to be at the stockyards?"

"Just hanging around. I like to watch the sales. Someday I'm going to have me a farm with cows and horses." Andy picked up their empty glasses and headed back inside. "Miz Mary Martha says dinner is ready."

It was much later before John was ready to pen his letter home. After Mrs. Archesson's bountiful dinner, he'd fallen asleep stretched out on top of his covers in his rented room. On waking, he yawned and splashed water on his face, scrubbing at the creases that confessed his laziness. He'd never slept this much at home, but a sodden lethargy had consumed him ever since the judge's pronouncement. Maybe he just couldn't bear to be fully awake.

He bent to open the window; fresh air would surely help. His knuckle struck a bell jar sitting on the sill and set it vibrating with a tinkle of sound. The white blooms of an African violet sheltered there quivered in reaction. A spider mite leaped down from the blossom. John had upset its equilibrium. He felt the need to apologize.

Sitting on the straight-backed chair beside his bedside table, he picked up the Bible his mother had given to him when he left home at eighteen. The cover was worn thin in places. John could almost see his mother's hands stroking the leather binding each time she picked it up. He remembered once when as a boy he'd carelessly knocked the Good Book to the floor and run on. His mother was a gentle woman not given to punishment or raising her voice, but she'd given him a good shaking that day. Now his hands caressed the Bible as hers once did.

The room darkened. He glanced at the clock. It was only three; a storm must be brewing. As if in answer, a mighty roll of thunder shook the window and rattled the bell jar. John put the Bible on the edge of his bed and went to the window.

He heard the plop of the book falling to the rug as he closed the window. Rain beaded on the sill. He should dry it off. After putting the Bible safely on the table, he took his towel from the washstand and blotted the rain, disturbing the violet as little as possible. With a sigh he turned back to the table; he'd dithered away the afternoon, and still the letter to Copper was not written.

The tablet paper was missing from his Bible. He guessed it came out when the Bible fell. On his knees he spied the paper and the marriage license underneath the bed. He raked them out, then leaned against the bed. The fluttering of his heart made him feel ill as it did each time he held the despised certificate. *Lord,* he prayed, seeking comfort, *will I never get over this?*

"Face your fears," he fancied he heard the Lord answer.

For the first time he studied the document. It was just an oblong piece of paper with a fancy design across the top. It proclaimed the marriage of John Daniel Pelfrey to Remy Rees Riddle on the fourteenth day of January 1884. There was the preacher's signature and that of his wife as witness. He swallowed hard to read his own bold mark on the paper, but it was there. And then Remy's on a line beside his. His heart beat hard, and he sat up straight. "What is this?"

Not trusting his eyes in the dark room, he paused to light the coal-oil lamp on the table. He'd noticed a magnifying glass nestled in the bedside drawer, and now he pulled the drawer out so fast and hard he nearly dislodged the lamp. Carefully, license in one hand, magnifier to his eye, he examined the paper.

Remy had not signed her name! Instead she had made a series of squiggles. Why, he reckoned, Remy Riddle couldn't read nor write, and she hadn't asked anyone to witness her *X.* Maybe she didn't know to. If you didn't look closely, you would swear it was a signature. John's heart thumped a different cadence—one of hope. He had his boots and hat on in seconds. He must show this to Benton Upchurch. It made all the difference in the world.

He'd just stopped to blow out the lamp when hail pelted the tin roof. A shrieking shearing sound like twisting metal filled the room; then a thin, mewling voice called, "Help me. Please, somebody, help."

Miss Emma, John thought. After sliding the certificate underneath his pillow, he hurried across the hall to her aid.

Miss Emma lay in a heap of sodden clothing and shattered glass. *Poor old thing.* John knelt beside her, careful of the glass. It looked as if her window had blown out and she'd been thrown across the room. A jagged piece of tin roof as sharp as a razor's edge seesawed on the window ledge. Had it struck her?

Gently John unfolded her tangled limbs and smoothed her clothing. He saw scratches and minor cuts but no frank bleeding.

"I was just putting my window down," she said as he bent over her.

"Can you get up?" he asked.

"I don't have a pup," Miss Emma said, confused. "Do you see my ear trumpet?"

"Hurry!" John heard Andy holler from the hallway. "Everybody to the cellar."

More hail, more screeching outside. The room was as black as midnight.

"Miss Emma," John yelled, "I'm going to carry you downstairs."

She was as light as a child, John thought as he raced down the stairs. All he could feel was clacking bones.

"This way." Andy directed with a lantern. "Down the cellar steps here."

Thankfully, John saw the rest of the household huddled together under the steps. He deposited Miss Emma on a pile of musty old rugs. "We'd better pray," he said.

CHAPTER 41

Fall hurried its way up Troublesome Creek. After a week of rain in mid-September, dry weather settled in and turned the trees into jeweled colors of orange and red and rust and gold seemingly overnight. Copper was on the porch each morning at sunrise, delaying milking just a bit until the mountain's majesty revealed itself. She loved this part of the day best, when ribbons of mist hung in the hollers like smoke dissipating raggedly as the sun rose.

While sitting on a bench to pull on her work shoes, Copper took stock. They needed to gather root vegetables today. Dimmert would spread clean straw on the floor of the cellar to bury turnips, parsnips, and sweet potatoes in. Yesterday Copper and Cara had swept the dirt floor clean of debris and wiped out the boxes where they'd store potatoes. Speaking of jeweled colors, sunlight streaming in through the open cellar door made row upon row of canned vegetables—green beans, pickled beets, tomatoes, sliced carrots, okra, and kraut—sparkle.

Soon they'd need to prepare apple butter and pear butter. They'd all ride to the orchards on the sled (wouldn't Lilly like that?) to pick the fruit, then haul full gunnysacks back to the house. The two little families would eat well this winter and have food left over to give away to those in need. Copper was very glad for the presence of Dimmert and Cara just across the creek. Many hands made light work, as the saying went.

Her mind ticked off a full list of chores as she tugged at Mazy's full teats. The milk streamed into the bucket. This would be a good day to beat the rugs. Wasn't Mam's old metal beater with the wooden handle up in the loft? She thought it hung on a nail beside the ladder. And she needed to get Dimmert to help her clean the chimneys. They could do hers, then go do his while they were both still covered in soot. Nobody needed a house on fire this winter.

It was much later when Copper and Faithful crossed the creek from Dimm and Cara's house. She'd stopped on their porch to wash her hands with some soft soap and to splash water on her face. It did little more than streak the soot that clung to her tenaciously. She reminded herself to give Cara some lye soap. Her hair was tied up in a scarf hastily torn from an old flannel shirt, and her dress was one fit only for the ragbag. She looked like a tramp, but the chimneys were ready for the fires of winter.

Oh, my. Spears Russell and two little girls were on the porch. "Hey, Spears," she called out. "You all okay?" Copper tucked her none-too-clean hands in her pockets.

"Looks like you been cleaning chimneys," Spears said in his honest way.

Copper laughed. "How could you tell?"

"It's a job I been putting off, I can tell you. Listen, Lolly and I need to beg a favor."

"Sure. Is Lolly here?"

"No, she stayed home with her mother and the baby. That's the problem—her mother."

"Do you need me to come? Do I have time to clean up a bit?"

"What would help us out is if you could mind the girls for a few days. Lolly's mother is . . . well, let's just say she's got a bad case of nerves along with terrible headaches. Lolly wants to take her to see her brother and sister down in Tennessee; sometimes that helps."

"We'll be happy to have the girls," Copper said.

Spears's face radiated relief. "I sure do thank you. The way her mother's acting and with the new baby and all, Lolly's at her wit's end."

"What about the horses and the farm? Do you need me to send Dimmert over?"

"My brother is there. He'll watch out for things." Spears turned and hugged his little girls. "You mind Miz Copper," he instructed.

"Wait just a minute. I've got something that might help those headaches." Copper hurried into the house and unlocked the doors to the cherry corner cupboard her grandfather had made. It was the sturdiest piece of furniture in the house and perfect for storing her herbs and medicines. She shook a portion of powder into a small medical envelope and secured it with an attached string. She wrote *Salicylate of soda for nervous headache. Take prescribed amount every three hours for first day, then every six hours for a few days thereafter.* After adding how many grains to dissolve in an ounce of water, she took the envelope out to Spears. "This and a change of scene should help," she said.

"I sure hope so," Spears replied. "She's feeling as rough as a cob today."

"You all take care, and don't worry about the girls."

There was a full table for supper with Flossie and Janie Russell seated on either side of Lilly, who refused to get in her high chair. Cara and Dimmert were there as well. The cookstove wouldn't draw, Cara related. After Dimm put the pipes back together, the house filled with smoke. They were letting it clear out before they tried to fix the stove.

"Maybe the damper is stuck closed," Copper said to Dimmert.

"Probably," he responded.

Flossie and Janie ate tiny bites of potato and one pinto bean a piece. Their little blonde heads stayed tucked into their chins. Lilly chattered away, too busy talking to eat.

"Girls," Copper said, "do you want to take your plates to the porch? You can play picnic."

At their nods, she picked up the girls' plates and fixed them a place outside.

"Maybe they'll eat better if we're not watching," she said when she returned to the table.

"Lilly will talk their ears off," Darcy said.

Cara sighed wistfully. "I'd like to have three little girls like that. Wouldn't you, Dimm?"

Dimm blushed the color of the cherry cobbler he was eating.

"Boys might be less trouble," Copper teased. "You should try for half a dozen at least."

"Are you going to the quilting circle tomorrow, Cara?" Darcy asked.

"I don't know." She glanced Dimm's way. "There's lots of work this time of year."

"We could probably spare half a day for quilting," Copper said. "What do you think, Dimm?"

"Surely," he said.

Copper smiled. She should talk to Cara about the subtle art of getting a man's permission to do almost anything. They just liked to be asked and have their opinions matter.

"Who's up for a game of Mother, may I?" Darcy asked, pushing away from the table. "It will be fun to play while we got the extra little girls."

"You all go on," Copper said. "I'll just put the dishes to soak before I come out."

As Copper scraped plates into the slop bucket and poured water over the stoneware cups and silverware in the granite pan, she let her mind wander. Would John ever be home again? His letter and one from Alice had come in the post this afternoon. Alice's letter was pessimistic, full of gloom and doom. Her words of anger at the judge who treated John's case so poorly scorched the fine-milled stationery in Copper's hand. John's letter she was saving for later, after everyone was in bed. She was fearful she would break down from the disappointment it would surely bring. Self-serving tears were better shed in private.

Soon little girls' squeals filled the evening. Lilly, Janie, and Flossie were perfect companions. Lilly at nearly three followed the six-year-old Janie like a lost puppy. She and four-year-old Flossie were happy to go along with Janie's stipulations about baby steps and backward steps and saying "Mother, may I?" in just the right tone.

After Dimmert and Cara went back across the creek, when it was almost too dark to see, Darcy filled a pan with rainwater from the barrel under the eave and washed three little faces, six little hands, and six little feet.

"But, Darcy," Lilly whined, "we wanna play."

"Don't fuss in front of your friends," Copper warned. "You girls get into your nightclothes, and we'll listen to the bug serenade."

"Yay," Lilly crowed, nearly twirling herself off the edge of the porch. "Sarah Nade."

"Who's Sarah?" Flossie asked, finally finding her tongue.

"Go in with Darcy and get ready for bed, and then come back and find out," Copper said as Darcy herded the girls through the door. "Don't forget to clean your teeth."

"Oh, Mama!" Lilly said.

"Oh, Mama," Janie mimicked, causing Lilly to get the giggles.

Copper fingered the letter in her apron pocket. It was good

to have some word of John close to hand. Would she ever get a minute's privacy to read it? Glad as she was to help the Russells out, the timing was not good. Her spirit was sore and afraid. But perhaps God sent the Russells' need to distract her from her fear. She remembered her daddy saying, "Nothing makes a body feel better than doing for someone else." He'd also say, "Leave it set" when she fretted over something. Paying attention to Daddy's advice, she'd let the letter and her fears set for the moment. The crickets were tuning up their fiddles, and the locusts their kazoos. The night was full of strange music.

Later, when the girls were finally tucked away, Copper and Darcy finished cleaning up the kitchen. They could hear laughing chatter from the bedroom.

"I don't know about having three girls like Cara wants," Darcy said. "Maybe boys would be better."

"My mam always told me boys were easier because they were too bold to sneak. You always knew when they were up to something. But with me . . . sometimes she wouldn't catch me for days."

"Miz Copper," Darcy said, pouring two cups of tea, "I cain't imagine you doing something wrong."

"My stepmother would tell you differently. Let's take our cups back outside. Maybe if the girls don't hear us they'll drift off."

Their rockers squeaked companionably. The lantern cast a golden glow. "How many children do you want?" Copper asked.

Darcy blew on her tea. She didn't answer for the longest time. Copper thought she was studying the question. As if a woman had much choice. Nursing for as long as possible was the only hope of spacing babies. No wonder so many women died young.

"Only as many as I can take good care of," Darcy finally said. "Some of the young'uns nearly starved before Mammaw took us in, and still times was lean." She took a bite of the blueberry muffin she and Copper shared. A dribble of butter slid down her chin. "Then God sent me and Dimmert to you. I been full as a tick ever since."

"I'm thankful He did. What would I have done without the two of you?"

"How about you? How many young'uns would you pick?"

Copper let go of worry long enough to dream. "I'd like a boy or two. My brothers were such fun. And one more daughter. That seems like a doable number, don't you think?"

Darcy counted fingers. "Four? Piece of cake. Or maybe blueberry muffin."

"Darcy Whitt, you're a sight."

"A sleepy sight." Darcy yawned. "I'm going in. Want me to take the lantern?"

"No, I'll sit here for a minute. It's so nice and quiet, and I've got some thinking to do."

"See you in the morning."

"Good night," Copper said. "Sleep well."

She waited a good fifteen minutes before she slipped the letter from her pocket. A moth beat its wings against the glass lantern. A hoot owl called to its mate. Copper shivered in her lightweight gown; she pulled a shawl from the back of the chair across her arms, then opened the envelope. John's bold and handsome scrawl made her smile. He was left-handed and held his pen in an awkward upside-down position to write. She'd watched him many times as children when they learned their lessons together at Mam's kitchen table.

Leaning toward the lantern, Copper unfolded the lined tablet paper and began to read.

Dear Copper,

It is with some hope I write to you this dark evening from Lexington. Today we had a terrible storm that ripped the roof from the front part of Mrs. Archesson's boardinghouse. Everyone is fine except for one old lady who got banged up some and also lost her ear trumpet. Now she can't hear it thunder, as the saying goes.

I was in my room before the storm hit, looking at the license I signed when I foolishly tied myself to Remy Riddle. Copper, here's the hope: Remy didn't sign the thing. It looked like a signature until I studied it under a magnifier; then I saw it was just R-scribble, R-scribble. *I take it Remy can't write, except for* R*s! Nor read. I reckon she was too proud to ask for help that day. And am I glad she was.*

Even though Judge Ledbetter practically threw me out of court the first time my case was presented, Benton Upchurch thinks we stand a good chance of getting another hearing!

I hurried on over to the Upchurches' as soon after the storm today as possible. We moved all the old ladies into the old folks' home until the roof is repaired. They are not happy, I can tell you.

Mrs. Archesson and Robert are staying in the kitchen part of the house. Tommy, Andy, and me are baching it in the washhouse.

Anyhow, as I was saying, Benton thinks the judge will have to look at this license and make a new ruling one way or the other. It will be a couple of weeks before we can get on the docket. That's some lawyerly term. I think it means the judge's calendar.

If words were drops of cool springwater, there wouldn't be enough to say how bad I miss you and Lilly and Faithful. I stay parched all the time.

I don't know if it is proper to say I love you when we're not sure how all this is going to go, but I do and I can't help but tell you. Wait for me.

Yours faithfully,
John

Copper sighed. More waiting. *Oh, well. I'm good at that.* Faithful nosed Copper's arm. She stroked the dog's bony head and velvet ears. "He'll be home soon, girl. I just know it."

CHAPTER 42

It was a pretty time of the year to be traveling. The days were as warm as bathwater, but at sundown a chill set in. Winter was hiding its cold face until fall played out. John had ridden over rolling hills and puny knobs until he was at the foothills of the mountains. "It won't be much longer now," he told the horse as he dismounted to set up camp. "We'll be home before you know it."

After walking a bit to stretch his legs, he shot a squirrel and dressed it for his supper. Soon the smell of fresh meat frying and coffee boiling over the campfire made his stomach growl. He had to say he liked these solitary times. If he'd lived in the earlier days, maybe he could have been like Daniel Boone or Simon Kenton, great men who helped to settle the wild land of Kentucky.

Man, John thought as he settled back, his granite cup full of black coffee, *if these mountains are this awesome now, what must they have been like in ol' Daniel's time? Buffalo so thick you couldn't count them, trees even thicker. It's a shame how fast things are changing. Trees cut down to make way for roads, and soon enough rails will be laid and trains will come chugging right through the mountains.* He shook his head to think on it. *They oughta put a fence around these hills and only let in the folks who want to live in peace and beauty.*

He was happy to be shaking the dust of Fayette County from his boots, that's for sure. No more city living for him. The only other thing he'd liked to have done before he left was finish Mrs. Archesson's washhouse. Once the roof on the house was replaced, he'd started right in on the old stone building. It was mostly done though, and some men from Mrs. Archesson's church had volunteered to finish it under the direction of Tommy. John had left money for supplies.

Well, there might be one more little thing he'd liked to have done before he left Lexington. He'd have liked to pop that Judge Ledbetter in the jaw. He was one sanctimonious character.

Judge Ledbetter's words came back as strong as the coffee John sipped. He wore these funny-looking half-glasses that kept sliding down his long nose while he studied the document Benton Upchurch had given him. At least they were in the judge's private chamber and not in court with all the riffraff and ne'er-do-wells when the judge scolded John.

First Judge Ledbetter took off his little ladylike glasses; then he pinched his nose between thumb and forefinger, as if John's business gave him a headache. He folded his arms over his black-robed chest and heaved a judgmental sigh. "You hill people are stupid as geese. You've come all this way, and you've taken the court's valuable time to have me annul a nonbinding union."

The judge waved the license in the air. "This, sir, is a bunch of hogwash. There's only one witness—a state-sanctioned marriage takes two—and this is not a legal signature."

John thought he might fall to the floor his relief was so great. At the time he didn't care what came out of the judge's mouth as long as he was set free. Anger didn't come until much later. He was well on his way home to Troublesome when the judge's parting words hit him like a slimy spitball right between the eyes. "How many other folks are living and breeding up in those hollows not married in the eyes of God or man?"

Now as John sat in front of a crackling fire, he figured he could let Judge Ledbetter's words sour in his belly like clabbered milk or he could let it go. Suddenly laughter rolled up his throat and boomed from his mouth. He laughed so hard he spilled his coffee and scared his horse. What did it matter as long as he had Copper? Other than a private word with Brother Jasper, he'd keep the judge's remarks to himself.

Copper waited and watched. Surely John would be home today or Mr. Bradley would bring a letter and she would know he wasn't coming. Her heart told her it would be good news—that God would answer her prayers. She longed for it to be so. She looked to the mountains as if they could answer. On the porch behind her, Lilly Gray played dollies with Janie and Flossie. Darcy churned butter. Cara embroidered a pillow slip.

Only Faithful stood watch with her. Copper put out a hand to pat her loyal companion and felt the dog tremble. Then Faithful was off and running out beyond the barn and up the road. Shading her eyes, Copper saw a swirl of dust in the distance. Her heart beat fast. Could it be?

And then John was handing off his horse to Dimmert. She thought to run to him but her knees gave way, and instead she sat in the rocker Darcy pushed behind her.

"Come, girls," she heard Cara say. "Let's go inside."

Faithful ran back and forth between them with her tongue hanging out. John walked across the yard as if they had all the time in the world, and from his smile Copper guessed they did.

"Come and sit a spell," Copper said as he reached the steps.

John pulled the other rocking chair up close to hers. He sat and stretched his long legs out, then reached for her hand. "Don't mind if I do, sweet girl. Don't mind if I do."

☙ ABOUT THE AUTHOR ☙

A retired registered nurse of twenty-five years, Jan Watson specialized in the care of newborns and their mothers. She is a charter member of Southern Acres Christian Church and lives in Lexington, Kentucky. Jan has three grown sons and a daughter-in-law.

Jan's awards include the 2004 Christian Writers Guild Operation First Novel contest and second place in the 2006 Inspirational Readers Choice Contest sponsored by the Faith, Hope, and Love Chapter of the Romance Writers of America. *Troublesome Creek* was also a nominee for the Kentucky Literary Awards in 2006. *Torrent Falls* is the sequel to *Troublesome Creek* and *Willow Springs*.

Jan's hobbies are reading, antiquing, and taking long walks with her Jack Russell terrier, Maggie.

Jan invites you to visit her Web site at www.janwatson.net. You can contact her through e-mail at author@janwatson.net.

CP0

have you visited tyndalefiction.com *lately?*

Only there can you find:

- → books hot off the press
- → first chapter excerpts
- → inside scoops on your favorite authors
- → author interviews
- → contests
- → fun facts
- → and much more!

Visit us today at: **tyndalefiction.com**

Sign up for your **free** newsletter!

Tyndale fiction does more than entertain.
- → It touches the heart.
- → It stirs the soul.
- → It changes lives.

That's why Tyndale is so committed to being first in fiction!

TYNDALE FICTION

CP0021